CROSS OVER

KIDS LOVE CHAINS ①

DONNY CATES
STORY

GEOFF SHAW
ART

DEE CUNNIFFE
COLORS

JOHN J. HILL
LETTERS & DESIGN

MARK WAID
STORY EDITS

Standard edition cover by
GEOFF SHAW w/**DAVE STEWART**

WERTHAM WAS RIGHT shirt design by
CHRISTOPHER SEBELA &
IBRAHIM MOUSTAFA

IMAGE COMICS, INC.

CROSSOVER VOL. 1. First printing. May 2021. Published by Image Comics, Inc. Office of publication: PO BOX 14457, Portland, OR 97293. Copyright © 2021 Donny Cates & Geoff Shaw. All rights reserved. Contains material originally published in single magazine form as CROSSOVER #1-6. "CROSSOVER," its logos, and the likenesses of all characters herein are trademarks of Donny Cates & Geoff Shaw, unless otherwise noted. "Madman" and the likenesses of all associated characters herein are TM & © 2021 Michael Allred. All rights reserved. "Atomahawk" and the likenesses of all associated characters herein are TM & © 2021 Donny Cates & Ian Bederman. All rights reserved. "Powers" and the likenesses of all associated characters herein are TM & © 2021 Jinxworld, Inc. All rights reserved. "Astro City" and the likenesses of all associated characters herein are TM & © 2021 Juke Box Productions. All rights reserved. "God Country" and the likenesses of all associated characters herein are TM & © 2021 Donny Cates & Geoff Shaw. All rights reserved. "The Wicked + The Divine" and the likenesses of all associated characters herein are TM & © 2021 Kieron Gillen Limited & Fiction & Feeling Ltd. All rights reserved. "Luther Strode" ed characters herein are TM & © 2021 Robert Kirkman & Tony Moore. All rights reserved. "Savage Dragon" and the likenesses of all associated characters herein are TM & © 2021 Erik Larsen. All rights reserved. "Chew" and the likenesses of all associated characters herein are TM & © 2021 Mighty Layman Productions, LLC. All rights reserved. "Black Hammer" and the likenesses of all associated characters herein are TM & © 2021 171 Studios, Inc., and Dean Ormston. All rights reserved. "Avengelyne," Berserkers," Bloodstrike," Bloodwulf," Brigade," Glory," and "Prophet" and the likenesses of all associated characters herein are TM & © 2021 Rob Liefeld. All rights reserved. "Hit-Girl" and the likenesses of all associated characters herein are TM & © 2021 Dave And Eggsy Ltd. & John S. Romita. All rights reserved. "The Paybacks" and the likenesses of all associated characters herein are TM & © 2021 Eliot Rahal, Donny Cates & Geoff Shaw. All rights reserved. "Buzzkill," and the likenesses of all associated characters herein are TM & © 2021 Mark Reznicek, Donny Cates & Geoff Shaw. All rights reserved. "Ghost" and "X" and the likenesses of all associated characters herein are TM & © 2021 Dark Horse Comics, Inc. All rights reserved. "The Darkness" and "Witchblade" and the likenesses of all associated characters herein are TM & © 2021 Top Cow Productions, Inc. All rights reserved. "Shadowhawk" and the likenesses of all associated characters herein are TM & © 2021 Jim Valentino. All rights reserved. "Incorruptible" and the likenesses of all associated characters herein are TM & © 2021 Boom Entertainment, Inc. All rights reserved. "I Hate Fairyland " and the likenesses of all associated characters herein are TM & © 2021 Skottie Young. All rights reserved. "Image" and the Image Comics logos are registered trademarks of Image Comics, Inc. No part of this publication may be reproduced or transmitted, in any form or by any means (except for short excerpts for journalistic or review purposes), without the express written permission of Donny Cates & Geoff Shaw, or Image Comics, Inc. All names, characters, events, and locales in this publication are entirely fictional. Any resemblance to actual persons (living or dead), events, or places, without satirical intent, is coincidental. Printed in the USA. For international rights, contact: foreignlicensing@imagecomics.com. ISBN: 978-1-5343-1893-9. ISBN, Diamond UK Exclusive: 978-1-5343-2043-7. ISBN, Sad Lemon Exclusive: 978-1-5343-2044-4. ISBN, Barnes & Noble Exclusive: 978-1-5343-2057-4.

IMAGECOMICS.COM

FROM THE AUTHOR...

Six years ago, I almost died.

I won't get into specifics. I've talked about it here and there on various podcasts and interviews. If you want to hear about it, I'm sure you can find it. Long story short: I was hospitalized. And for the first time in my life, I truly thought I wasn't going to make it out of there alive.

And when I finally did, I had a lot to say about the nature of death and family and legacy. All of those feelings were channeled into a book called GOD COUNTRY. Some of you may have read it, and I thank all of you for doing so. That book truly changed my life.

Until, well, just recently...I kinda almost died again...

I found myself hospitalized this past summer. And for a brief moment there, I thought I wouldn't make it out. Again.

Except this time, when I got back on my feet...it was different. I didn't want to talk about death anymore. I wasn't consumed with those notions of eternal darkness that have peppered so much of my work these last few years.

This time, I awoke wanting to talk about the things I loved. The things that made my life **worth living**. I wanted to talk about **comics**.

I wanted to make something that captured the **excitement** I felt at eleven years old, rabid and huddled in my room reading dog-eared copies of YOUNGBLOOD and WILDC.A.T.S. and SPAWN and SAVAGE DRAGON!

In short, I wanted to make something big and bombastic, but also...small, and intimate and connected to a larger, almost infinite world filled with shocking guest stars, that...man, I'm still pinching myself that we get to play with.

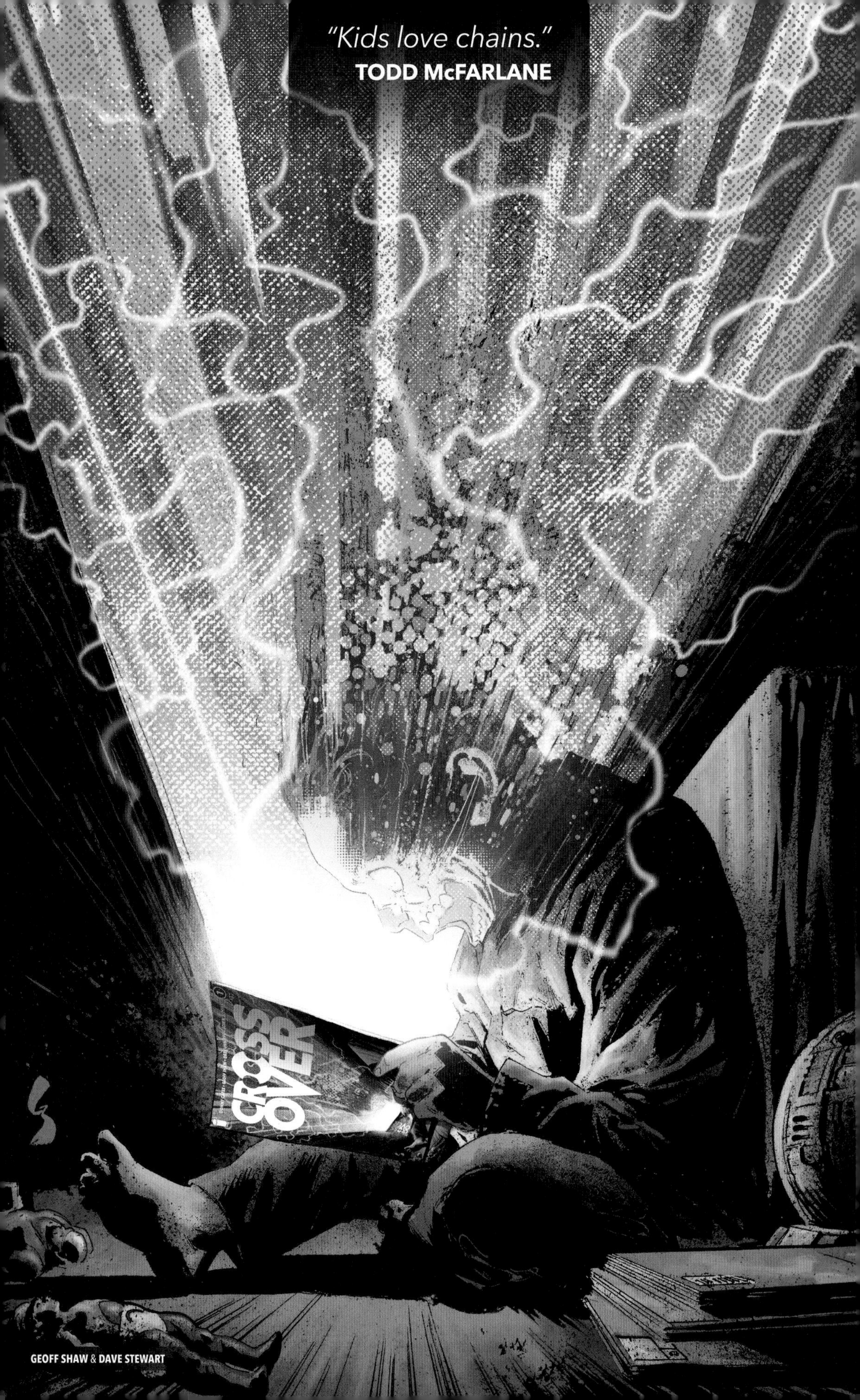
"Kids love chains."
TODD McFARLANE
CROSS OVER

GEOFF SHAW & DAVE STEWART

"The world of the comic book is the world of the strong, the ruthless, the bluffer, the shrewd deceiver, the torturer and the thief...

In comic books life is worth nothing; there is no dignity of a human being."

FREDRIC WERTHAM
SEDUCTION OF THE INNOCENT

KIDS LOVE CHAINS

CHAPTER ONE

● ● ●

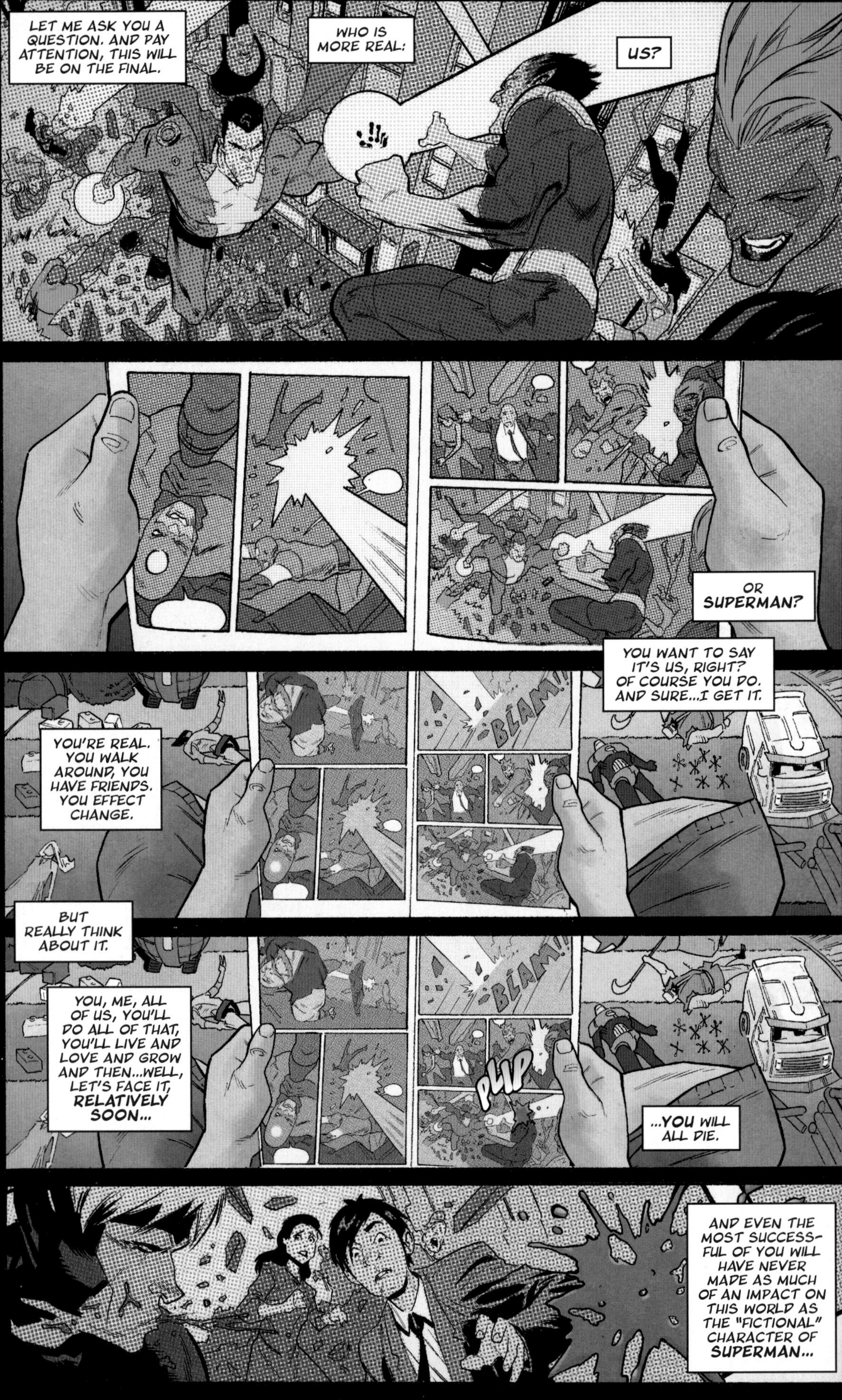
LET ME ASK YOU A QUESTION. AND PAY ATTENTION, THIS WILL BE ON THE FINAL.
WHO IS MORE REAL:
US?
OR SUPERMAN?
YOU WANT TO SAY IT'S US, RIGHT? OF COURSE YOU DO. AND SURE...I GET IT.
BLAM!!
YOU'RE REAL. YOU WALK AROUND, YOU HAVE FRIENDS. YOU EFFECT CHANGE.
BUT REALLY THINK ABOUT IT.
YOU, ME, ALL OF US, YOU'LL DO ALL OF THAT, YOU'LL LIVE AND LOVE AND GROW AND THEN...WELL, LET'S FACE IT, RELATIVELY SOON...
BLAM!!
PLIP
...YOU WILL ALL DIE.
AND EVEN THE MOST SUCCESSFUL OF YOU WILL HAVE NEVER MADE AS MUCH OF AN IMPACT ON THIS WORLD AS THE "FICTIONAL" CHARACTER OF SUPERMAN...

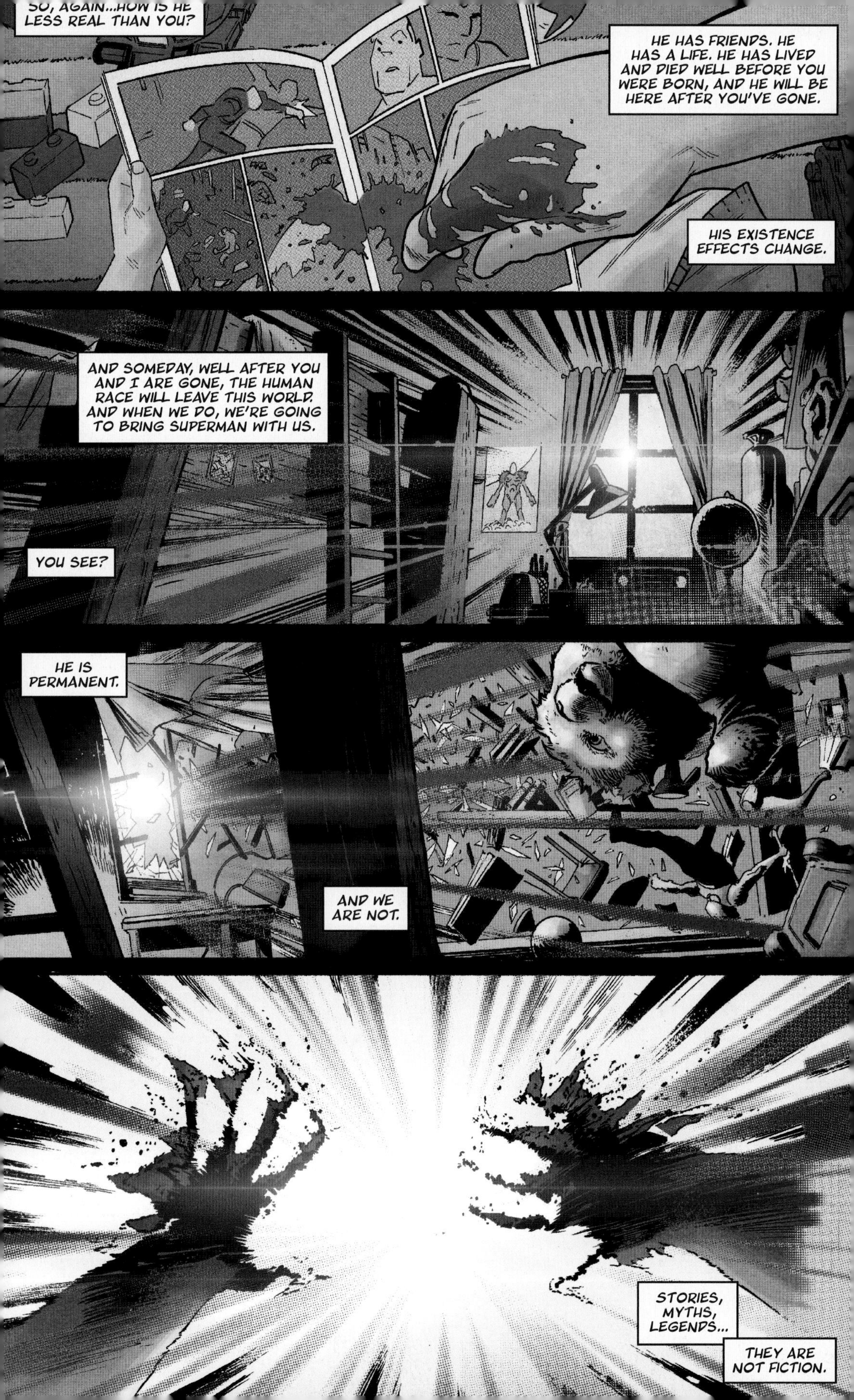
SO, AGAIN...HOW IS HE LESS REAL THAN YOU?
HE HAS FRIENDS. HE HAS A LIFE. HE HAS LIVED AND DIED WELL BEFORE YOU WERE BORN, AND HE WILL BE HERE AFTER YOU'VE GONE.
HIS EXISTENCE EFFECTS CHANGE.
AND SOMEDAY, WELL AFTER YOU AND I ARE GONE, THE HUMAN RACE WILL LEAVE THIS WORLD. AND WHEN WE DO, WE'RE GOING TO BRING SUPERMAN WITH US.
YOU SEE?
HE IS PERMANENT.
AND WE ARE NOT.
STORIES, MYTHS, LEGENDS...
THEY ARE NOT FICTION.

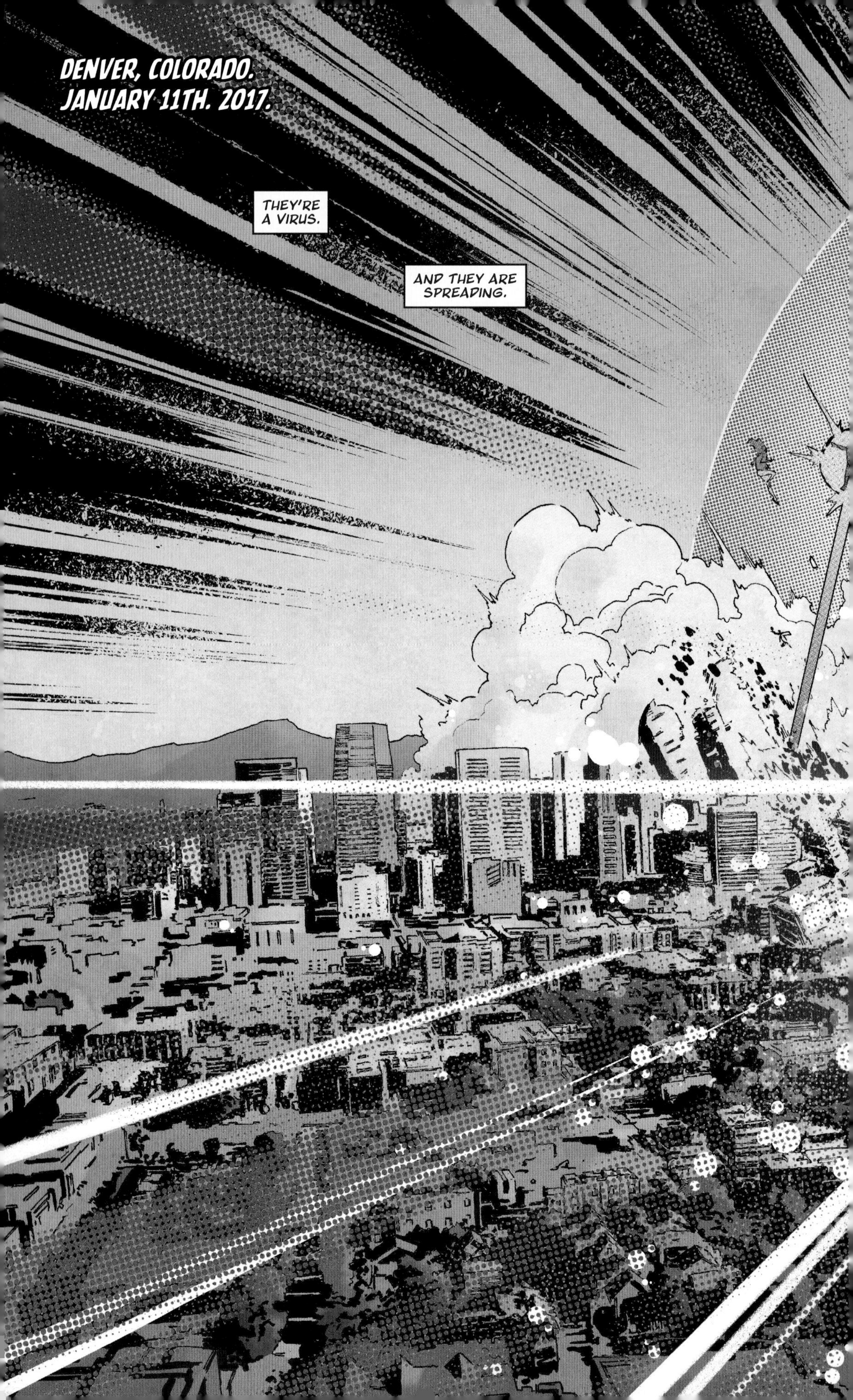
DENVER, COLORADO.
JANUARY 11TH. 2017.
THEY'RE A VIRUS.
AND THEY ARE SPREADING.

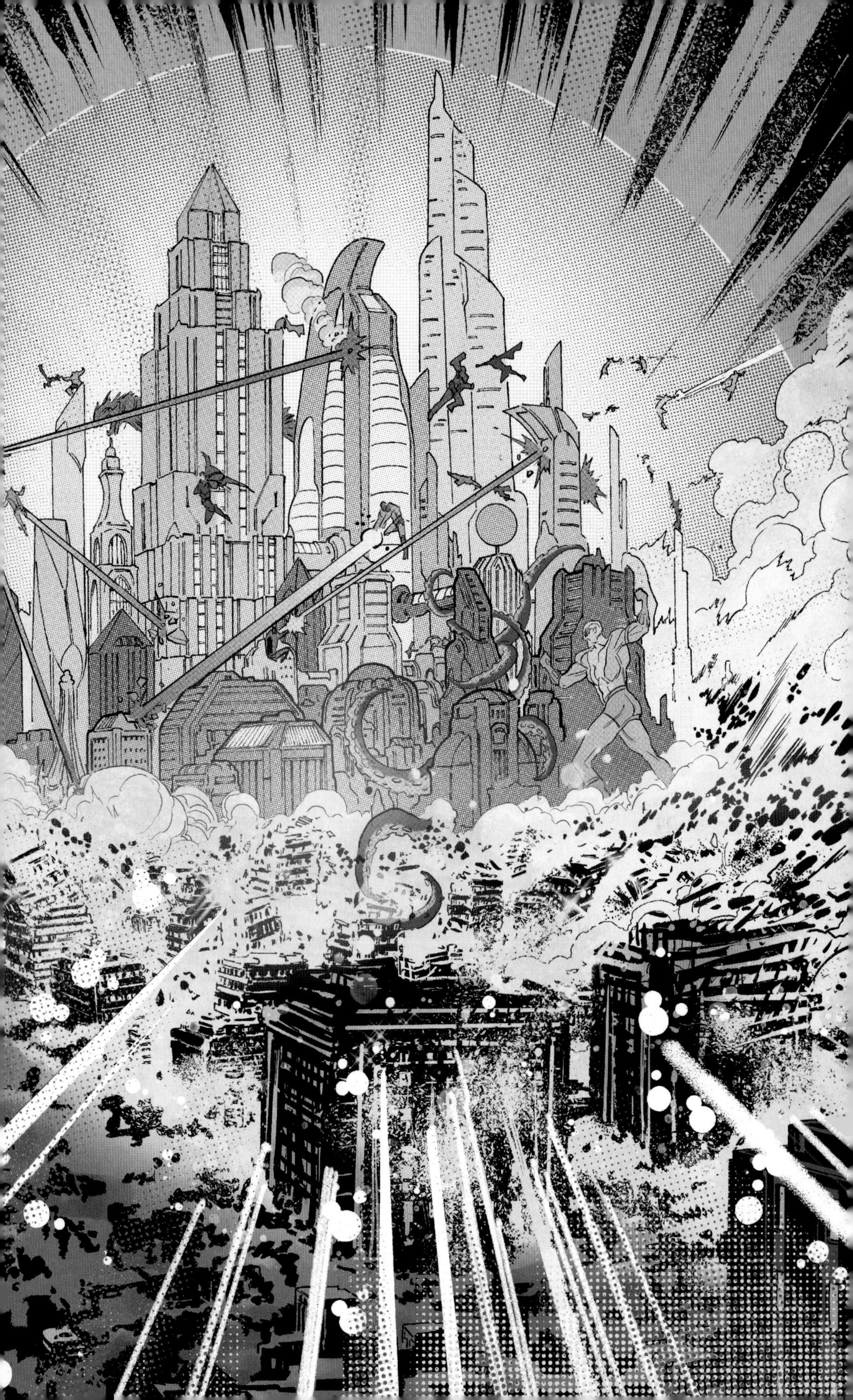

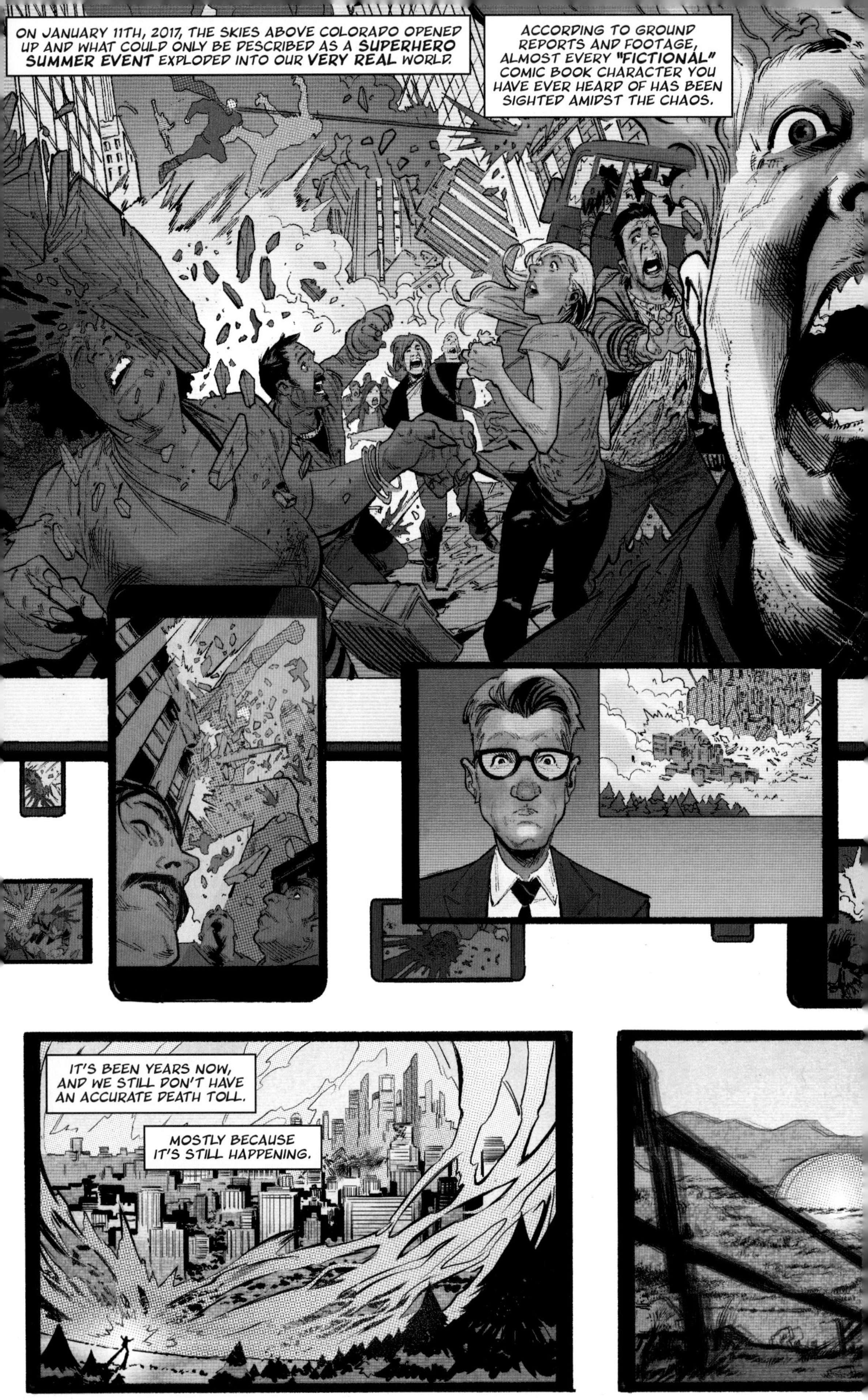
ON JANUARY 11TH, 2017, THE SKIES ABOVE COLORADO OPENED UP AND WHAT COULD ONLY BE DESCRIBED AS A SUPERHERO SUMMER EVENT EXPLODED INTO OUR VERY REAL WORLD.
ACCORDING TO GROUND REPORTS AND FOOTAGE, ALMOST EVERY "FICTIONAL" COMIC BOOK CHARACTER YOU HAVE EVER HEARD OF HAS BEEN SIGHTED AMIDST THE CHAOS.
IT'S BEEN YEARS NOW, AND WE STILL DON'T HAVE AN ACCURATE DEATH TOLL.
MOSTLY BECAUSE IT'S STILL HAPPENING.

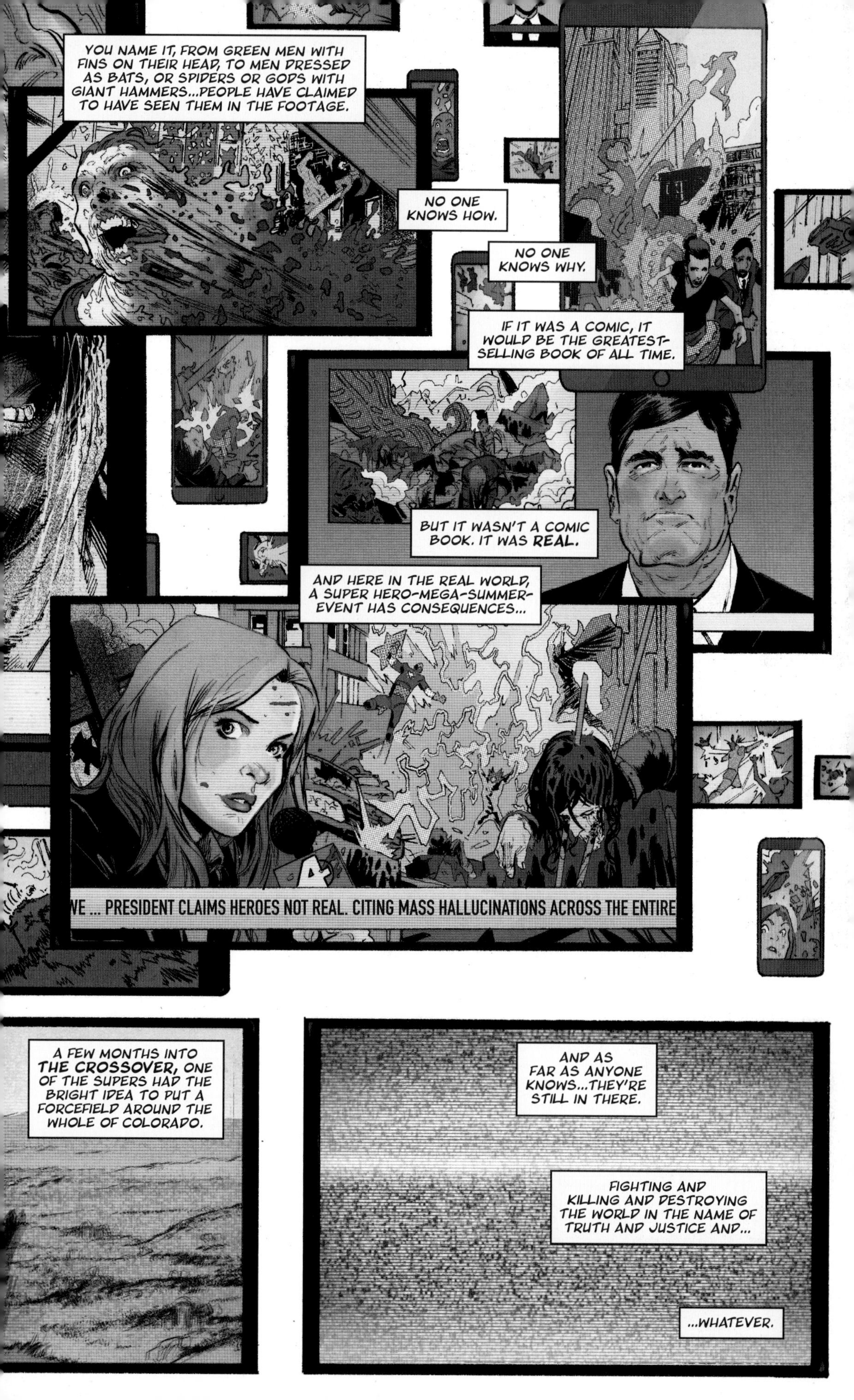
YOU NAME IT, FROM GREEN MEN WITH FINS ON THEIR HEAD, TO MEN DRESSED AS BATS, OR SPIDERS OR GODS WITH GIANT HAMMERS...PEOPLE HAVE CLAIMED TO HAVE SEEN THEM IN THE FOOTAGE.
NO ONE KNOWS HOW.
NO ONE KNOWS WHY.
IF IT WAS A COMIC, IT WOULD BE THE GREATEST-SELLING BOOK OF ALL TIME.
BUT IT WASN'T A COMIC BOOK. IT WAS **REAL.**
AND HERE IN THE REAL WORLD, A SUPER HERO-MEGA-SUMMER-EVENT HAS CONSEQUENCES...
VE ... PRESIDENT CLAIMS HEROES NOT REAL. CITING MASS HALLUCINATIONS ACROSS THE ENTIRE
A FEW MONTHS INTO **THE CROSSOVER,** ONE OF THE SUPERS HAD THE BRIGHT IDEA TO PUT A FORCEFIELD AROUND THE WHOLE OF COLORADO.
AND AS FAR AS ANYONE KNOWS...THEY'RE STILL IN THERE.
FIGHTING AND KILLING AND DESTROYING THE WORLD IN THE NAME OF TRUTH AND JUSTICE AND...
...WHATEVER.

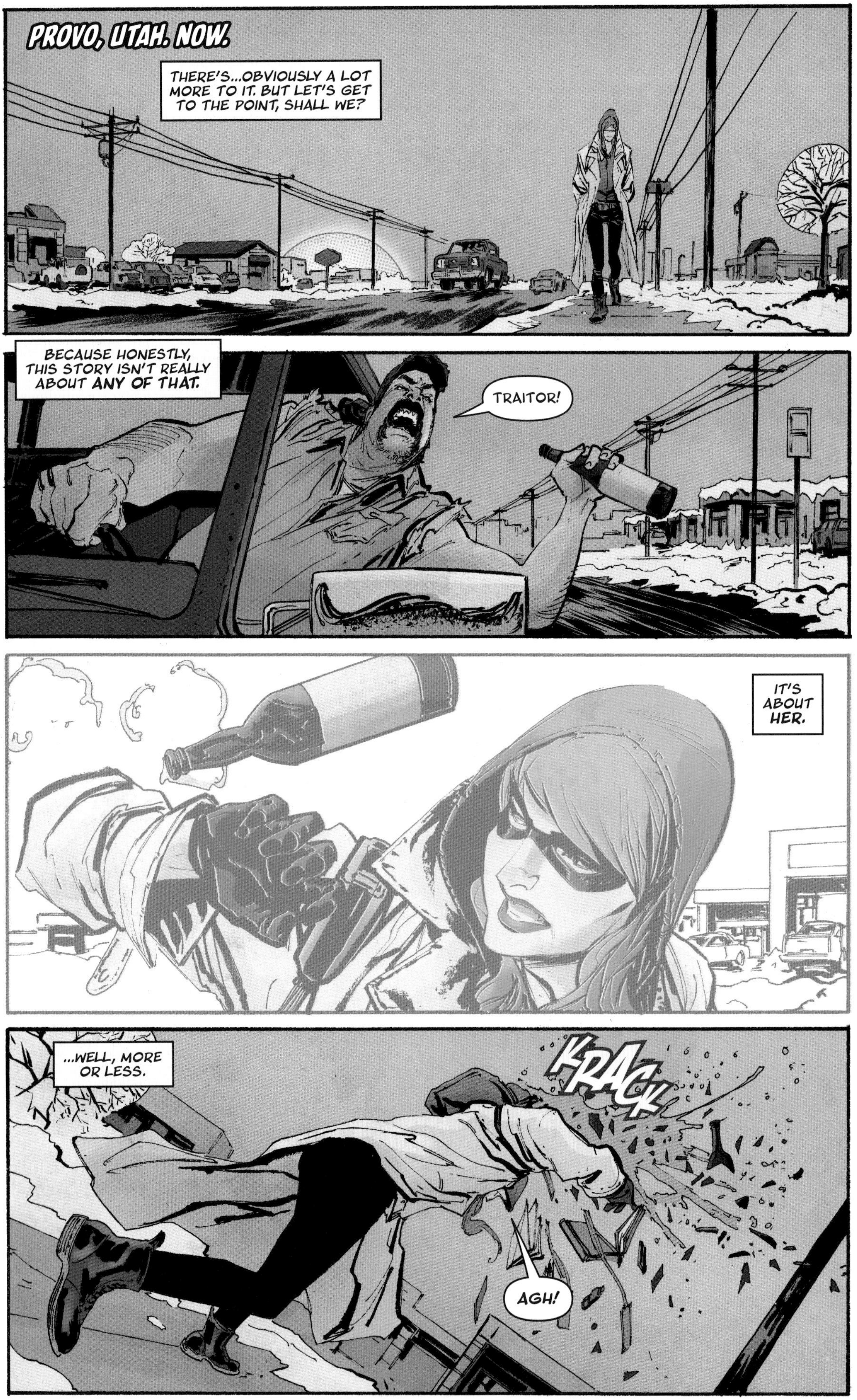
PROVO, UTAH. NOW.
THERE'S...OBVIOUSLY A LOT MORE TO IT. BUT LET'S GET TO THE POINT, SHALL WE?
BECAUSE HONESTLY, THIS STORY ISN'T REALLY ABOUT ANY OF THAT.
TRAITOR!
IT'S ABOUT HER.
...WELL, MORE OR LESS.
KRACK
AGH!

THIS IS ELLIPSIS HOWELL.

SHE GOES BY ELLIE.

OR EL.

MAN... DAMMIT.

AND YEAH, "ELLIPSIS" IS A WEIRD NAME.

HER PARENTS, THEY WERE BOTH WRITERS. THEY THOUGHT IT SOUNDED HEROIC. LIKE SOME KIND OF GREEK HERO OR SOMETHING...

REDNECK PIECE OF...

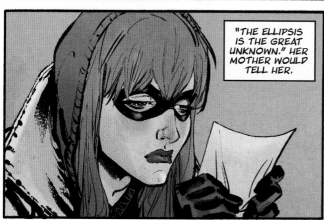

"THE ELLIPSIS IS THE GREAT UNKNOWN." HER MOTHER WOULD TELL HER.

"THOSE *THREE* LITTLE DOTS..."

...

God hates masks.

lowebaptistministry.com

"THEY CAN BECOME ANYTHING."

PRAY THE CAPES AWAY

I SHOULD ADD THAT ELLIE IS NOT VERY POPULAR IN THIS STRANGE NEW WORLD.

HERETIC!!

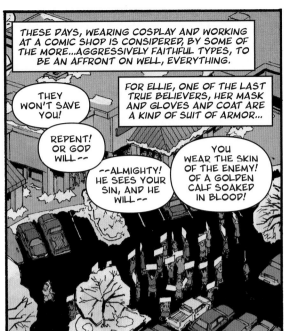

THESE DAYS, WEARING COSPLAY AND WORKING AT A COMIC SHOP IS CONSIDERED, BY SOME OF THE MORE...AGGRESSIVELY FAITHFUL TYPES, TO BE AN AFFRONT ON WELL, EVERYTHING.

THEY WON'T SAVE YOU!

REPENT! OR GOD WILL --

--ALMIGHTY! HE SEES YOUR SIN, AND HE WILL --

FOR ELLIE, ONE OF THE LAST TRUE BELIEVERS, HER MASK AND GLOVES AND COAT ARE A KIND OF SUIT OF ARMOR...

YOU WEAR THE SKIN OF THE ENEMY! OF A GOLDEN CALF SOAKED IN BLOOD!

YOU SELL THE DEVIL'S SCRIPTURE! HE HAS SENT THESE DEMONS TO CLEANSE THE EARTH OF--

THERE IS ONLY ONE GOD, AND HIS WRATH IS--

READ YOUR WAY TO HELL

OKAY! I GET IT! SUPER-HEROES BAD! GOD GOOD.

COSPLAY EVIL. COMIC BOOKS FROM THE DEVIL!

SHE LIKES TO THINK THEY PROTECT HER...

...FROM A WORLD WHERE BOTH FICTION...

...AND REALITY...

JESUS CHRIST, EVEN YOUR GOD TOOK A DAY OFF ONCE IN A WHILE, GUYS.

...ARE DEAD.

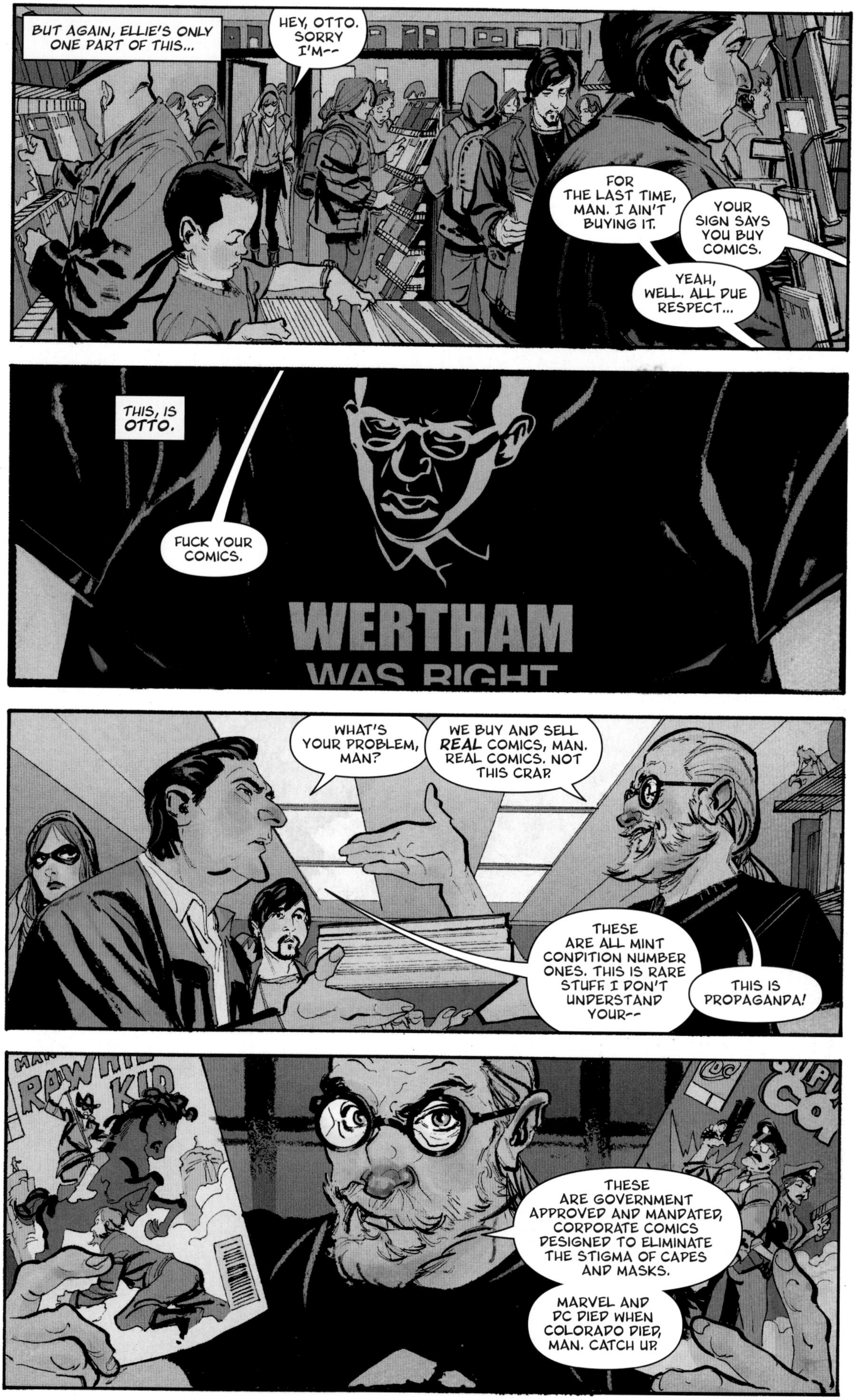
BUT AGAIN, ELLIE'S ONLY ONE PART OF THIS...
HEY, OTTO. SORRY I'M--
FOR THE LAST TIME, MAN. I AIN'T BUYING IT.
YOUR SIGN SAYS YOU BUY COMICS.
YEAH, WELL. ALL DUE RESPECT...
THIS, IS OTTO.
FUCK YOUR COMICS.
WERTHAM
WAS RIGHT
WHAT'S YOUR PROBLEM, MAN?
WE BUY AND SELL REAL COMICS, MAN. REAL COMICS. NOT THIS CRAP.
THESE ARE ALL MINT CONDITION NUMBER ONES. THIS IS RARE STUFF. I DON'T UNDERSTAND YOUR--
THIS IS PROPAGANDA!
RAWHIDE KID
THESE ARE GOVERNMENT APPROVED AND MANDATED, CORPORATE COMICS DESIGNED TO ELIMINATE THE STIGMA OF CAPES AND MASKS.
MARVEL AND DC DIED WHEN COLORADO DIED, MAN. CATCH UP.

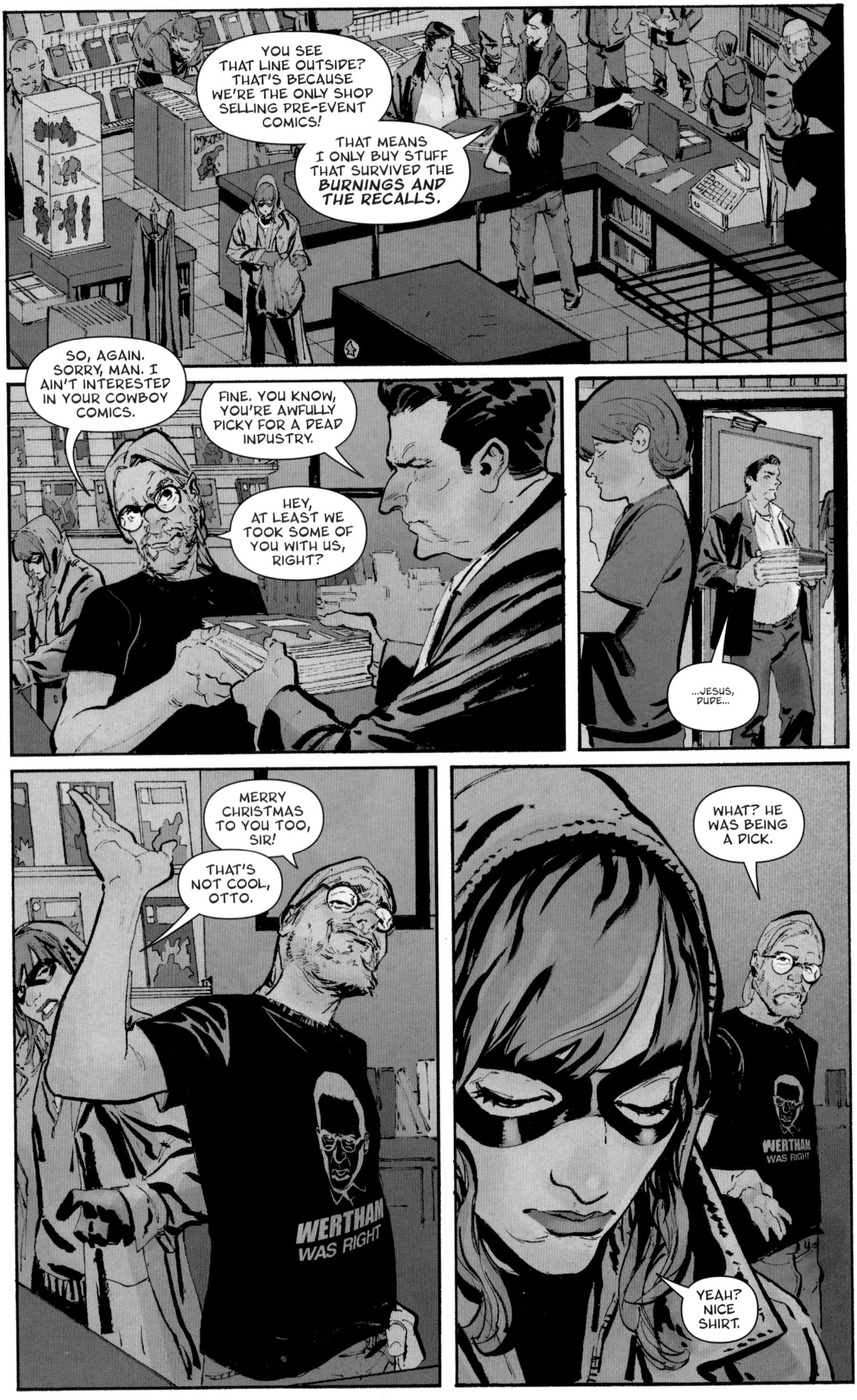
YOU SEE THAT LINE OUTSIDE? THAT'S BECAUSE WE'RE THE ONLY SHOP SELLING PRE-EVENT COMICS!
THAT MEANS I ONLY BUY STUFF THAT SURVIVED THE BURNINGS AND THE RECALLS.
SO, AGAIN. SORRY, MAN. I AIN'T INTERESTED IN YOUR COWBOY COMICS.
FINE. YOU KNOW, YOU'RE AWFULLY PICKY FOR A DEAD INDUSTRY.
HEY, AT LEAST WE TOOK SOME OF YOU WITH US, RIGHT?
...JESUS, DUDE...
MERRY CHRISTMAS TO YOU TOO, SIR!
THAT'S NOT COOL, OTTO.
WERTHAM WAS RIGHT
WHAT? HE WAS BEING A DICK.
WERTHAM WAS RIGHT
YEAH? NICE SHIRT.

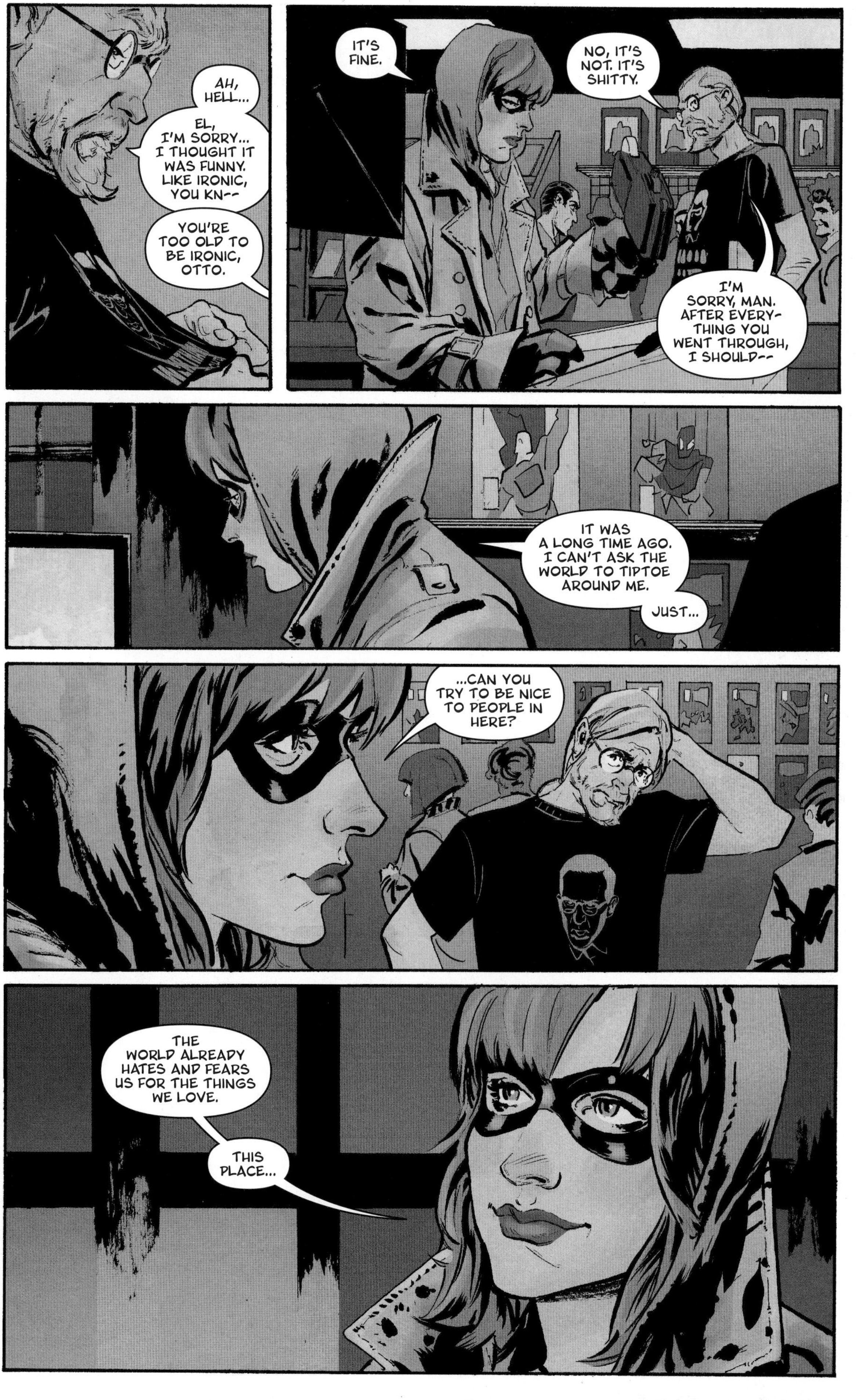
AH, HELL...
EL, I'M SORRY... I THOUGHT IT WAS FUNNY. LIKE IRONIC, YOU KN--
YOU'RE TOO OLD TO BE IRONIC, OTTO.
IT'S FINE.
NO, IT'S NOT. IT'S SHITTY.
I'M SORRY, MAN. AFTER EVERY-THING YOU WENT THROUGH, I SHOULD--
IT WAS A LONG TIME AGO. I CAN'T ASK THE WORLD TO TIPTOE AROUND ME.
JUST...
...CAN YOU TRY TO BE NICE TO PEOPLE IN HERE?
THE WORLD ALREADY HATES AND FEARS US FOR THE THINGS WE LOVE.
THIS PLACE...

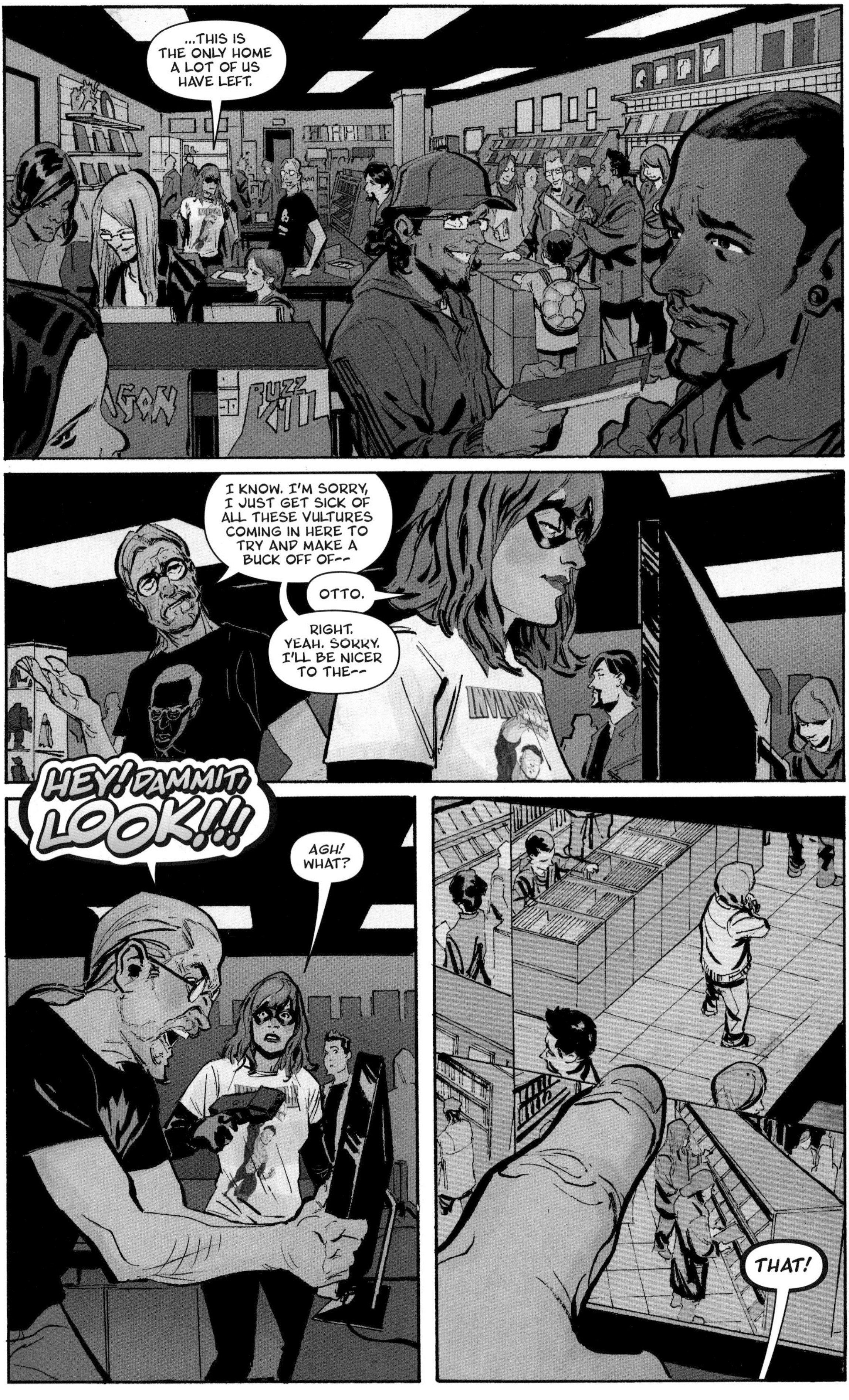
...THIS IS THE ONLY HOME A LOT OF US HAVE LEFT.
I KNOW. I'M SORRY, I JUST GET SICK OF ALL THESE VULTURES COMING IN HERE TO TRY AND MAKE A BUCK OFF OF--
OTTO.
RIGHT. YEAH. SORRY. I'LL BE NICER TO THE--
HEY! DAMMIT, LOOK!!!
AGH! WHAT?
THAT!

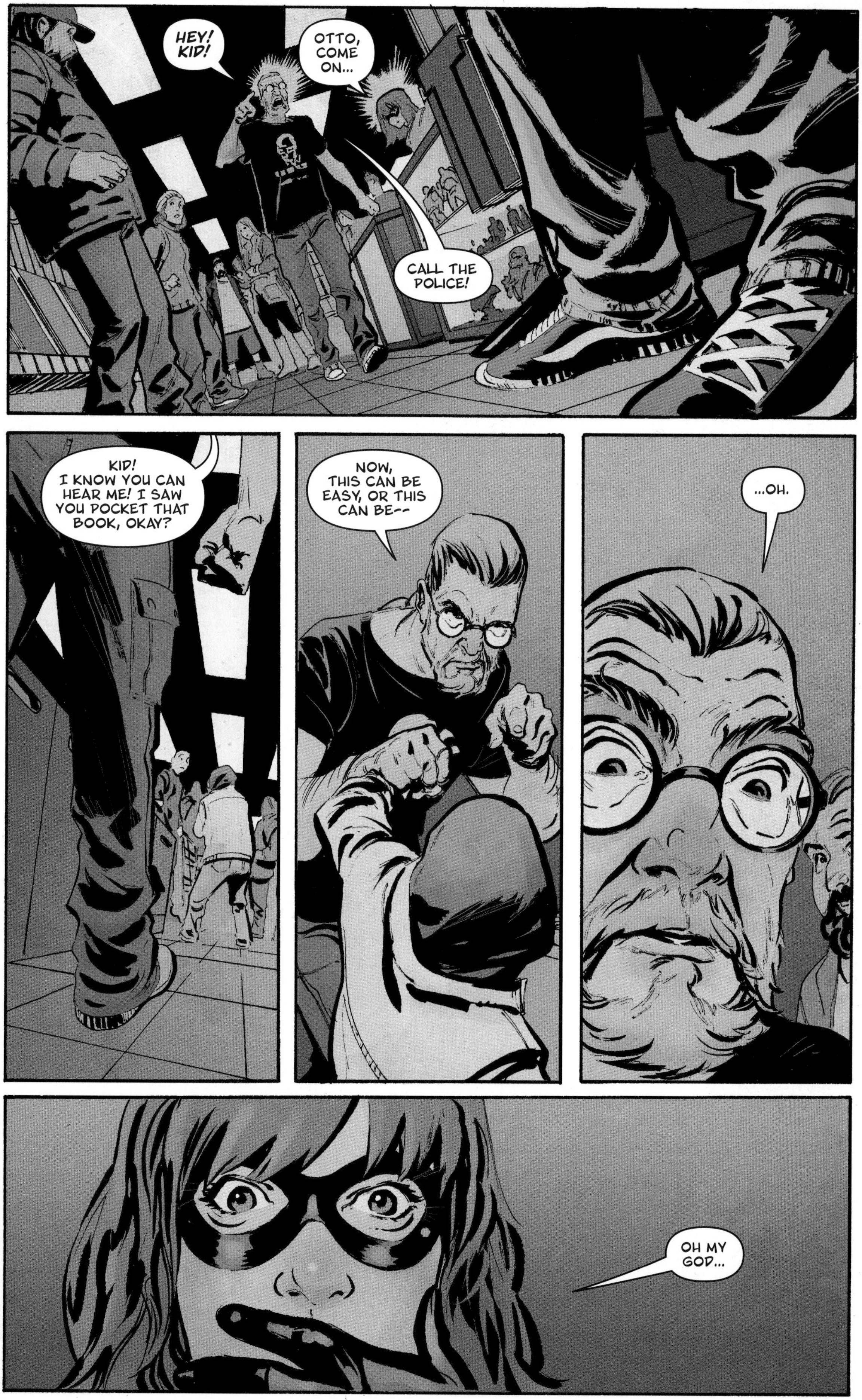
HEY! KID!
OTTO, COME ON...
CALL THE POLICE!
KID! I KNOW YOU CAN HEAR ME! I SAW YOU POCKET THAT BOOK, OKAY?
NOW, THIS CAN BE EASY, OR THIS CAN BE--
...OH.
OH MY GOD...

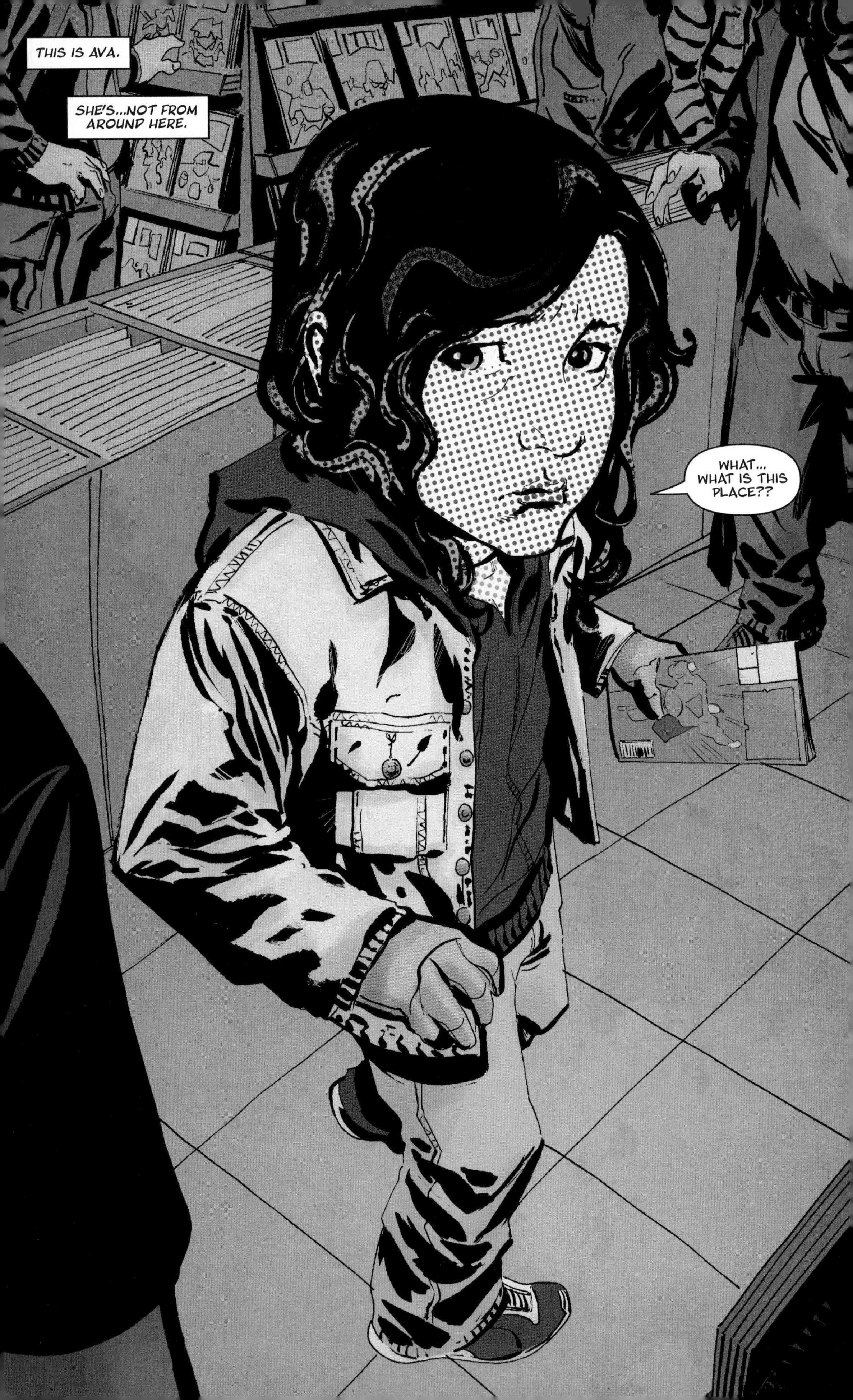
THIS IS AVA.
SHE'S...NOT FROM AROUND HERE.
WHAT... WHAT IS THIS PLACE??

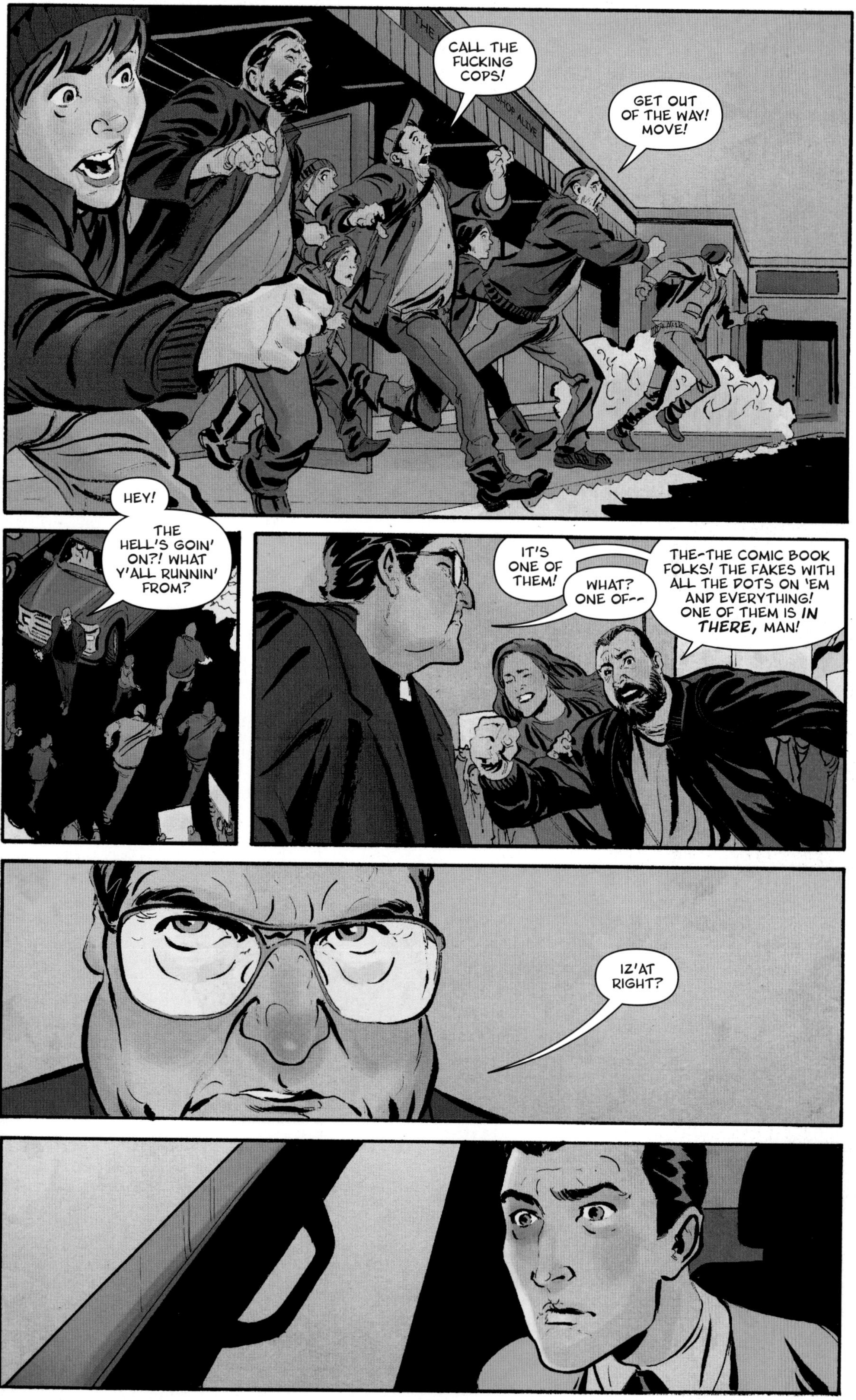
CALL THE FUCKING COPS!
GET OUT OF THE WAY! MOVE!
HEY!
THE HELL'S GOIN' ON?! WHAT Y'ALL RUNNIN' FROM?
IT'S ONE OF THEM!
WHAT? ONE OF--
THE-THE COMIC BOOK FOLKS! THE FAKES WITH ALL THE DOTS ON 'EM AND EVERYTHING! ONE OF THEM IS IN THERE, MAN!
IZ'AT RIGHT?

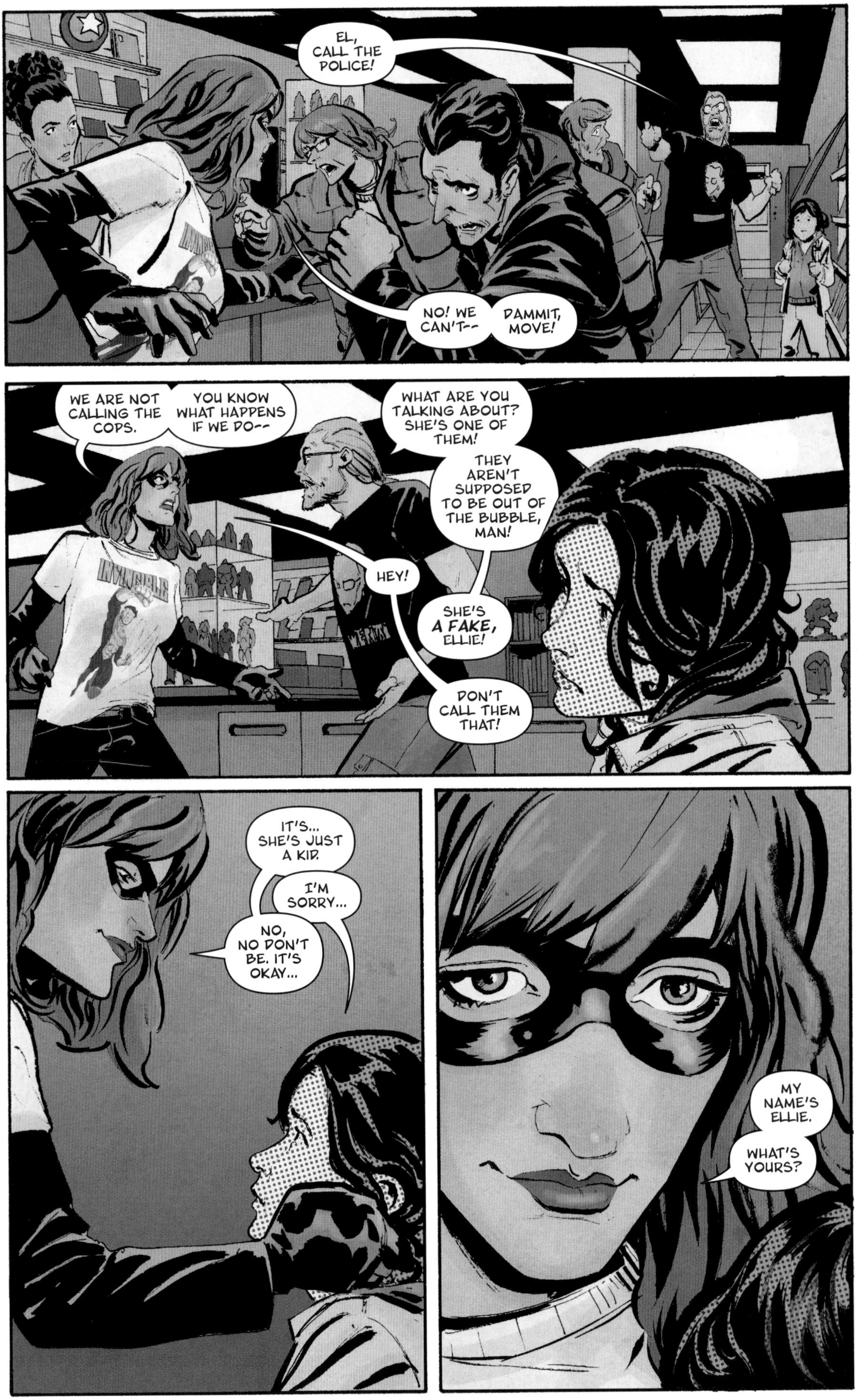
EL, CALL THE POLICE!
NO! WE CAN'T--
DAMMIT, MOVE!
WE ARE NOT CALLING THE COPS.
YOU KNOW WHAT HAPPENS IF WE DO--
WHAT ARE YOU TALKING ABOUT? SHE'S ONE OF THEM!
THEY AREN'T SUPPOSED TO BE OUT OF THE BUBBLE, MAN!
HEY!
SHE'S **A FAKE,** ELLIE!
DON'T CALL THEM THAT!
IT'S... SHE'S JUST A KID.
I'M SORRY...
NO, NO DON'T BE. IT'S OKAY...
MY NAME'S ELLIE.
WHAT'S YOURS?

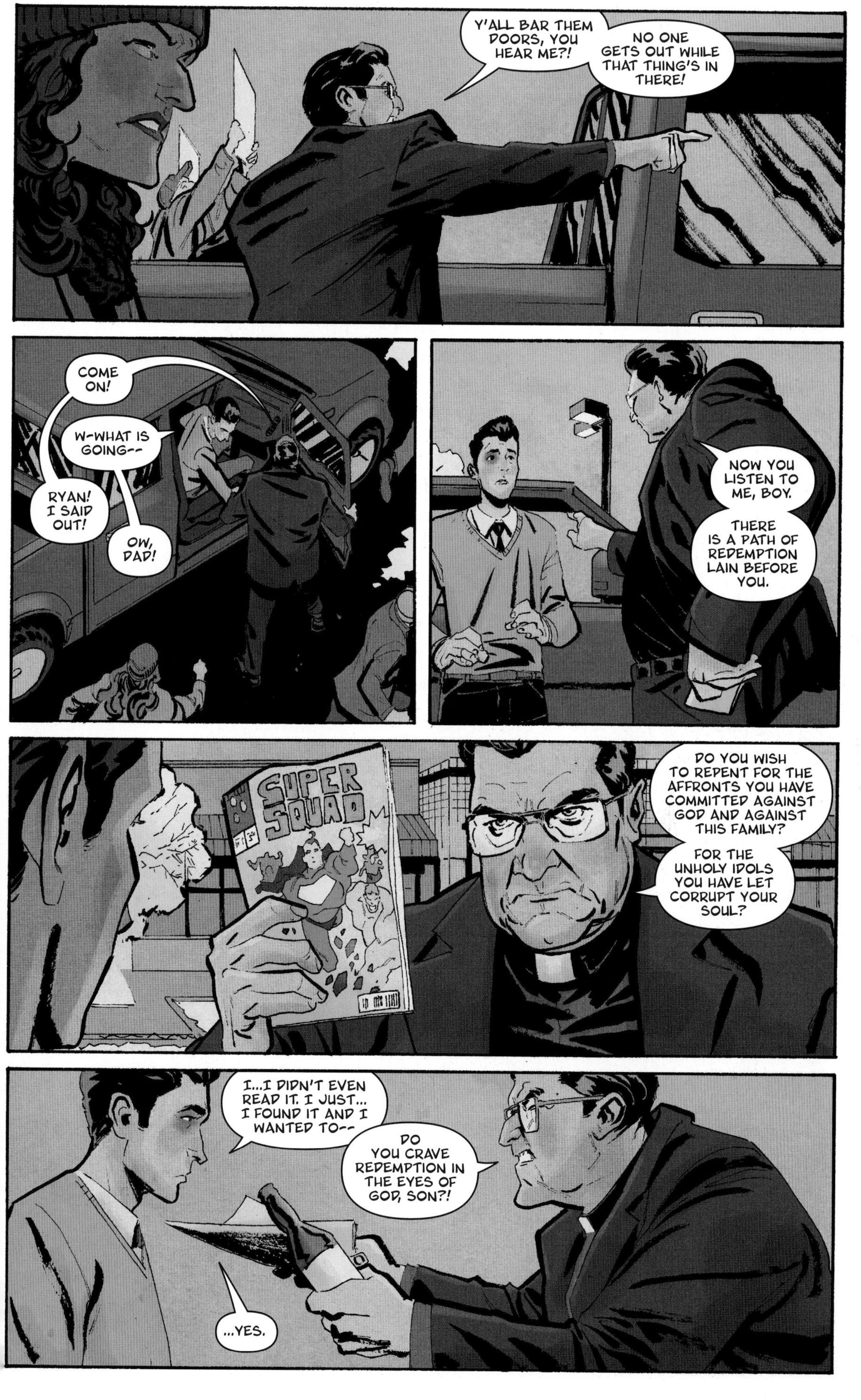
Y'ALL BAR THEM DOORS, YOU HEAR ME?!
NO ONE GETS OUT WHILE THAT THING'S IN THERE!
COME ON!
W-WHAT IS GOING--
RYAN! I SAID OUT!
OW, DAD!
NOW YOU LISTEN TO ME, BOY.
THERE IS A PATH OF REDEMPTION LAIN BEFORE YOU.
SUPER SQUAD
DO YOU WISH TO REPENT FOR THE AFFRONTS YOU HAVE COMMITTED AGAINST GOD AND AGAINST THIS FAMILY?
FOR THE UNHOLY IDOLS YOU HAVE LET CORRUPT YOUR SOUL?
I...I DIDN'T EVEN READ IT. I JUST... I FOUND IT AND I WANTED TO--
DO YOU CRAVE REDEMPTION IN THE EYES OF GOD, SON?!
...YES.

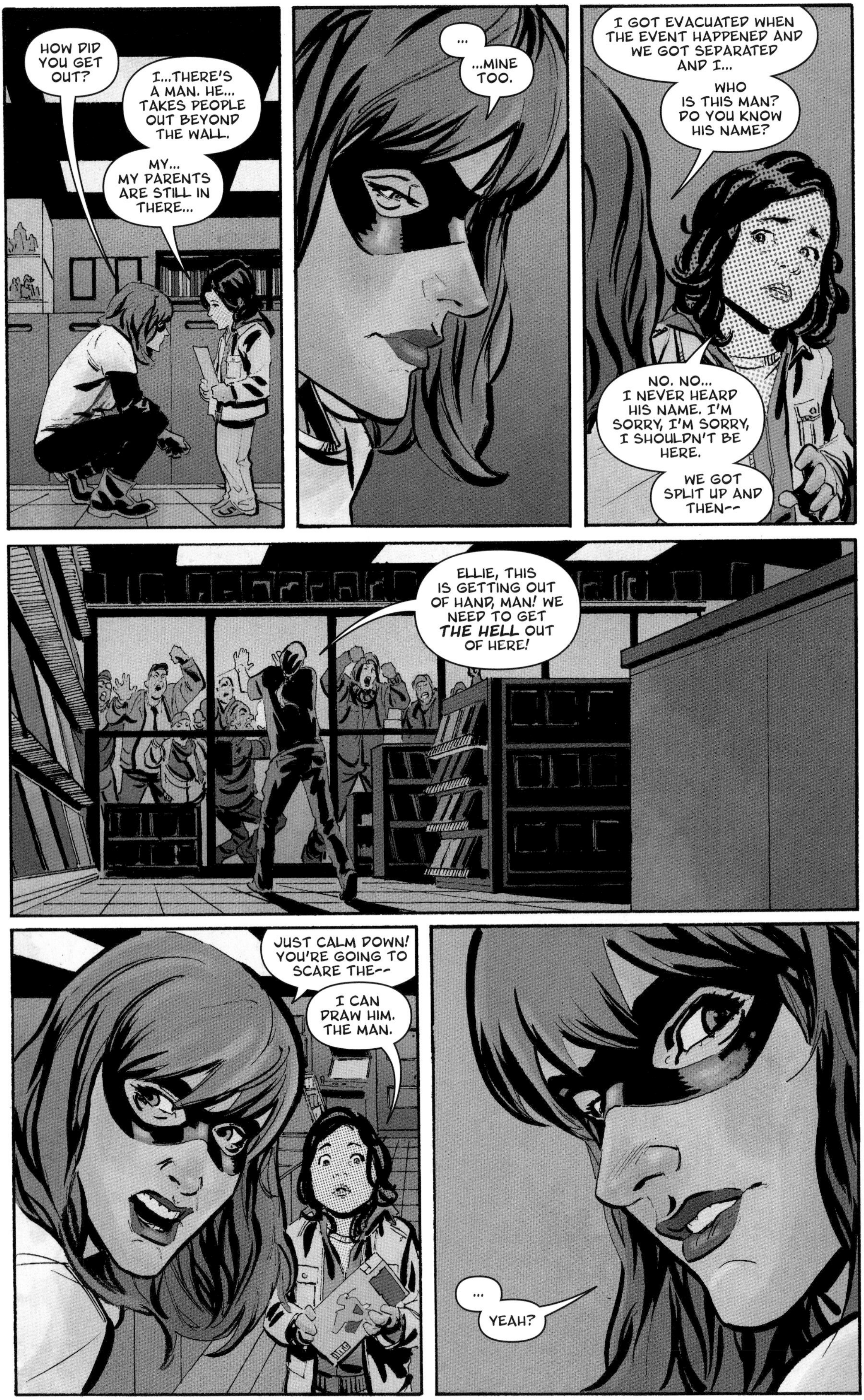

HOW DID YOU GET OUT?
I...THERE'S A MAN. HE... TAKES PEOPLE OUT BEYOND THE WALL.
MY... MY PARENTS ARE STILL IN THERE...
...
...MINE TOO.
I GOT EVACUATED WHEN THE EVENT HAPPENED AND WE GOT SEPARATED AND I...
WHO IS THIS MAN? DO YOU KNOW HIS NAME?
NO. NO... I NEVER HEARD HIS NAME. I'M SORRY, I'M SORRY, I SHOULDN'T BE HERE.
WE GOT SPLIT UP AND THEN--
ELLIE, THIS IS GETTING OUT OF HAND, MAN! WE NEED TO GET ***THE HELL*** OUT OF HERE!
JUST CALM DOWN! YOU'RE GOING TO SCARE THE--
I CAN DRAW HIM. THE MAN.
...
YEAH?

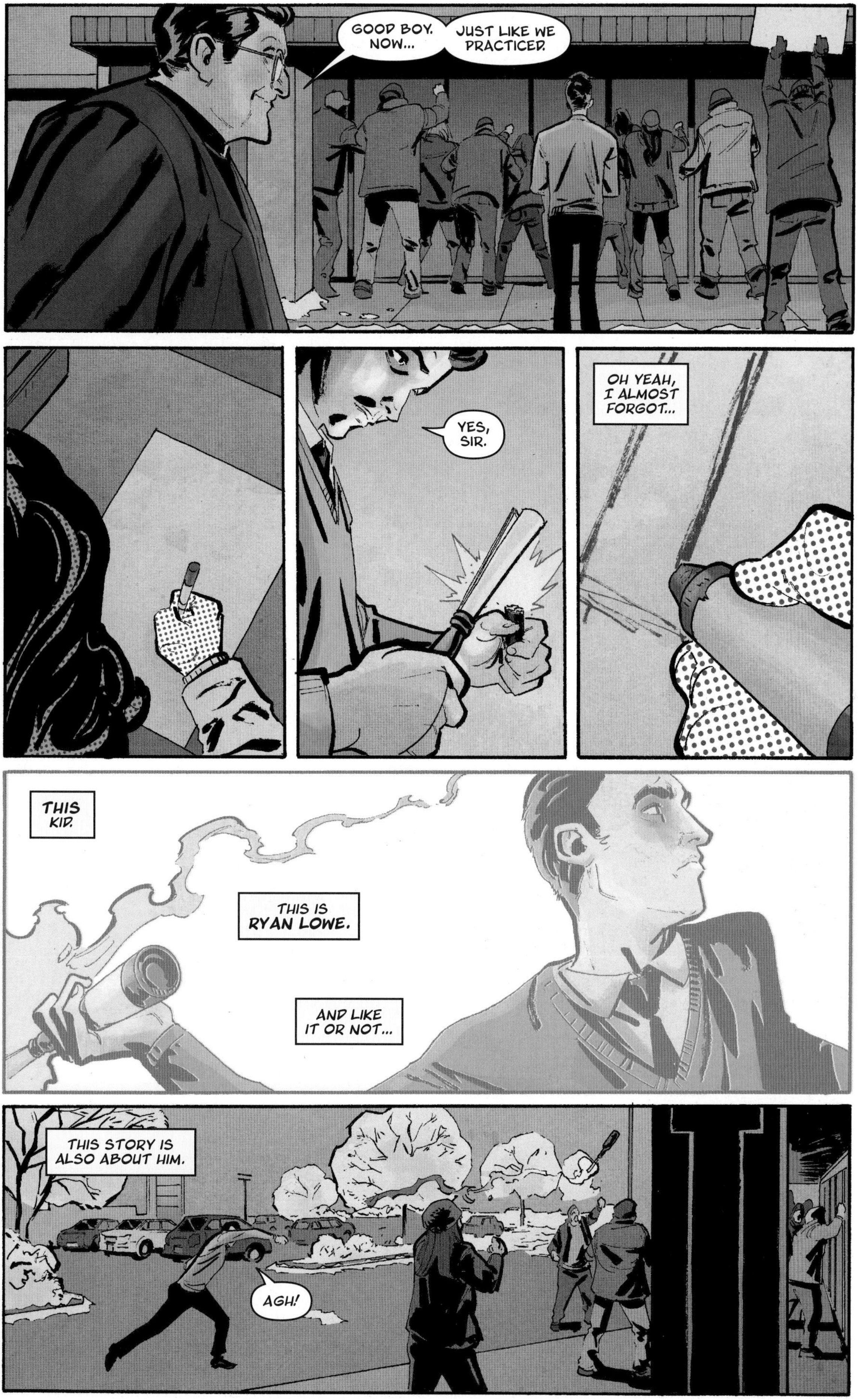
GOOD BOY. NOW...
JUST LIKE WE PRACTICED.
YES, SIR.
OH YEAH, I ALMOST FORGOT...
THIS KID.
THIS IS RYAN LOWE.
AND LIKE IT OR NOT...
THIS STORY IS ALSO ABOUT HIM.
AGH!

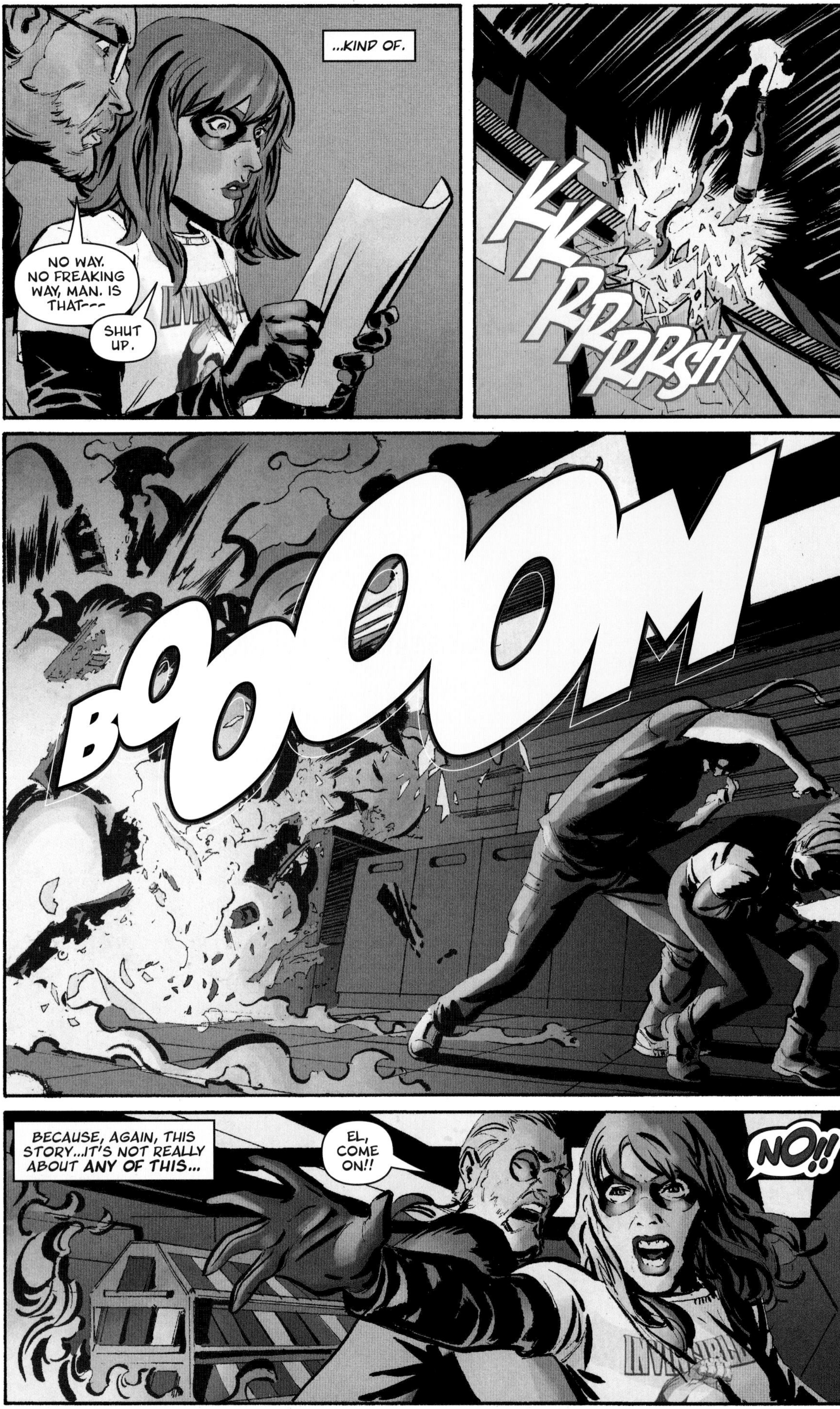
...KIND OF.
NO WAY. NO FREAKING WAY, MAN. IS THAT---
SHUT UP.
KKRRRRSH
BOOOOM
BECAUSE, AGAIN, THIS STORY...IT'S NOT REALLY ABOUT ANY OF THIS...
EL, COME ON!!
NO!!

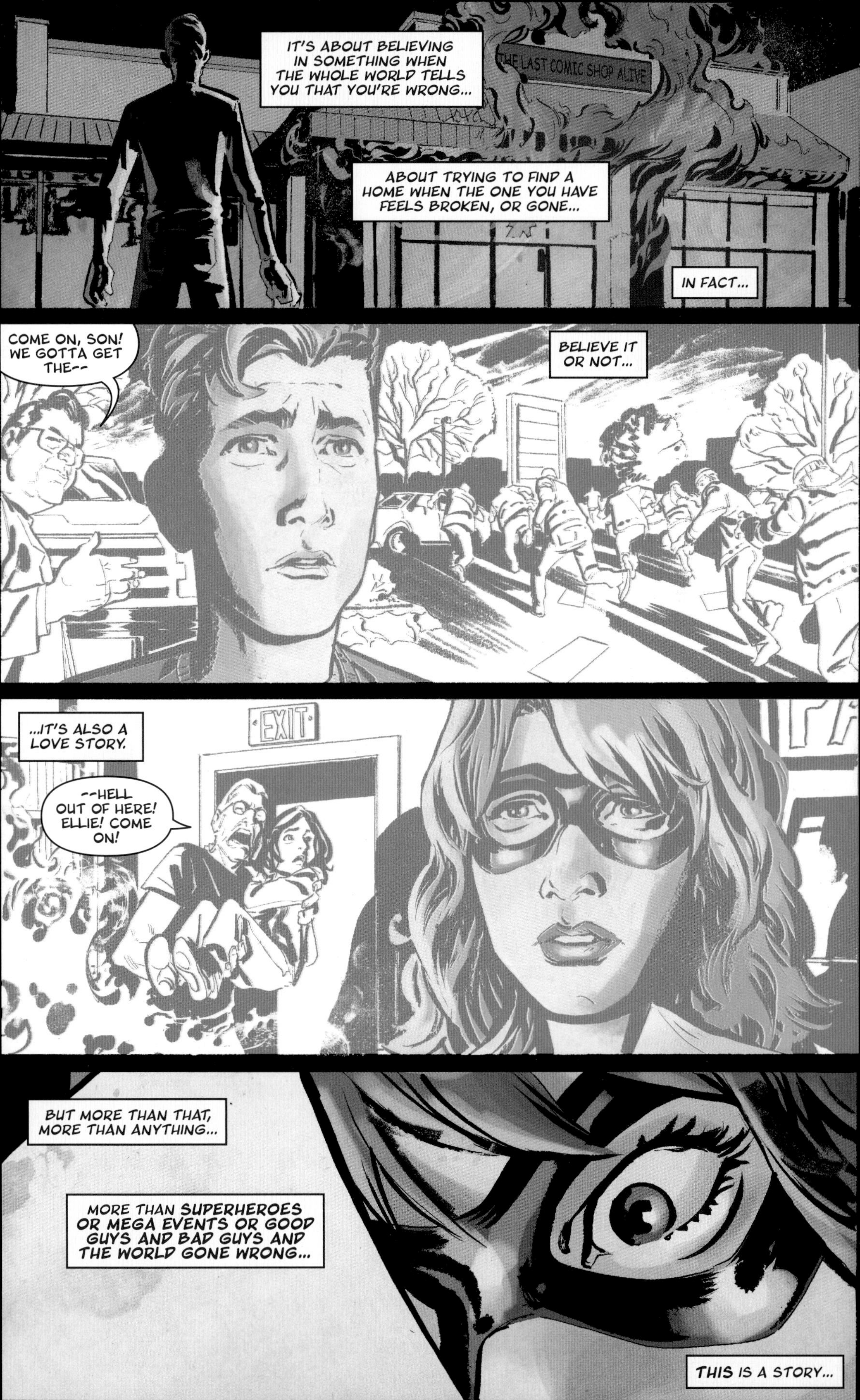

IT'S ABOUT BELIEVING IN SOMETHING WHEN THE WHOLE WORLD TELLS YOU THAT YOU'RE WRONG...
THE LAST COMIC SHOP ALIVE
ABOUT TRYING TO FIND A HOME WHEN THE ONE YOU HAVE FEELS BROKEN, OR GONE...
IN FACT...
COME ON, SON! WE GOTTA GET THE--
BELIEVE IT OR NOT...
...IT'S ALSO A LOVE STORY.
EXIT
--HELL OUT OF HERE! ELLIE! COME ON!
BUT MORE THAN THAT, MORE THAN ANYTHING...
MORE THAN SUPERHEROES OR MEGA EVENTS OR GOOD GUYS AND BAD GUYS AND THE WORLD GONE WRONG...
THIS IS A STORY...

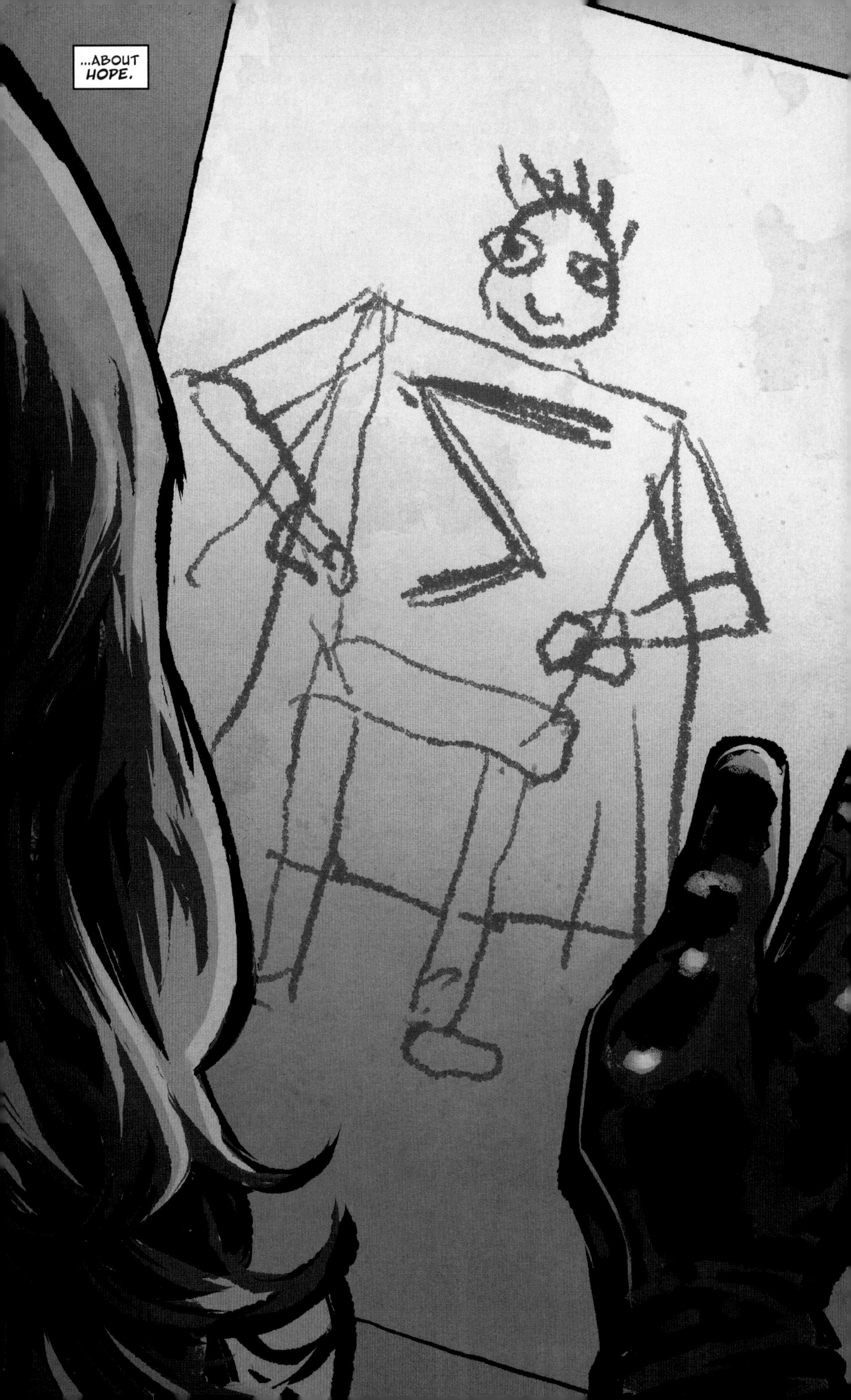
...ABOUT HOPE.

GEOFF SHAW

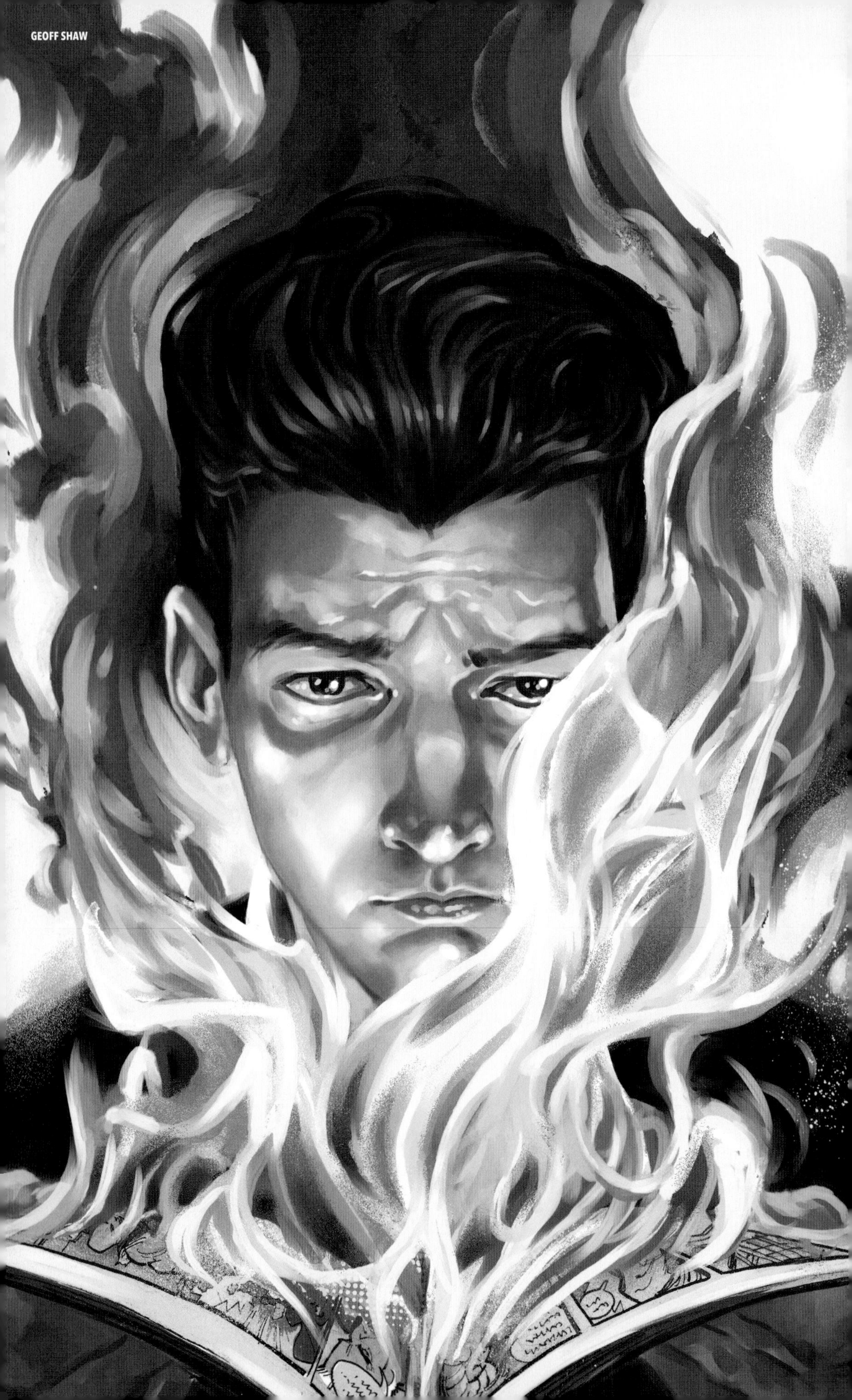

KIDS LOVE
CHAINS

CHAPTER TWO

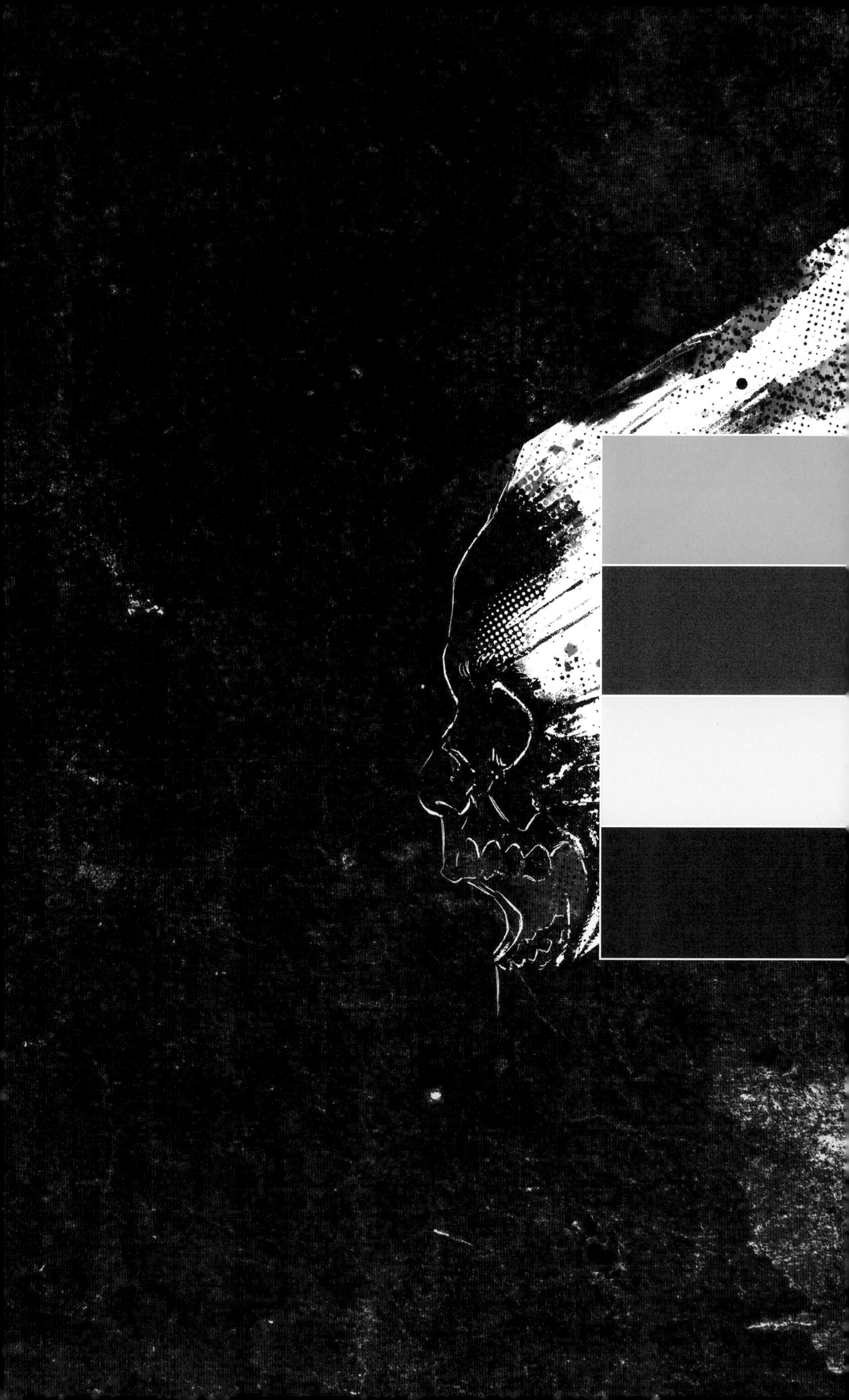

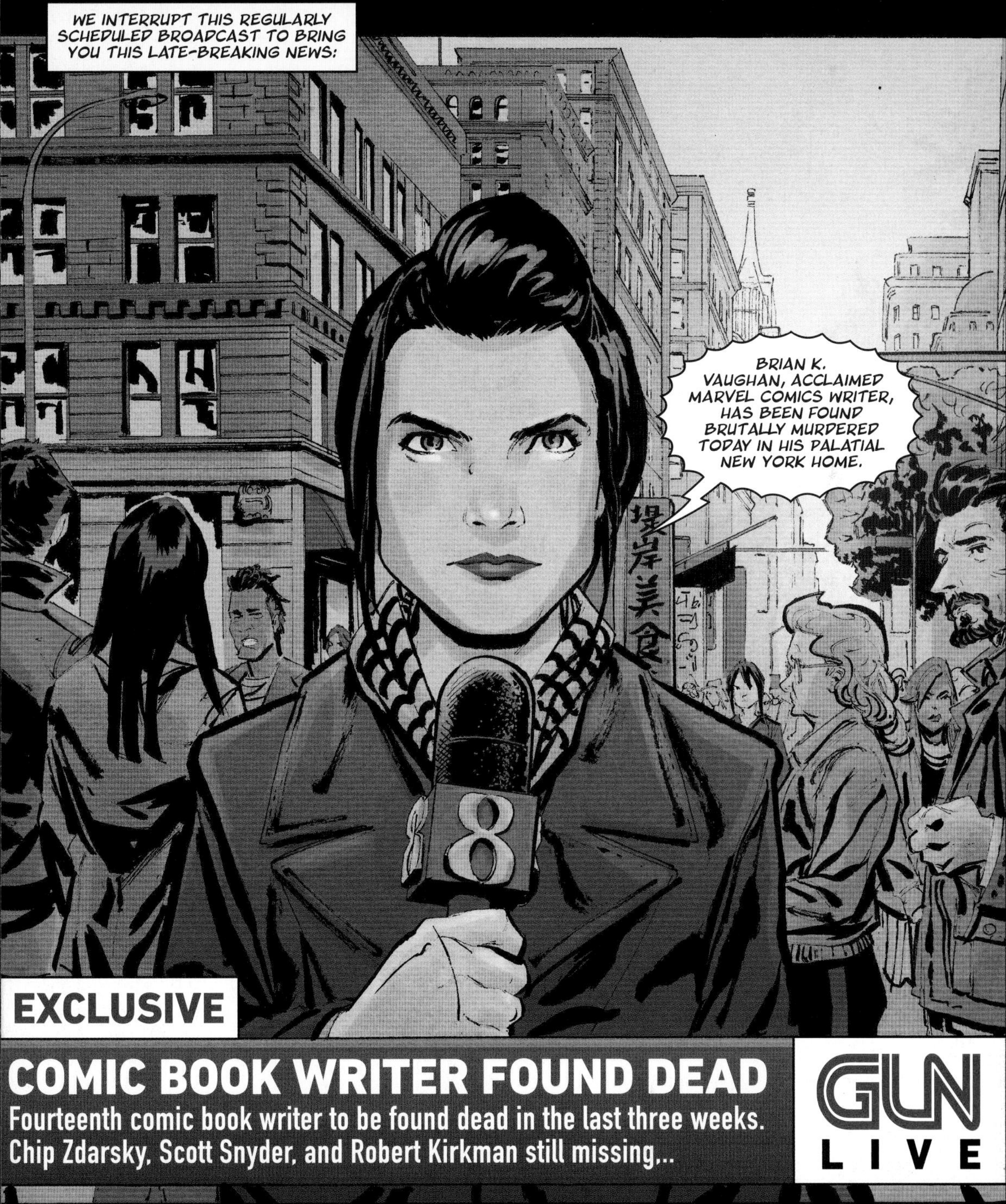
WE INTERRUPT THIS REGULARLY SCHEDULED BROADCAST TO BRING YOU THIS LATE-BREAKING NEWS:
BRIAN K. VAUGHAN, ACCLAIMED MARVEL COMICS WRITER, HAS BEEN FOUND BRUTALLY MURDERED TODAY IN HIS PALATIAL NEW YORK HOME.
8
EXCLUSIVE
COMIC BOOK WRITER FOUND DEAD
Fourteenth comic book writer to be found dead in the last three weeks.
Chip Zdarsky, Scott Snyder, and Robert Kirkman still missing...
GLN
LIVE

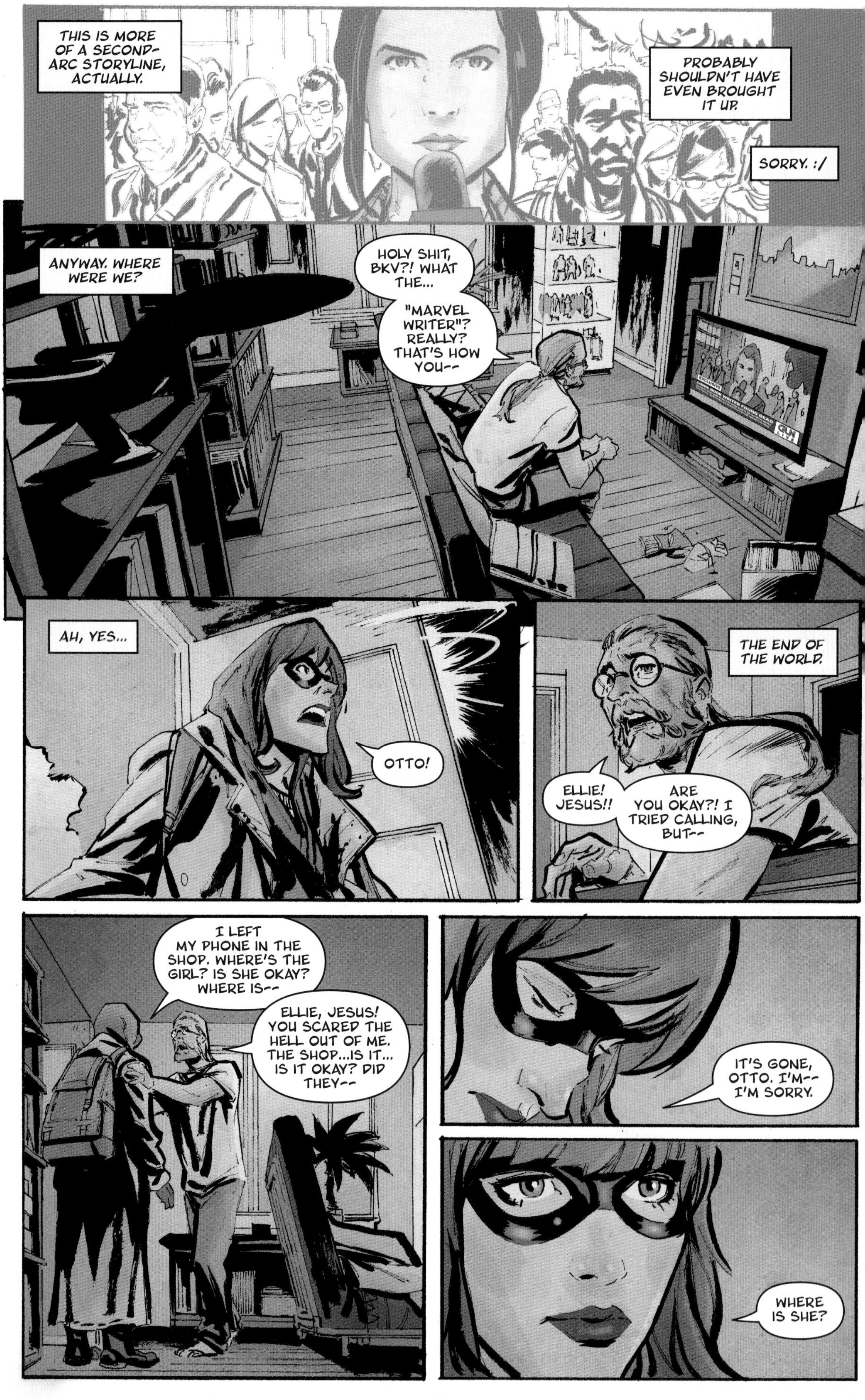
THIS IS MORE OF A SECOND-ARC STORYLINE, ACTUALLY.
PROBABLY SHOULDN'T HAVE EVEN BROUGHT IT UP.
SORRY. :/
ANYWAY. WHERE WERE WE?
HOLY SHIT, BKV?! WHAT THE...
"MARVEL WRITER"? REALLY? THAT'S HOW YOU--
AH, YES...
OTTO!
THE END OF THE WORLD.
ELLIE! JESUS!!
ARE YOU OKAY?! I TRIED CALLING, BUT--
I LEFT MY PHONE IN THE SHOP. WHERE'S THE GIRL? IS SHE OKAY? WHERE IS--
ELLIE, JESUS! YOU SCARED THE HELL OUT OF ME. THE SHOP...IS IT... IS IT OKAY? DID THEY--
IT'S GONE, OTTO. I'M-- I'M SORRY.
WHERE IS SHE?

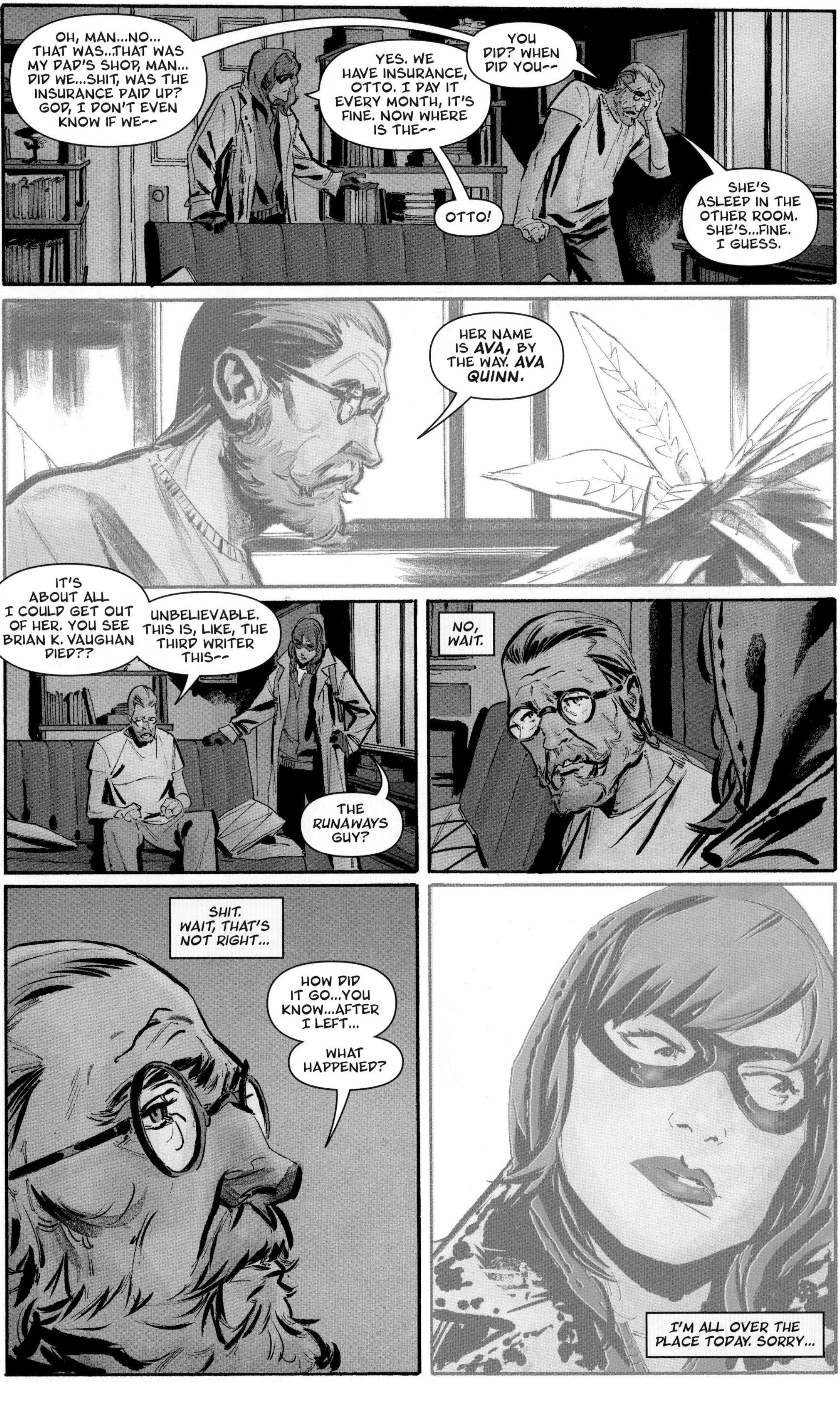
OH, MAN...NO... THAT WAS...THAT WAS MY DAD'S SHOP, MAN... DID WE...SHIT, WAS THE INSURANCE PAID UP? GOD, I DON'T EVEN KNOW IF WE--
YOU DID? WHEN DID YOU--
YES. WE HAVE INSURANCE, OTTO. I PAY IT EVERY MONTH, IT'S FINE. NOW WHERE IS THE--
OTTO!
SHE'S ASLEEP IN THE OTHER ROOM. SHE'S...FINE. I GUESS.
HER NAME IS AVA, BY THE WAY. AVA QUINN.
IT'S ABOUT ALL I COULD GET OUT OF HER. YOU SEE BRIAN K. VAUGHAN DIED??
UNBELIEVABLE. THIS IS, LIKE, THE THIRD WRITER THIS--
THE RUNAWAYS GUY?
NO, WAIT.
SHIT. WAIT, THAT'S NOT RIGHT...
HOW DID IT GO...YOU KNOW...AFTER I LEFT...
WHAT HAPPENED?
I'M ALL OVER THE PLACE TODAY. SORRY...

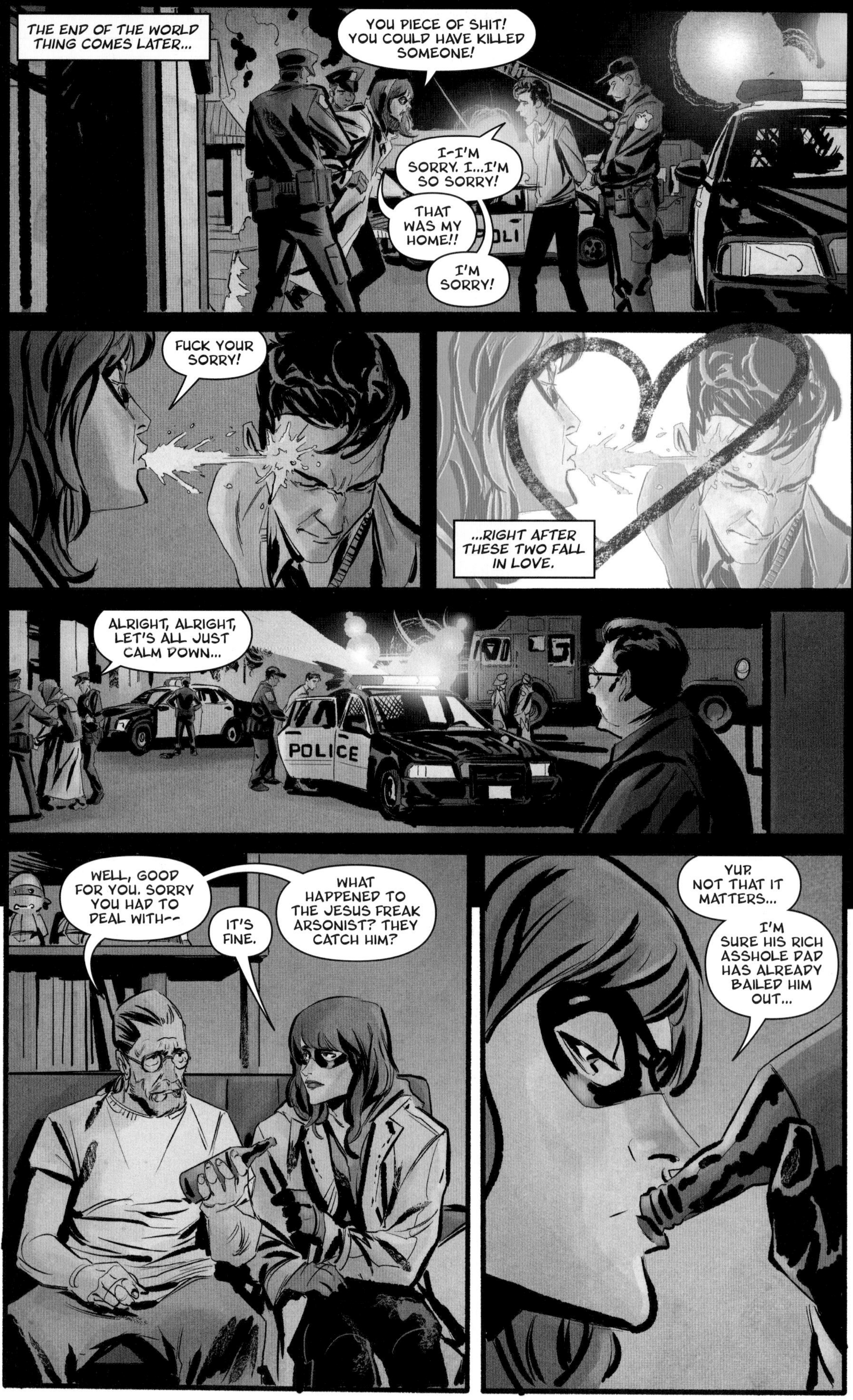

THE END OF THE WORLD THING COMES LATER...
YOU PIECE OF SHIT! YOU COULD HAVE KILLED SOMEONE!
I-I'M SORRY. I...I'M SO SORRY!
THAT WAS MY HOME!!
I'M SORRY!
FUCK YOUR SORRY!
...RIGHT AFTER THESE TWO FALL IN LOVE.
ALRIGHT, ALRIGHT, LET'S ALL JUST CALM DOWN...
POLICE
WELL, GOOD FOR YOU. SORRY YOU HAD TO DEAL WITH--
IT'S FINE.
WHAT HAPPENED TO THE JESUS FREAK ARSONIST? THEY CATCH HIM?
YUP. NOT THAT IT MATTERS...
I'M SURE HIS RICH ASSHOLE DAD HAS ALREADY BAILED HIM OUT...

HA! REALLY? YOU DON'T WANT ME TO CALL PSYCHOPATH MILLIONAIRE *FATHER LOWE* TO COME AND BAIL YOU OUT?

LOOK, KID, YOU'RE NOT GETTING ANY ARGUMENT FROM ME.

YOU KNOW HE'S NOT EVEN ORDAINED, RIGHT?

ALL THAT "FATHER" STUFF IS JUST BULLSHIT, IT'S JUST A CULT. KID, WE CAN HELP YOU--

NO...

PLEASE DON'T CALL MY FATHER.

I JUST... I WANT TO CONFESS.

I DESERVE TO BE PUNISHED FOR WHAT I DID.

I COULD HAVE HURT SOMEONE AND I--I JUST...DON'T WANT TO GO HOME...

RYAN. LOOK. HOLD UP, OKAY. CALM DOWN.

YOU'RE NOT EVEN OUR PROBLEM ANY-MORE...WE'RE JUST MAKING THE TRANSFER.

SO, YOU WANNA LAWYER? YOU WANNA TRY AND CUT A DEAL?

MAYBE GIVE US SOMETHING ON THAT PSYCHO GUN-HOARDING COMPOUND OF YOUR DAD'S HE THINKS WE DON'T KNOW ABOUT?

THIS AIN'T THAT. YOU'RE OFFICIALLY OUT OF OUR JURIS-DICTION...

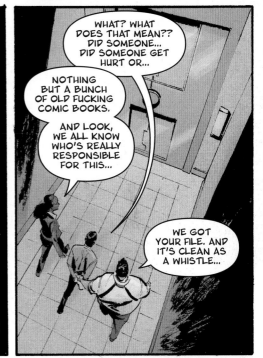

WHAT? WHAT DOES THAT MEAN?? DID SOMEONE... DID SOMEONE GET HURT OR...

NOTHING BUT A BUNCH OF OLD FUCKING COMIC BOOKS.

AND LOOK, WE ALL KNOW WHO'S REALLY RESPONSIBLE FOR THIS...

WE GOT YOUR FILE. AND IT'S CLEAN AS A WHISTLE...

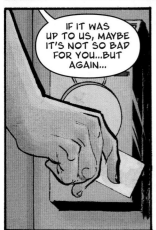

IF IT WAS UP TO US, MAYBE IT'S NOT SO BAD FOR YOU...BUT AGAIN...

YOU HAVE, FOR WHATEVER REASON, OFFICIALLY MADE THE HIGHEST OF SHIT LISTS...

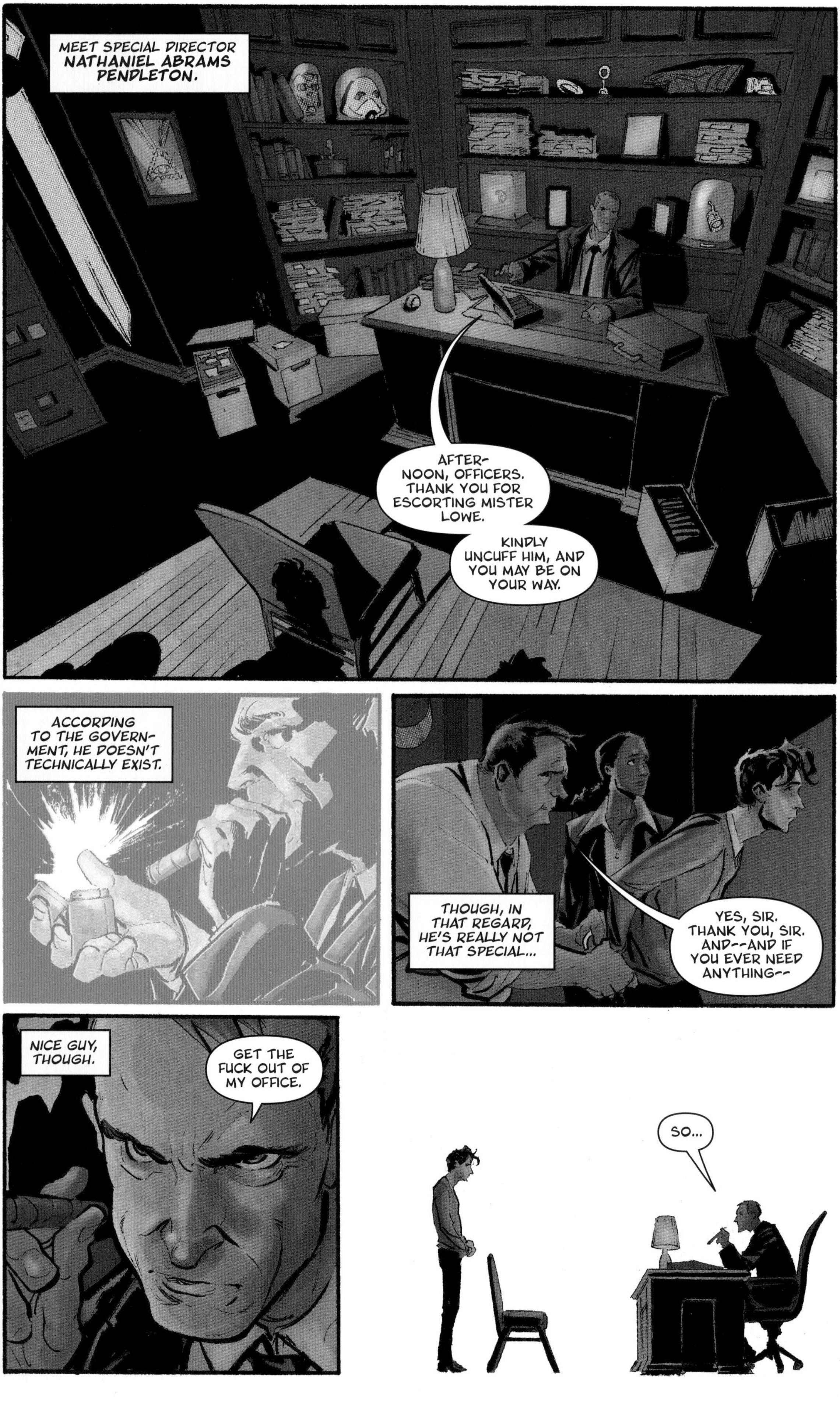

MEET SPECIAL DIRECTOR NATHANIEL ABRAMS PENDLETON.
AFTER-NOON, OFFICERS. THANK YOU FOR ESCORTING MISTER LOWE.
KINDLY UNCUFF HIM, AND YOU MAY BE ON YOUR WAY.
ACCORDING TO THE GOVERN-MENT, HE DOESN'T TECHNICALLY EXIST.
THOUGH, IN THAT REGARD, HE'S REALLY NOT THAT SPECIAL...
YES, SIR. THANK YOU, SIR. AND--AND IF YOU EVER NEED ANYTHING--
NICE GUY, THOUGH.
GET THE FUCK OUT OF MY OFFICE.
SO...

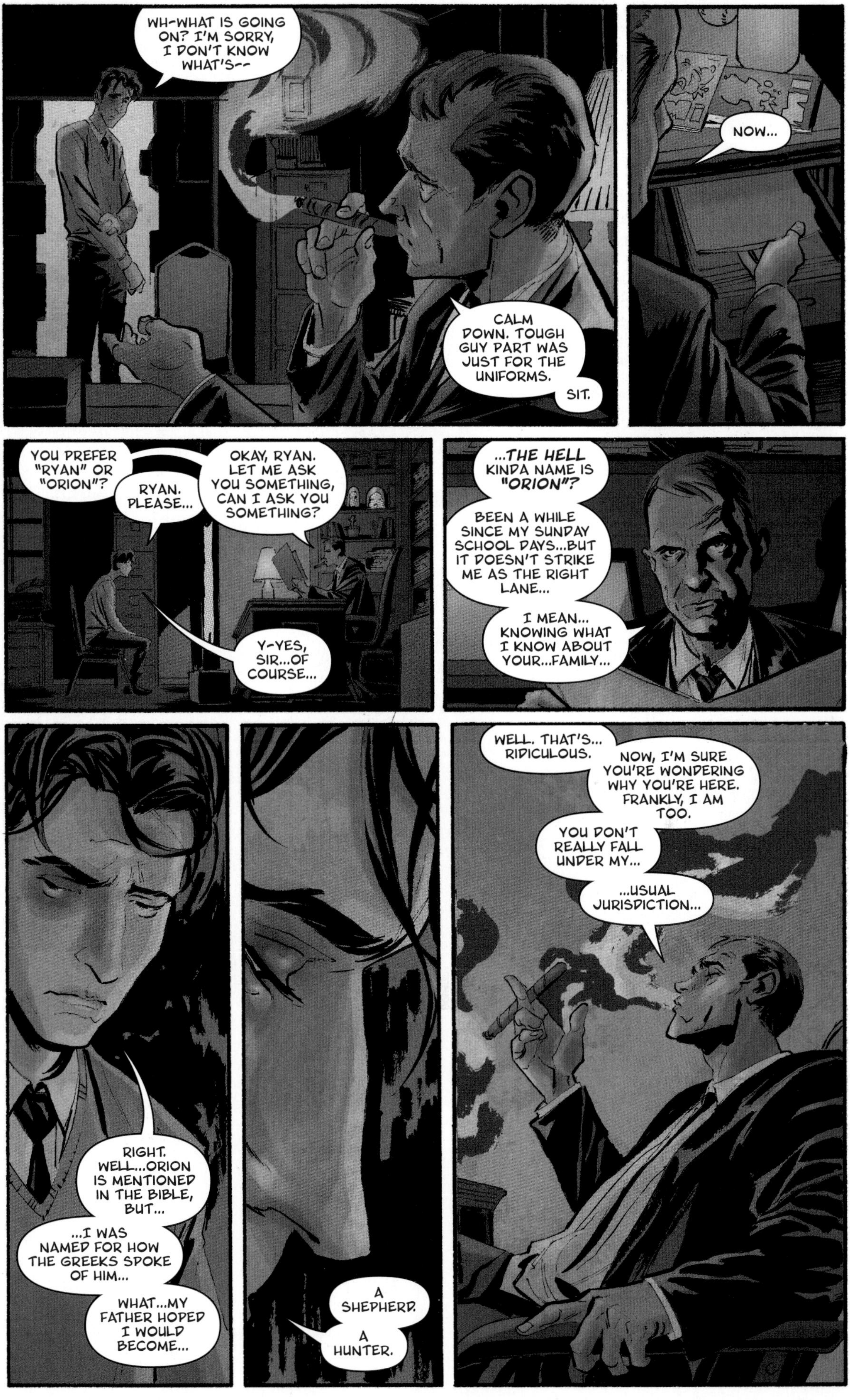
WH-WHAT IS GOING ON? I'M SORRY, I DON'T KNOW WHAT'S--
CALM DOWN. TOUGH GUY PART WAS JUST FOR THE UNIFORMS.
SIT.
NOW...
YOU PREFER "RYAN" OR "ORION"?
RYAN. PLEASE...
OKAY, RYAN. LET ME ASK YOU SOMETHING, CAN I ASK YOU SOMETHING?
Y-YES, SIR...OF COURSE...
...THE HELL KINDA NAME IS "ORION"?
BEEN A WHILE SINCE MY SUNDAY SCHOOL DAYS...BUT IT DOESN'T STRIKE ME AS THE RIGHT LANE...
I MEAN... KNOWING WHAT I KNOW ABOUT YOUR...FAMILY...
RIGHT. WELL...ORION IS MENTIONED IN THE BIBLE, BUT...
...I WAS NAMED FOR HOW THE GREEKS SPOKE OF HIM...
WHAT...MY FATHER HOPED I WOULD BECOME...
A SHEPHERD.
A HUNTER.
WELL. THAT'S... RIDICULOUS.
NOW, I'M SURE YOU'RE WONDERING WHY YOU'RE HERE. FRANKLY, I AM TOO.
YOU DON'T REALLY FALL UNDER MY...
...USUAL JURISDICTION...

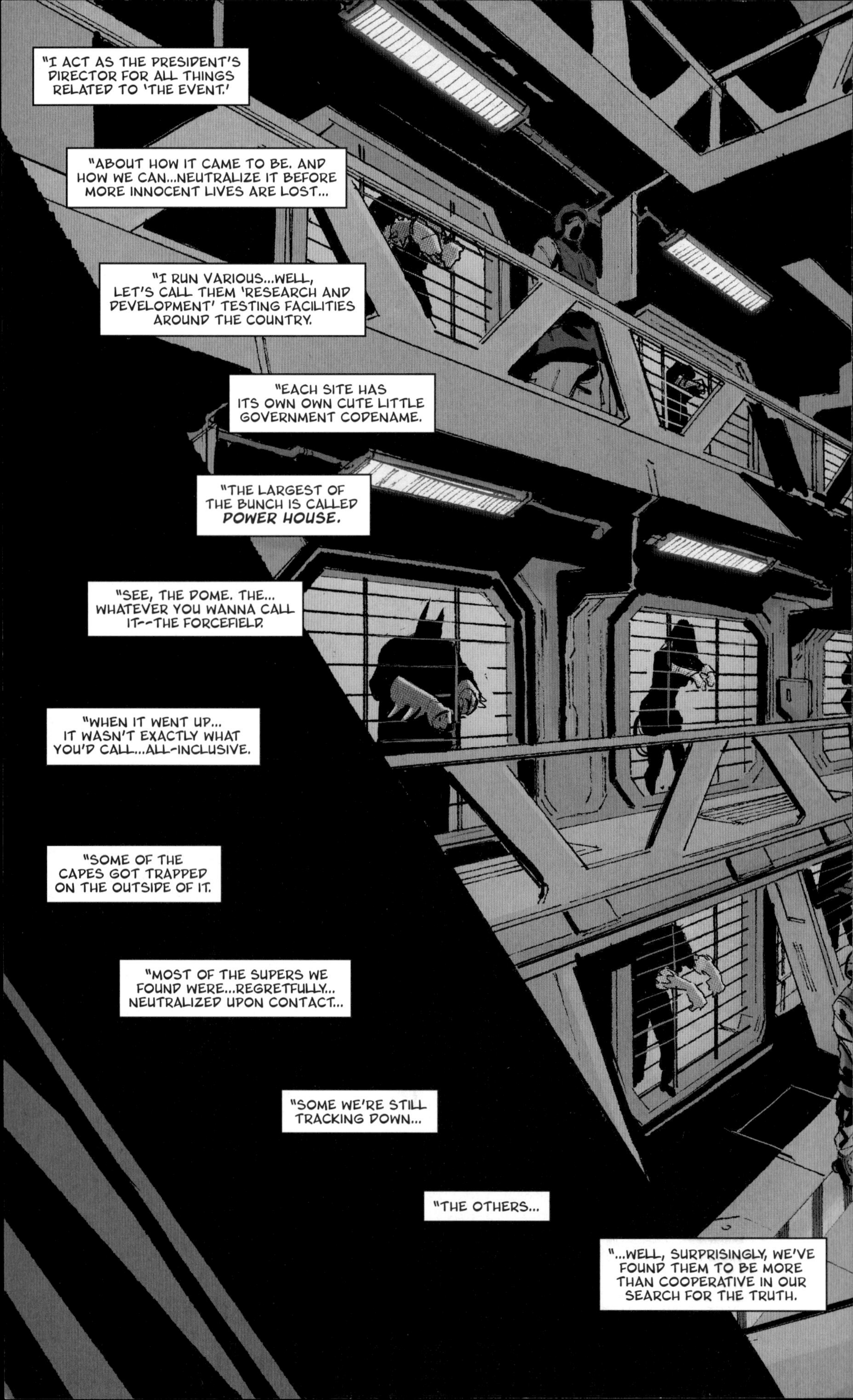
"I ACT AS THE PRESIDENT'S DIRECTOR FOR ALL THINGS RELATED TO 'THE EVENT.'
"ABOUT HOW IT CAME TO BE. AND HOW WE CAN...NEUTRALIZE IT BEFORE MORE INNOCENT LIVES ARE LOST...
"I RUN VARIOUS...WELL, LET'S CALL THEM 'RESEARCH AND DEVELOPMENT' TESTING FACILITIES AROUND THE COUNTRY.
"EACH SITE HAS ITS OWN OWN CUTE LITTLE GOVERNMENT CODENAME.
"THE LARGEST OF THE BUNCH IS CALLED *POWER HOUSE.*
"SEE, THE DOME. THE... WHATEVER YOU WANNA CALL IT--THE FORCEFIELD.
"WHEN IT WENT UP... IT WASN'T EXACTLY WHAT YOU'D CALL...ALL-INCLUSIVE.
"SOME OF THE CAPES GOT TRAPPED ON THE OUTSIDE OF IT.
"MOST OF THE SUPERS WE FOUND WERE...REGRETFULLY... NEUTRALIZED UPON CONTACT...
"SOME WE'RE STILL TRACKING DOWN...
"THE OTHERS...
"...WELL, SURPRISINGLY, WE'VE FOUND THEM TO BE MORE THAN COOPERATIVE IN OUR SEARCH FOR THE TRUTH.

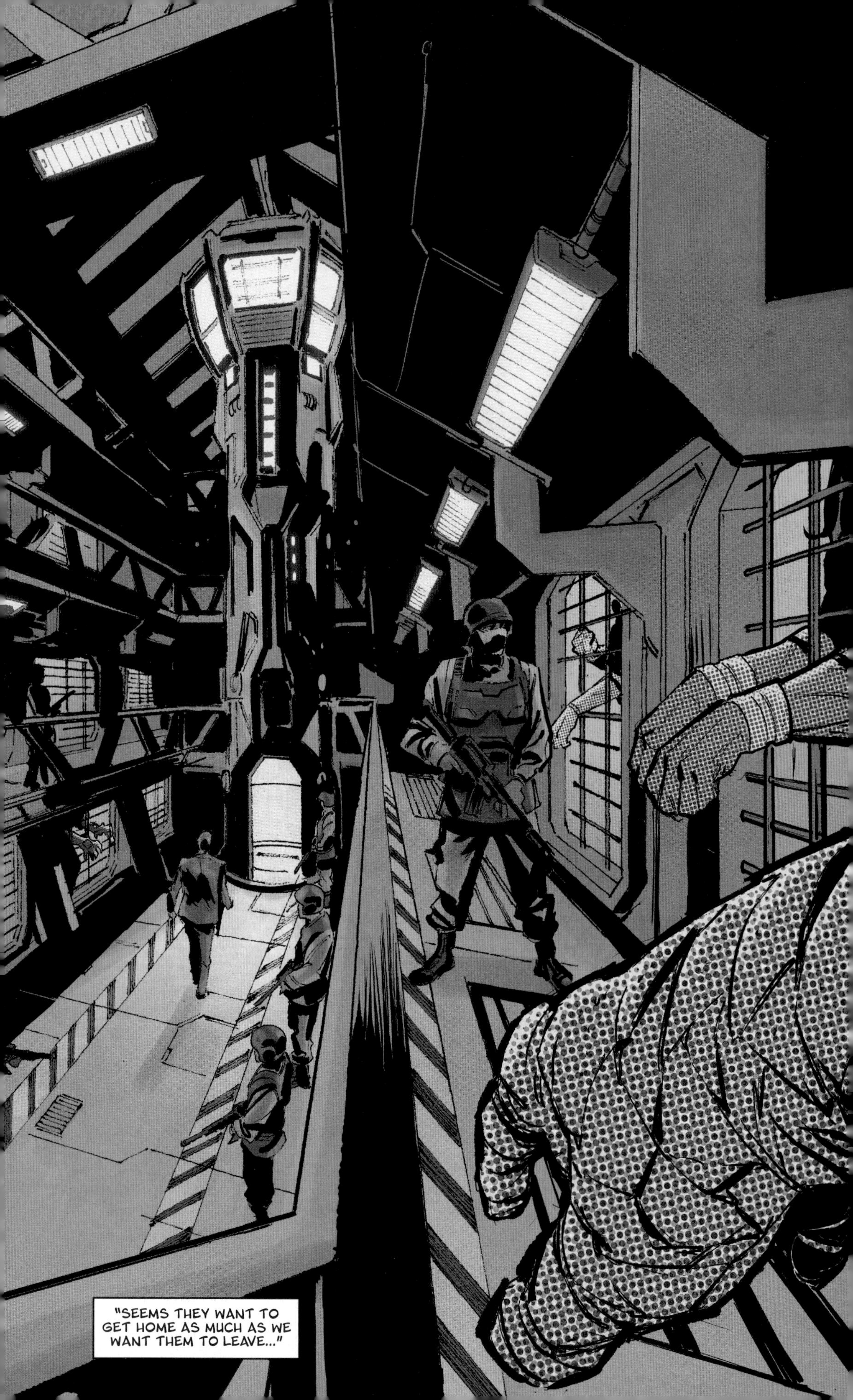
"SEEMS THEY WANT TO GET HOME AS MUCH AS WE WANT THEM TO LEAVE..."

WHICH BRINGS US TO YOU...

"YOU SEE, ALL OF OUR CELLS ARE EQUIPPED WITH THESE...*DRAINING LAMPS* THAT REMOVE THE SUBJECT'S *POWERS.*

"(LITTLE STROKE OF GOOD LUCK WE GOT ON LOAN FROM A FEW OF *THEIR KIND* WILLING TO HELP US IN EXCHANGE FOR A FEW...FAVORS.)

"ANYWAY, DAMN THINGS HAVE BEEN CRUCIAL IN THE MORE...SCIENTIFIC STUDIES OF THEIR KIND...

"BUT SEE, HERE'S THE THING....

"WE HAVE, IN OUR POSSESSION, AN... INDIVIDUAL WHOSE POWERS ARE, FOR WHATEVER REASON, *NOT DAMPENED BY THE LAMPS.*

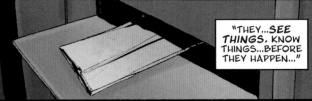

"THEY...*SEE THINGS.* KNOW THINGS...BEFORE THEY HAPPEN..."

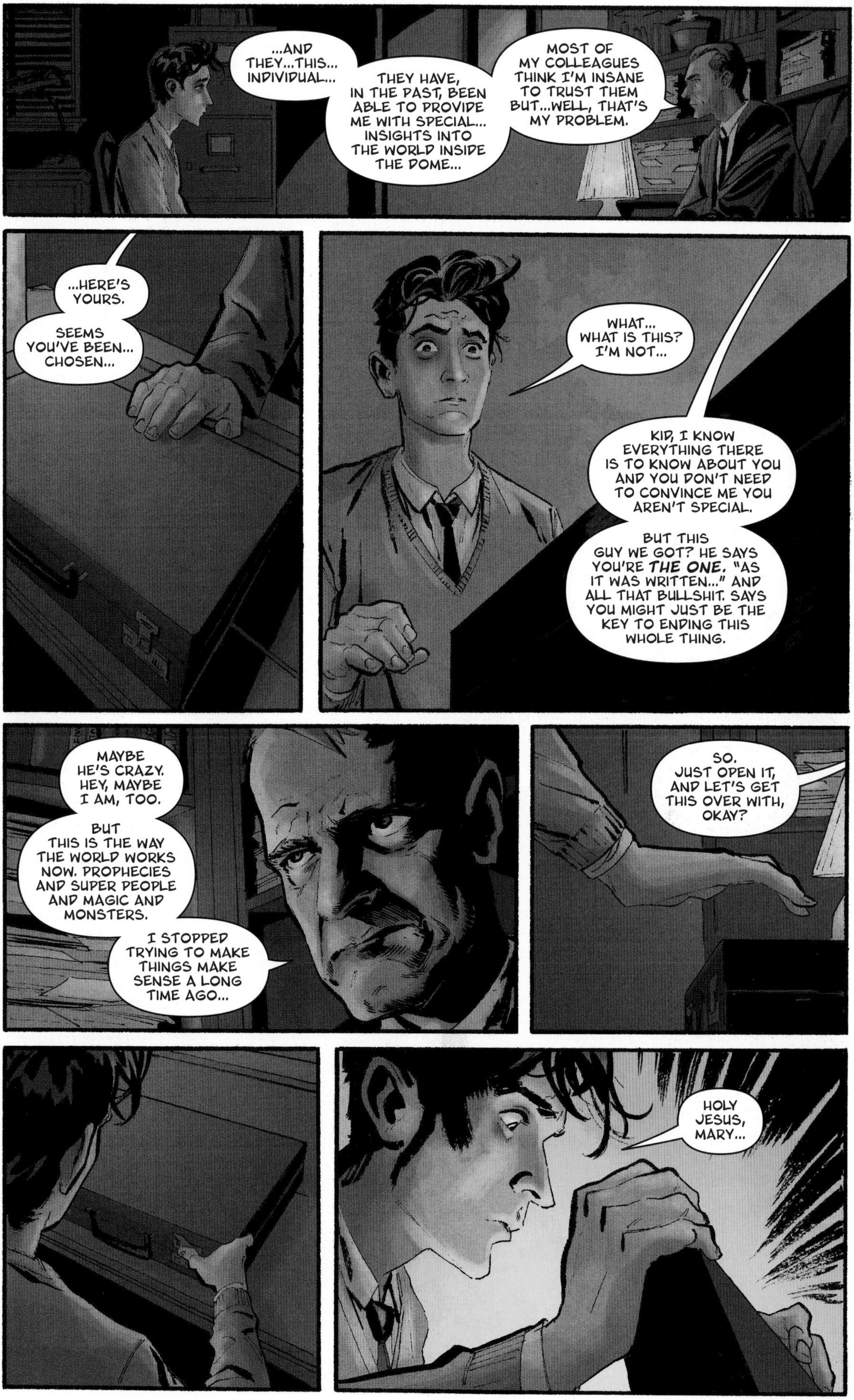
...AND THEY...THIS... INDIVIDUAL...
THEY HAVE, IN THE PAST, BEEN ABLE TO PROVIDE ME WITH SPECIAL... INSIGHTS INTO THE WORLD INSIDE THE DOME...
MOST OF MY COLLEAGUES THINK I'M INSANE TO TRUST THEM BUT...WELL, THAT'S MY PROBLEM.
...HERE'S YOURS.
SEEMS YOU'VE BEEN... CHOSEN...
WHAT... WHAT IS THIS? I'M NOT...
KID, I KNOW EVERYTHING THERE IS TO KNOW ABOUT YOU AND YOU DON'T NEED TO CONVINCE ME YOU AREN'T SPECIAL.
BUT THIS GUY WE GOT? HE SAYS YOU'RE ***THE ONE.*** "AS IT WAS WRITTEN..." AND ALL THAT BULLSHIT. SAYS YOU MIGHT JUST BE THE KEY TO ENDING THIS WHOLE THING.
MAYBE HE'S CRAZY. HEY, MAYBE I AM, TOO.
BUT THIS IS THE WAY THE WORLD WORKS NOW. PROPHECIES AND SUPER PEOPLE AND MAGIC AND MONSTERS.
I STOPPED TRYING TO MAKE THINGS MAKE SENSE A LONG TIME AGO...
SO. JUST OPEN IT, AND LET'S GET THIS OVER WITH, OKAY?
HOLY JESUS, MARY...

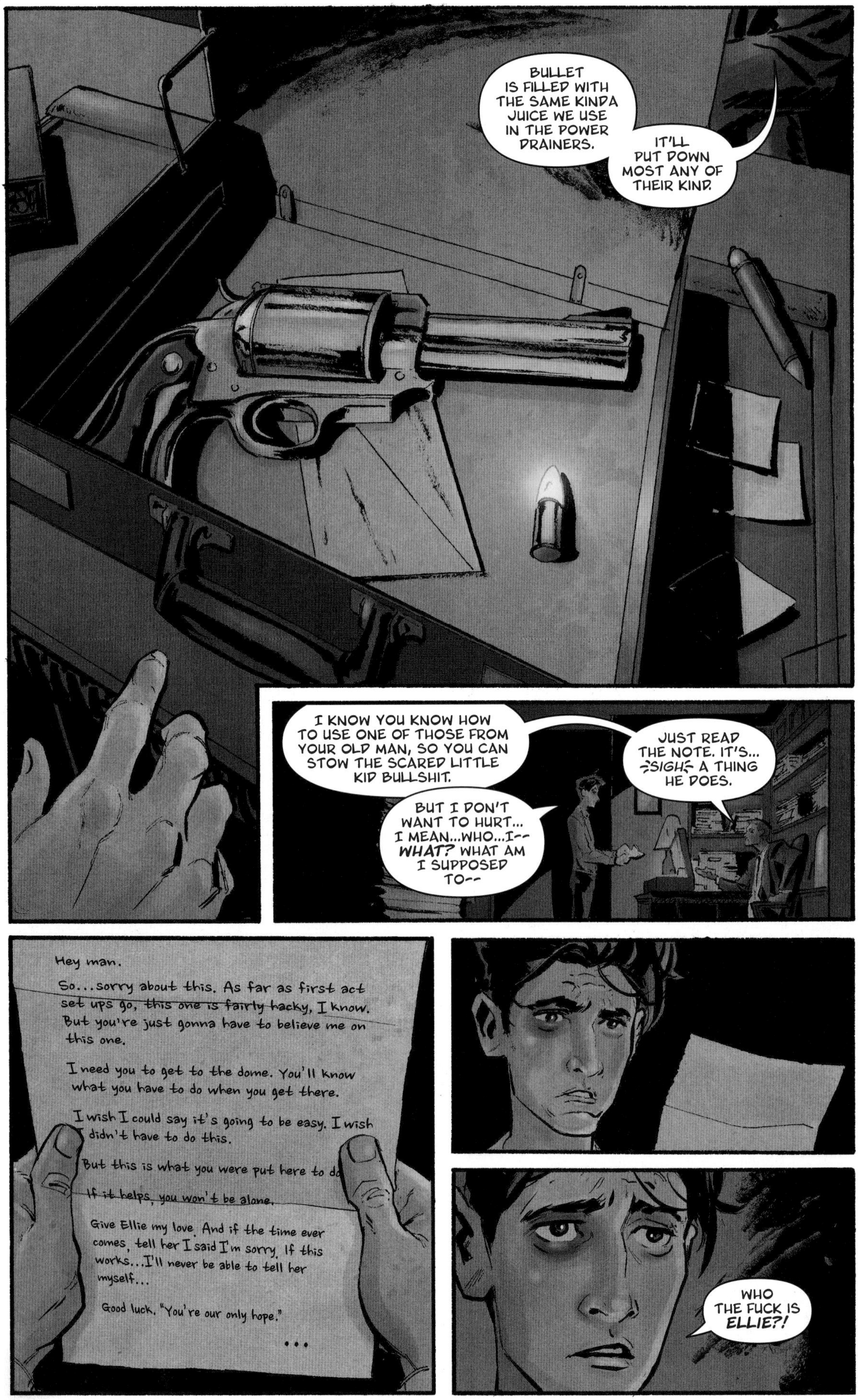
BULLET IS FILLED WITH THE SAME KINDA JUICE WE USE IN THE POWER DRAINERS.
IT'LL PUT DOWN MOST ANY OF THEIR KIND.
I KNOW YOU KNOW HOW TO USE ONE OF THOSE FROM YOUR OLD MAN, SO YOU CAN STOW THE SCARED LITTLE KID BULLSHIT.
JUST READ THE NOTE. IT'S... ~SIGH~ A THING HE DOES.
BUT I DON'T WANT TO HURT... I MEAN...WHO...I-- WHAT? WHAT AM I SUPPOSED TO--
Hey man.
So...sorry about this. As far as first act set ups go, this one is fairly hacky, I know. But you're just gonna have to believe me on this one.
I need you to get to the dome. You'll know what you have to do when you get there.
I wish I could say it's going to be easy. I wish I didn't have to do this.
But this is what you were put here to do
If it helps, you won't be alone.
Give Ellie my love. And if the time ever comes, tell her I said I'm sorry. If this works...I'll never be able to tell her myself...
Good luck. "You're our only hope."
...
WHO THE FUCK IS ELLIE?!

YOU OFFICIALLY KNOW EXACTLY THE SAME AMOUNT OF INFORMATION I DO CONCERNING THAT NOTE AND BRIEFCASE.

WAIT, NO... HOW, HOW DO I GET THERE? WHAT ABOUT MY DAD? HE'S NOT JUST GOING TO LET ME LEAVE!

AND--AND I'M SUPPOSED TO SHOOT SOMEONE?! THIS DOESN'T MAKE ANY--

HEY. WHAT DID I JUST SAY? THIS IS THE DEAL.

YOU THINK I'M JUST GOING TO LET YOU RUN OUT OF HERE, KNOWING WHAT I JUST TOLD YOU? SORRY...

BUT YOU BELONG TO ME.

YOU DO THIS... OR YOU GO AWAY TO A PLACE SO DEEP NOT EVEN YOUR DADDY WILL FIND YOU.

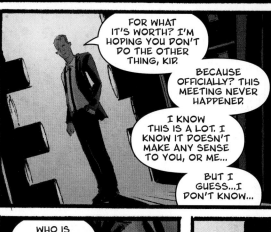

FOR WHAT IT'S WORTH? I'M HOPING YOU DON'T DO THE OTHER THING, KID.

BECAUSE OFFICIALLY? THIS MEETING NEVER HAPPENED.

I KNOW THIS IS A LOT. I KNOW IT DOESN'T MAKE ANY SENSE TO YOU, OR ME...

BUT I GUESS...I DON'T KNOW...

...MAYBE HAVE A LITTLE FAITH.

WHO IS HE? THE MAN WHO WROTE THE NOTE.

IS HE A...LIKE, A CHARACTER?

LIKE, WOULD I... KNOW HIM? FROM THE COMICS OR--

÷SIGH÷ LISTEN...

...GO DO YOUR JOB. OR DON'T. BUT TRUST ME...

THERE'RE THINGS IN THIS NEW WORLD OF OURS...

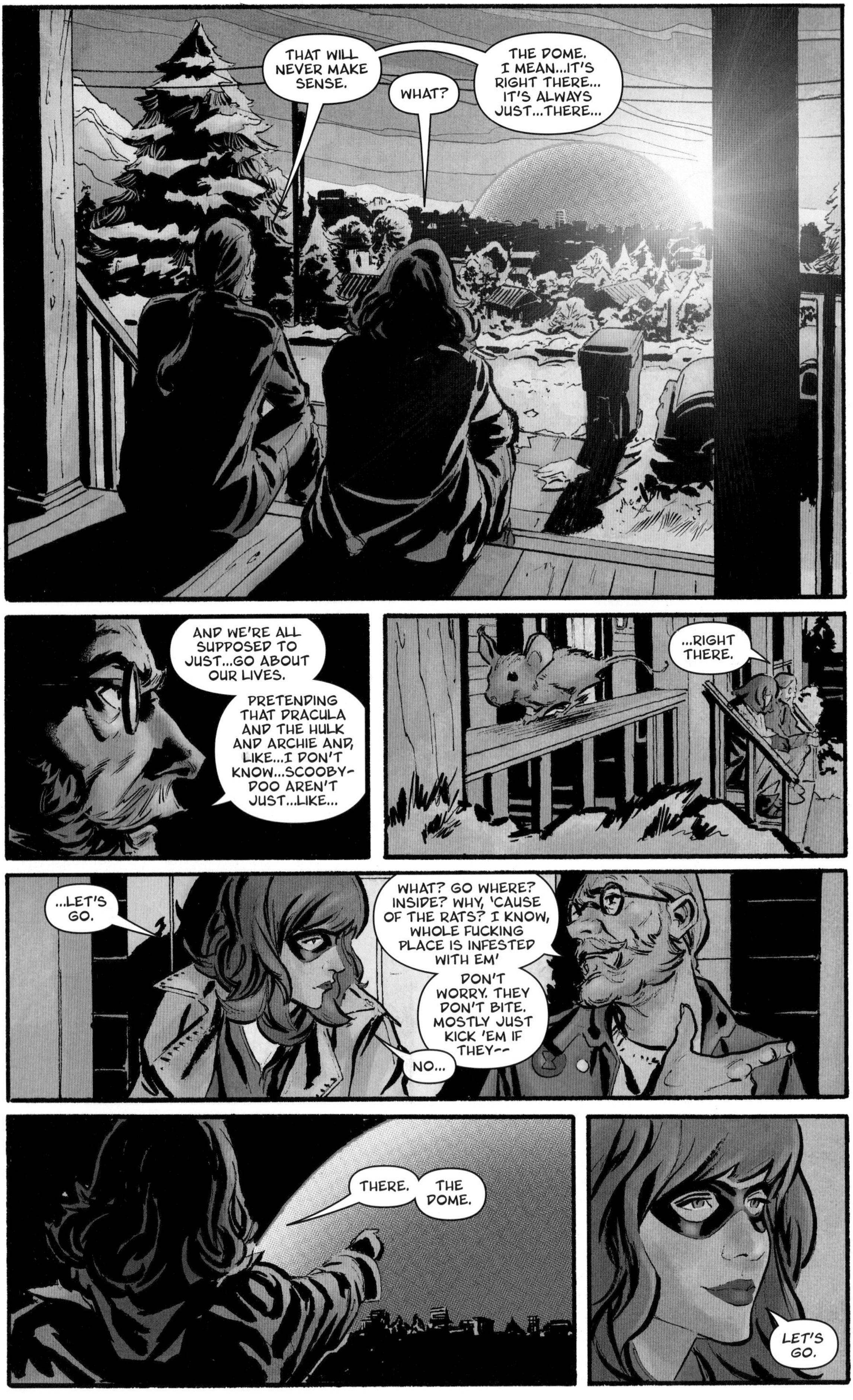
THAT WILL NEVER MAKE SENSE.
WHAT?
THE DOME. I MEAN...IT'S RIGHT THERE... IT'S ALWAYS JUST...THERE...
AND WE'RE ALL SUPPOSED TO JUST...GO ABOUT OUR LIVES.
PRETENDING THAT DRACULA AND THE HULK AND ARCHIE AND, LIKE...I DON'T KNOW...SCOOBY-DOO AREN'T JUST...LIKE...
...RIGHT THERE.
...LET'S GO.
WHAT? GO WHERE? INSIDE? WHY, 'CAUSE OF THE RATS? I KNOW, WHOLE FUCKING PLACE IS INFESTED WITH EM'
DON'T WORRY. THEY DON'T BITE. MOSTLY JUST KICK 'EM IF THEY--
NO...
THERE.
THE DOME.
LET'S GO.

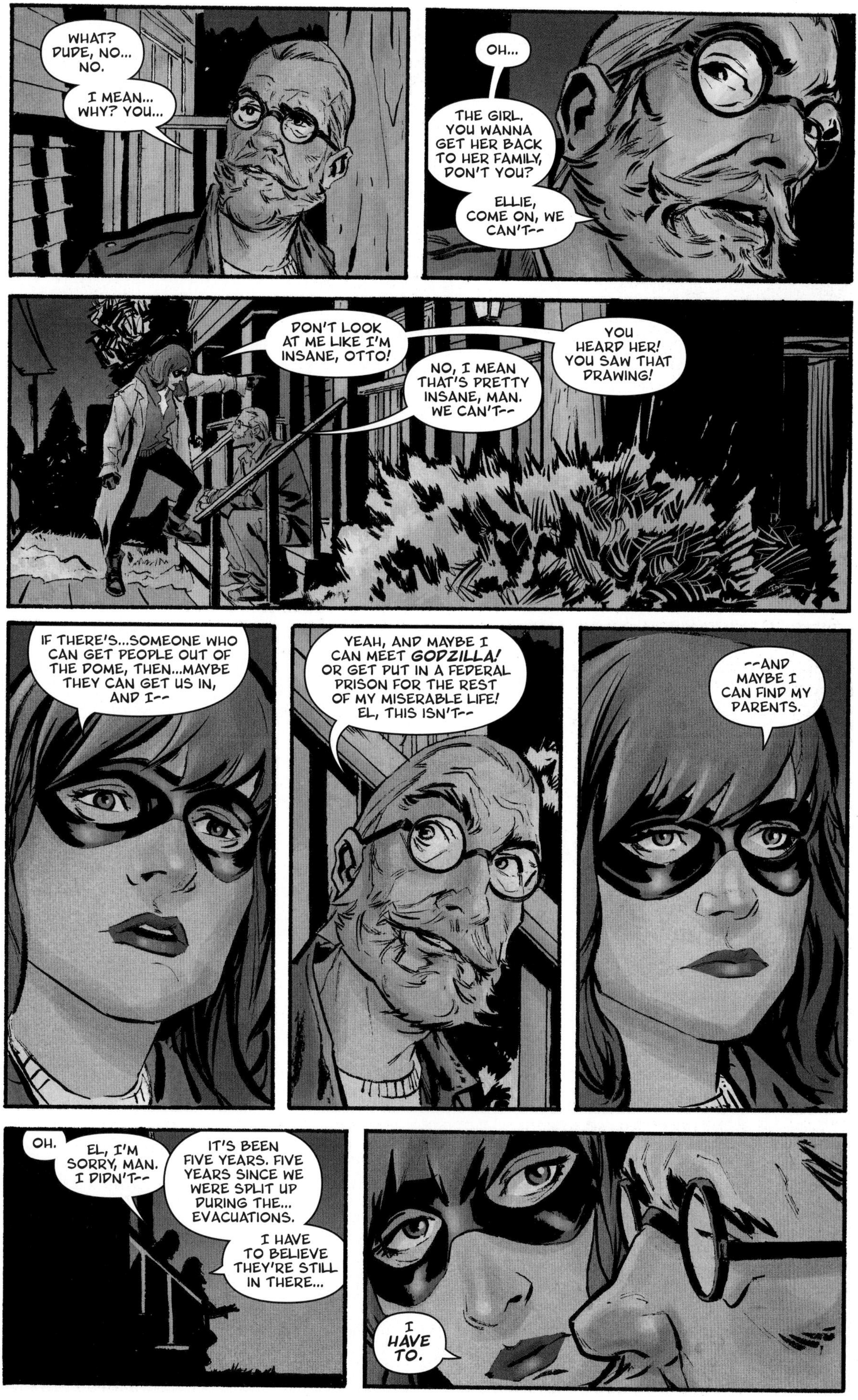
WHAT? DUDE, NO... NO.
I MEAN... WHY? YOU...
OH...
THE GIRL. YOU WANNA GET HER BACK TO HER FAMILY, DON'T YOU?
ELLIE, COME ON, WE CAN'T--
DON'T LOOK AT ME LIKE I'M INSANE, OTTO!
YOU HEARD HER! YOU SAW THAT DRAWING!
NO, I MEAN THAT'S PRETTY INSANE, MAN. WE CAN'T--
IF THERE'S...SOMEONE WHO CAN GET PEOPLE OUT OF THE DOME, THEN...MAYBE THEY CAN GET US IN, AND I--
YEAH, AND MAYBE I CAN MEET GODZILLA! OR GET PUT IN A FEDERAL PRISON FOR THE REST OF MY MISERABLE LIFE! EL, THIS ISN'T--
--AND MAYBE I CAN FIND MY PARENTS.
OH.
EL, I'M SORRY, MAN. I DIDN'T--
IT'S BEEN FIVE YEARS. FIVE YEARS SINCE WE WERE SPLIT UP DURING THE... EVACUATIONS.
I HAVE TO BELIEVE THEY'RE STILL IN THERE...
I HAVE TO.

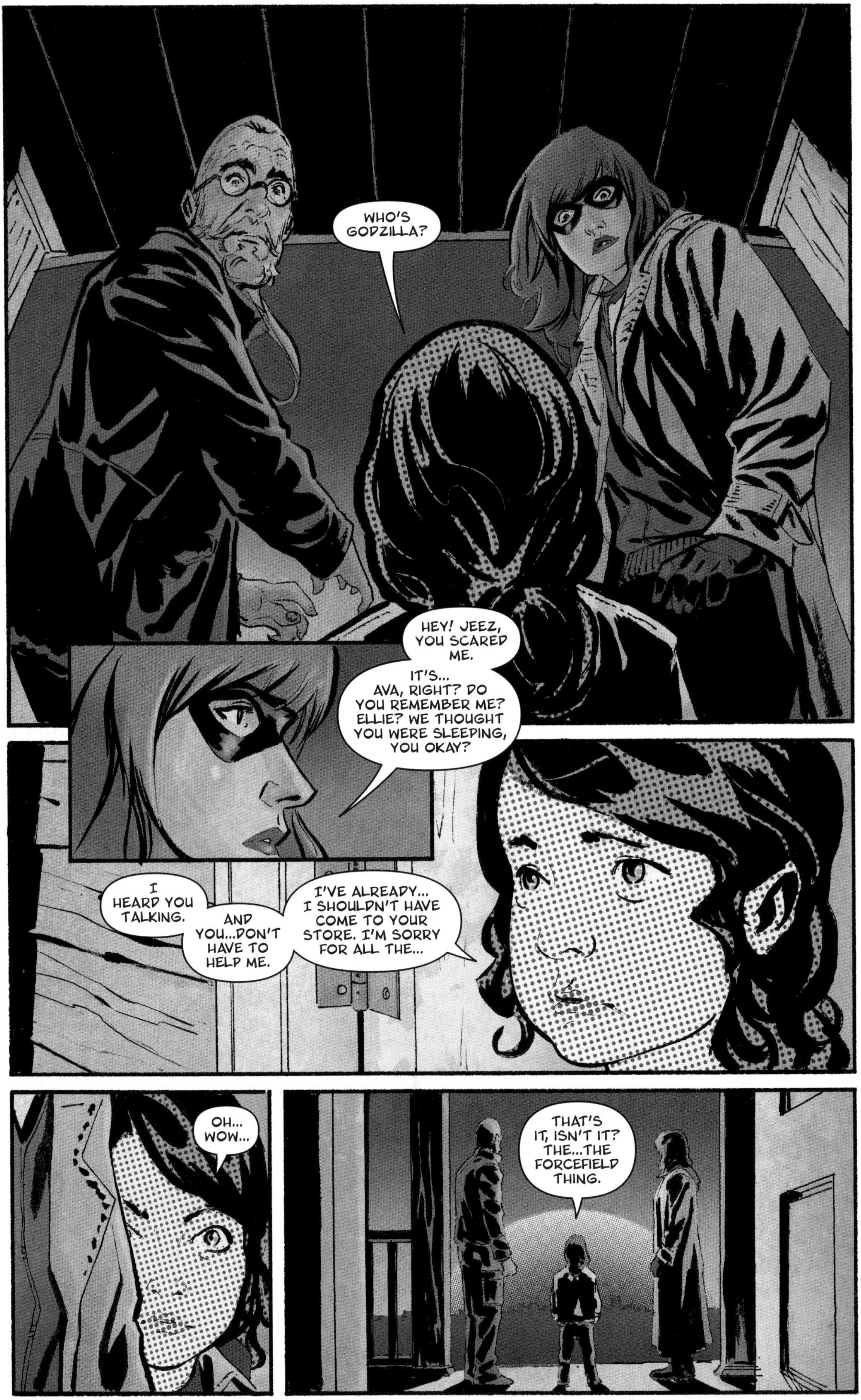
WHO'S GODZILLA?
HEY! JEEZ, YOU SCARED ME.
IT'S... AVA, RIGHT? DO YOU REMEMBER ME? ELLIE? WE THOUGHT YOU WERE SLEEPING, YOU OKAY?
I HEARD YOU TALKING.
AND YOU...DON'T HAVE TO HELP ME.
I'VE ALREADY... I SHOULDN'T HAVE COME TO YOUR STORE. I'M SORRY FOR ALL THE...
OH... WOW...
THAT'S IT, ISN'T IT? THE...THE FORCEFIELD THING.

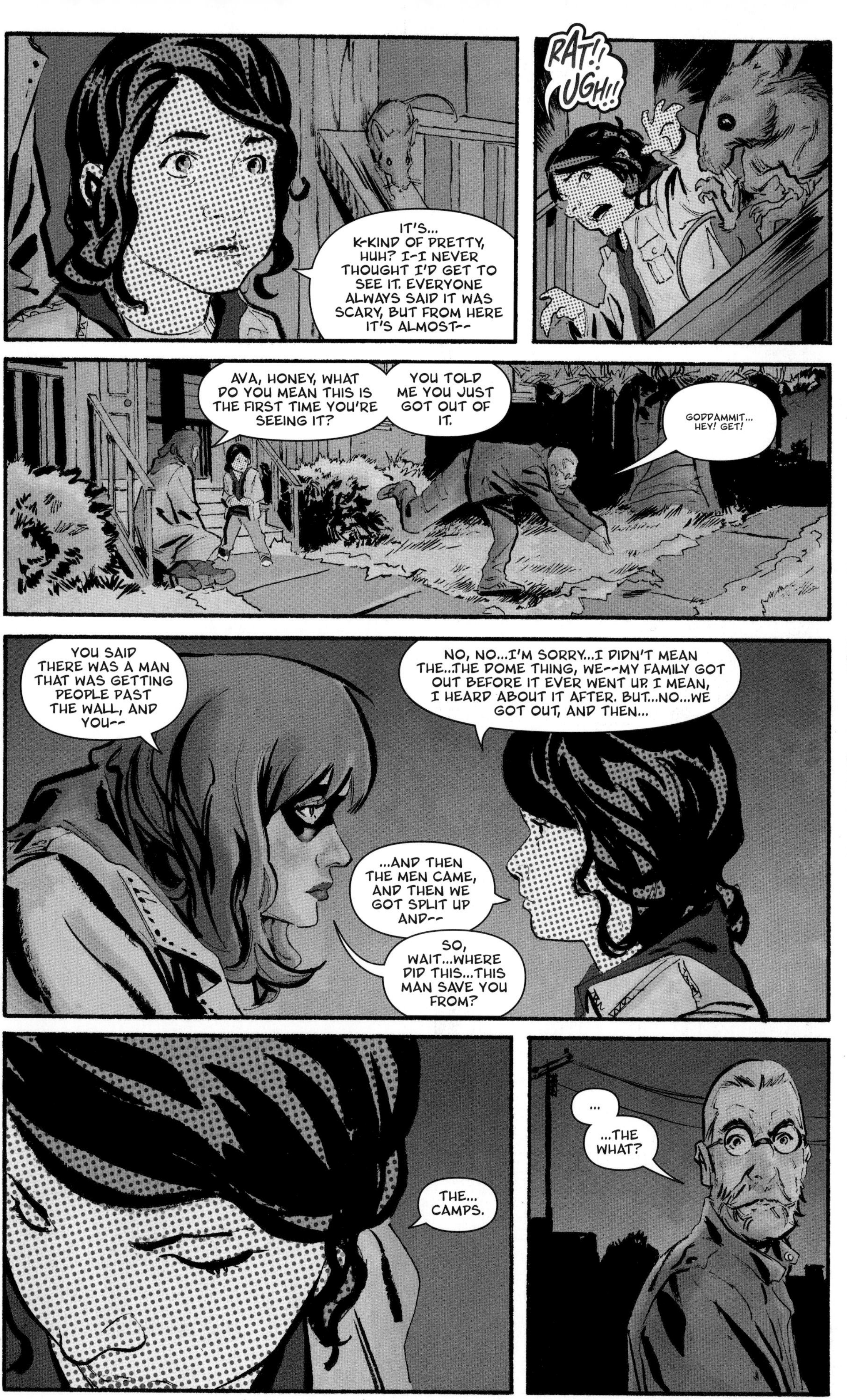
IT'S... K-KIND OF PRETTY, HUH? I-I NEVER THOUGHT I'D GET TO SEE IT. EVERYONE ALWAYS SAID IT WAS SCARY, BUT FROM HERE IT'S ALMOST--
RAT!! UGH!!
AVA, HONEY, WHAT DO YOU MEAN THIS IS THE FIRST TIME YOU'RE SEEING IT?
YOU TOLD ME YOU JUST GOT OUT OF IT.
GODDAMMIT... HEY! GET!
YOU SAID THERE WAS A MAN THAT WAS GETTING PEOPLE PAST THE WALL, AND YOU--
NO, NO...I'M SORRY...I DIDN'T MEAN THE...THE DOME THING, WE--MY FAMILY GOT OUT BEFORE IT EVER WENT UP. I MEAN, I HEARD ABOUT IT AFTER. BUT...NO...WE GOT OUT, AND THEN...
...AND THEN THE MEN CAME, AND THEN WE GOT SPLIT UP AND--
SO, WAIT...WHERE DID THIS...THIS MAN SAVE YOU FROM?
THE... CAMPS.
...
...THE WHAT?

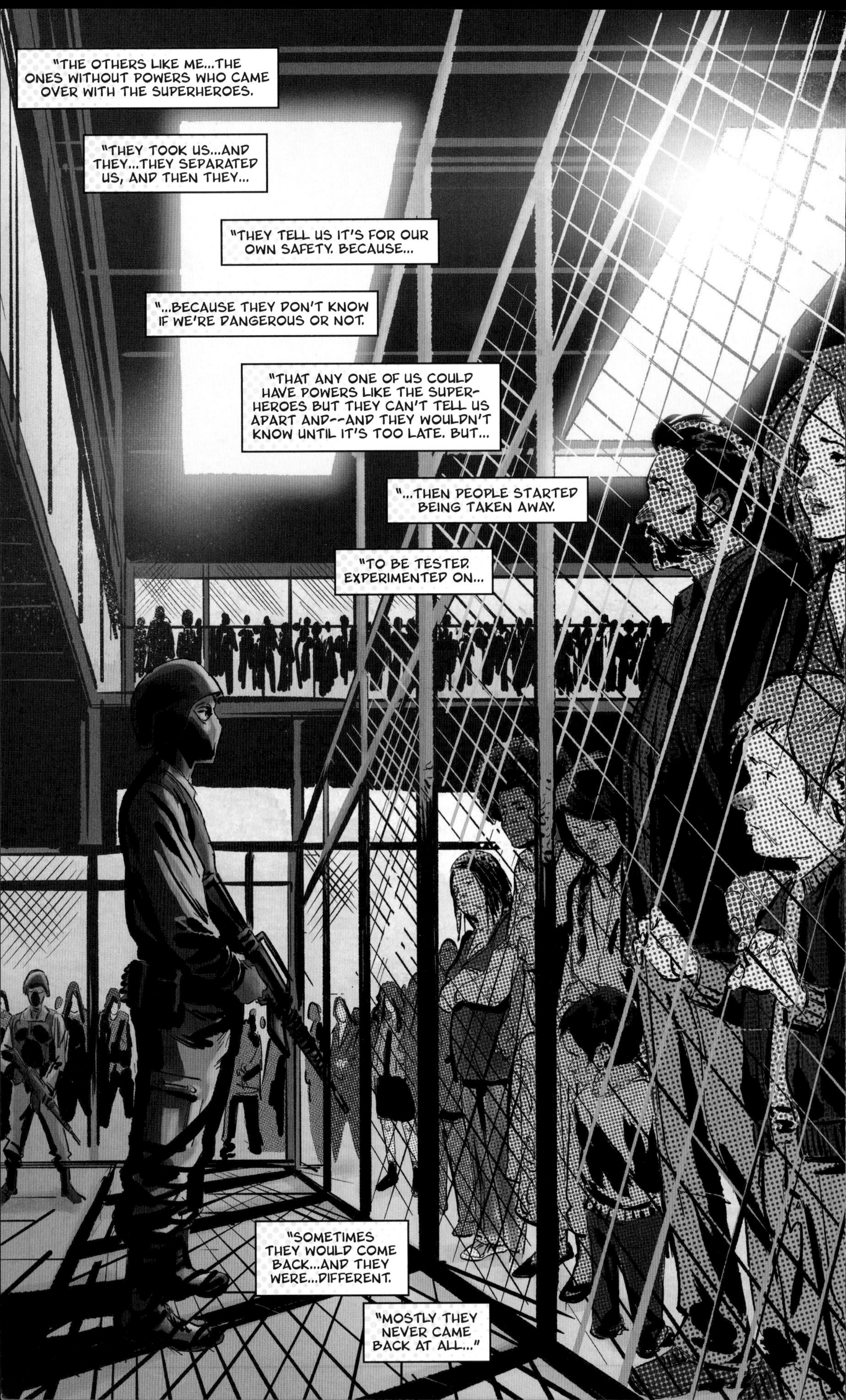
"THE OTHERS LIKE ME...THE ONES WITHOUT POWERS WHO CAME OVER WITH THE SUPERHEROES.
"THEY TOOK US...AND THEY...THEY SEPARATED US, AND THEN THEY...
"THEY TELL US IT'S FOR OUR OWN SAFETY. BECAUSE...
"...BECAUSE THEY DON'T KNOW IF WE'RE DANGEROUS OR NOT.
"THAT ANY ONE OF US COULD HAVE POWERS LIKE THE SUPER-HEROES BUT THEY CAN'T TELL US APART AND--AND THEY WOULDN'T KNOW UNTIL IT'S TOO LATE. BUT...
"...THEN PEOPLE STARTED BEING TAKEN AWAY.
"TO BE TESTED. EXPERIMENTED ON...
"SOMETIMES THEY WOULD COME BACK...AND THEY WERE...DIFFERENT.
"MOSTLY THEY NEVER CAME BACK AT ALL..."

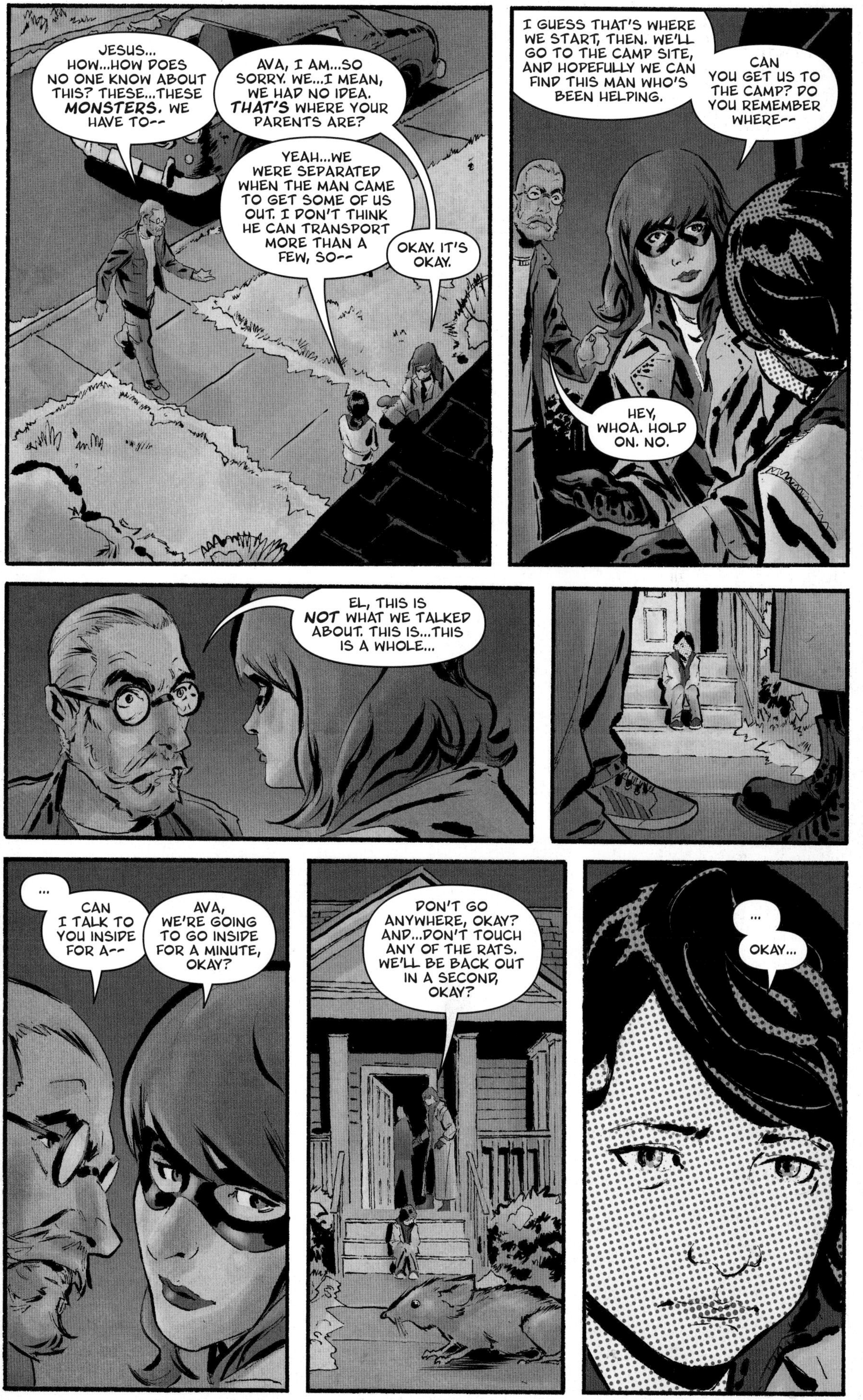
JESUS... HOW...HOW DOES NO ONE KNOW ABOUT THIS? THESE...THESE MONSTERS. WE HAVE TO--
AVA, I AM...SO SORRY. WE...I MEAN, WE HAD NO IDEA. THAT'S WHERE YOUR PARENTS ARE?
YEAH...WE WERE SEPARATED WHEN THE MAN CAME TO GET SOME OF US OUT. I DON'T THINK HE CAN TRANSPORT MORE THAN A FEW, SO--
OKAY. IT'S OKAY.
I GUESS THAT'S WHERE WE START, THEN. WE'LL GO TO THE CAMP SITE, AND HOPEFULLY WE CAN FIND THIS MAN WHO'S BEEN HELPING.
CAN YOU GET US TO THE CAMP? DO YOU REMEMBER WHERE--
HEY, WHOA. HOLD ON. NO.
EL, THIS IS NOT WHAT WE TALKED ABOUT. THIS IS...THIS IS A WHOLE...
...
CAN I TALK TO YOU INSIDE FOR A--
AVA, WE'RE GOING TO GO INSIDE FOR A MINUTE, OKAY?
DON'T GO ANYWHERE, OKAY? AND...DON'T TOUCH ANY OF THE RATS. WE'LL BE BACK OUT IN A SECOND, OKAY?
...
OKAY...

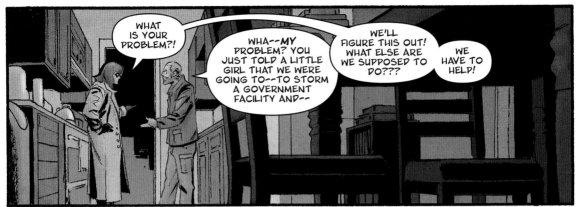

WHAT IS YOUR PROBLEM?!

WHA--MY PROBLEM? YOU JUST TOLD A LITTLE GIRL THAT WE WERE GOING TO--TO STORM A GOVERNMENT FACILITY AND--

WE'LL FIGURE THIS OUT! WHAT ELSE ARE WE SUPPOSED TO DO???

WE HAVE TO HELP!

WE READ THESE COMICS AND ACT LIKE WE'RE THE GOOD GUYS, BUT NOW WHEN IT COMES TO ACTUALLY DOING SOMETHING GOOD, YOU WANT TO RUN?

I'M HELPING HER, OTTO. BECAUSE SHE DOESN'T HAVE ANYWHERE TO RUN.

SHE DOESN'T HAVE A HOME, AND NEITHER DO I, SO WITH YOU OR WITHOUT YOU--

WAIT. WHAT DOES THAT MEAN? YOU "DON'T HAVE A HOME"?

...

DAMMIT. I WAS GOING TO TELL YOU... I--

YOU WERE LIVING IN THE STORE. I KNEW IT! I KNEW SOMETHING WAS WEIRD WHEN YOU STARTED WORKING--

I'M SORRY! I SHOULD HAVE TOLD YOU, BUT--

YOU KNOW WHAT? THAT'S GREAT, NOW I HAVE TWO REFUGEES IN MY HOUSE...

"...AND ONE OF THEM COULD BE AN ATOM BOMB."

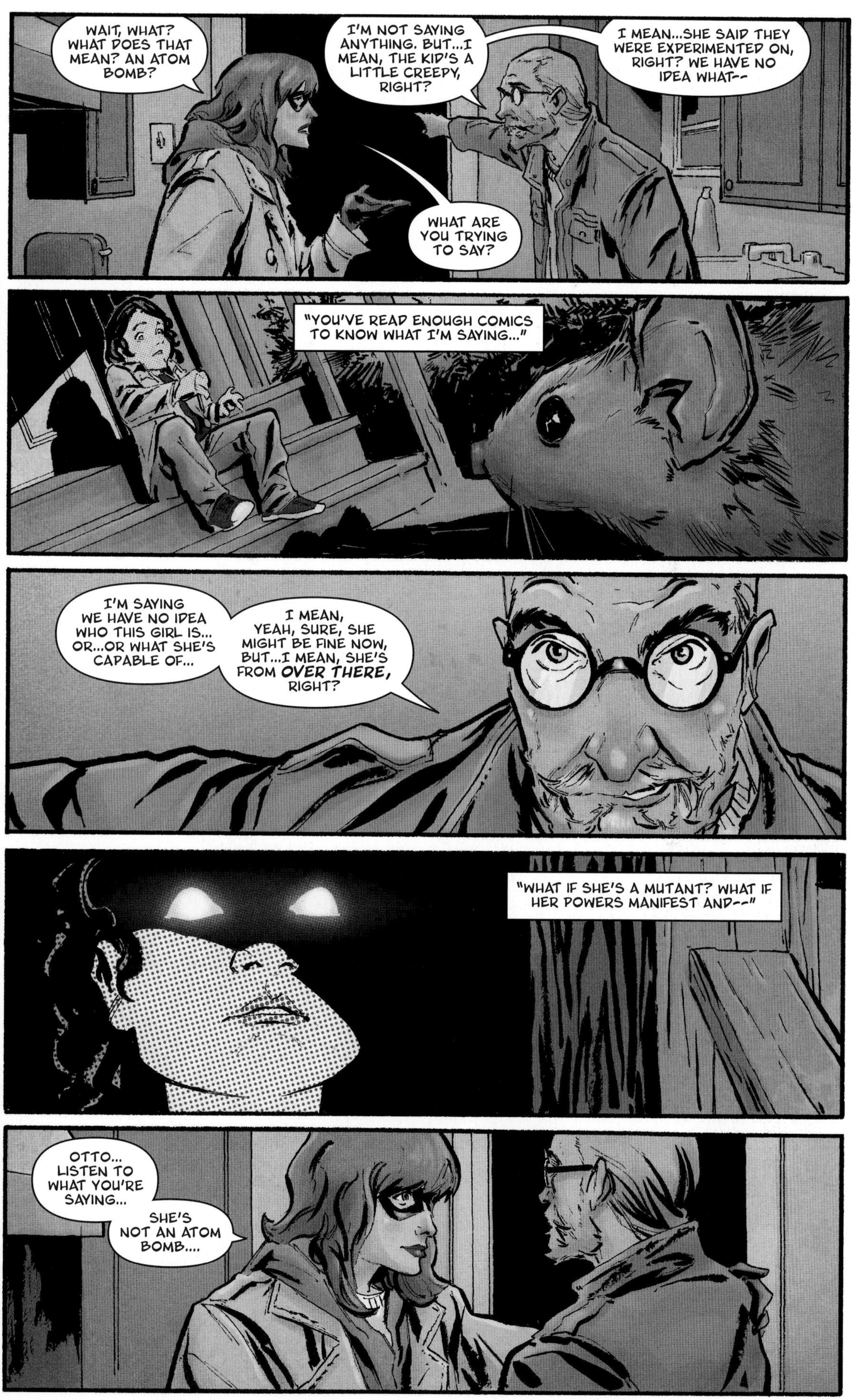
WAIT, WHAT? WHAT DOES THAT MEAN? AN ATOM BOMB?
I'M NOT SAYING ANYTHING. BUT...I MEAN, THE KID'S A LITTLE CREEPY, RIGHT?
I MEAN...SHE SAID THEY WERE EXPERIMENTED ON, RIGHT? WE HAVE NO IDEA WHAT--
WHAT ARE YOU TRYING TO SAY?
"YOU'VE READ ENOUGH COMICS TO KNOW WHAT I'M SAYING..."
I'M SAYING WE HAVE NO IDEA WHO THIS GIRL IS... OR...OR WHAT SHE'S CAPABLE OF...
I MEAN, YEAH, SURE, SHE MIGHT BE FINE NOW, BUT...I MEAN, SHE'S FROM ***OVER THERE,*** RIGHT?
"WHAT IF SHE'S A MUTANT? WHAT IF HER POWERS MANIFEST AND--"
OTTO... LISTEN TO WHAT YOU'RE SAYING...
SHE'S NOT AN ATOM BOMB....

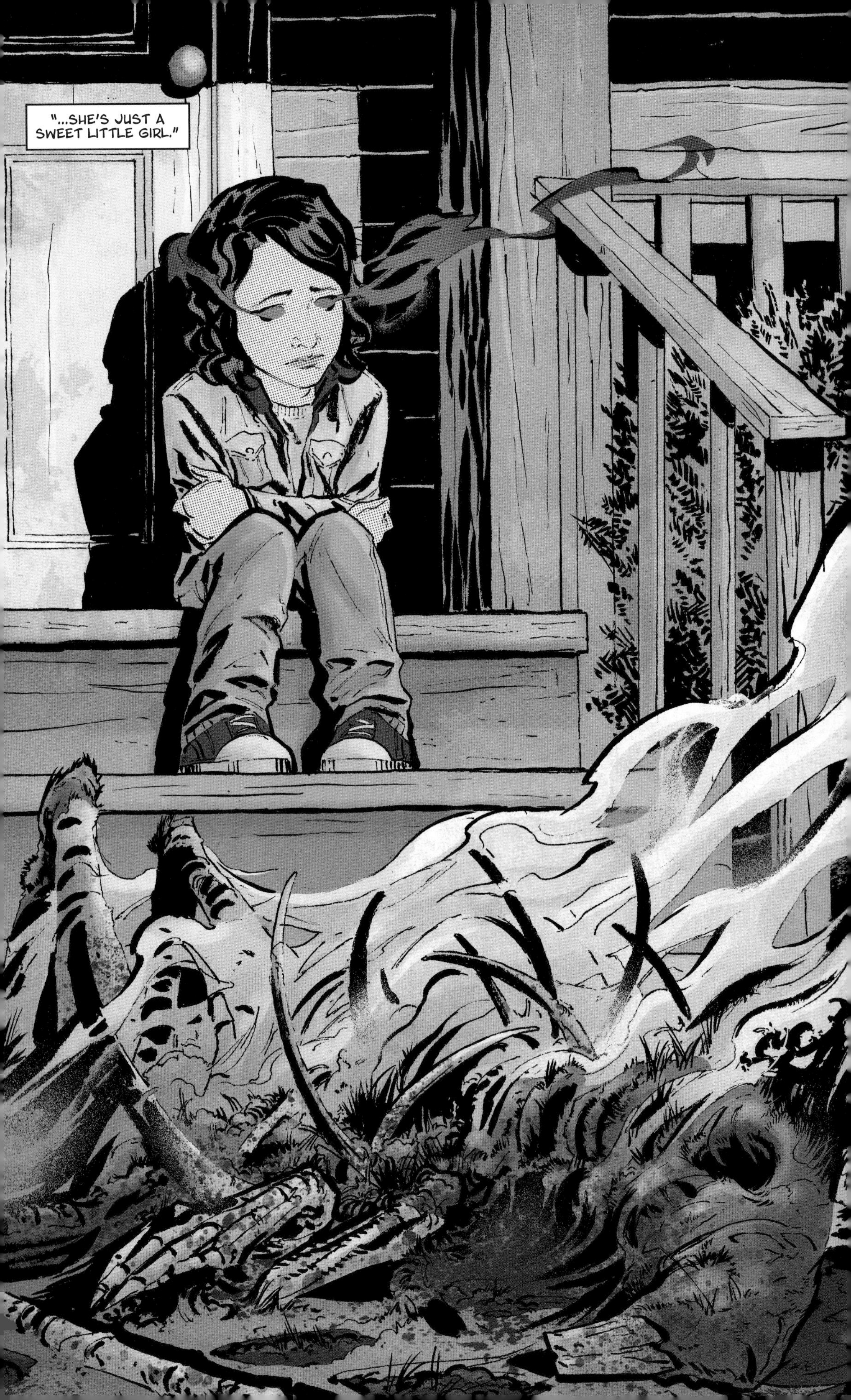
"...SHE'S JUST A SWEET LITTLE GIRL."

GEOFF SHAW & DEE CUNNIFFE

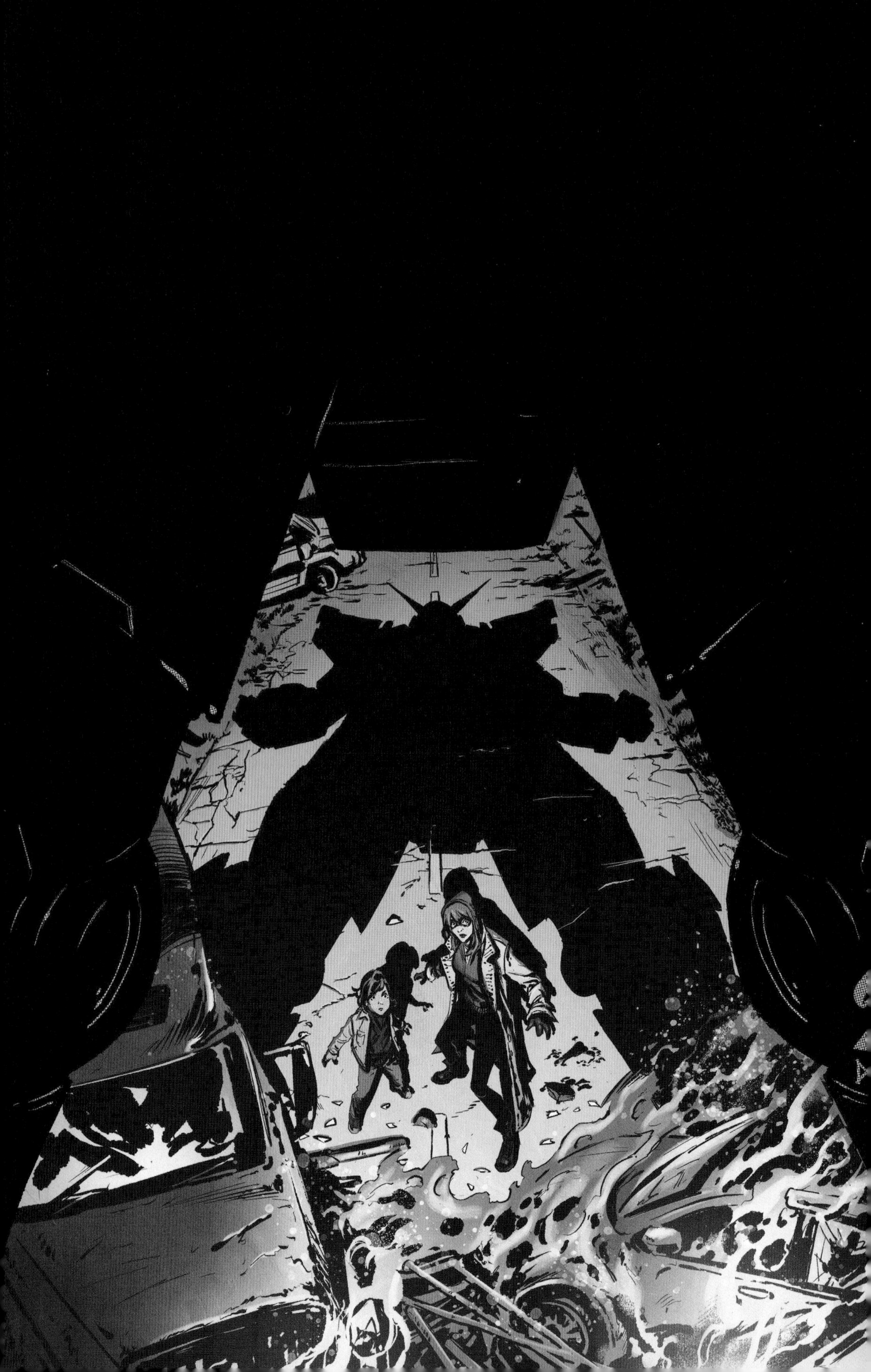

KIDS LOVE CHAINS

CHAPTER THREE

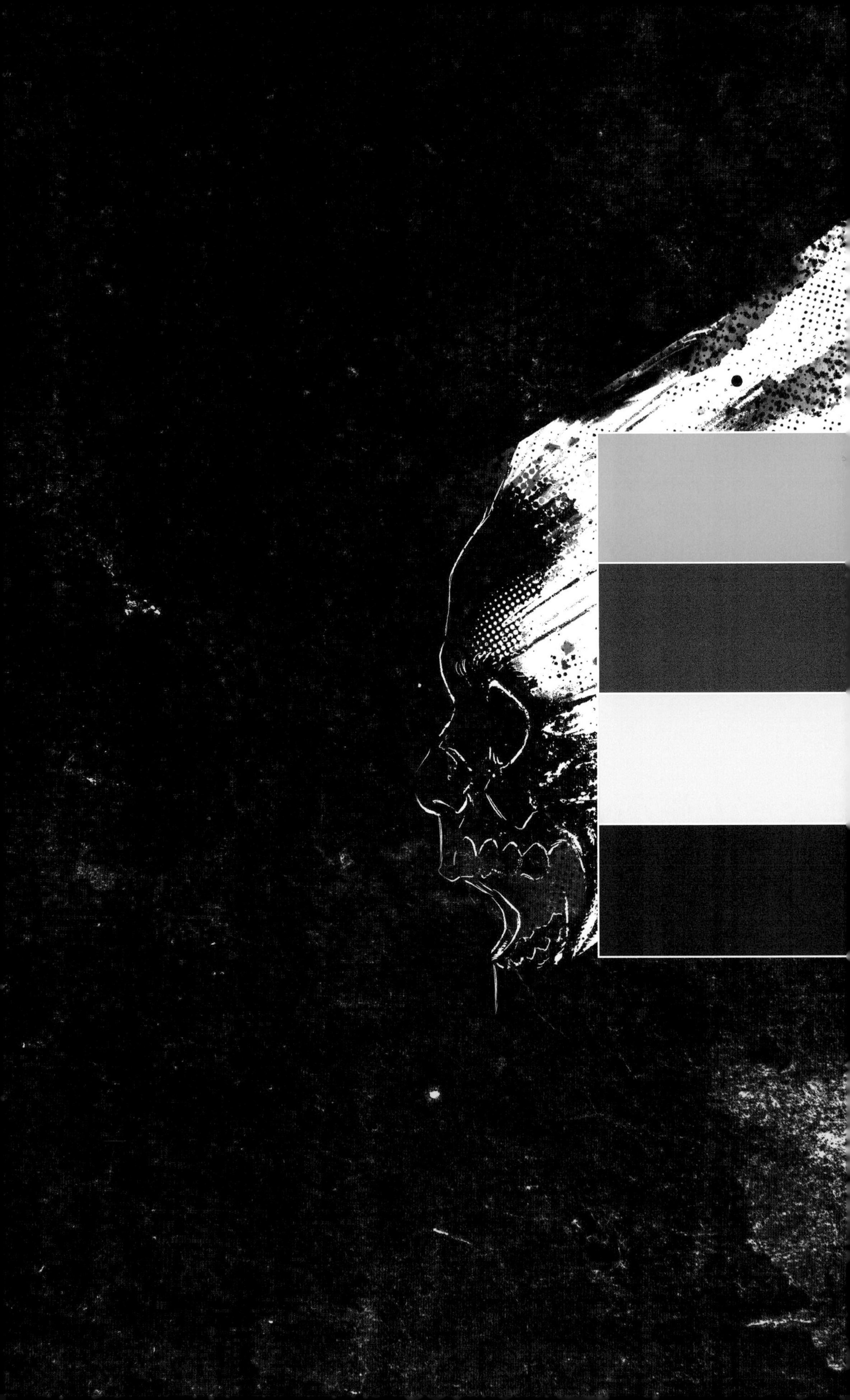

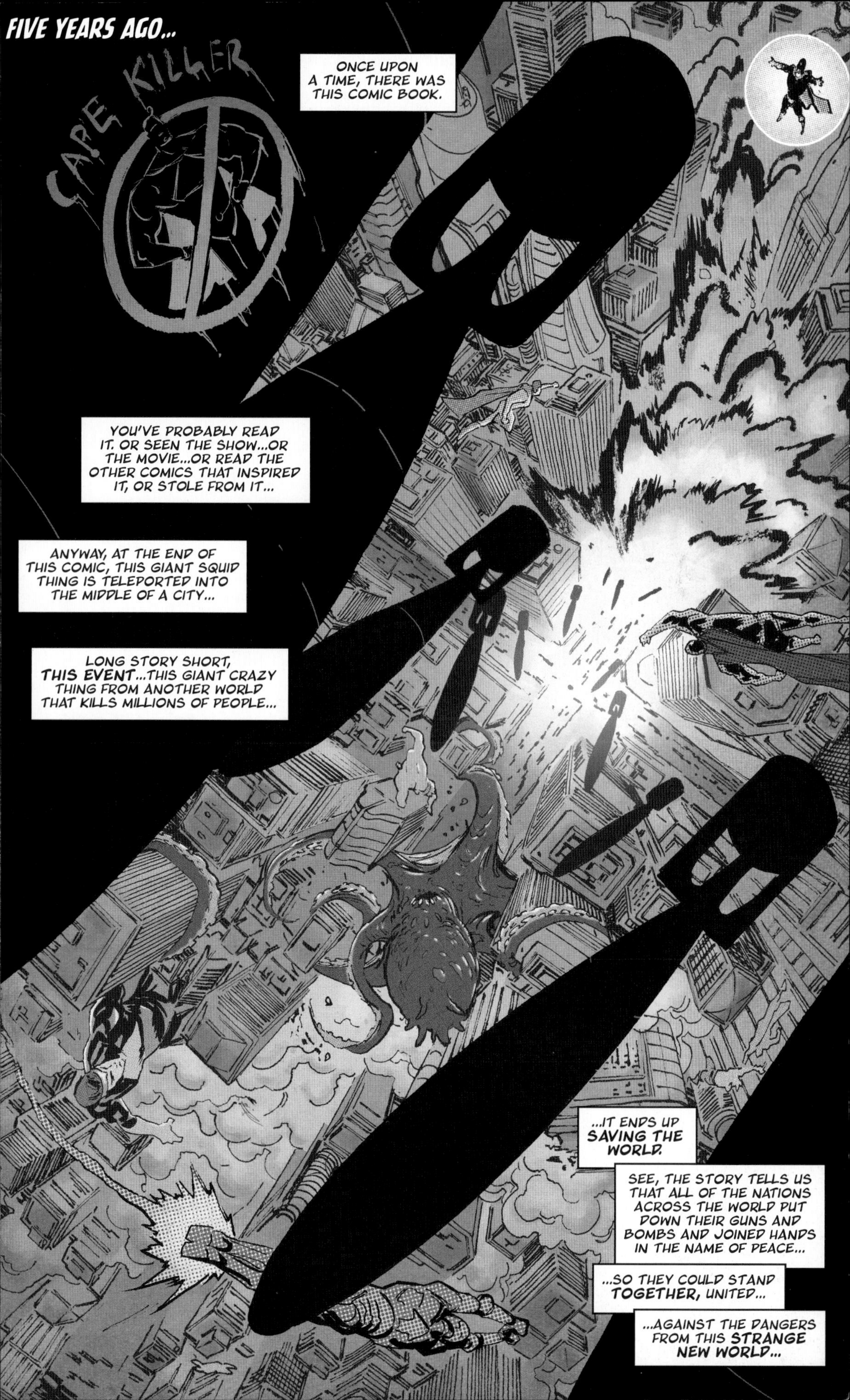
FIVE YEARS AGO...
CAPE KILLER
ONCE UPON A TIME, THERE WAS THIS COMIC BOOK.
YOU'VE PROBABLY READ IT. OR SEEN THE SHOW...OR THE MOVIE...OR READ THE OTHER COMICS THAT INSPIRED IT, OR STOLE FROM IT...
ANYWAY, AT THE END OF THIS COMIC, THIS GIANT SQUID THING IS TELEPORTED INTO THE MIDDLE OF A CITY...
LONG STORY SHORT, THIS EVENT...THIS GIANT CRAZY THING FROM ANOTHER WORLD THAT KILLS MILLIONS OF PEOPLE...
...IT ENDS UP SAVING THE WORLD.
SEE, THE STORY TELLS US THAT ALL OF THE NATIONS ACROSS THE WORLD PUT DOWN THEIR GUNS AND BOMBS AND JOINED HANDS IN THE NAME OF PEACE...
...SO THEY COULD STAND TOGETHER, UNITED...
...AGAINST THE DANGERS FROM THIS STRANGE NEW WORLD...

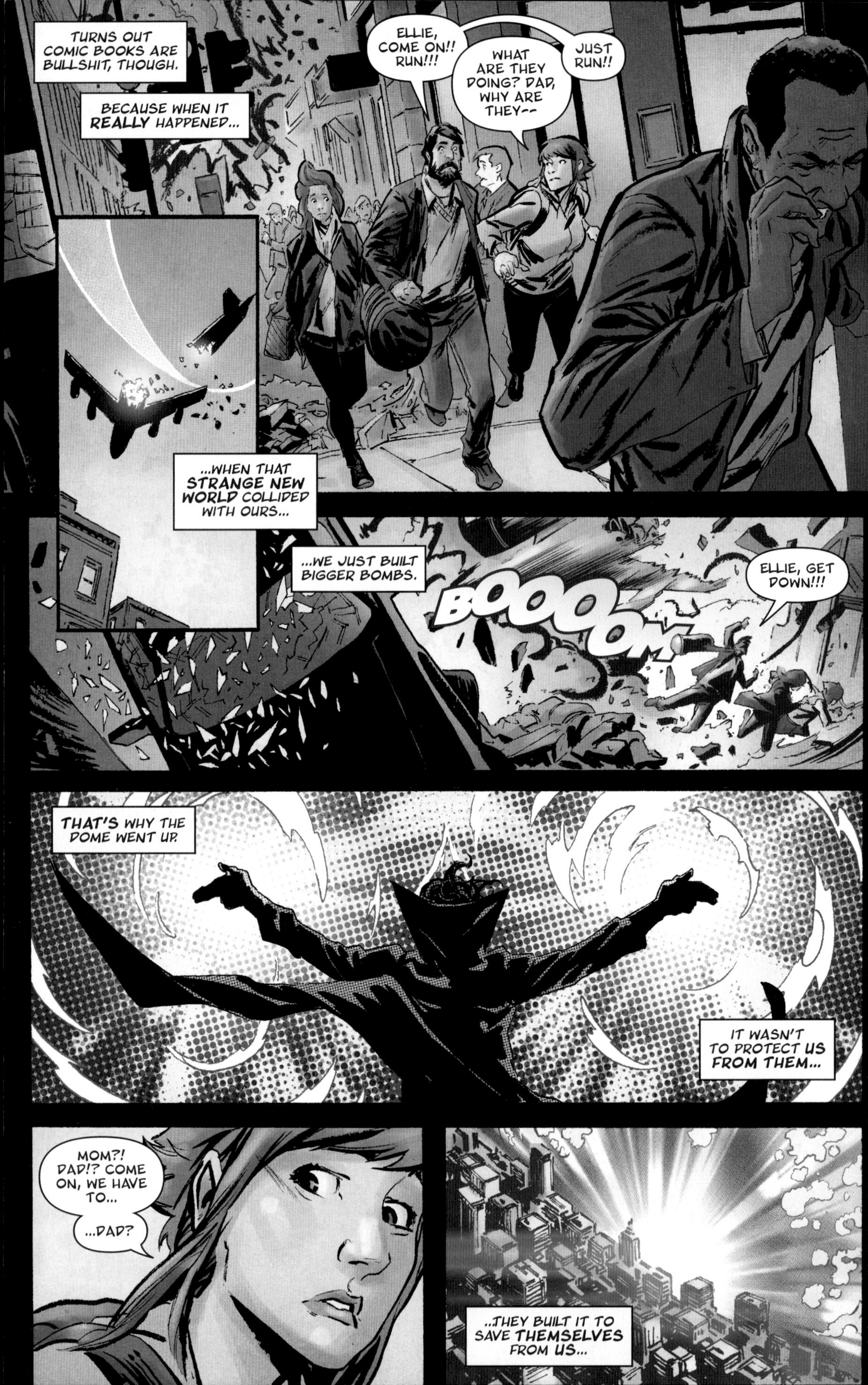
TURNS OUT COMIC BOOKS ARE BULLSHIT, THOUGH.
BECAUSE WHEN IT REALLY HAPPENED...
ELLIE, COME ON!! RUN!!!
WHAT ARE THEY DOING? DAD, WHY ARE THEY--
JUST RUN!!
...WHEN THAT STRANGE NEW WORLD COLLIDED WITH OURS...
...WE JUST BUILT BIGGER BOMBS.
BOOOOOM
ELLIE, GET DOWN!!!
THAT'S WHY THE DOME WENT UP.
IT WASN'T TO PROTECT US FROM THEM...
MOM?! DAD!? COME ON, WE HAVE TO...
...DAD?
...THEY BUILT IT TO SAVE THEMSELVES FROM US...

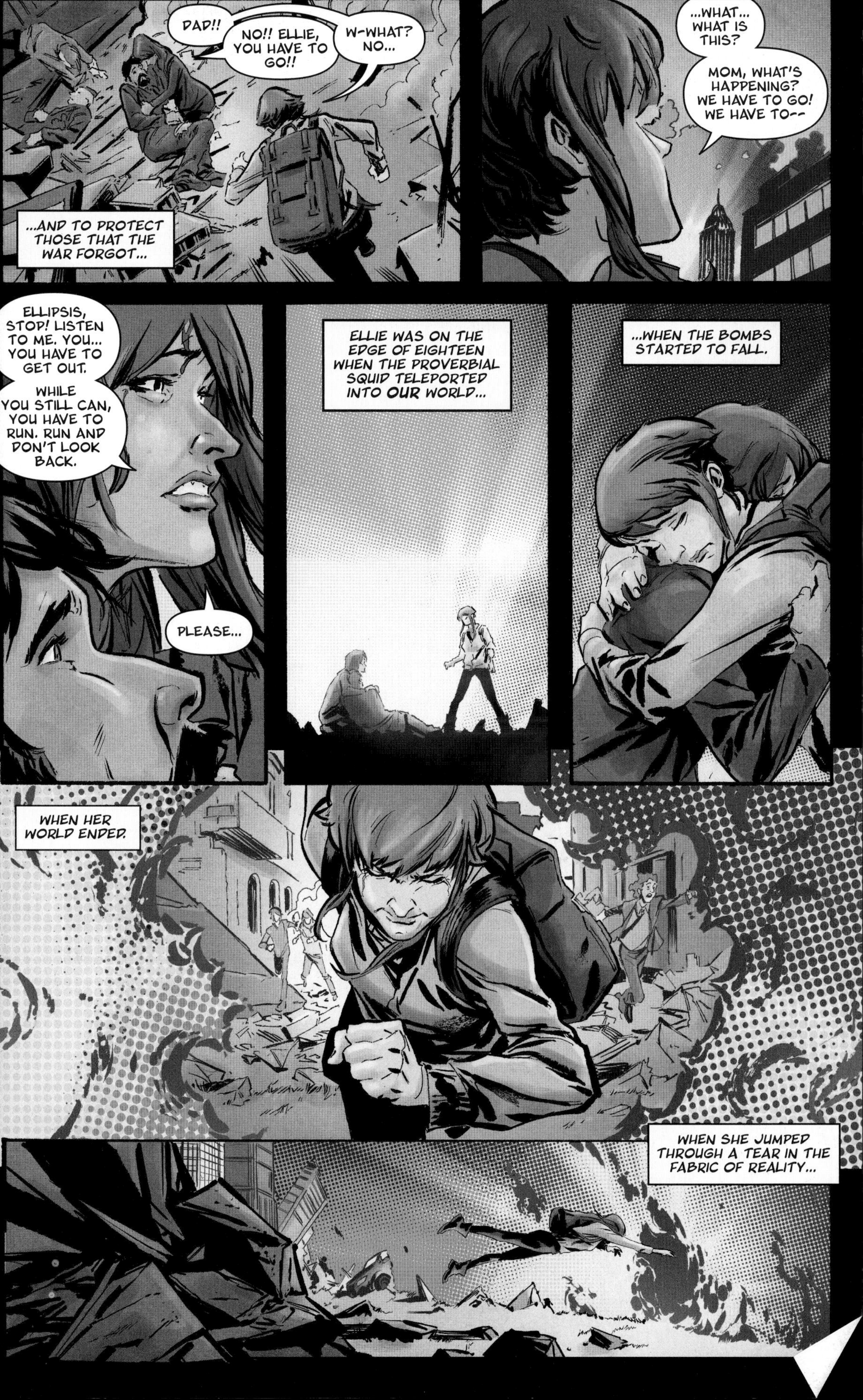
DAD!!
NO!! ELLIE, YOU HAVE TO GO!!
W-WHAT? NO...
...AND TO PROTECT THOSE THAT THE WAR FORGOT...
...WHAT... WHAT IS THIS?
MOM, WHAT'S HAPPENING? WE HAVE TO GO! WE HAVE TO--
ELLIPSIS, STOP! LISTEN TO ME. YOU... YOU HAVE TO GET OUT.
WHILE YOU STILL CAN, YOU HAVE TO RUN. RUN AND DON'T LOOK BACK.
PLEASE...
ELLIE WAS ON THE EDGE OF EIGHTEEN WHEN THE PROVERBIAL SQUID TELEPORTED INTO OUR WORLD...
...WHEN THE BOMBS STARTED TO FALL.
WHEN HER WORLD ENDED.
WHEN SHE JUMPED THROUGH A TEAR IN THE FABRIC OF REALITY...

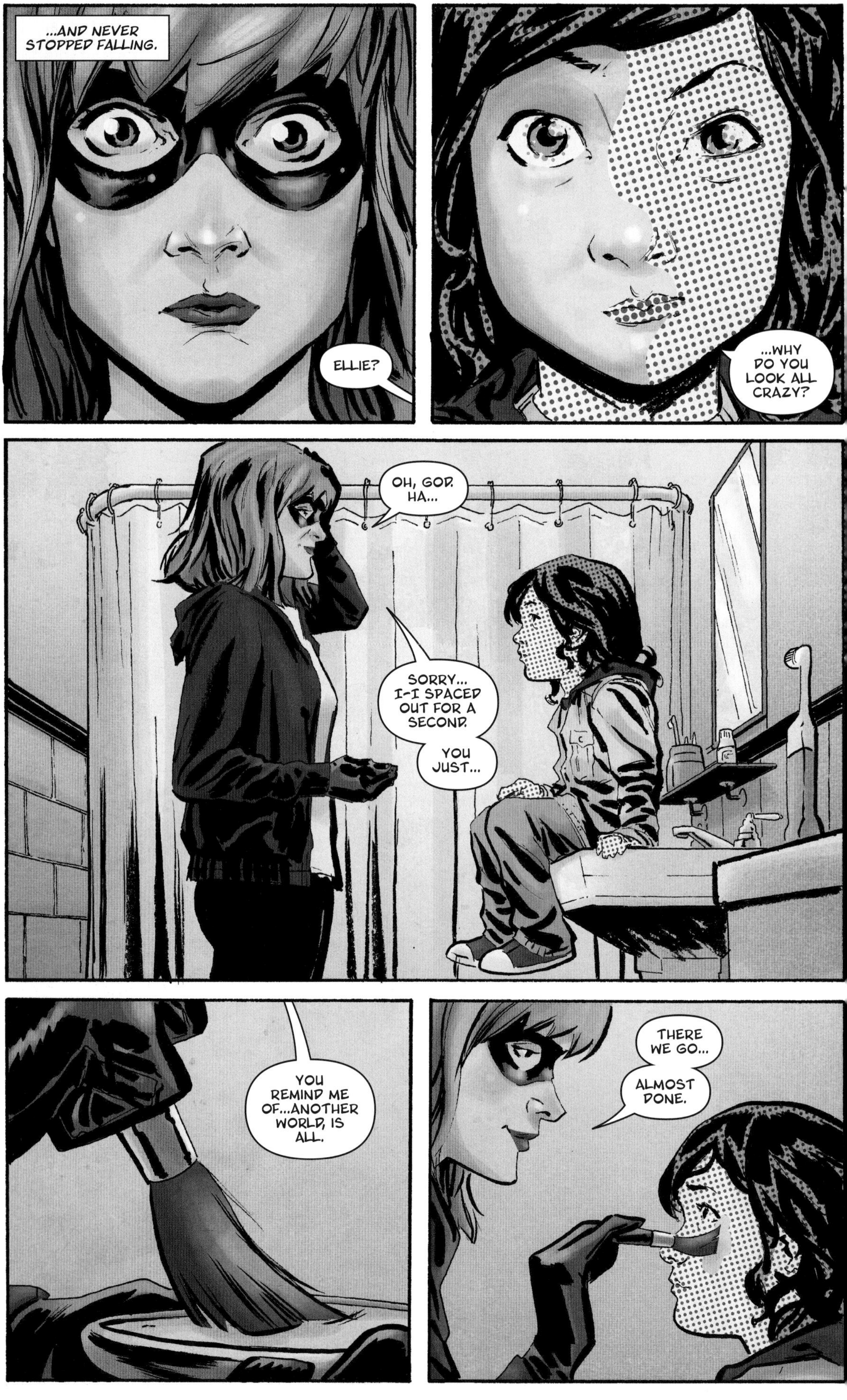
...AND NEVER STOPPED FALLING.
ELLIE?
...WHY DO YOU LOOK ALL CRAZY?
OH, GOD. HA...
SORRY... I-I SPACED OUT FOR A SECOND.
YOU JUST...
YOU REMIND ME OF...ANOTHER WORLD, IS ALL.
THERE WE GO...
ALMOST DONE.

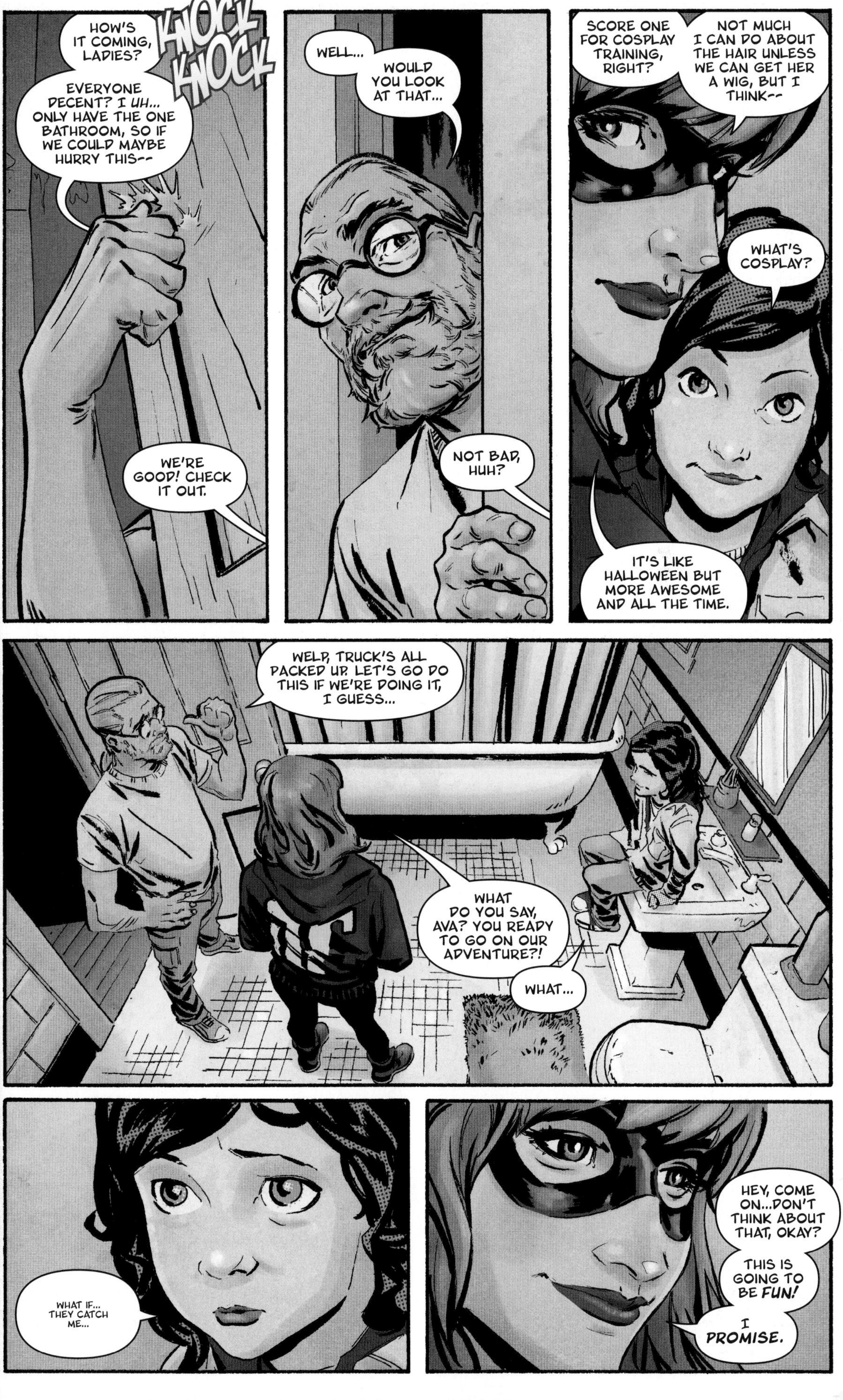
HOW'S IT COMING, LADIES?
KNOCK KNOCK
EVERYONE DECENT? I UH... ONLY HAVE THE ONE BATHROOM, SO IF WE COULD MAYBE HURRY THIS--
WE'RE GOOD! CHECK IT OUT.
WELL...
WOULD YOU LOOK AT THAT...
NOT BAD, HUH?
SCORE ONE FOR COSPLAY TRAINING, RIGHT?
NOT MUCH I CAN DO ABOUT THE HAIR UNLESS WE CAN GET HER A WIG, BUT I THINK--
WHAT'S COSPLAY?
IT'S LIKE HALLOWEEN BUT MORE AWESOME AND ALL THE TIME.
WELP, TRUCK'S ALL PACKED UP. LET'S GO DO THIS IF WE'RE DOING IT, I GUESS...
WHAT DO YOU SAY, AVA? YOU READY TO GO ON OUR ADVENTURE?!
WHAT...
WHAT IF... THEY CATCH ME...
HEY, COME ON...DON'T THINK ABOUT THAT, OKAY?
THIS IS GOING TO BE FUN!
I PROMISE.

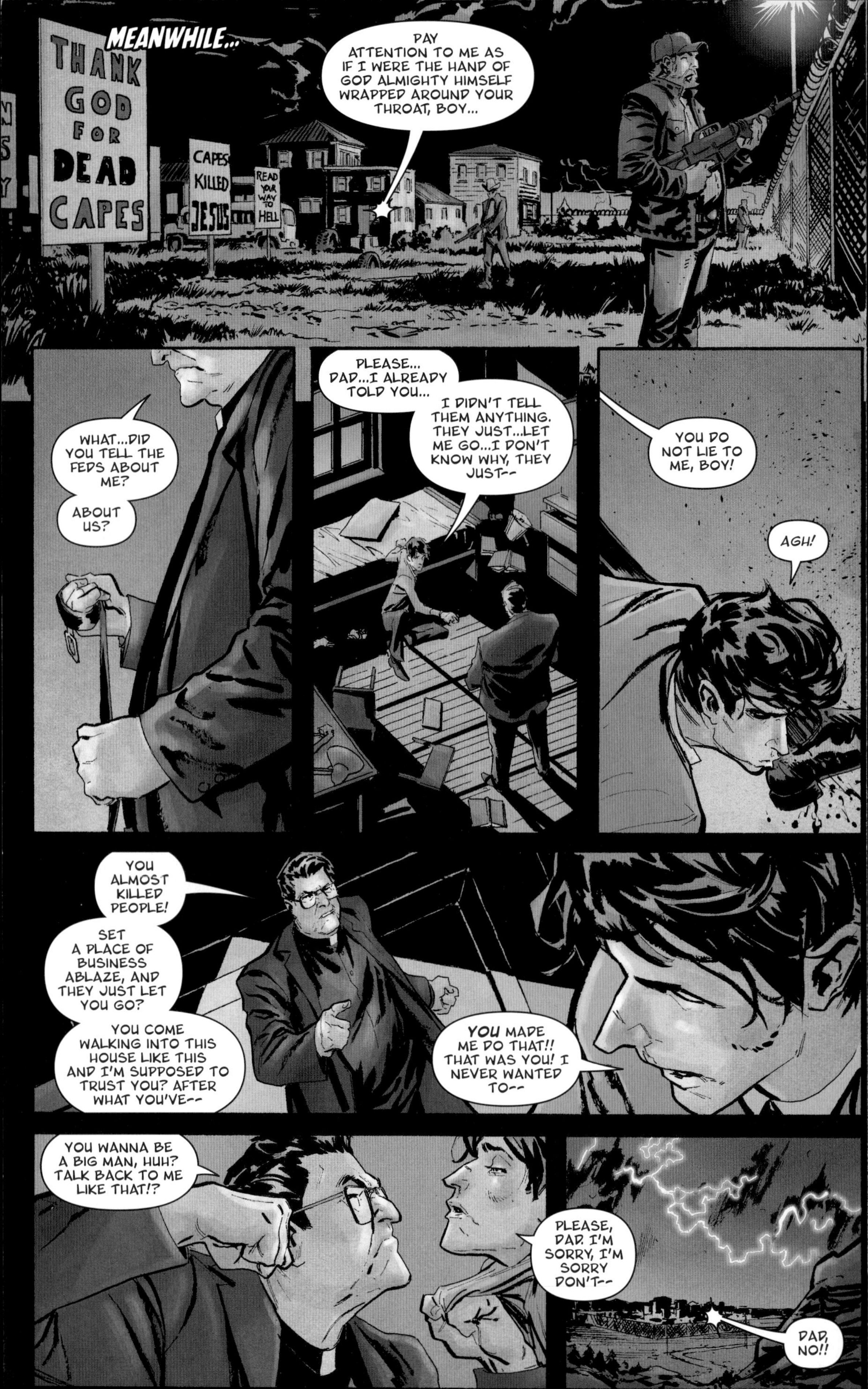
MEANWHILE...
THANK GOD FOR DEAD CAPES
CAPES KILLED JESUS
READ YOUR WAY TO HELL
PAY ATTENTION TO ME AS IF I WERE THE HAND OF GOD ALMIGHTY HIMSELF WRAPPED AROUND YOUR THROAT, BOY...
WHAT...DID YOU TELL THE FEDS ABOUT ME?
ABOUT US?
PLEASE... DAD...I ALREADY TOLD YOU...
I DIDN'T TELL THEM ANYTHING. THEY JUST...LET ME GO...I DON'T KNOW WHY, THEY JUST--
YOU DO NOT LIE TO ME, BOY!
AGH!
YOU ALMOST KILLED PEOPLE!
SET A PLACE OF BUSINESS ABLAZE, AND THEY JUST LET YOU GO?
YOU COME WALKING INTO THIS HOUSE LIKE THIS AND I'M SUPPOSED TO TRUST YOU? AFTER WHAT YOU'VE--
YOU MADE ME DO THAT!! THAT WAS YOU! I NEVER WANTED TO--
YOU WANNA BE A BIG MAN, HUH? TALK BACK TO ME LIKE THAT!?
PLEASE, DAD. I'M SORRY, I'M SORRY DON'T--
DAD, NO!!

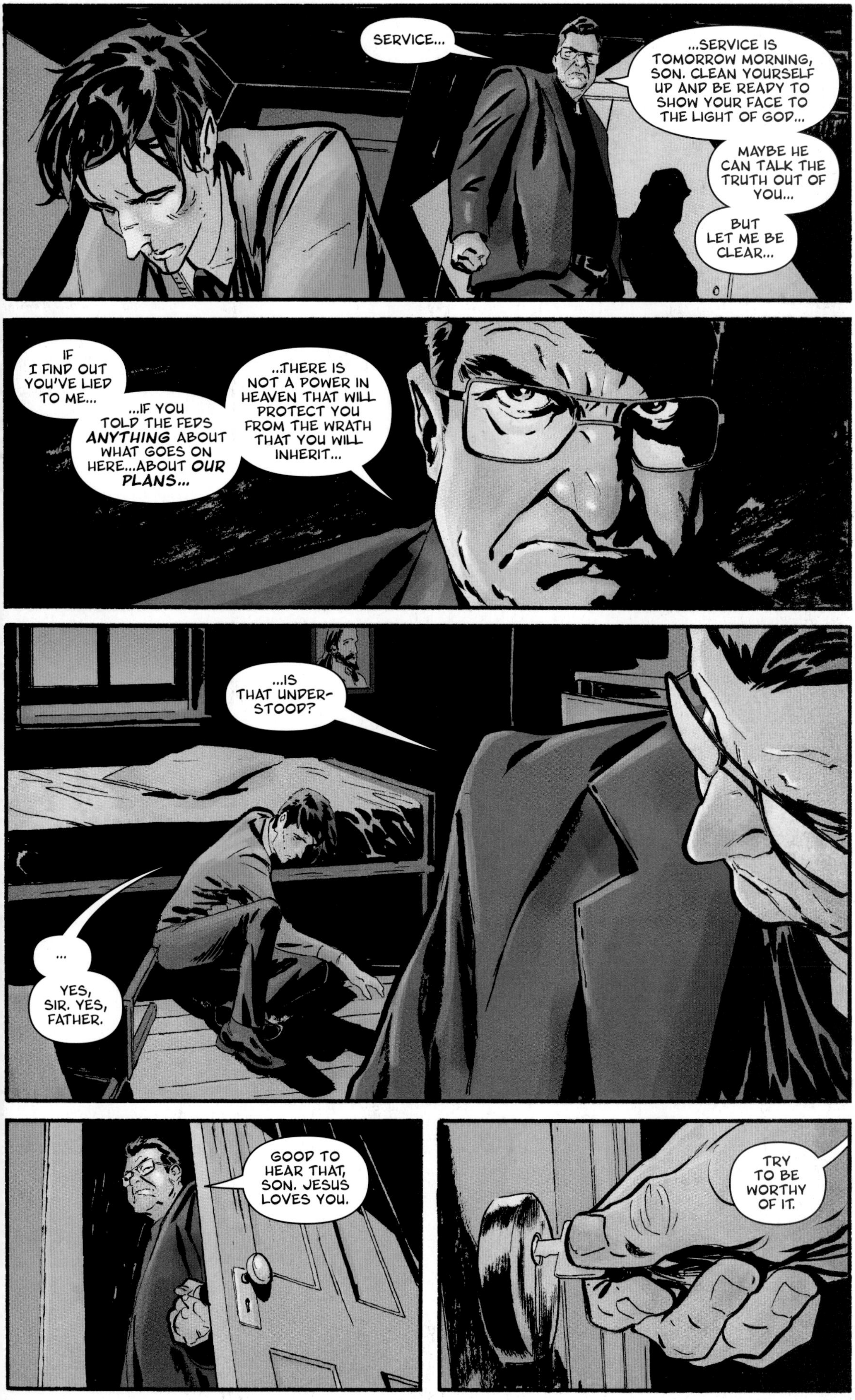
SERVICE...
...SERVICE IS TOMORROW MORNING, SON. CLEAN YOURSELF UP AND BE READY TO SHOW YOUR FACE TO THE LIGHT OF GOD...
MAYBE HE CAN TALK THE TRUTH OUT OF YOU...
BUT LET ME BE CLEAR...
IF I FIND OUT YOU'VE LIED TO ME...
...IF YOU TOLD THE FEDS ANYTHING ABOUT WHAT GOES ON HERE...ABOUT OUR PLANS...
...THERE IS NOT A POWER IN HEAVEN THAT WILL PROTECT YOU FROM THE WRATH THAT YOU WILL INHERIT...
...IS THAT UNDERSTOOD?
...
YES, SIR. YES, FATHER.
GOOD TO HEAR THAT, SON. JESUS LOVES YOU.
TRY TO BE WORTHY OF IT.

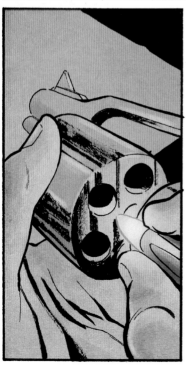

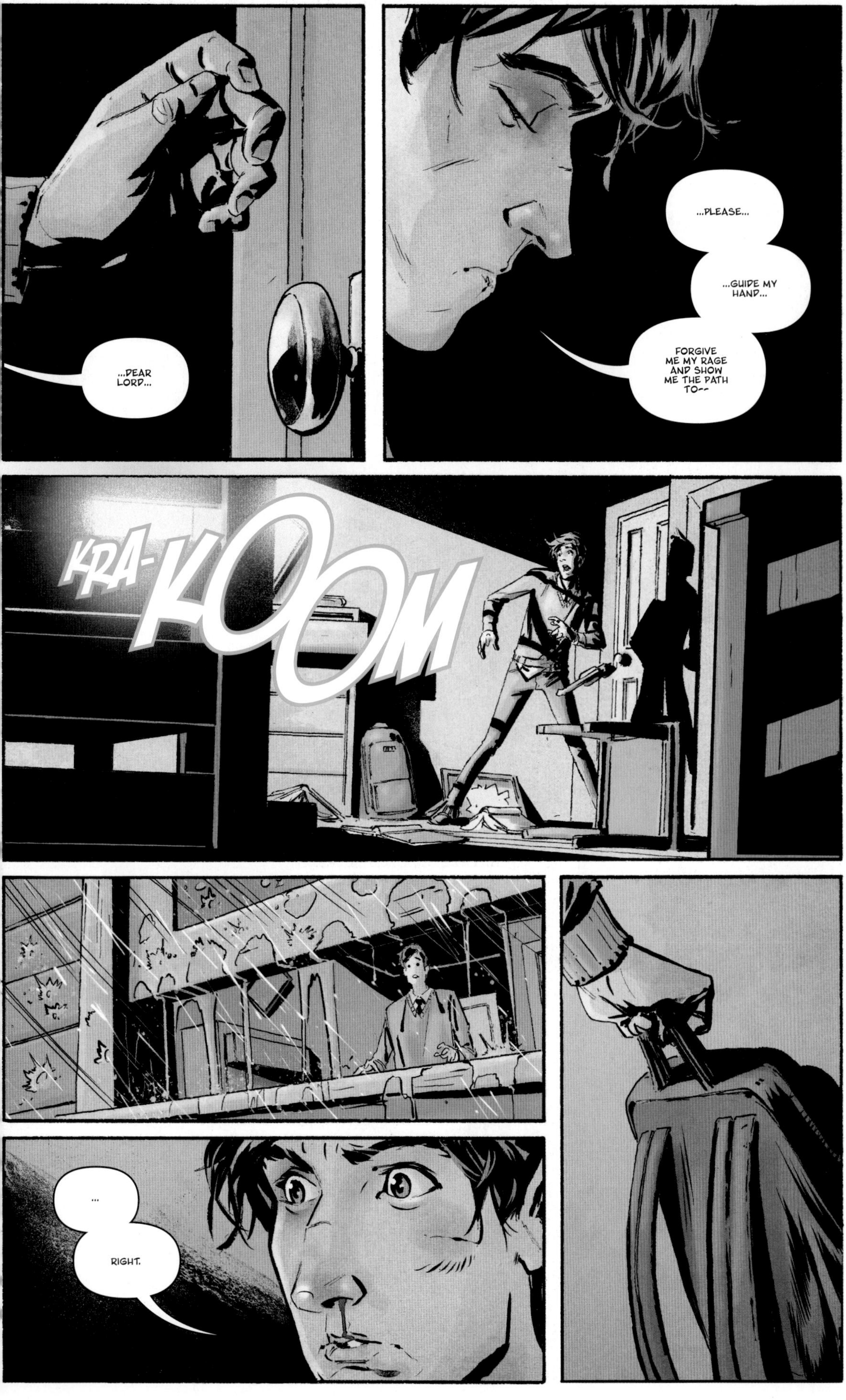
...DEAR LORD...
...PLEASE...
...GUIDE MY HAND...
FORGIVE ME MY RAGE AND SHOW ME THE PATH TO--
KRA-KOOOM
...
RIGHT.

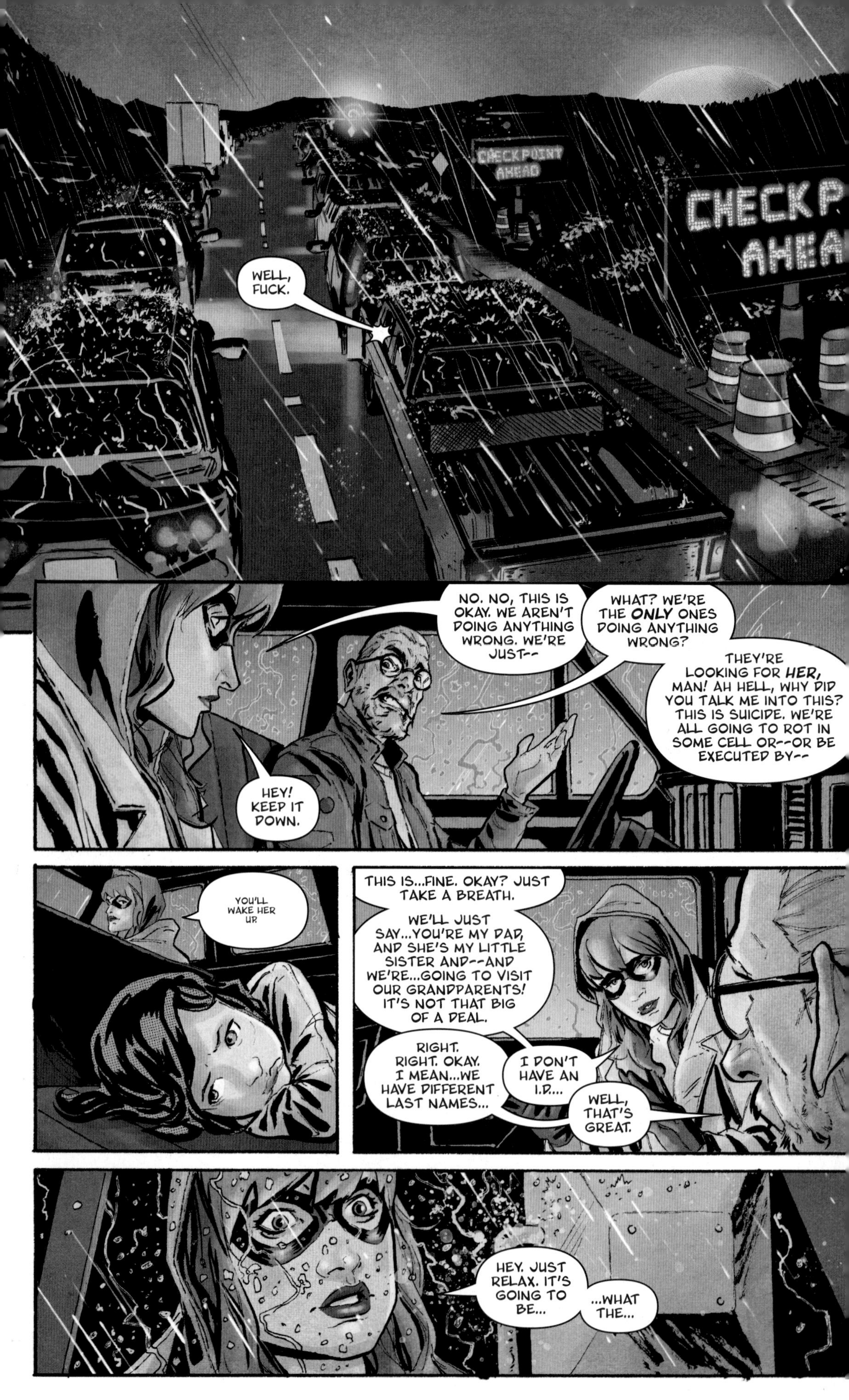
CHECKPOINT AHEAD
CHECKP AHEA
WELL, FUCK.
NO. NO, THIS IS OKAY. WE AREN'T DOING ANYTHING WRONG. WE'RE JUST--
WHAT? WE'RE THE ONLY ONES DOING ANYTHING WRONG?
THEY'RE LOOKING FOR HER, MAN! AH HELL, WHY DID YOU TALK ME INTO THIS? THIS IS SUICIDE. WE'RE ALL GOING TO ROT IN SOME CELL OR--OR BE EXECUTED BY--
HEY! KEEP IT DOWN.
YOU'LL WAKE HER UP.
THIS IS...FINE. OKAY? JUST TAKE A BREATH.
WE'LL JUST SAY...YOU'RE MY DAD, AND SHE'S MY LITTLE SISTER AND--AND WE'RE...GOING TO VISIT OUR GRANDPARENTS! IT'S NOT THAT BIG OF A DEAL.
RIGHT. RIGHT. OKAY. I MEAN...WE HAVE DIFFERENT LAST NAMES...
I DON'T HAVE AN I.D....
WELL, THAT'S GREAT.
HEY. JUST RELAX. IT'S GOING TO BE...
...WHAT THE...

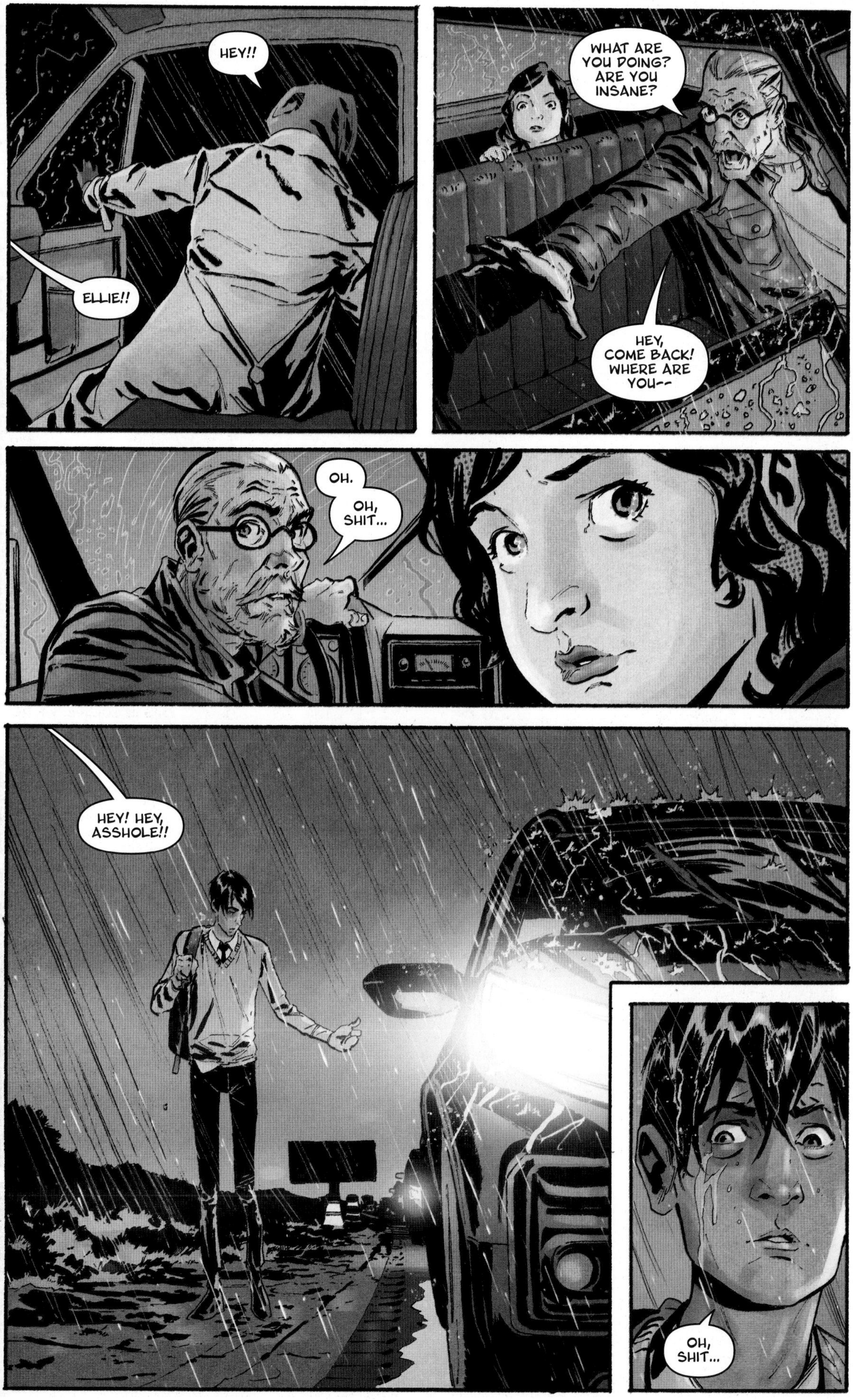
HEY!!
ELLIE!!
WHAT ARE YOU DOING? ARE YOU INSANE?
HEY, COME BACK! WHERE ARE YOU--
OH.
OH, SHIT...
HEY! HEY, ASSHOLE!!
OH, SHIT...

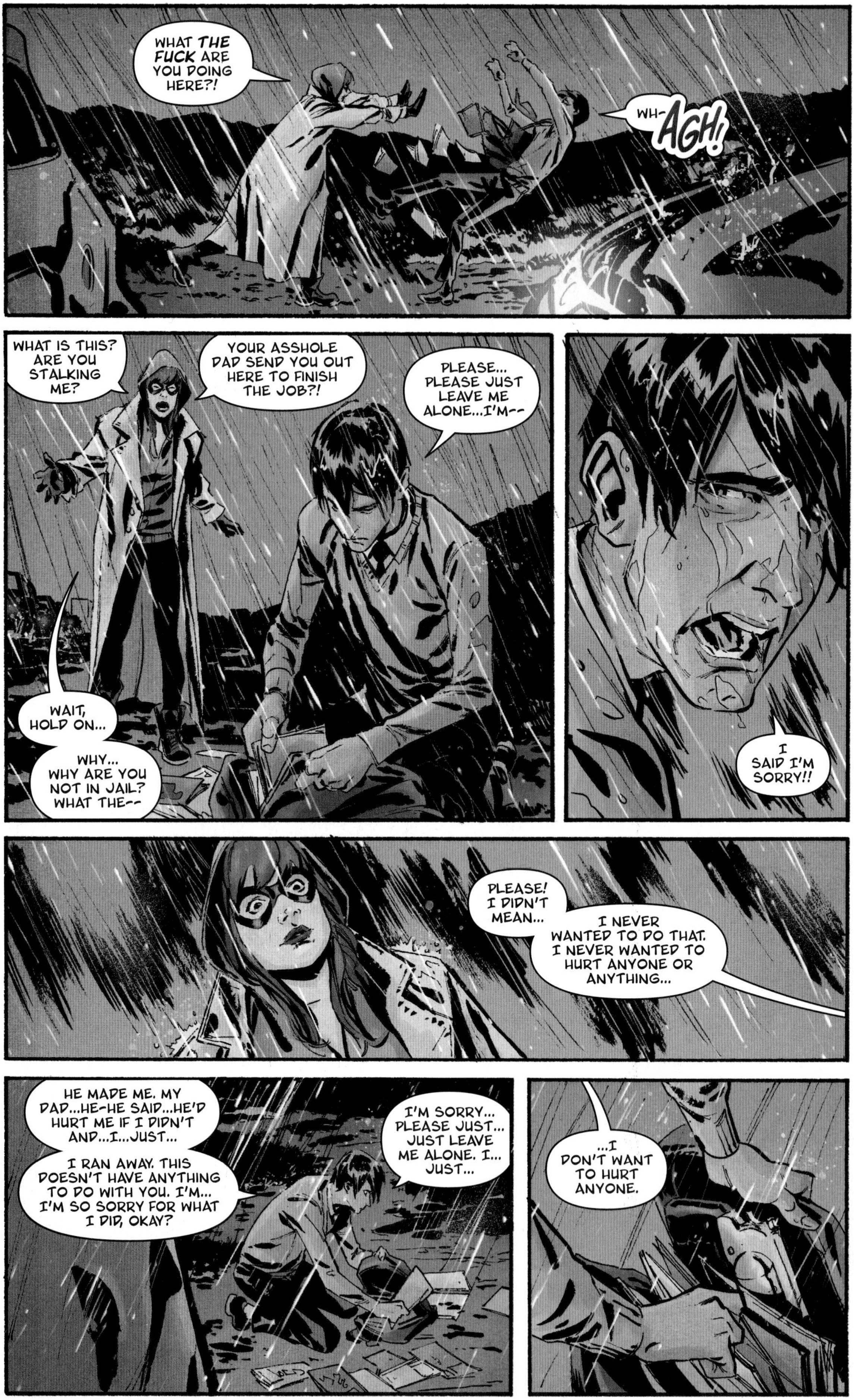
WHAT THE FUCK ARE YOU DOING HERE?!
WH-AGH!
WHAT IS THIS? ARE YOU STALKING ME?
YOUR ASSHOLE DAD SEND YOU OUT HERE TO FINISH THE JOB?!
PLEASE... PLEASE JUST LEAVE ME ALONE...I'M--
WAIT, HOLD ON...
WHY... WHY ARE YOU NOT IN JAIL? WHAT THE--
I SAID I'M SORRY!!
PLEASE! I DIDN'T MEAN...
I NEVER WANTED TO DO THAT. I NEVER WANTED TO HURT ANYONE OR ANYTHING...
HE MADE ME. MY DAD...HE-HE SAID...HE'D HURT ME IF I DIDN'T AND...I...JUST...
I RAN AWAY. THIS DOESN'T HAVE ANYTHING TO DO WITH YOU. I'M... I'M SO SORRY FOR WHAT I DID, OKAY?
I'M SORRY... PLEASE JUST... JUST LEAVE ME ALONE. I... JUST...
...I DON'T WANT TO HURT ANYONE.

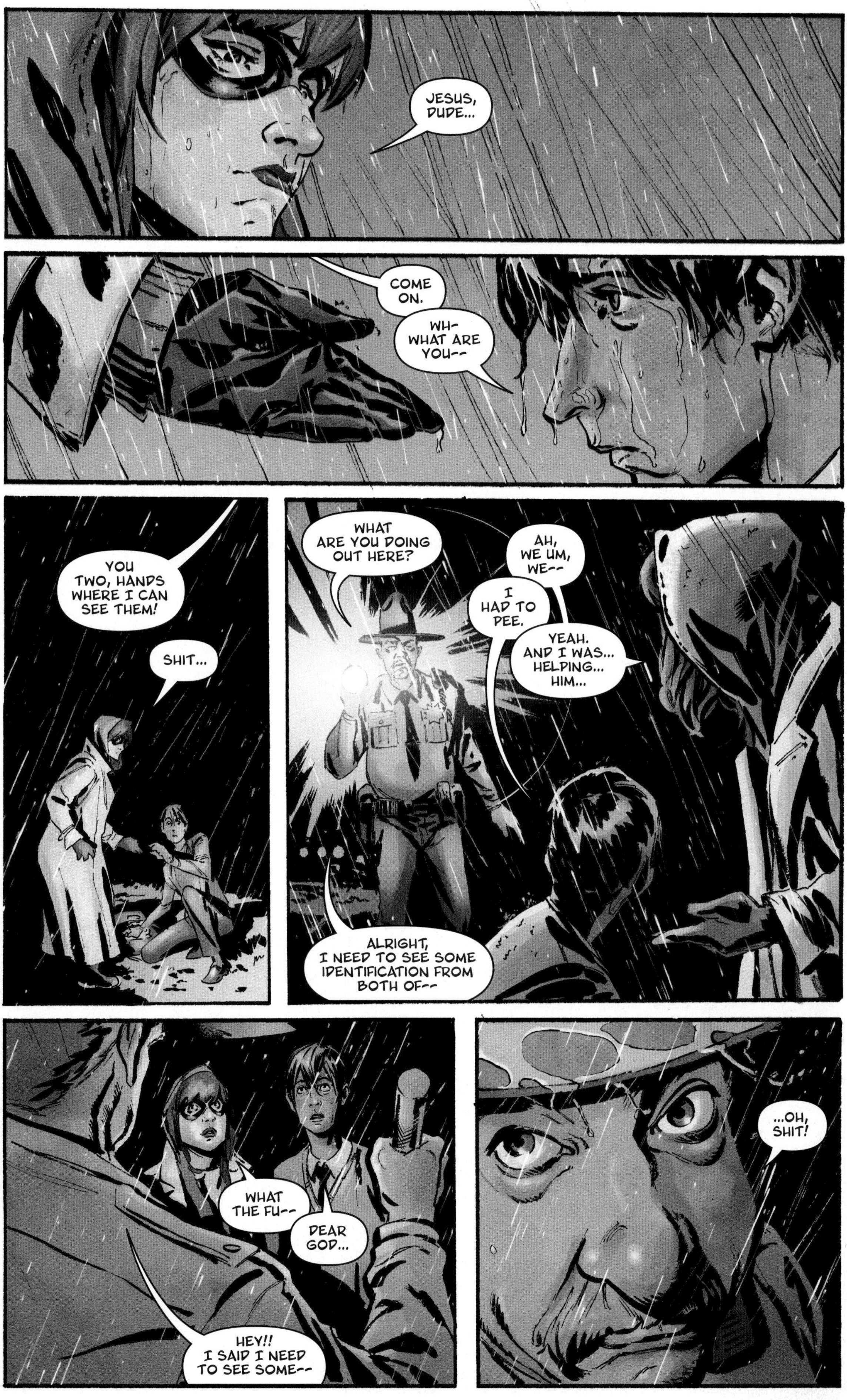
JESUS, DUDE...
COME ON.
WH- WHAT ARE YOU--
YOU TWO, HANDS WHERE I CAN SEE THEM!
SHIT...
WHAT ARE YOU DOING OUT HERE?
AH, WE UM, WE--
I HAD TO PEE.
YEAH. AND I WAS... HELPING... HIM...
ALRIGHT, I NEED TO SEE SOME IDENTIFICATION FROM BOTH OF--
WHAT THE FU--
DEAR GOD...
HEY!! I SAID I NEED TO SEE SOME--
...OH, SHIT!

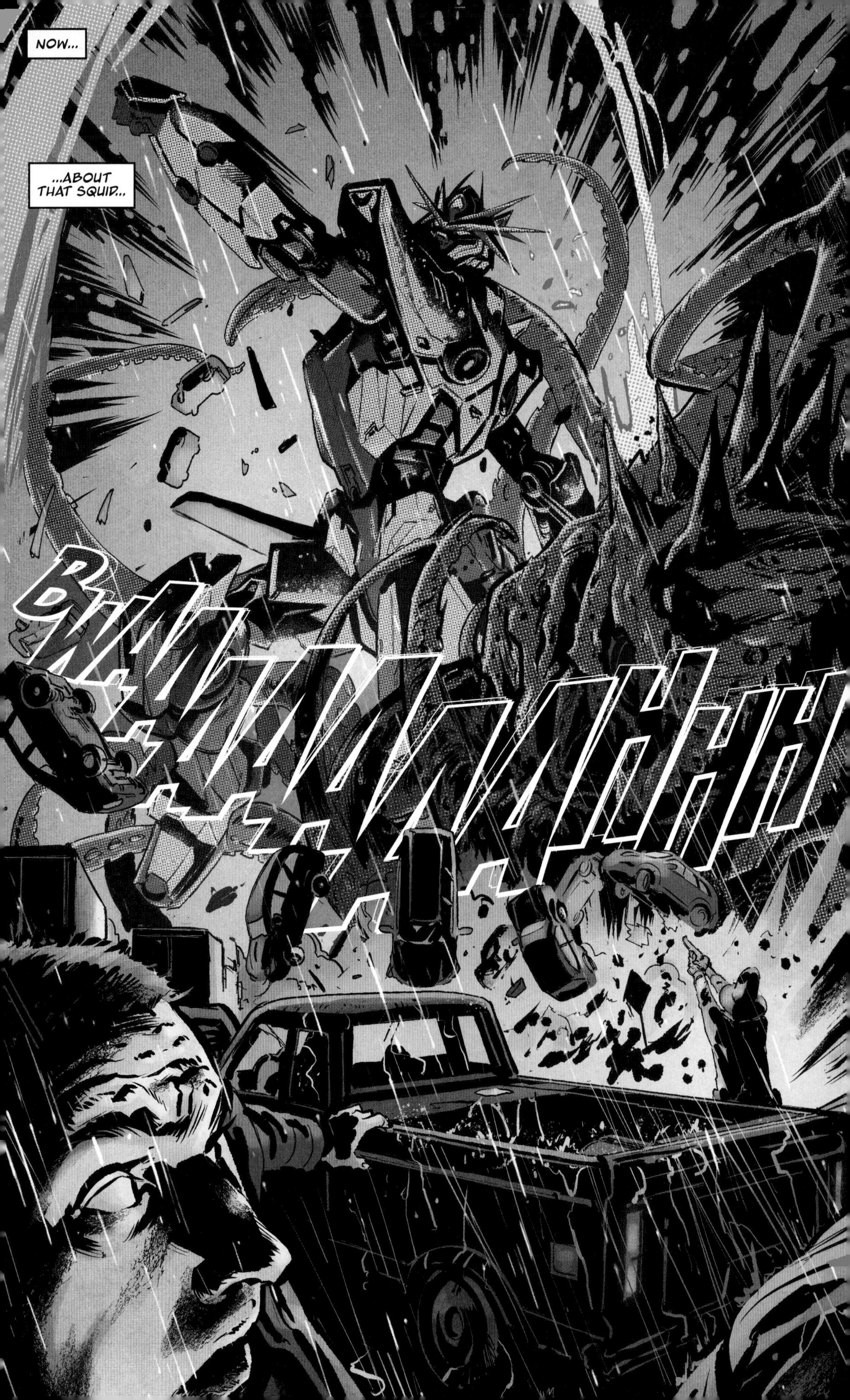
NOW...
...ABOUT THAT SQUID...

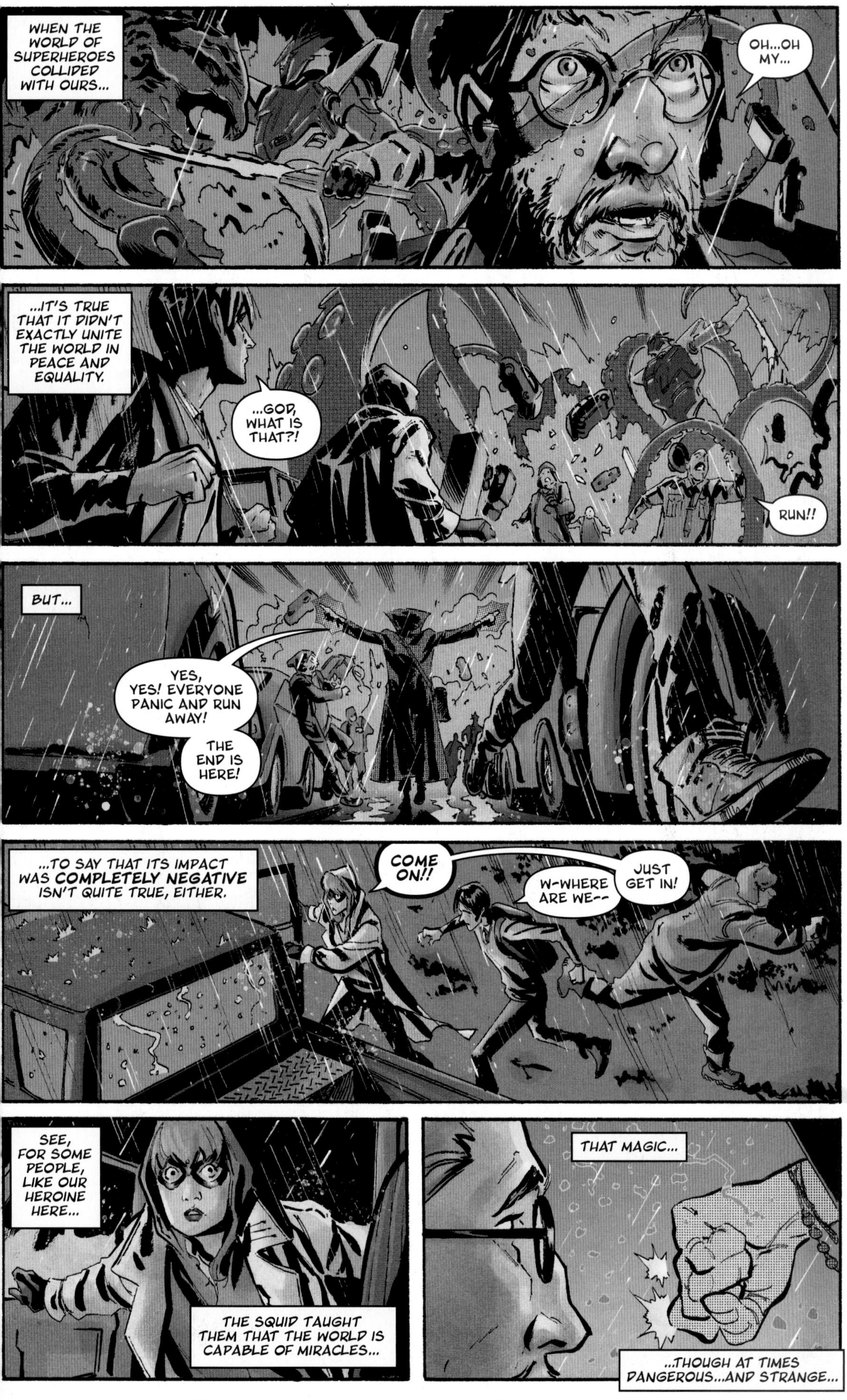
WHEN THE WORLD OF SUPERHEROES COLLIDED WITH OURS...
OH...OH MY...
...IT'S TRUE THAT IT DIDN'T EXACTLY UNITE THE WORLD IN PEACE AND EQUALITY.
...GOD, WHAT IS THAT?!
RUN!!
BUT...
YES, YES! EVERYONE PANIC AND RUN AWAY!
THE END IS HERE!
...TO SAY THAT ITS IMPACT WAS **COMPLETELY NEGATIVE** ISN'T QUITE TRUE, EITHER.
COME ON!!
W-WHERE ARE WE--
JUST GET IN!
SEE, FOR SOME PEOPLE, LIKE OUR HEROINE HERE...
THE SQUID TAUGHT THEM THAT THE WORLD IS CAPABLE OF MIRACLES...
THAT MAGIC...
...THOUGH AT TIMES DANGEROUS...AND STRANGE...

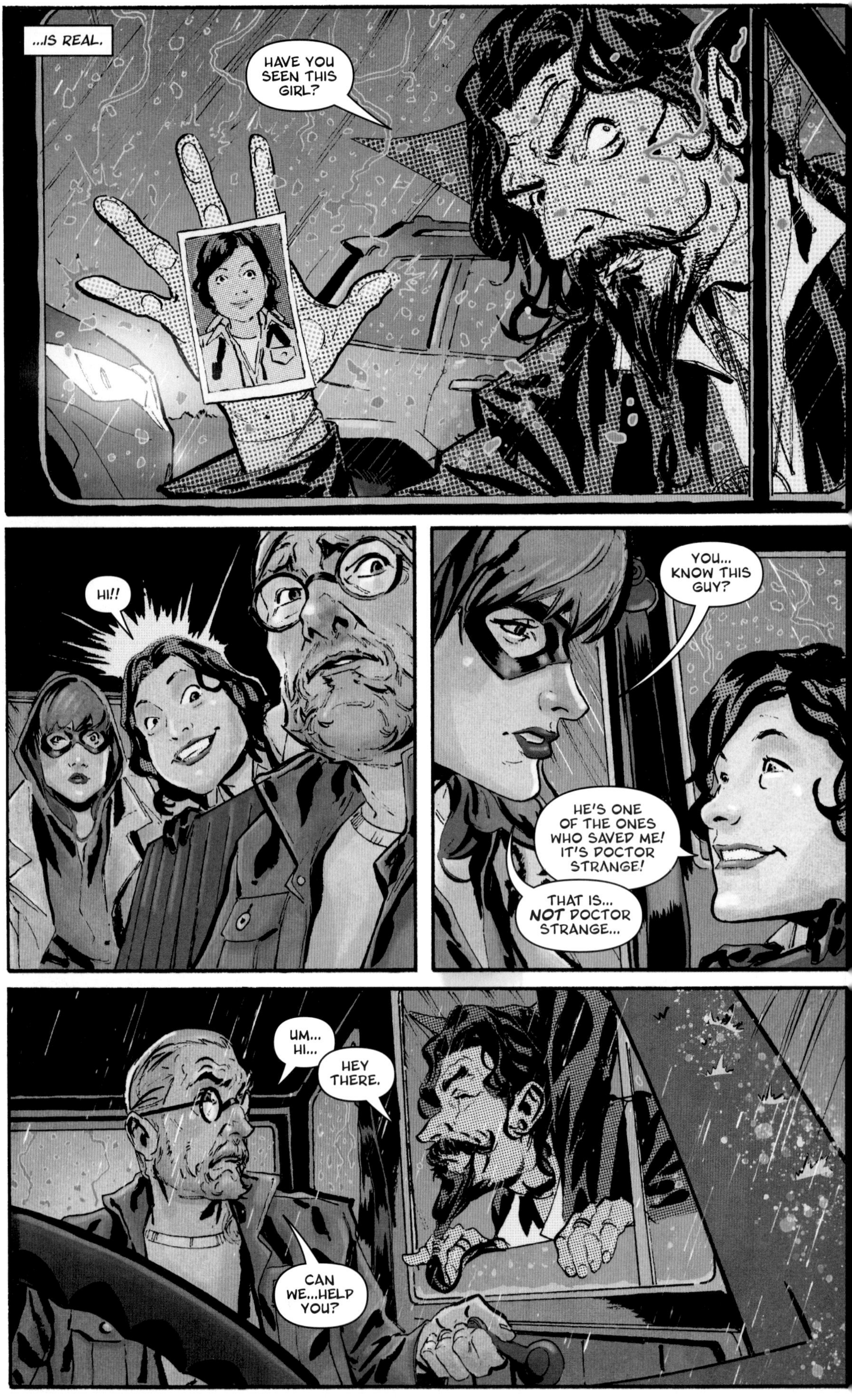
...IS REAL.
HAVE YOU SEEN THIS GIRL?
HI!!
YOU... KNOW THIS GUY?
HE'S ONE OF THE ONES WHO SAVED ME! IT'S DOCTOR STRANGE!
THAT IS... NOT DOCTOR STRANGE...
UM... HI...
HEY THERE.
CAN WE...HELP YOU?

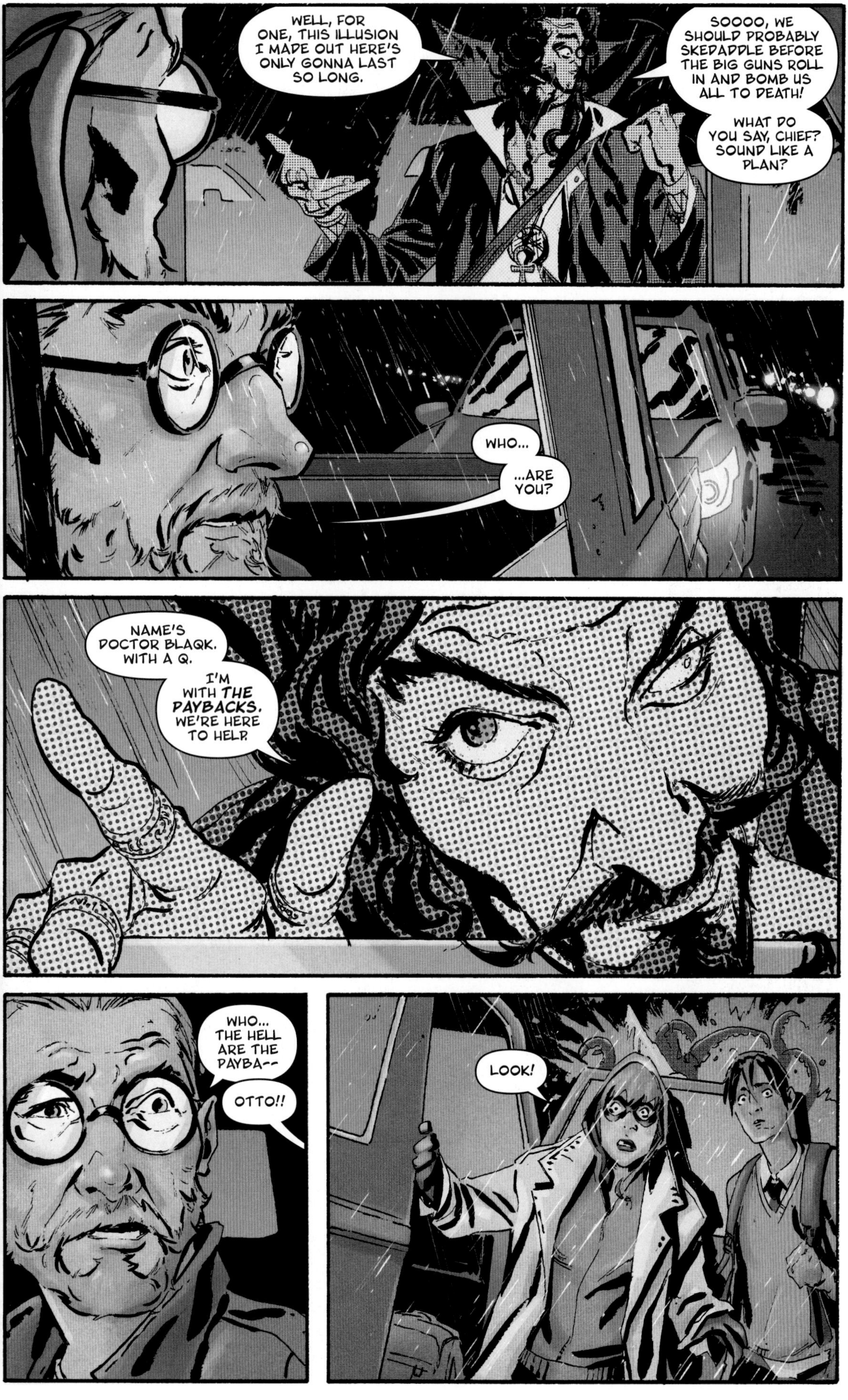
WELL, FOR ONE, THIS ILLUSION I MADE OUT HERE'S ONLY GONNA LAST SO LONG.
SOOOO, WE SHOULD PROBABLY SKEDADDLE BEFORE THE BIG GUNS ROLL IN AND BOMB US ALL TO DEATH!
WHAT DO YOU SAY, CHIEF? SOUND LIKE A PLAN?
WHO...
...ARE YOU?
NAME'S DOCTOR BLAQK. WITH A Q.
I'M WITH **THE PAYBACKS.** WE'RE HERE TO HELP.
WHO... THE HELL ARE THE PAYBA--
OTTO!!
LOOK!

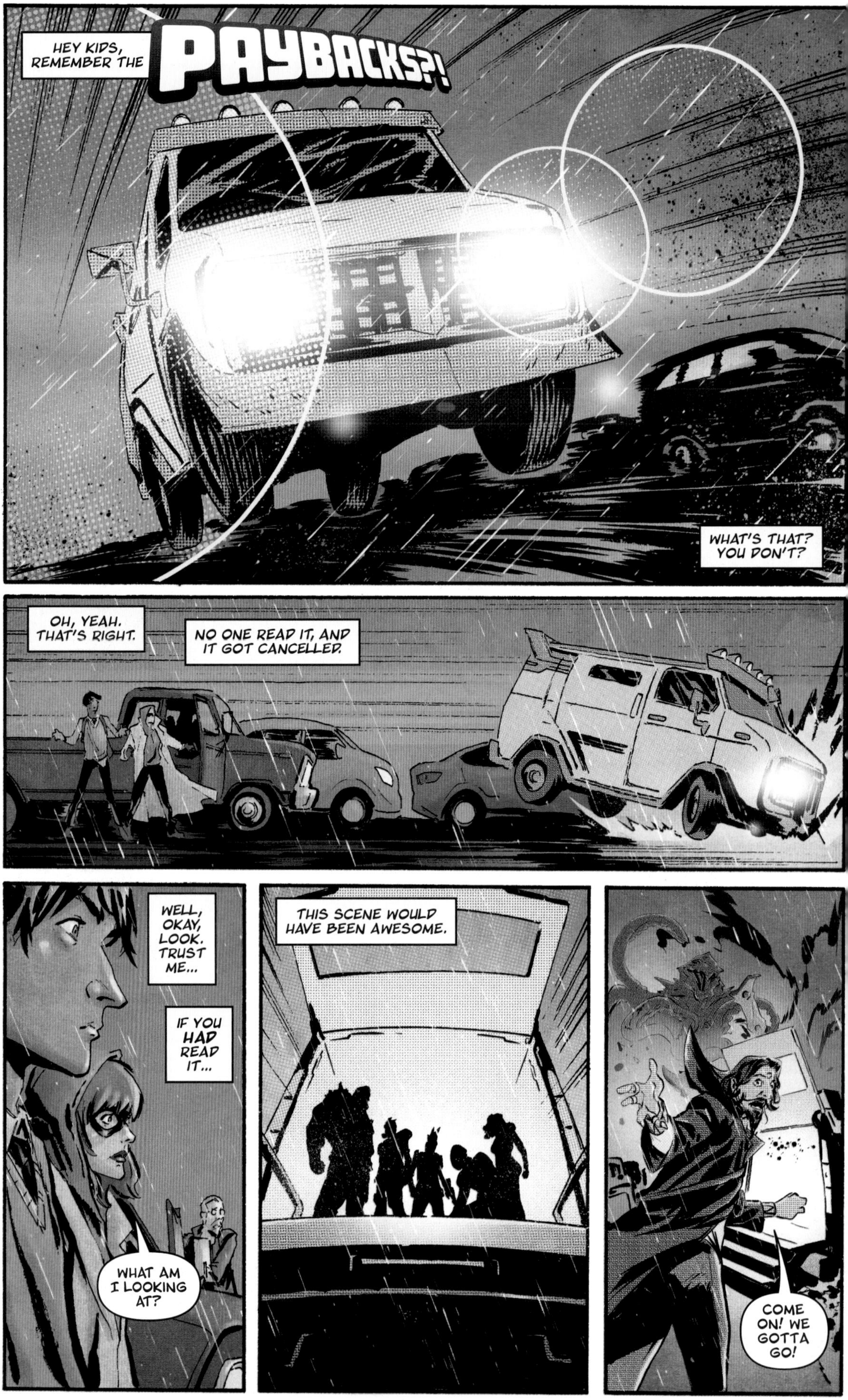
HEY KIDS, REMEMBER THE
PAYBACKS?!
WHAT'S THAT? YOU DON'T?
OH, YEAH. THAT'S RIGHT.
NO ONE READ IT, AND IT GOT CANCELLED.
WELL, OKAY, LOOK. TRUST ME...
IF YOU HAD READ IT...
WHAT AM I LOOKING AT?
THIS SCENE WOULD HAVE BEEN AWESOME.
COME ON! WE GOTTA GO!

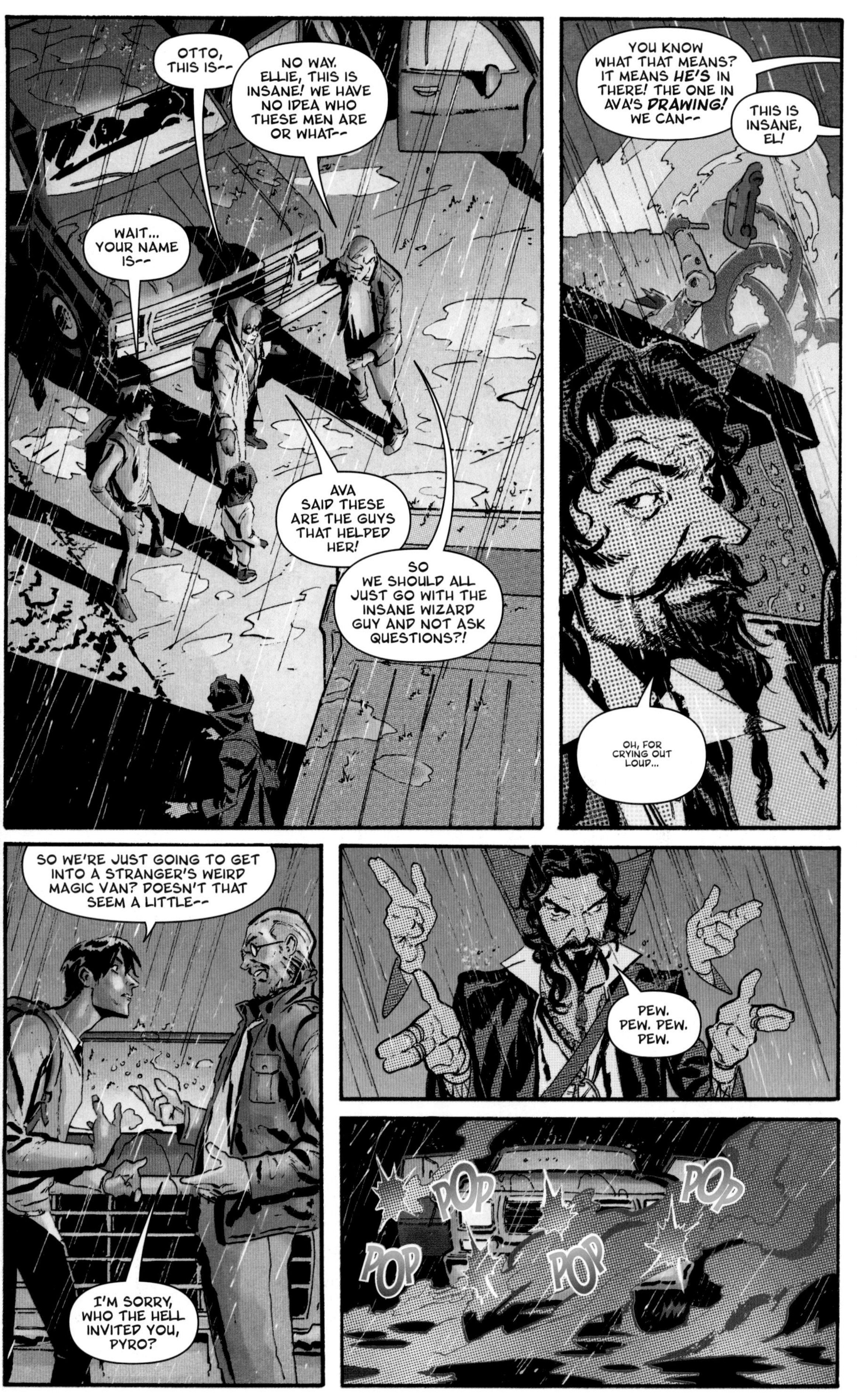
OTTO, THIS IS--
NO WAY. ELLIE, THIS IS INSANE! WE HAVE NO IDEA WHO THESE MEN ARE OR WHAT--
WAIT... YOUR NAME IS--
AVA SAID THESE ARE THE GUYS THAT HELPED HER!
SO WE SHOULD ALL JUST GO WITH THE INSANE WIZARD GUY AND NOT ASK QUESTIONS?!
YOU KNOW WHAT THAT MEANS? IT MEANS HE'S IN THERE! THE ONE IN AVA'S DRAWING! WE CAN--
THIS IS INSANE, EL!
OH, FOR CRYING OUT LOUD...
SO WE'RE JUST GOING TO GET INTO A STRANGER'S WEIRD MAGIC VAN? DOESN'T THAT SEEM A LITTLE--
I'M SORRY, WHO THE HELL INVITED YOU, PYRO?
PEW. PEW. PEW. PEW.
POP
POP
POP
POP

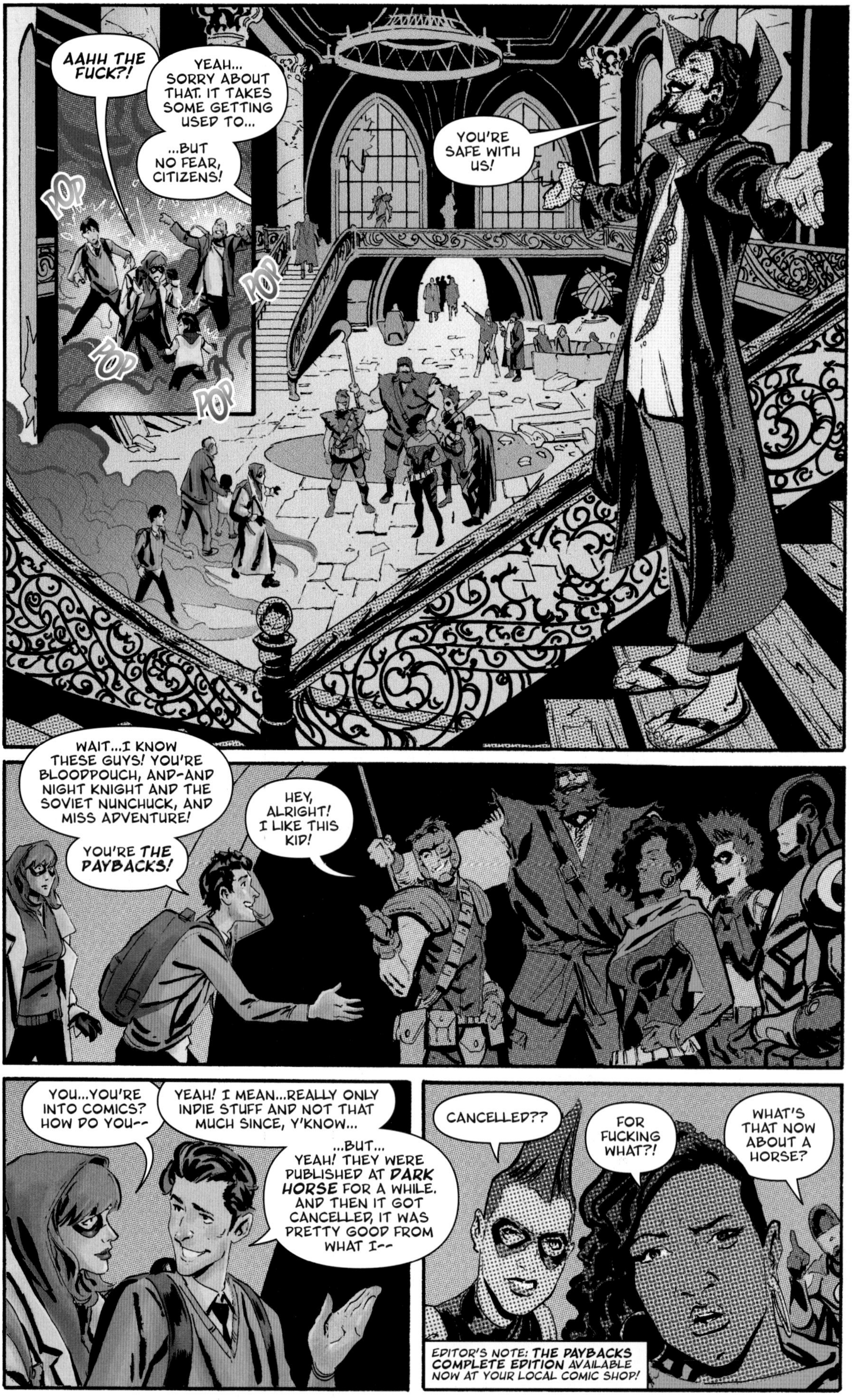
AAHH THE FUCK?!
YEAH... SORRY ABOUT THAT. IT TAKES SOME GETTING USED TO...
...BUT NO FEAR, CITIZENS!
POP
POP
POP
POP
YOU'RE SAFE WITH US!
WAIT...I KNOW THESE GUYS! YOU'RE BLOODPOUCH, AND-AND NIGHT KNIGHT AND THE SOVIET NUNCHUCK, AND MISS ADVENTURE!
YOU'RE THE PAYBACKS!
HEY, ALRIGHT! I LIKE THIS KID!
YOU...YOU'RE INTO COMICS? HOW DO YOU--
YEAH! I MEAN...REALLY ONLY INDIE STUFF AND NOT THAT MUCH SINCE, Y'KNOW...
...BUT... YEAH! THEY WERE PUBLISHED AT DARK HORSE FOR A WHILE. AND THEN IT GOT CANCELLED, IT WAS PRETTY GOOD FROM WHAT I--
CANCELLED??
FOR FUCKING WHAT?!
WHAT'S THAT NOW ABOUT A HORSE?
EDITOR'S NOTE: THE PAYBACKS COMPLETE EDITION AVAILABLE NOW AT YOUR LOCAL COMIC SHOP!

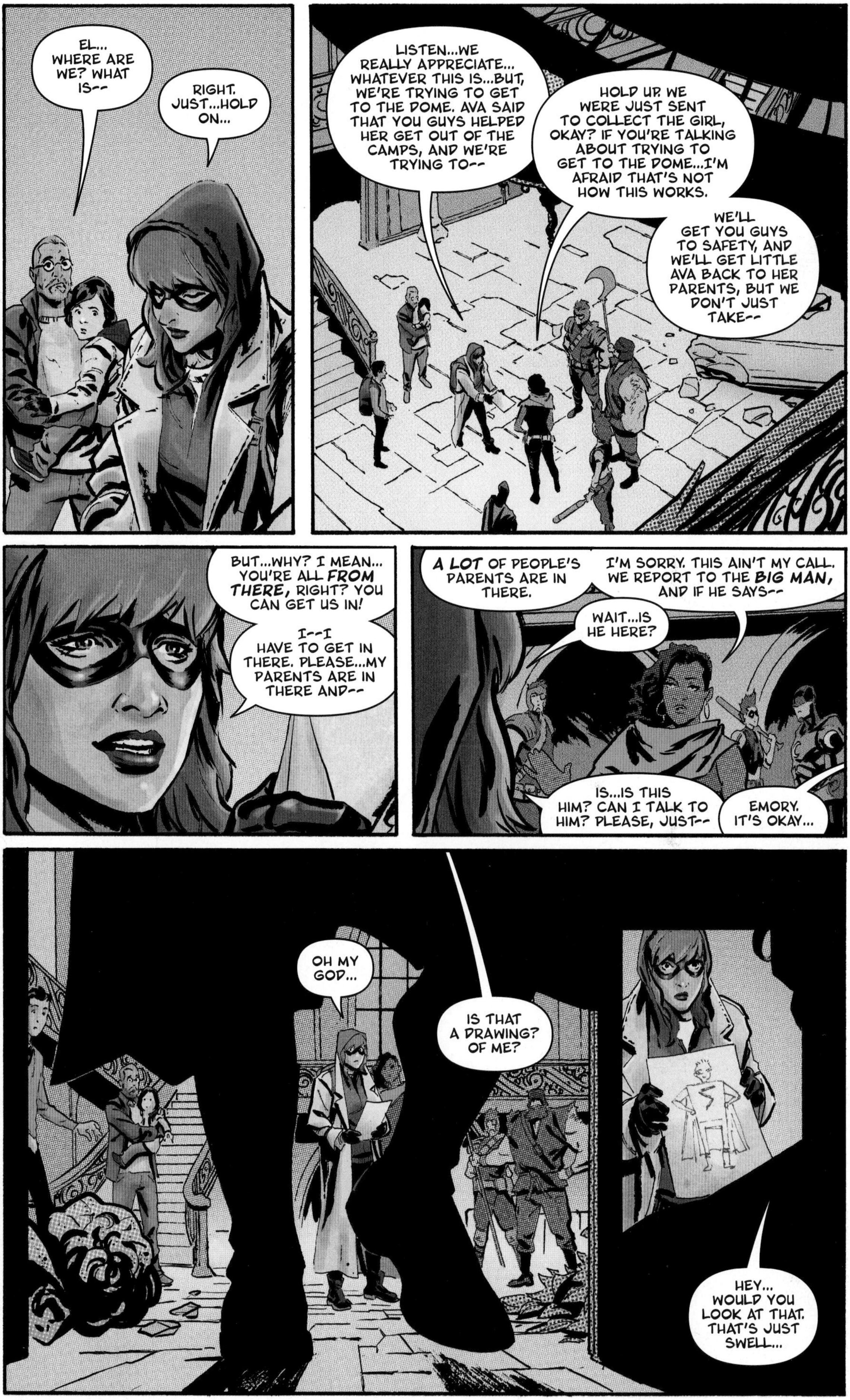
EL... WHERE ARE WE? WHAT IS--
RIGHT. JUST...HOLD ON...
LISTEN...WE REALLY APPRECIATE... WHATEVER THIS IS...BUT, WE'RE TRYING TO GET TO THE DOME. AVA SAID THAT YOU GUYS HELPED HER GET OUT OF THE CAMPS, AND WE'RE TRYING TO--
HOLD UP. WE WERE JUST SENT TO COLLECT THE GIRL, OKAY? IF YOU'RE TALKING ABOUT TRYING TO GET TO THE DOME...I'M AFRAID THAT'S NOT HOW THIS WORKS.
WE'LL GET YOU GUYS TO SAFETY, AND WE'LL GET LITTLE AVA BACK TO HER PARENTS, BUT WE DON'T JUST TAKE--
BUT...WHY? I MEAN... YOU'RE ALL FROM THERE, RIGHT? YOU CAN GET US IN!
I--I HAVE TO GET IN THERE. PLEASE...MY PARENTS ARE IN THERE AND--
A LOT OF PEOPLE'S PARENTS ARE IN THERE.
I'M SORRY. THIS AIN'T MY CALL. WE REPORT TO THE BIG MAN, AND IF HE SAYS--
WAIT...IS HE HERE?
IS...IS THIS HIM? CAN I TALK TO HIM? PLEASE, JUST--
EMORY. IT'S OKAY...
OH MY GOD...
IS THAT A DRAWING? OF ME?
HEY... WOULD YOU LOOK AT THAT. THAT'S JUST SWELL...

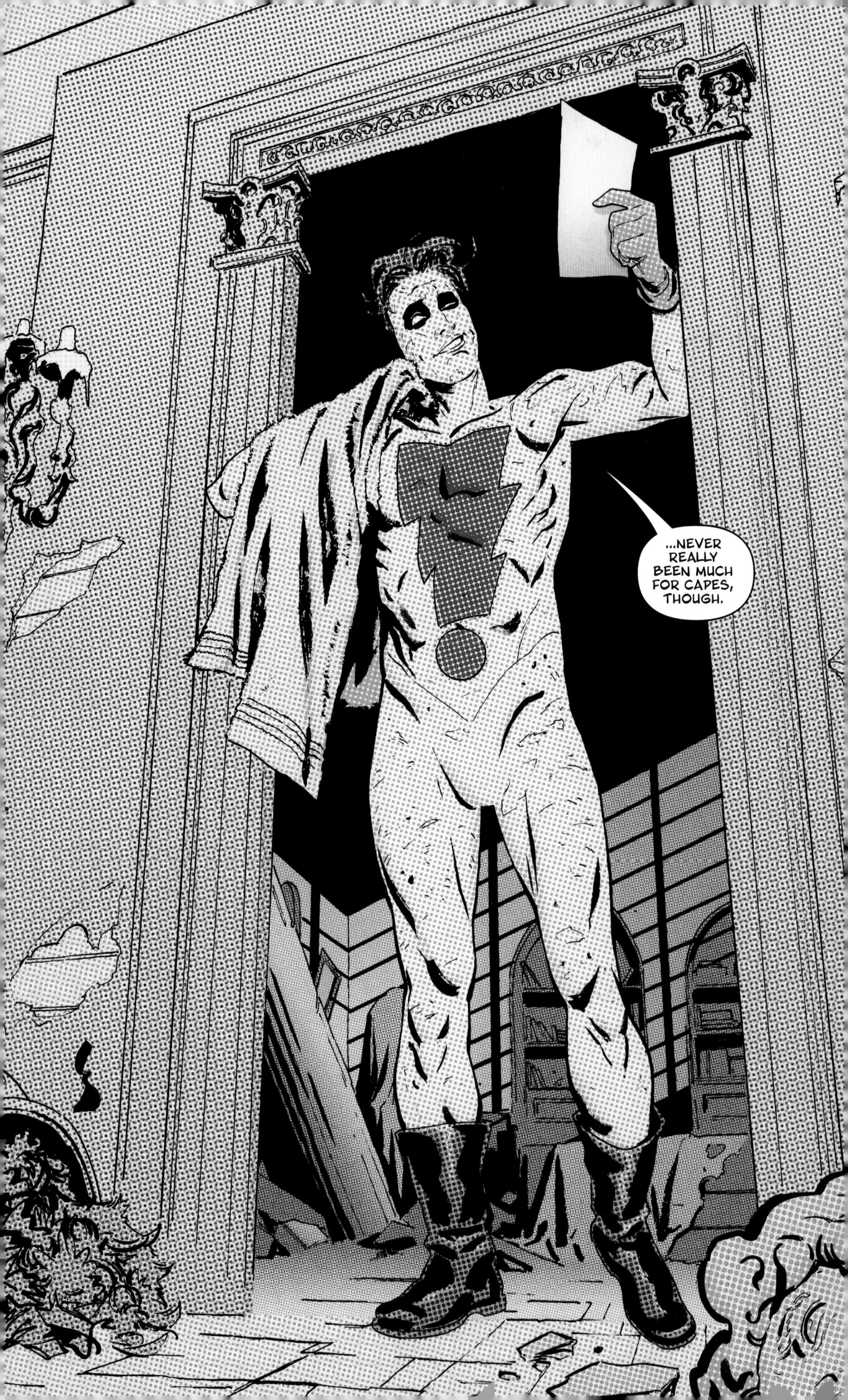
...NEVER REALLY BEEN MUCH FOR CAPES, THOUGH.

GEOFF SHAW, DEE CUNNIFFE & JOHN J. HILL

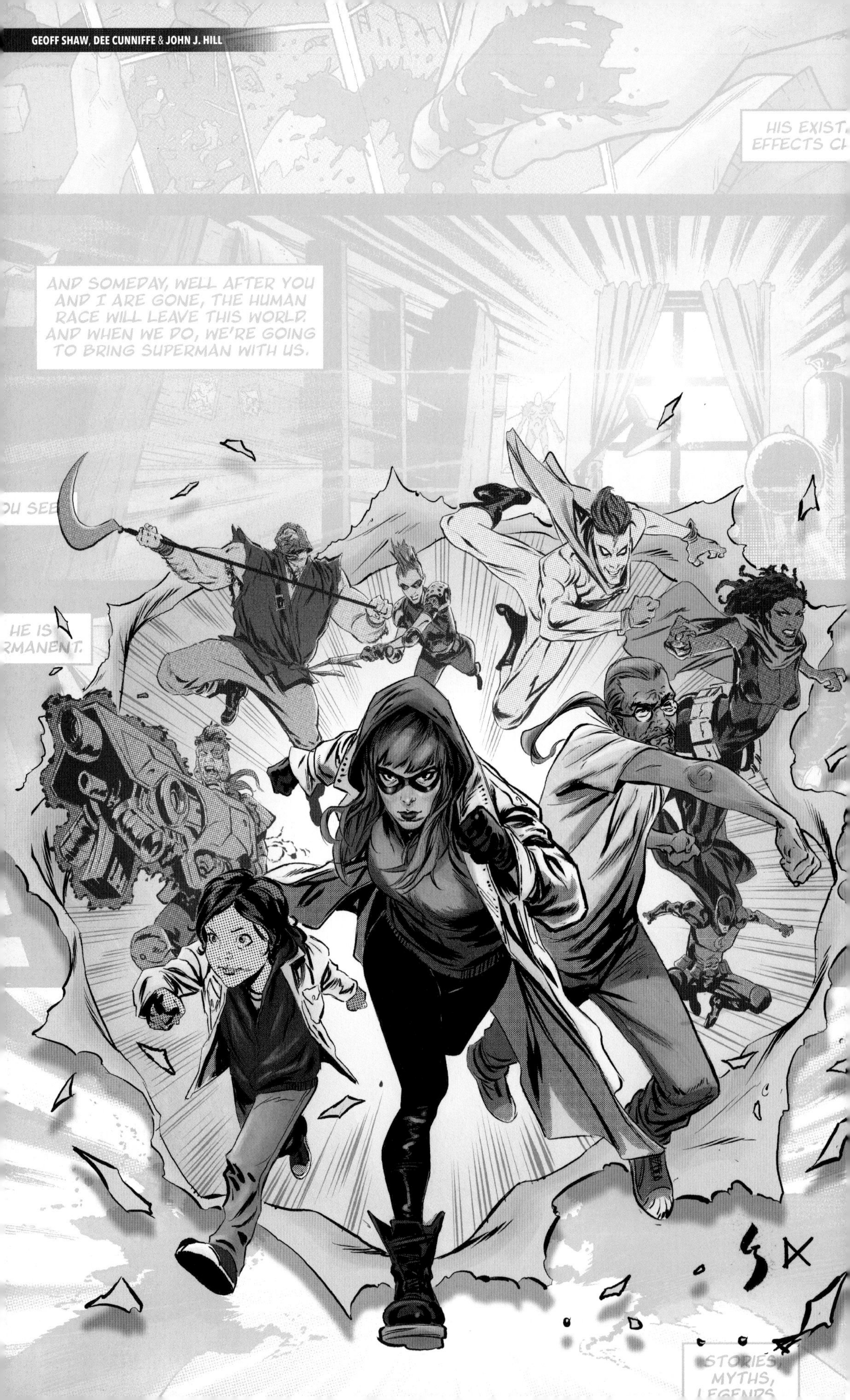
AND SOMEDAY, WELL AFTER YOU AND I ARE GONE, THE HUMAN RACE WILL LEAVE THIS WORLD. AND WHEN WE DO, WE'RE GOING TO BRING SUPERMAN WITH US.

KIDS LOVE CHAINS

CHAPTER FOUR

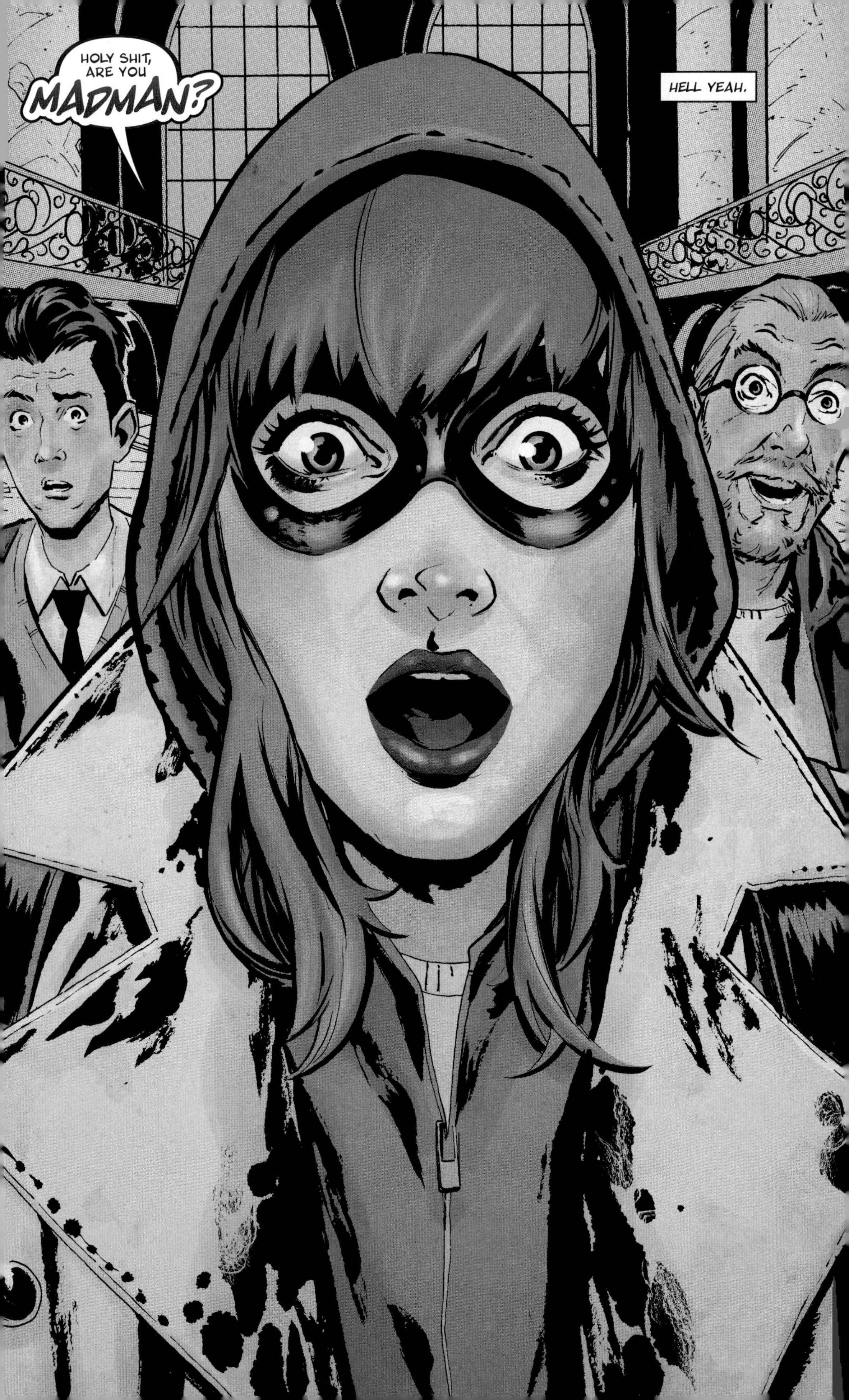
HOLY SHIT, ARE YOU MADMAN?
HELL YEAH.

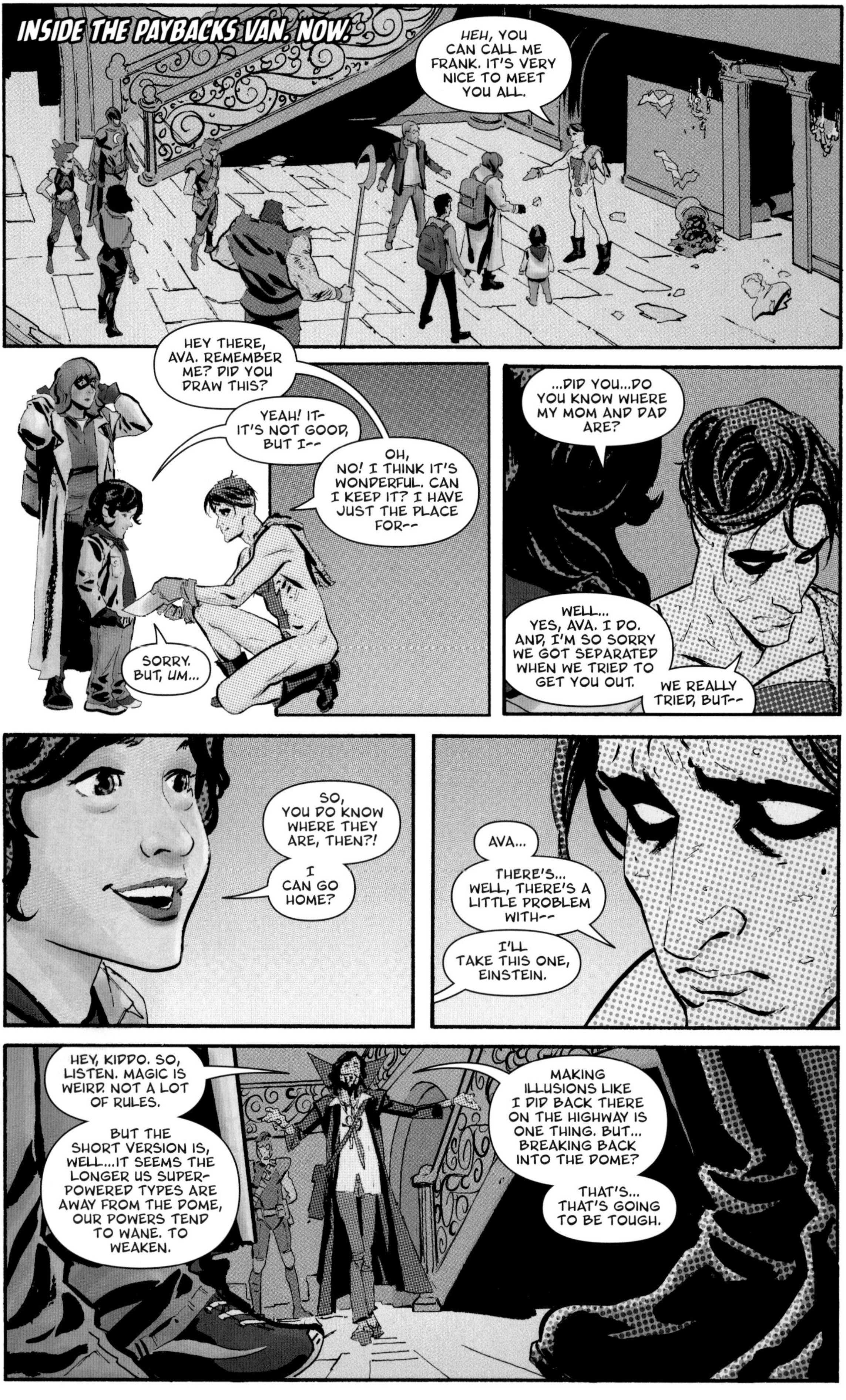
INSIDE THE PAYBACKS VAN. NOW.
HEH, YOU CAN CALL ME FRANK. IT'S VERY NICE TO MEET YOU ALL.
HEY THERE, AVA. REMEMBER ME? DID YOU DRAW THIS?
YEAH! IT-IT'S NOT GOOD, BUT I--
OH, NO! I THINK IT'S WONDERFUL. CAN I KEEP IT? I HAVE JUST THE PLACE FOR--
SORRY. BUT, UM...
...DID YOU...DO YOU KNOW WHERE MY MOM AND DAD ARE?
WELL... YES, AVA. I DO. AND, I'M SO SORRY WE GOT SEPARATED WHEN WE TRIED TO GET YOU OUT.
WE REALLY TRIED, BUT--
SO, YOU DO KNOW WHERE THEY ARE, THEN?!
I CAN GO HOME?
AVA...
THERE'S... WELL, THERE'S A LITTLE PROBLEM WITH--
I'LL TAKE THIS ONE, EINSTEIN.
HEY, KIDDO. SO, LISTEN. MAGIC IS WEIRD. NOT A LOT OF RULES.
BUT THE SHORT VERSION IS, WELL...IT SEEMS THE LONGER US SUPER-POWERED TYPES ARE AWAY FROM THE DOME, OUR POWERS TEND TO WANE. TO WEAKEN.
MAKING ILLUSIONS LIKE I DID BACK THERE ON THE HIGHWAY IS ONE THING. BUT... BREAKING BACK INTO THE DOME?
THAT'S... THAT'S GOING TO BE TOUGH.

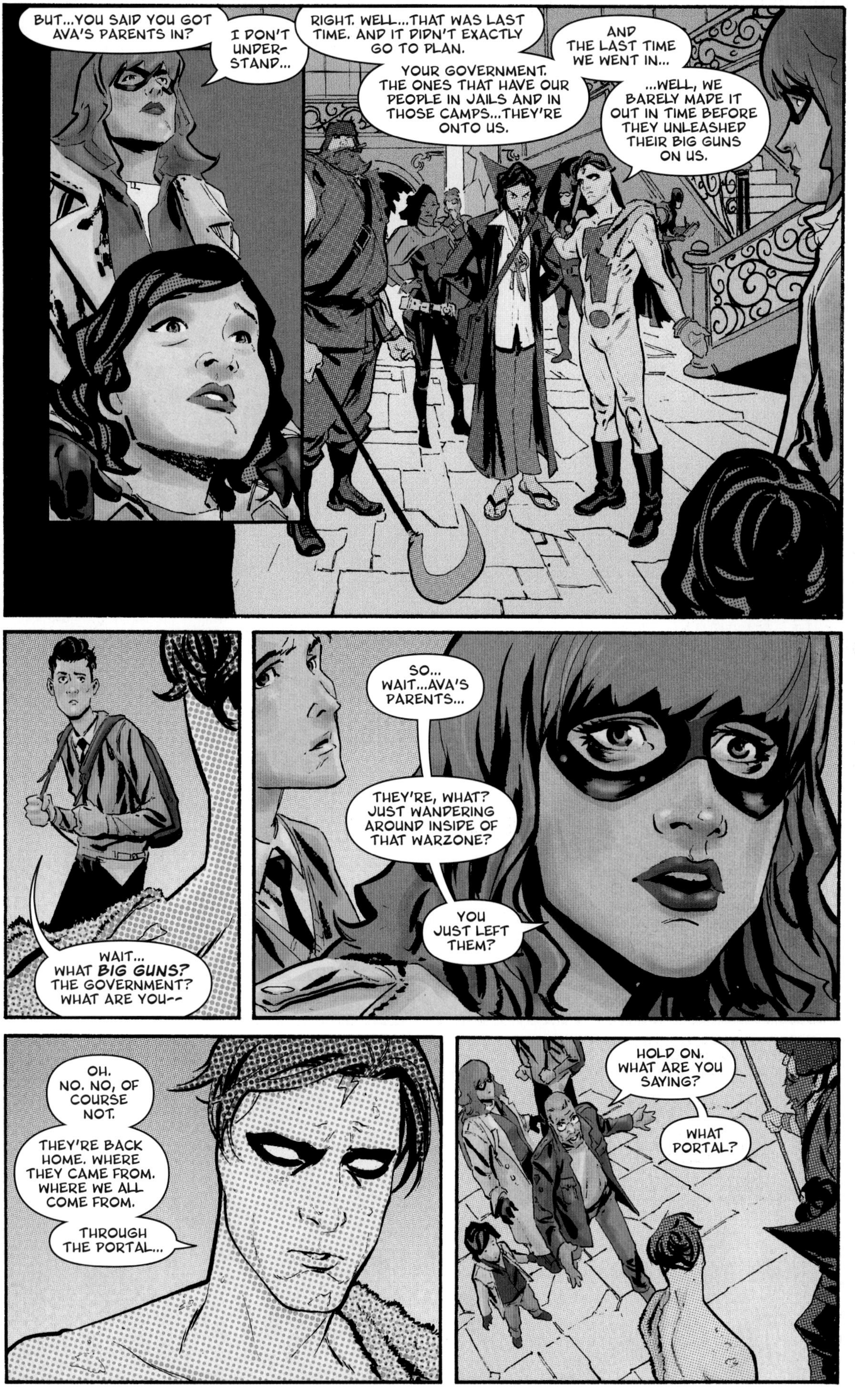
BUT...YOU SAID YOU GOT AVA'S PARENTS IN?
I DON'T UNDER-STAND...
RIGHT. WELL...THAT WAS LAST TIME. AND IT DIDN'T EXACTLY GO TO PLAN.
YOUR GOVERNMENT. THE ONES THAT HAVE OUR PEOPLE IN JAILS AND IN THOSE CAMPS...THEY'RE ONTO US.
AND THE LAST TIME WE WENT IN...
...WELL, WE BARELY MADE IT OUT IN TIME BEFORE THEY UNLEASHED THEIR BIG GUNS ON US.
WAIT... WHAT **BIG GUNS?** THE GOVERNMENT? WHAT ARE YOU--
SO... WAIT...AVA'S PARENTS...
THEY'RE, WHAT? JUST WANDERING AROUND INSIDE OF THAT WARZONE?
YOU JUST LEFT THEM?
OH. NO. NO, OF COURSE NOT.
THEY'RE BACK HOME. WHERE THEY CAME FROM. WHERE WE ALL COME FROM.
THROUGH THE PORTAL...
HOLD ON. WHAT ARE YOU SAYING?
WHAT PORTAL?

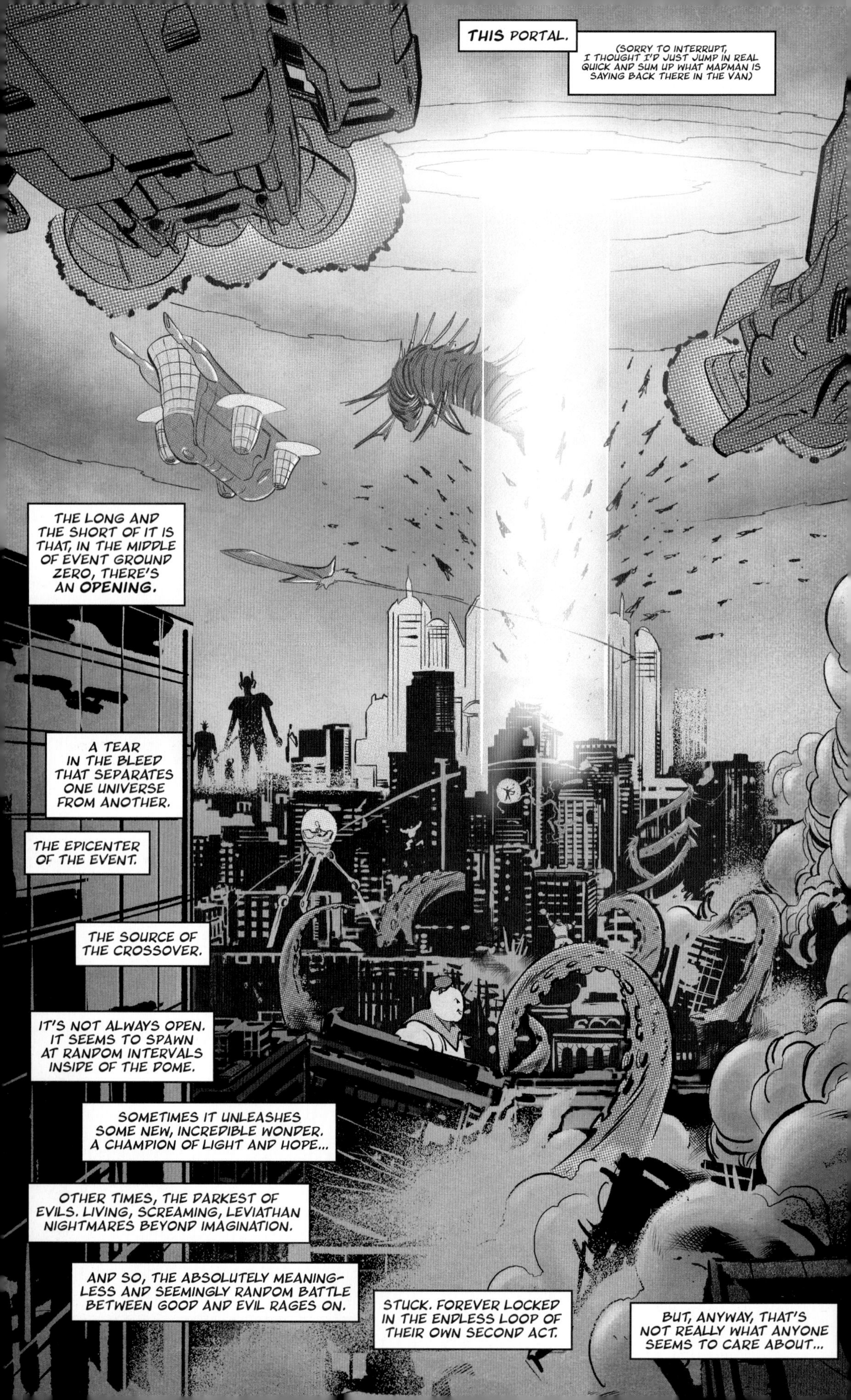
THIS PORTAL.
(SORRY TO INTERRUPT, I THOUGHT I'D JUST JUMP IN REAL QUICK AND SUM UP WHAT MADMAN IS SAYING BACK THERE IN THE VAN)
THE LONG AND THE SHORT OF IT IS THAT, IN THE MIDDLE OF EVENT GROUND ZERO, THERE'S AN OPENING.
A TEAR IN THE BLEED THAT SEPARATES ONE UNIVERSE FROM ANOTHER.
THE EPICENTER OF THE EVENT.
THE SOURCE OF THE CROSSOVER.
IT'S NOT ALWAYS OPEN. IT SEEMS TO SPAWN AT RANDOM INTERVALS INSIDE OF THE DOME.
SOMETIMES IT UNLEASHES SOME NEW, INCREDIBLE WONDER. A CHAMPION OF LIGHT AND HOPE...
OTHER TIMES, THE DARKEST OF EVILS. LIVING, SCREAMING, LEVIATHAN NIGHTMARES BEYOND IMAGINATION.
AND SO, THE ABSOLUTELY MEANING-LESS AND SEEMINGLY RANDOM BATTLE BETWEEN GOOD AND EVIL RAGES ON.
STUCK. FOREVER LOCKED IN THE ENDLESS LOOP OF THEIR OWN SECOND ACT.
BUT, ANYWAY, THAT'S NOT REALLY WHAT ANYONE SEEMS TO CARE ABOUT...

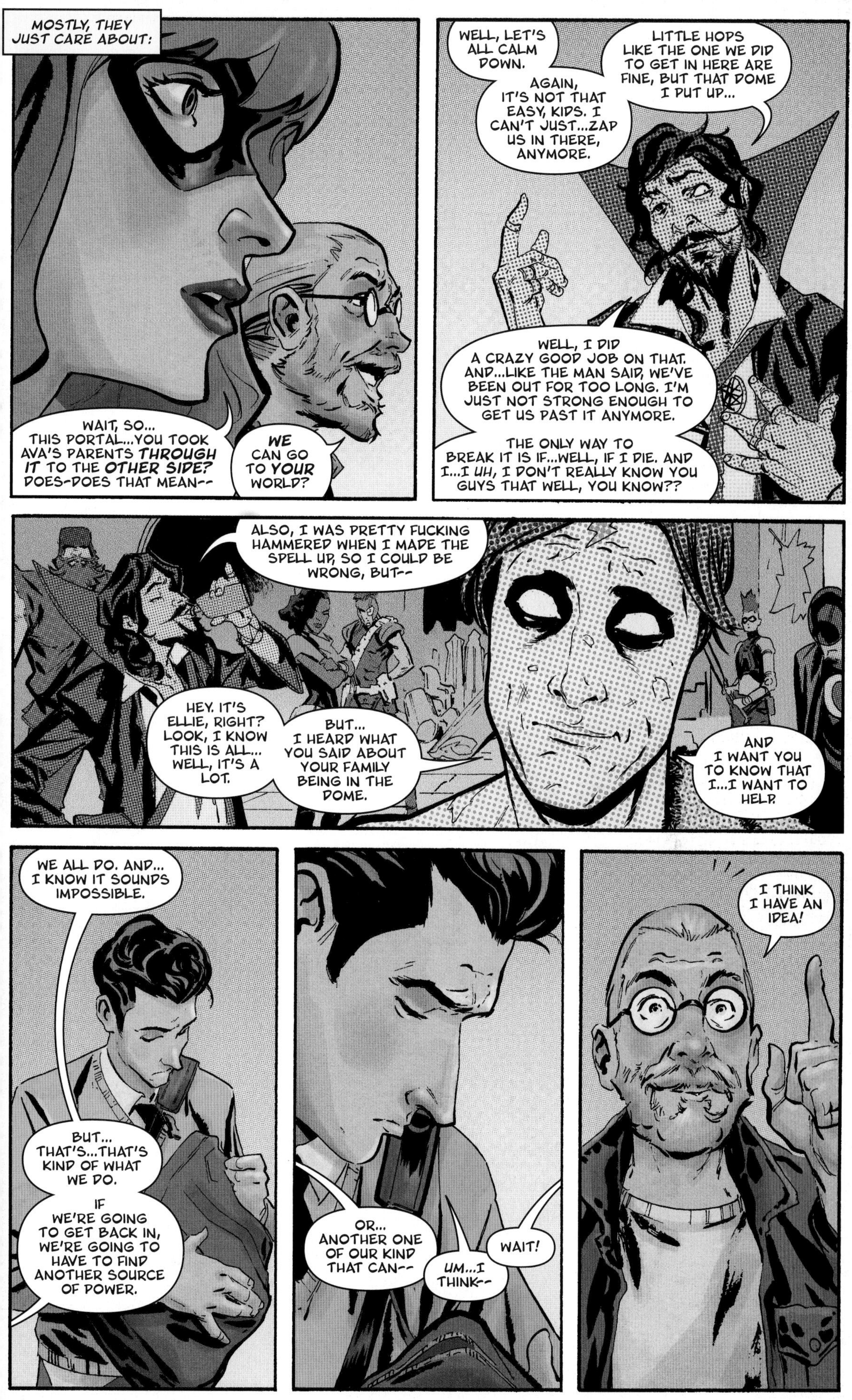
MOSTLY, THEY JUST CARE ABOUT:
WAIT, SO... THIS PORTAL...YOU TOOK AVA'S PARENTS *THROUGH IT* TO THE *OTHER SIDE?* DOES-DOES THAT MEAN--
WE CAN GO TO *YOUR* WORLD?
WELL, LET'S ALL CALM DOWN.
AGAIN, IT'S NOT THAT EASY, KIDS. I CAN'T JUST...ZAP US IN THERE, ANYMORE.
LITTLE HOPS LIKE THE ONE WE DID TO GET IN HERE ARE FINE, BUT THAT DOME I PUT UP...
WELL, I DID A CRAZY GOOD JOB ON THAT. AND...LIKE THE MAN SAID, WE'VE BEEN OUT FOR TOO LONG. I'M JUST NOT STRONG ENOUGH TO GET US PAST IT ANYMORE.
THE ONLY WAY TO BREAK IT IS IF...WELL, IF I DIE. AND I...I *UH*, I DON'T REALLY KNOW YOU GUYS THAT WELL, YOU KNOW??
ALSO, I WAS PRETTY FUCKING HAMMERED WHEN I MADE THE SPELL UP, SO I COULD BE WRONG, BUT--
HEY. IT'S ELLIE, RIGHT? LOOK, I KNOW THIS IS ALL... WELL, IT'S A LOT.
BUT... I HEARD WHAT YOU SAID ABOUT YOUR FAMILY BEING IN THE DOME.
AND I WANT YOU TO KNOW THAT I...I WANT TO HELP.
WE ALL DO. AND... I KNOW IT SOUNDS IMPOSSIBLE.
BUT... THAT'S...THAT'S KIND OF WHAT WE DO.
IF WE'RE GOING TO GET BACK IN, WE'RE GOING TO HAVE TO FIND ANOTHER SOURCE OF POWER.
OR... ANOTHER ONE OF OUR KIND THAT CAN--
UM...I THINK--
WAIT!
I THINK I HAVE AN IDEA!

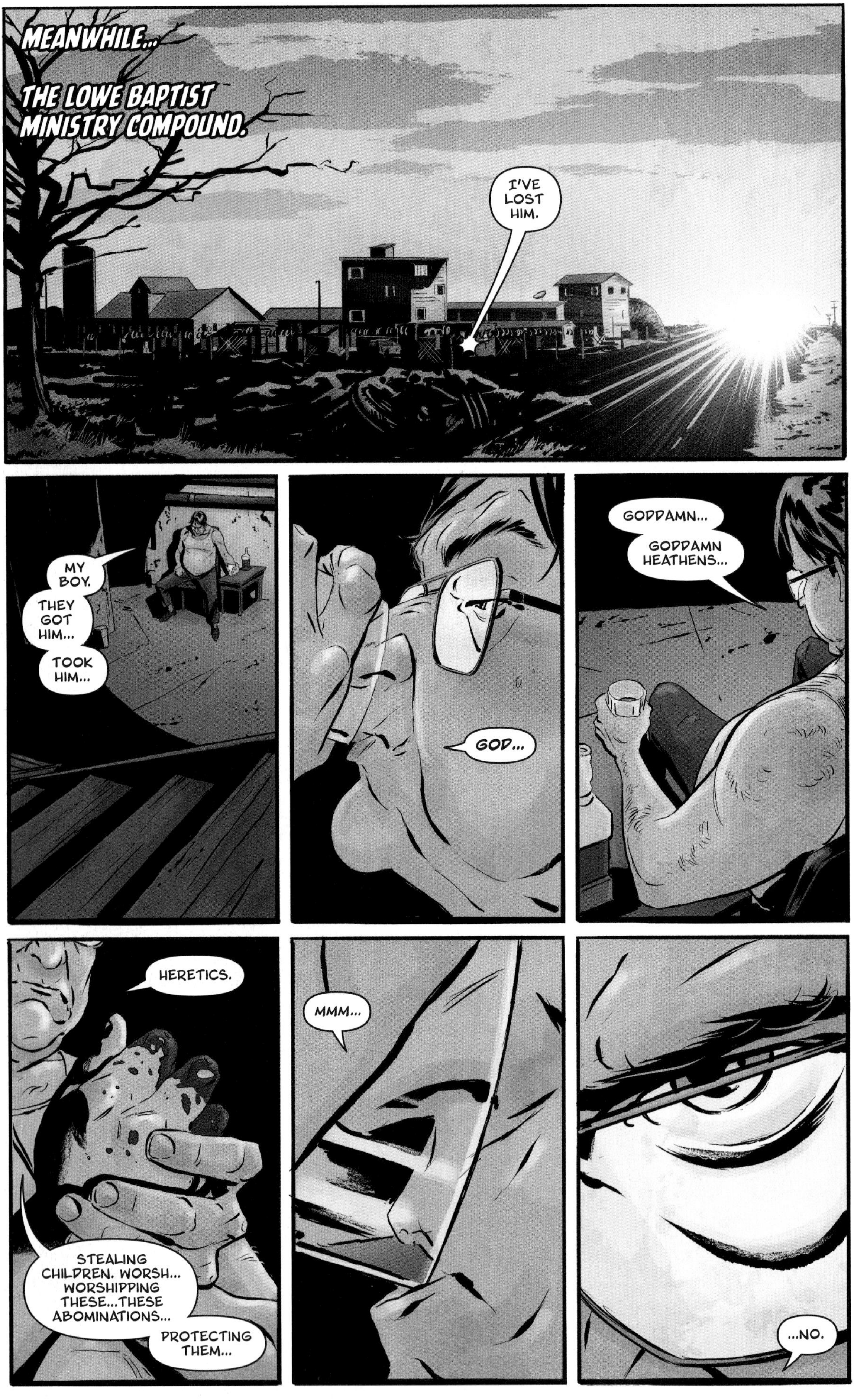
MEANWHILE...
THE LOWE BAPTIST MINISTRY COMPOUND.
I'VE LOST HIM.
MY BOY.
THEY GOT HIM...
TOOK HIM...
GOD...
GODDAMN...
GODDAMN HEATHENS...
HERETICS.
STEALING CHILDREN. WORSH... WORSHIPPING THESE...THESE ABOMINATIONS...
PROTECTING THEM...
MMM...
...NO.

NO.

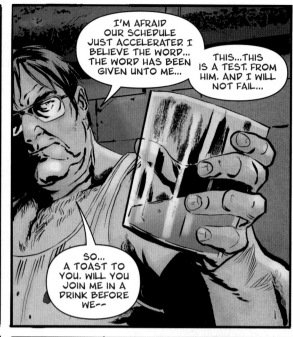

I'M AFRAID OUR SCHEDULE JUST ACCELERATED. I BELIEVE THE WORD... THE WORD HAS BEEN GIVEN UNTO ME...

THIS...THIS IS A TEST. FROM HIM. AND I WILL NOT FAIL...

SO... A TOAST TO YOU. WILL YOU JOIN ME IN A DRINK BEFORE WE--

P-PLEASE...

N-NO MORE...

WELL...IF THAT'S HOW YOU WANT IT, FRIEND...

HEHE... SUIT YOURSELF.

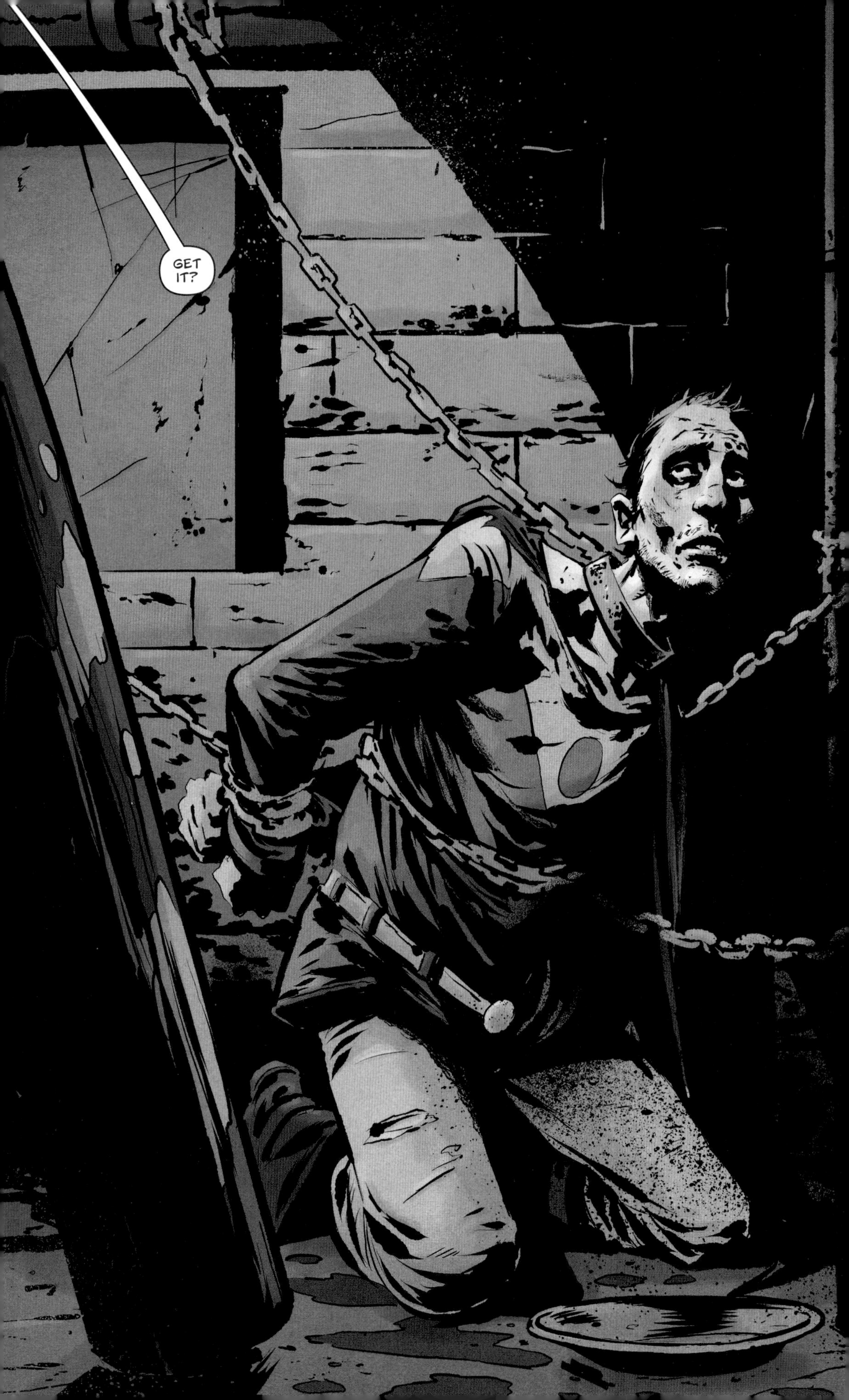
GET IT?

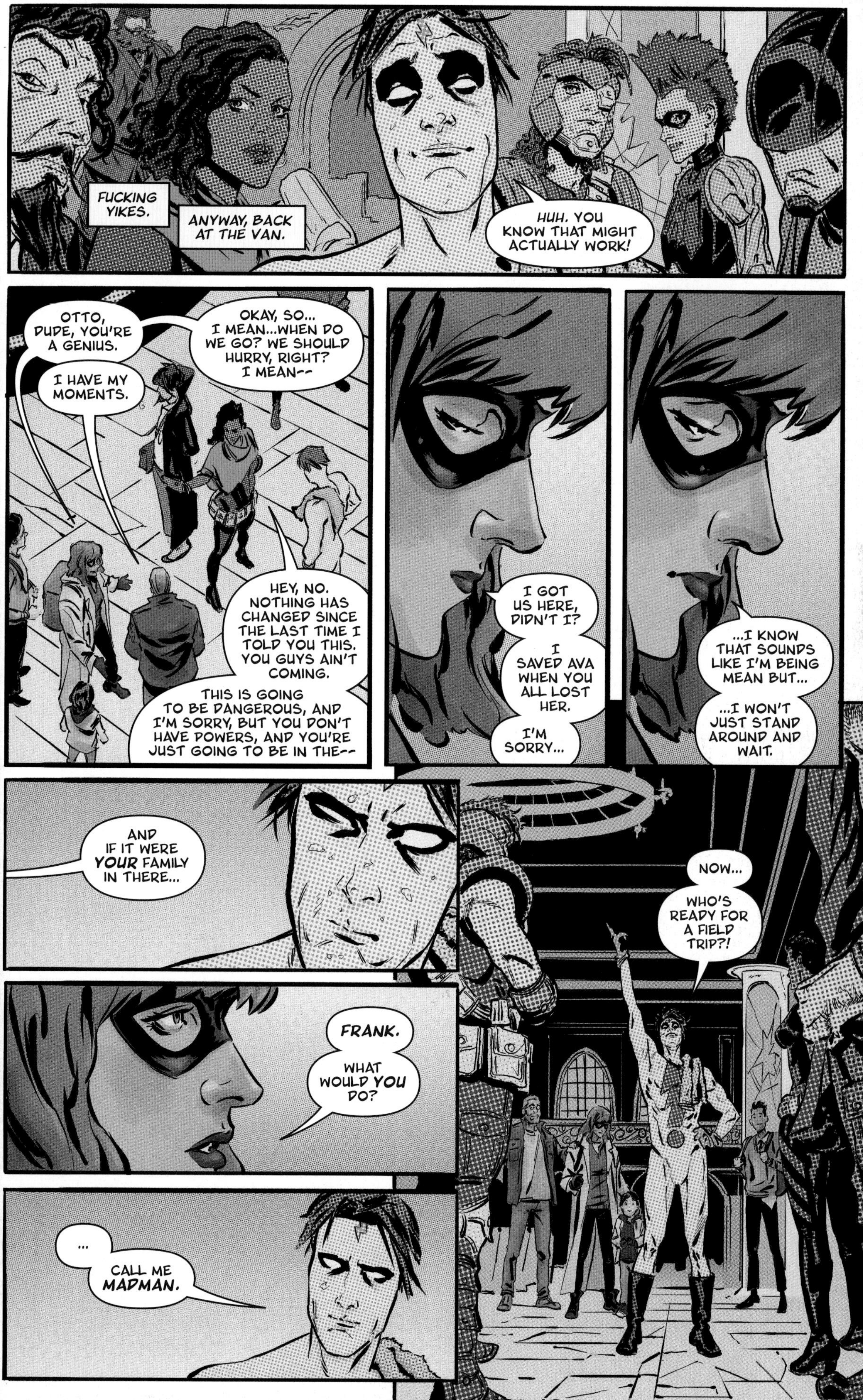
FUCKING YIKES.
ANYWAY, BACK AT THE VAN.
HUH. YOU KNOW THAT MIGHT ACTUALLY WORK!
OTTO, DUDE, YOU'RE A GENIUS.
I HAVE MY MOMENTS.
OKAY, SO... I MEAN...WHEN DO WE GO? WE SHOULD HURRY, RIGHT? I MEAN--
HEY, NO. NOTHING HAS CHANGED SINCE THE LAST TIME I TOLD YOU THIS. YOU GUYS AIN'T COMING.
THIS IS GOING TO BE DANGEROUS, AND I'M SORRY, BUT YOU DON'T HAVE POWERS, AND YOU'RE JUST GOING TO BE IN THE--
I GOT US HERE, DIDN'T I?
I SAVED AVA WHEN YOU ALL LOST HER.
I'M SORRY...
...I KNOW THAT SOUNDS LIKE I'M BEING MEAN BUT...
...I WON'T JUST STAND AROUND AND WAIT.
AND IF IT WERE YOUR FAMILY IN THERE...
FRANK.
WHAT WOULD YOU DO?
...
CALL ME MADMAN.
NOW...
WHO'S READY FOR A FIELD TRIP?!

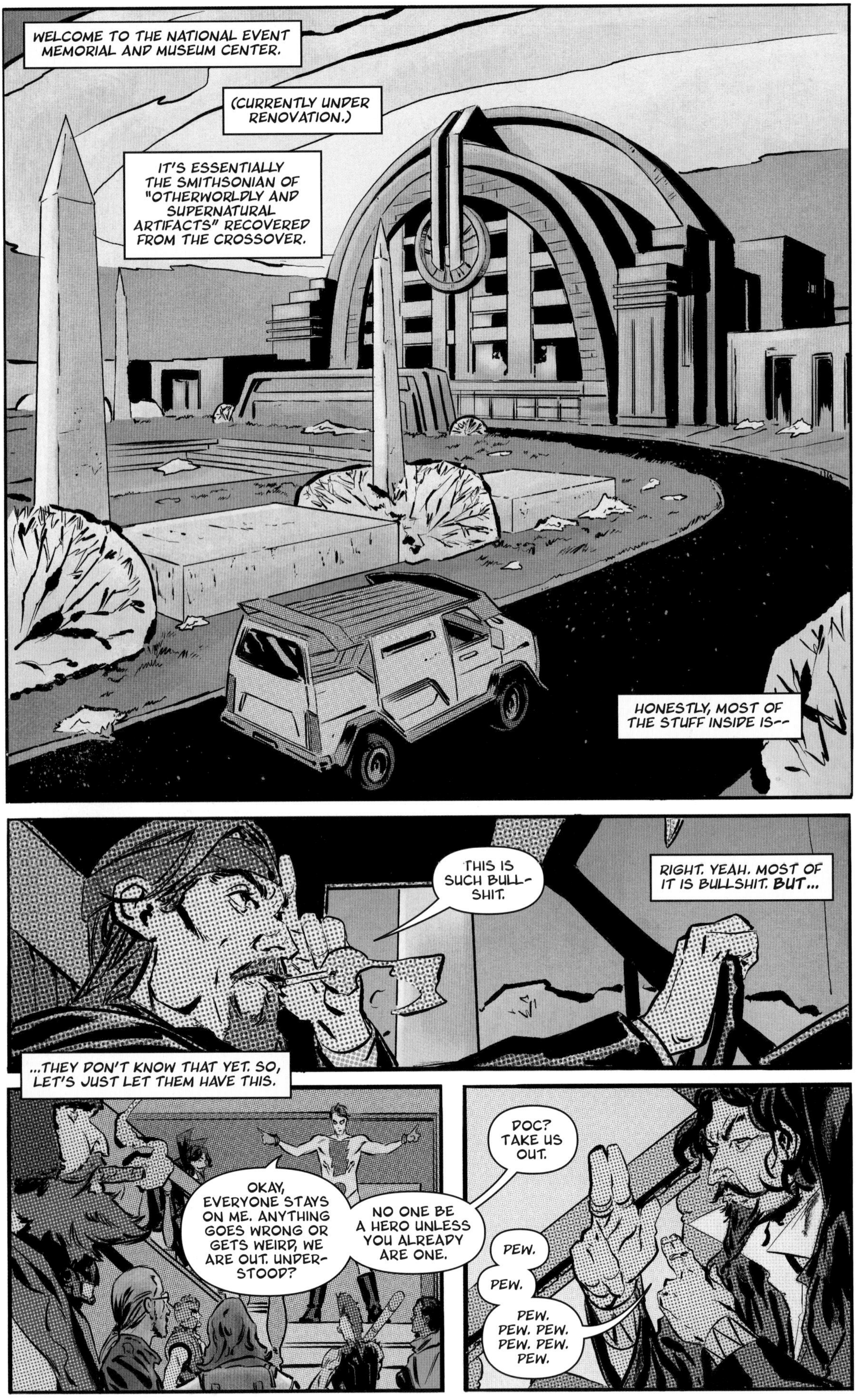
WELCOME TO THE NATIONAL EVENT MEMORIAL AND MUSEUM CENTER.
(CURRENTLY UNDER RENOVATION.)
IT'S ESSENTIALLY THE SMITHSONIAN OF "OTHERWORLDLY AND SUPERNATURAL ARTIFACTS" RECOVERED FROM THE CROSSOVER.
HONESTLY, MOST OF THE STUFF INSIDE IS--
THIS IS SUCH BULL-SHIT.
RIGHT. YEAH. MOST OF IT IS BULLSHIT. BUT...
...THEY DON'T KNOW THAT YET. SO, LET'S JUST LET THEM HAVE THIS.
OKAY, EVERYONE STAYS ON ME. ANYTHING GOES WRONG OR GETS WEIRD, WE ARE OUT. UNDER-STOOD?
NO ONE BE A HERO UNLESS YOU ALREADY ARE ONE.
DOC? TAKE US OUT.
PEW.
PEW.
PEW. PEW. PEW. PEW. PEW. PEW.

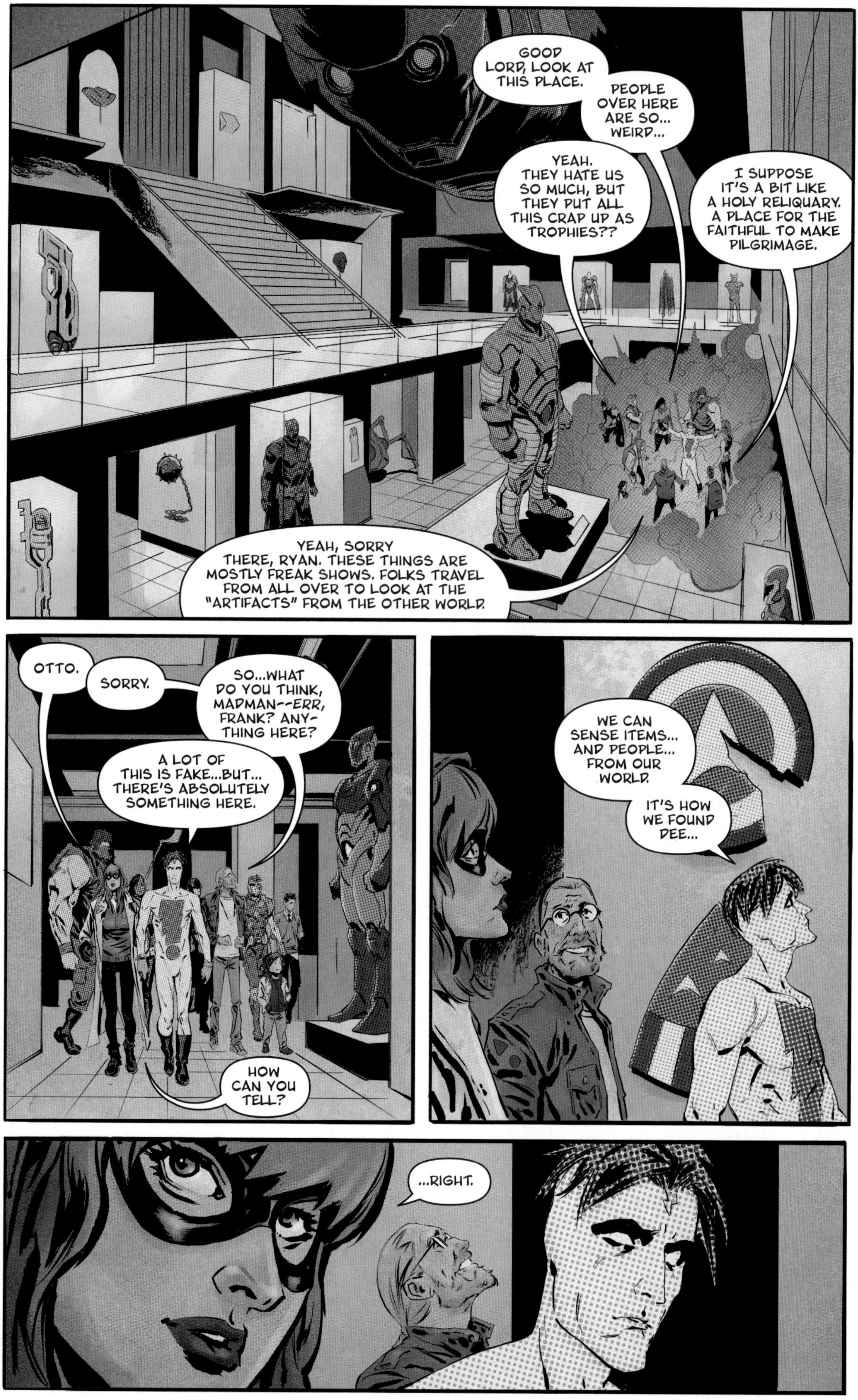
GOOD LORD, LOOK AT THIS PLACE.
PEOPLE OVER HERE ARE SO... WEIRD...
YEAH. THEY HATE US SO MUCH, BUT THEY PUT ALL THIS CRAP UP AS TROPHIES??
I SUPPOSE IT'S A BIT LIKE A HOLY RELIQUARY. A PLACE FOR THE FAITHFUL TO MAKE PILGRIMAGE.
YEAH, SORRY THERE, RYAN. THESE THINGS ARE MOSTLY FREAK SHOWS. FOLKS TRAVEL FROM ALL OVER TO LOOK AT THE "ARTIFACTS" FROM THE OTHER WORLD.
OTTO.
SORRY.
SO...WHAT DO YOU THINK, MADMAN--ERR, FRANK? ANYTHING HERE?
A LOT OF THIS IS FAKE...BUT... THERE'S ABSOLUTELY SOMETHING HERE.
HOW CAN YOU TELL?
WE CAN SENSE ITEMS... AND PEOPLE... FROM OUR WORLD.
IT'S HOW WE FOUND DEE...
...RIGHT.

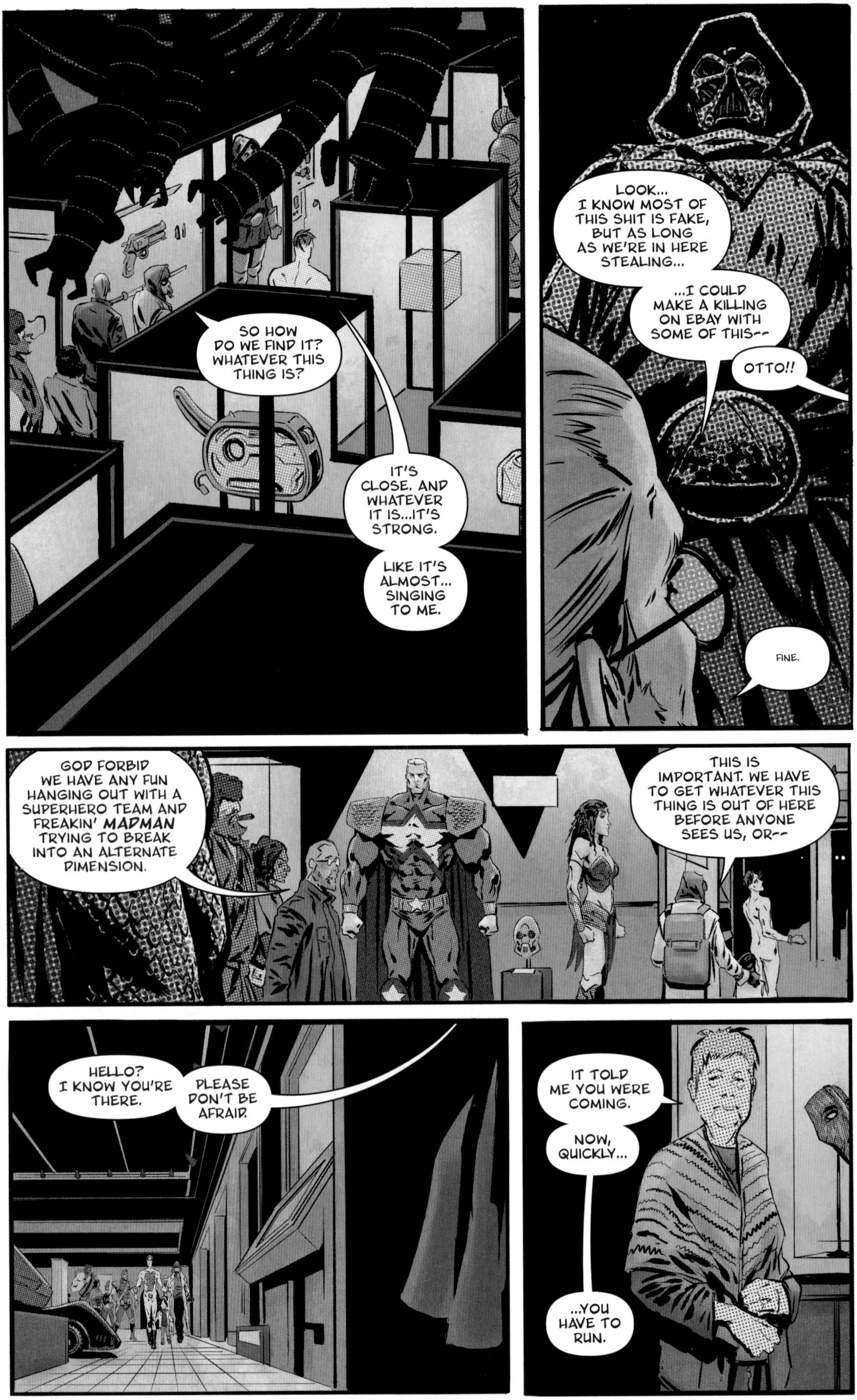
SO HOW DO WE FIND IT? WHATEVER THIS THING IS?
IT'S CLOSE. AND WHATEVER IT IS...IT'S STRONG.
LIKE IT'S ALMOST... SINGING TO ME.
LOOK... I KNOW MOST OF THIS SHIT IS FAKE, BUT AS LONG AS WE'RE IN HERE STEALING...
...I COULD MAKE A KILLING ON EBAY WITH SOME OF THIS--
OTTO!!
FINE.
GOD FORBID WE HAVE ANY FUN HANGING OUT WITH A SUPERHERO TEAM AND FREAKIN' MADMAN TRYING TO BREAK INTO AN ALTERNATE DIMENSION.
THIS IS IMPORTANT. WE HAVE TO GET WHATEVER THIS THING IS OUT OF HERE BEFORE ANYONE SEES US, OR--
HELLO? I KNOW YOU'RE THERE.
PLEASE DON'T BE AFRAID.
IT TOLD ME YOU WERE COMING.
NOW, QUICKLY...
...YOU HAVE TO RUN.

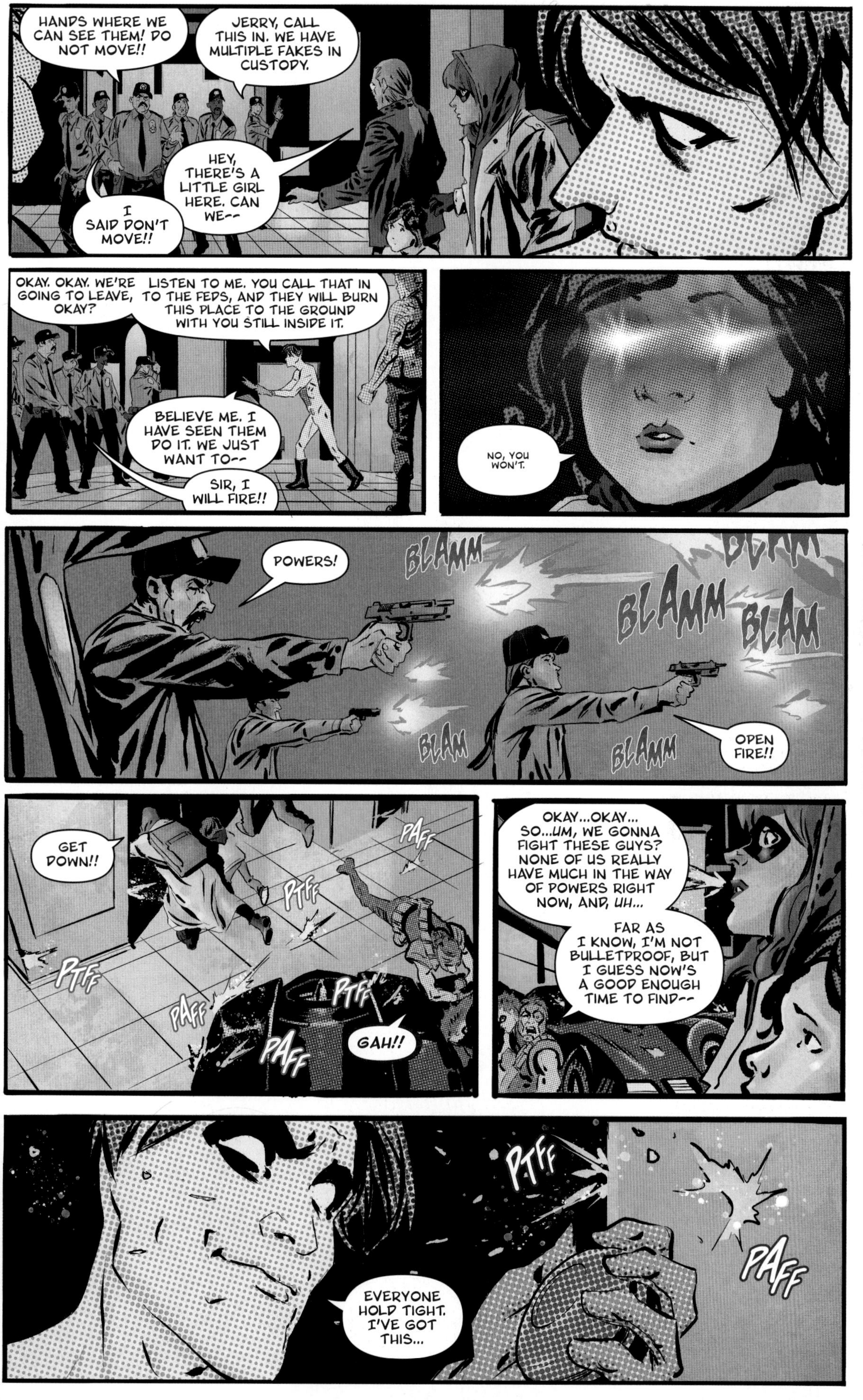
HANDS WHERE WE CAN SEE THEM! DO NOT MOVE!!
JERRY, CALL THIS IN. WE HAVE MULTIPLE FAKES IN CUSTODY.
HEY, THERE'S A LITTLE GIRL HERE. CAN WE--
I SAID DON'T MOVE!!
OKAY. OKAY. WE'RE GOING TO LEAVE, OKAY?
LISTEN TO ME. YOU CALL THAT IN TO THE FEDS, AND THEY WILL BURN THIS PLACE TO THE GROUND WITH YOU STILL INSIDE IT.
BELIEVE ME. I HAVE SEEN THEM DO IT. WE JUST WANT TO--
SIR, I WILL FIRE!!
NO, YOU WON'T.
POWERS!
BLAMM
BLAMM
BLAM
BLAM
BLAMM
OPEN FIRE!!
GET DOWN!!
PAFF
PTFF
PTFF
PAFF
PTFF
PAFF
GAH!!
OKAY...OKAY... SO...UM, WE GONNA FIGHT THESE GUYS? NONE OF US REALLY HAVE MUCH IN THE WAY OF POWERS RIGHT NOW, AND, UH...
FAR AS I KNOW, I'M NOT BULLETPROOF, BUT I GUESS NOW'S A GOOD ENOUGH TIME TO FIND--
PTFF
PAFF
EVERYONE HOLD TIGHT. I'VE GOT THIS...

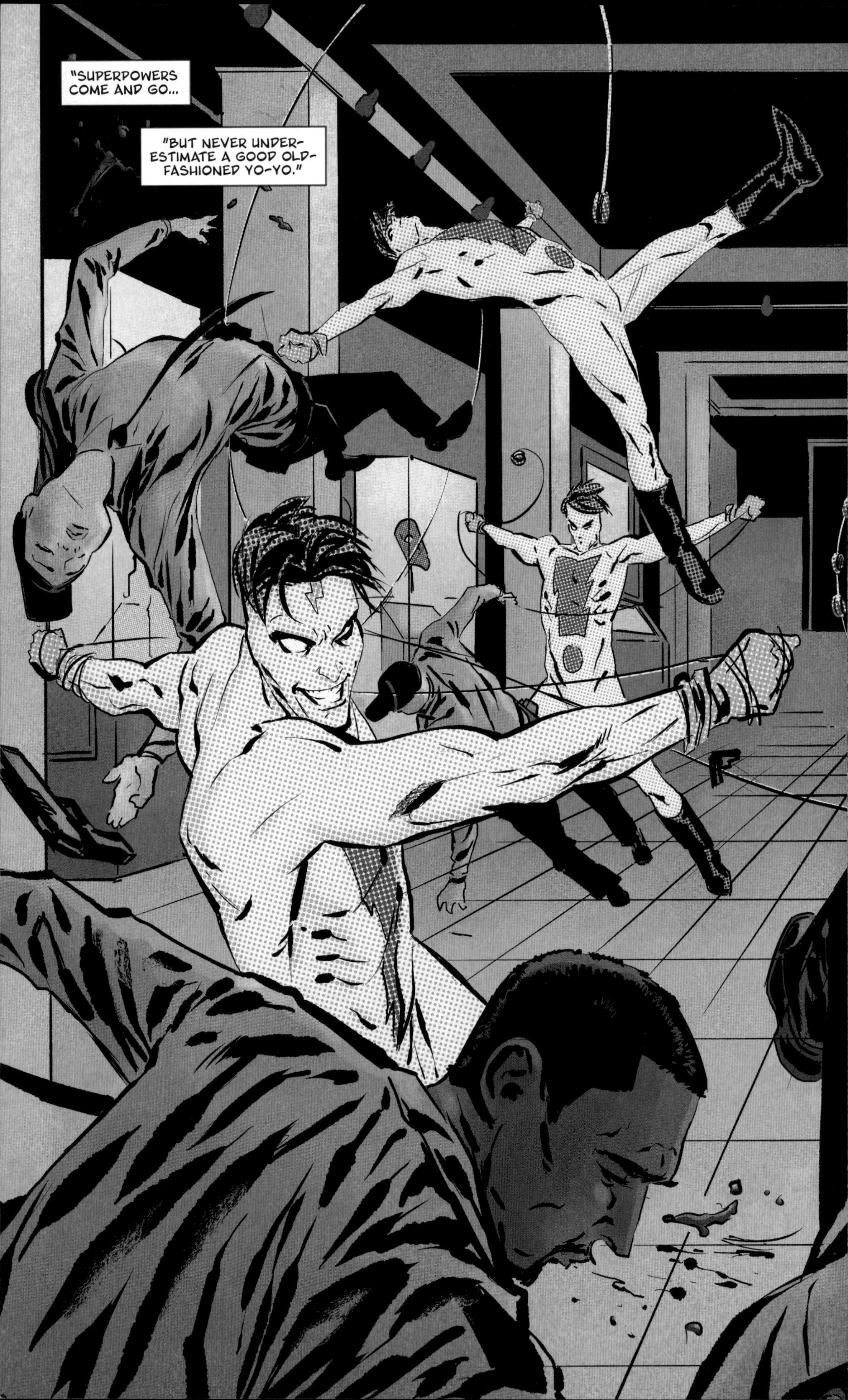
"SUPERPOWERS COME AND GO...
"BUT NEVER UNDER-ESTIMATE A GOOD OLD-FASHIONED YO-YO."

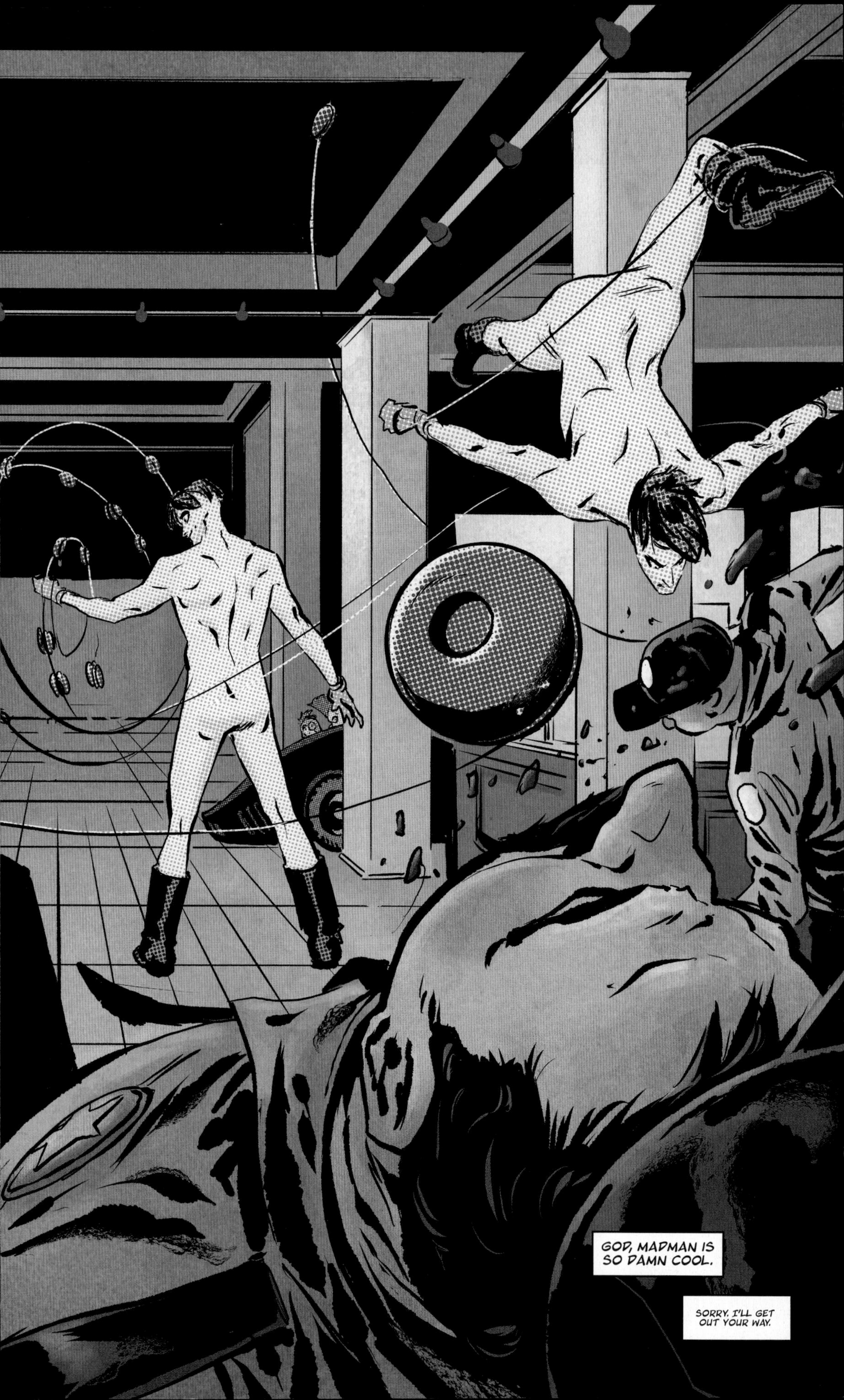
GOD, MADMAN IS SO DAMN COOL.
SORRY. I'LL GET OUT YOUR WAY.

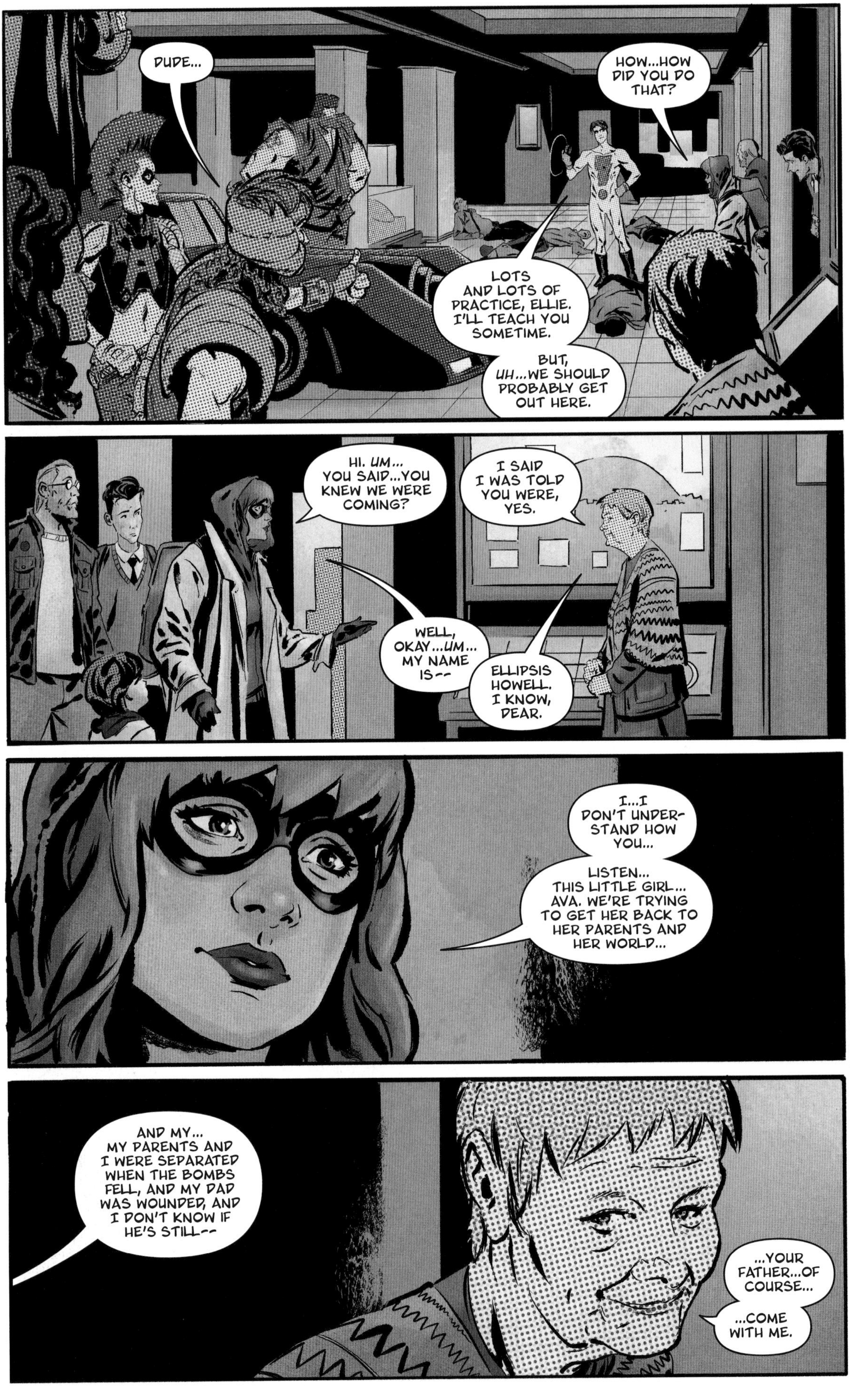
DUDE...
HOW...HOW DID YOU DO THAT?
LOTS AND LOTS OF PRACTICE, ELLIE. I'LL TEACH YOU SOMETIME.
BUT, UH...WE SHOULD PROBABLY GET OUT HERE.
HI. UM... YOU SAID...YOU KNEW WE WERE COMING?
I SAID I WAS TOLD YOU WERE, YES.
WELL, OKAY...UM... MY NAME IS--
ELLIPSIS HOWELL. I KNOW, DEAR.
I...I DON'T UNDER-STAND HOW YOU...
LISTEN... THIS LITTLE GIRL... AVA. WE'RE TRYING TO GET HER BACK TO HER PARENTS AND HER WORLD...
AND MY... MY PARENTS AND I WERE SEPARATED WHEN THE BOMBS FELL, AND MY DAD WAS WOUNDED, AND I DON'T KNOW IF HE'S STILL--
...YOUR FATHER...OF COURSE...
...COME WITH ME.

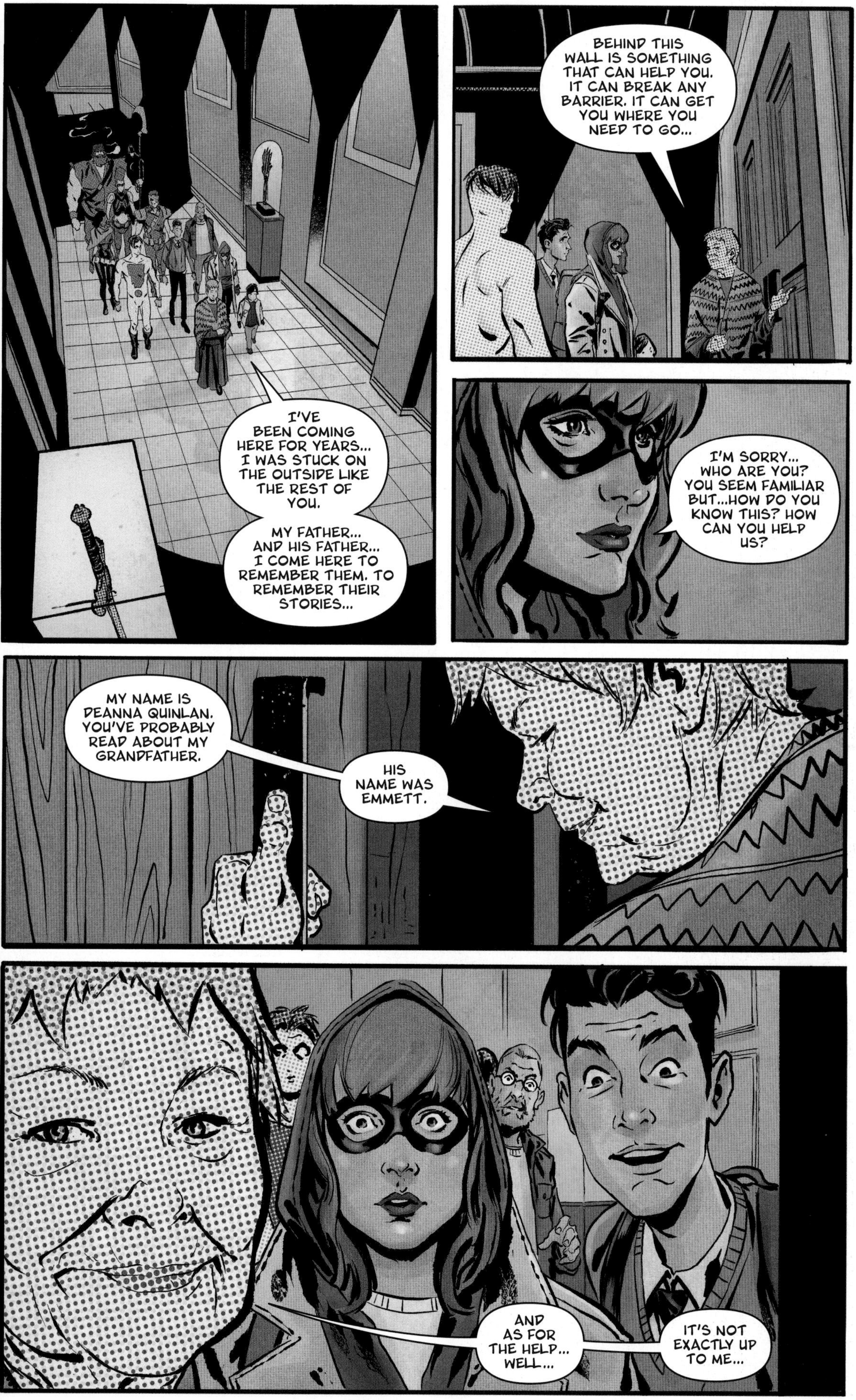
I'VE BEEN COMING HERE FOR YEARS... I WAS STUCK ON THE OUTSIDE LIKE THE REST OF YOU.
MY FATHER... AND HIS FATHER... I COME HERE TO REMEMBER THEM. TO REMEMBER THEIR STORIES...
BEHIND THIS WALL IS SOMETHING THAT CAN HELP YOU. IT CAN BREAK ANY BARRIER. IT CAN GET YOU WHERE YOU NEED TO GO...
I'M SORRY... WHO ARE YOU? YOU SEEM FAMILIAR BUT...HOW DO YOU KNOW THIS? HOW CAN YOU HELP US?
MY NAME IS DEANNA QUINLAN. YOU'VE PROBABLY READ ABOUT MY GRANDFATHER.
HIS NAME WAS EMMETT.
AND AS FOR THE HELP... WELL...
IT'S NOT EXACTLY UP TO ME...

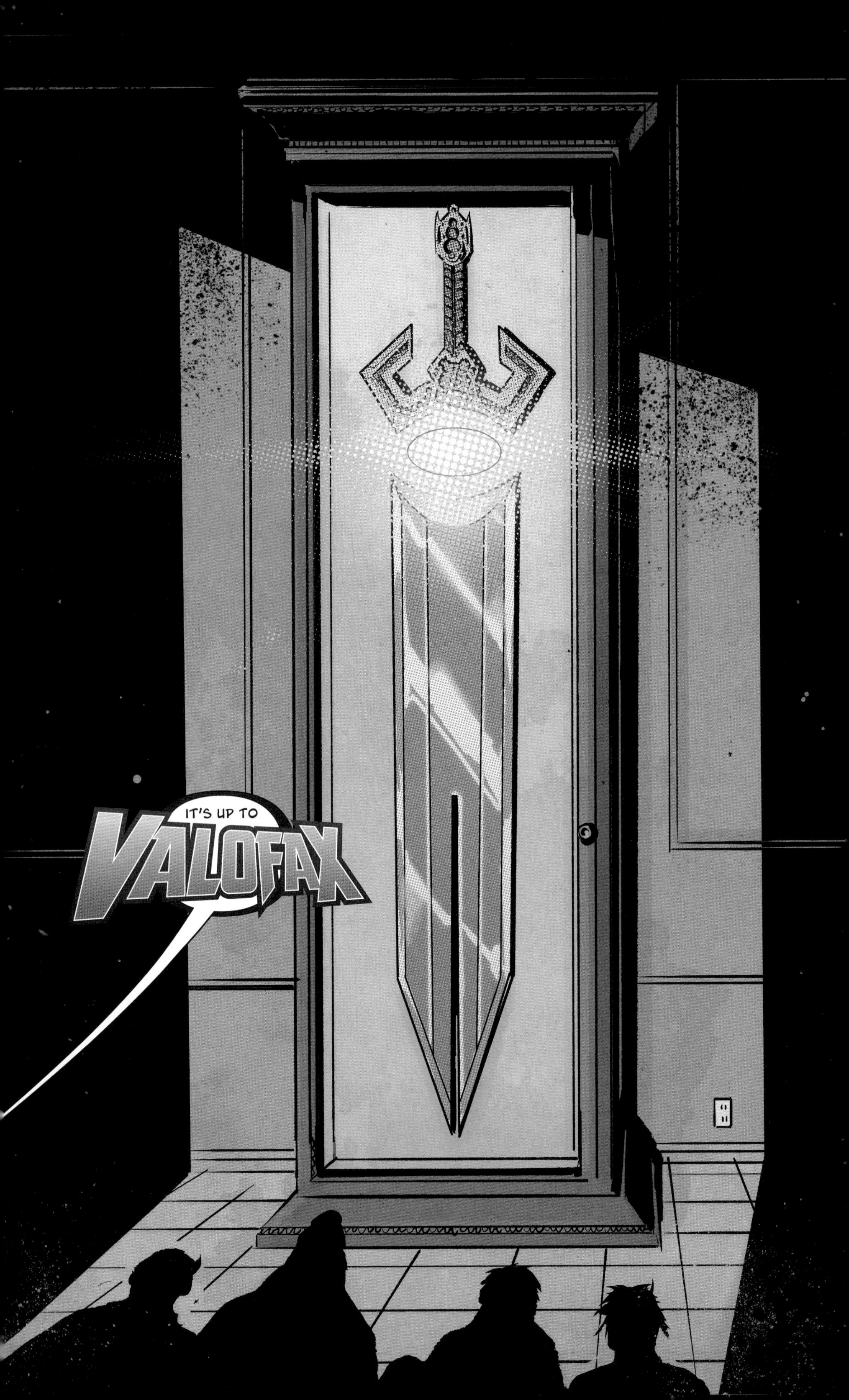
IT'S UP TO
VALOFAX

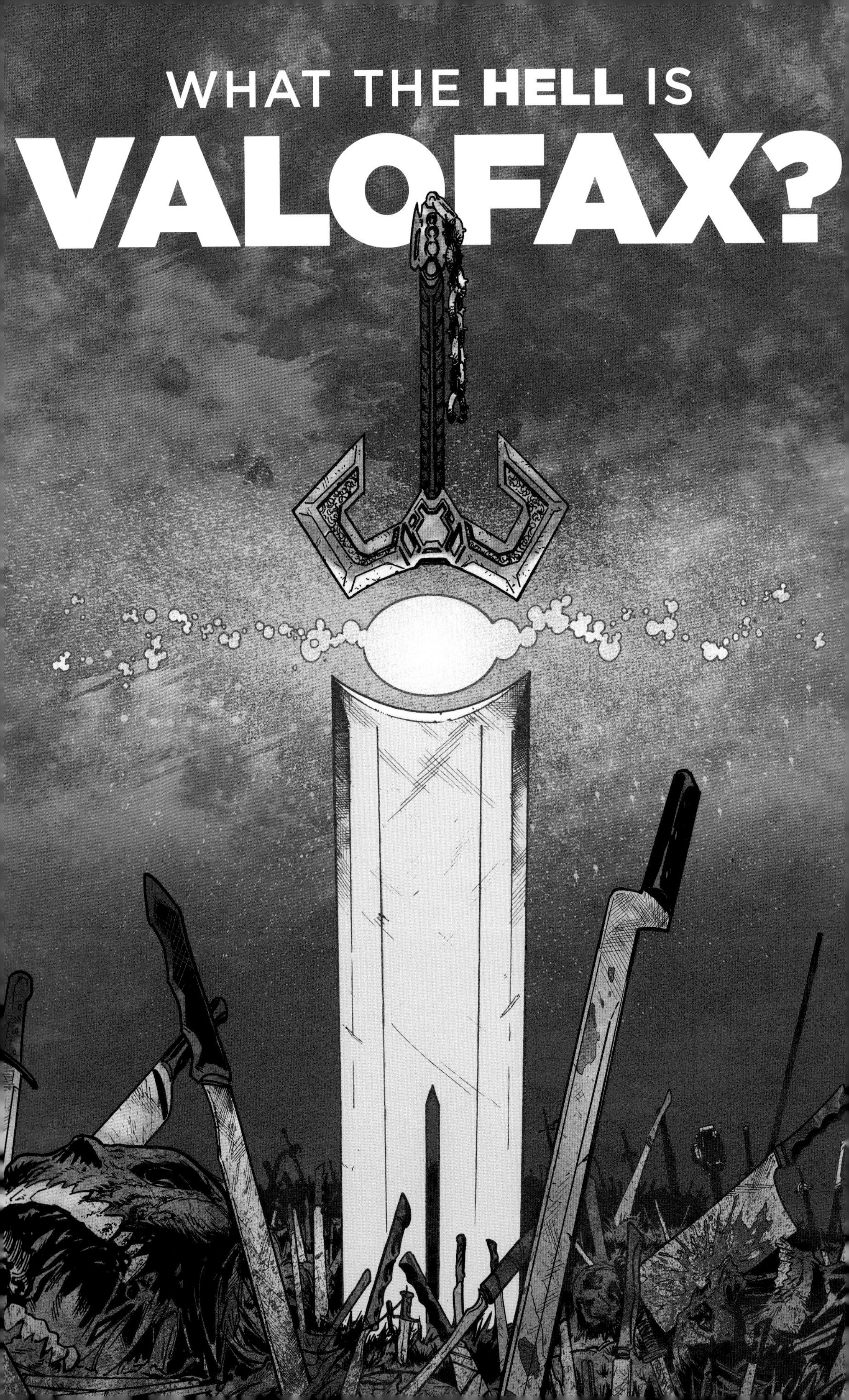
WHAT THE HELL IS
VALOFAX?

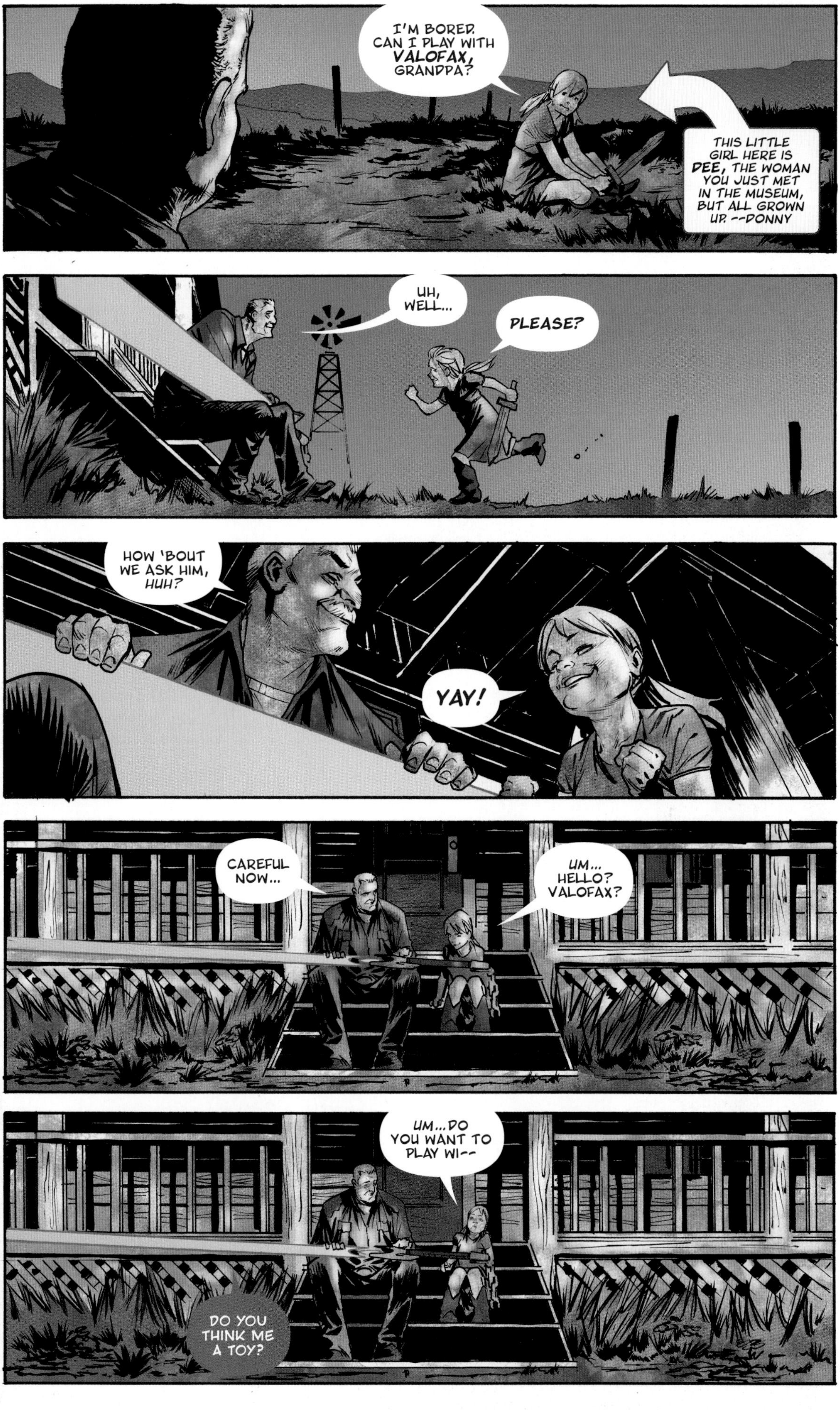
I'M BORED. CAN I PLAY WITH VALOFAX, GRANDPA?
THIS LITTLE GIRL HERE IS DEE, THE WOMAN YOU JUST MET IN THE MUSEUM, BUT ALL GROWN UP. --DONNY
UH, WELL...
PLEASE?
HOW 'BOUT WE ASK HIM, HUH?
YAY!
CAREFUL NOW...
UM... HELLO? VALOFAX?
UM...DO YOU WANT TO PLAY WI--
DO YOU THINK ME A TOY?

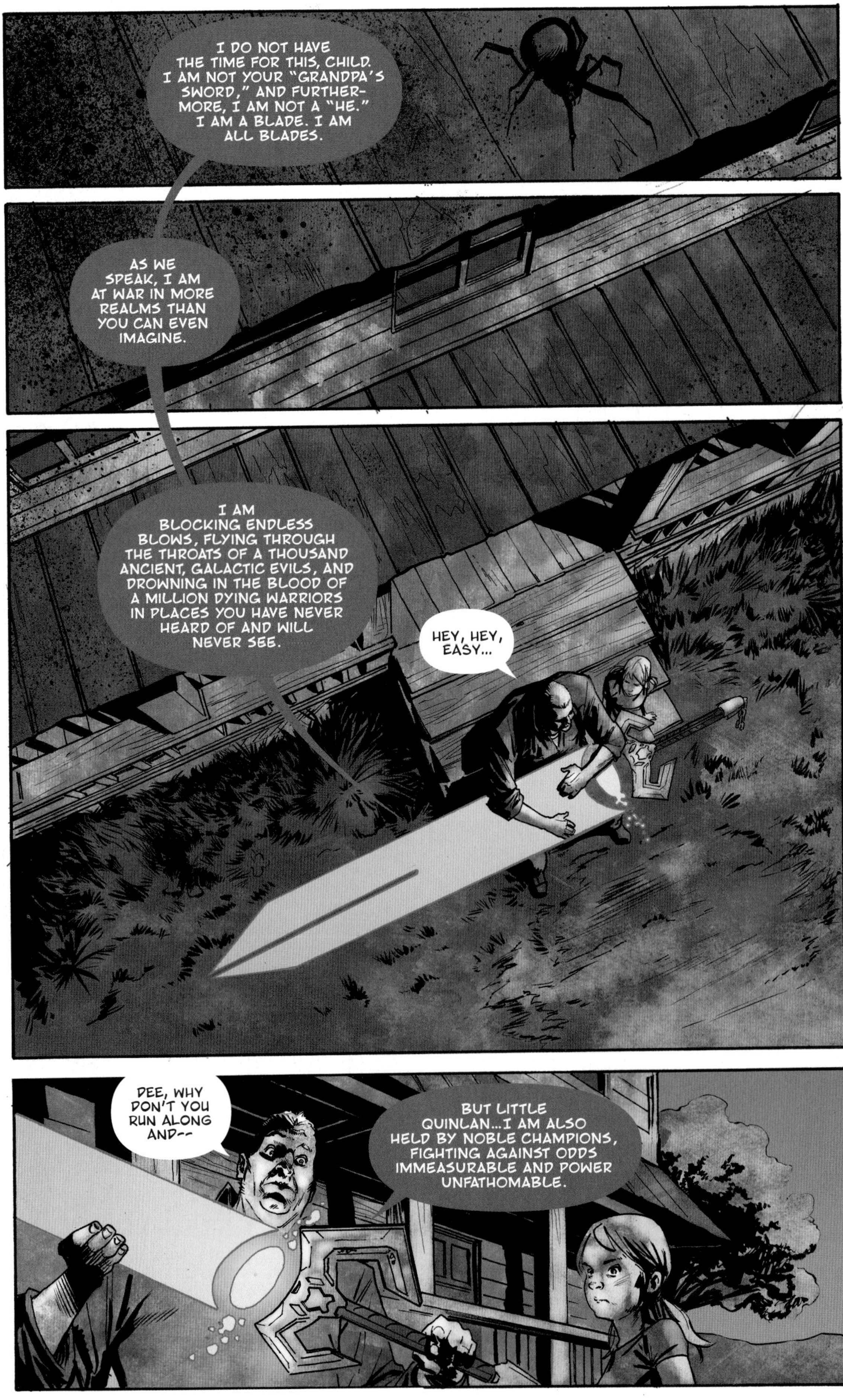

I DO NOT HAVE THE TIME FOR THIS, CHILD. I AM NOT YOUR "GRANDPA'S SWORD," AND FURTHER-MORE, I AM NOT A "HE." I AM A BLADE. I AM ALL BLADES.
AS WE SPEAK, I AM AT WAR IN MORE REALMS THAN YOU CAN EVEN IMAGINE.
I AM BLOCKING ENDLESS BLOWS, FLYING THROUGH THE THROATS OF A THOUSAND ANCIENT, GALACTIC EVILS, AND DROWNING IN THE BLOOD OF A MILLION DYING WARRIORS IN PLACES YOU HAVE NEVER HEARD OF AND WILL NEVER SEE.
HEY, HEY, EASY...
DEE, WHY DON'T YOU RUN ALONG AND--
BUT LITTLE QUINLAN...I AM ALSO HELD BY NOBLE CHAMPIONS, FIGHTING AGAINST ODDS IMMEASURABLE AND POWER UNFATHOMABLE.

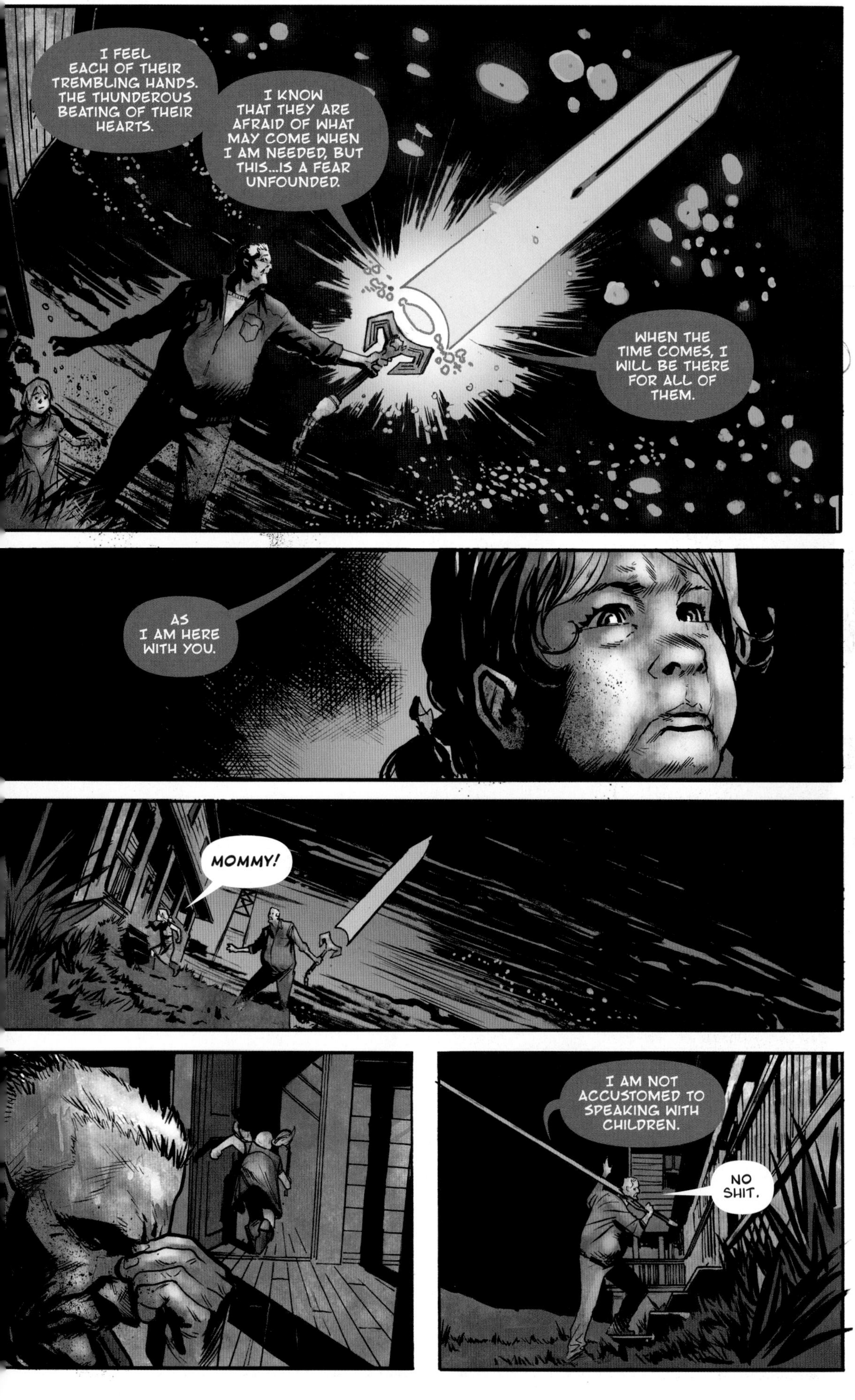
I FEEL EACH OF THEIR TREMBLING HANDS. THE THUNDEROUS BEATING OF THEIR HEARTS.
I KNOW THAT THEY ARE AFRAID OF WHAT MAY COME WHEN I AM NEEDED, BUT THIS...IS A FEAR UNFOUNDED.
WHEN THE TIME COMES, I WILL BE THERE FOR ALL OF THEM.
AS I AM HERE WITH YOU.
MOMMY!
I AM NOT ACCUSTOMED TO SPEAKING WITH CHILDREN.
NO SHIT.

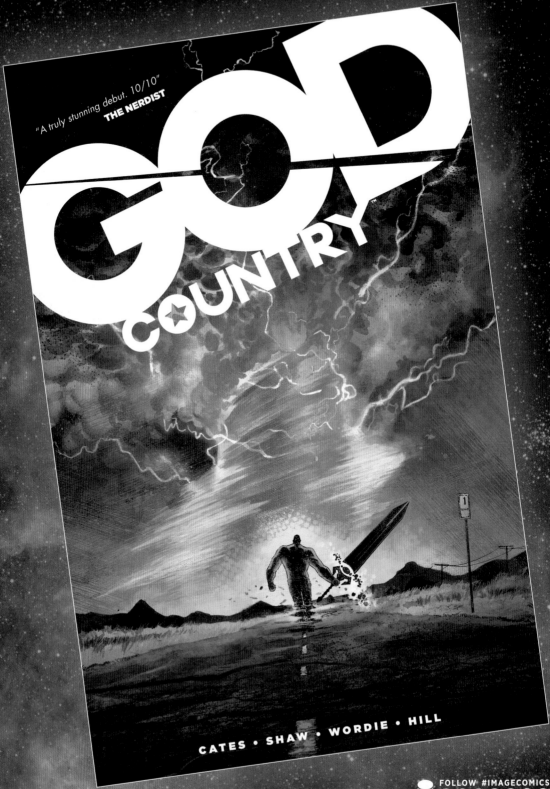

MEANWHILE...

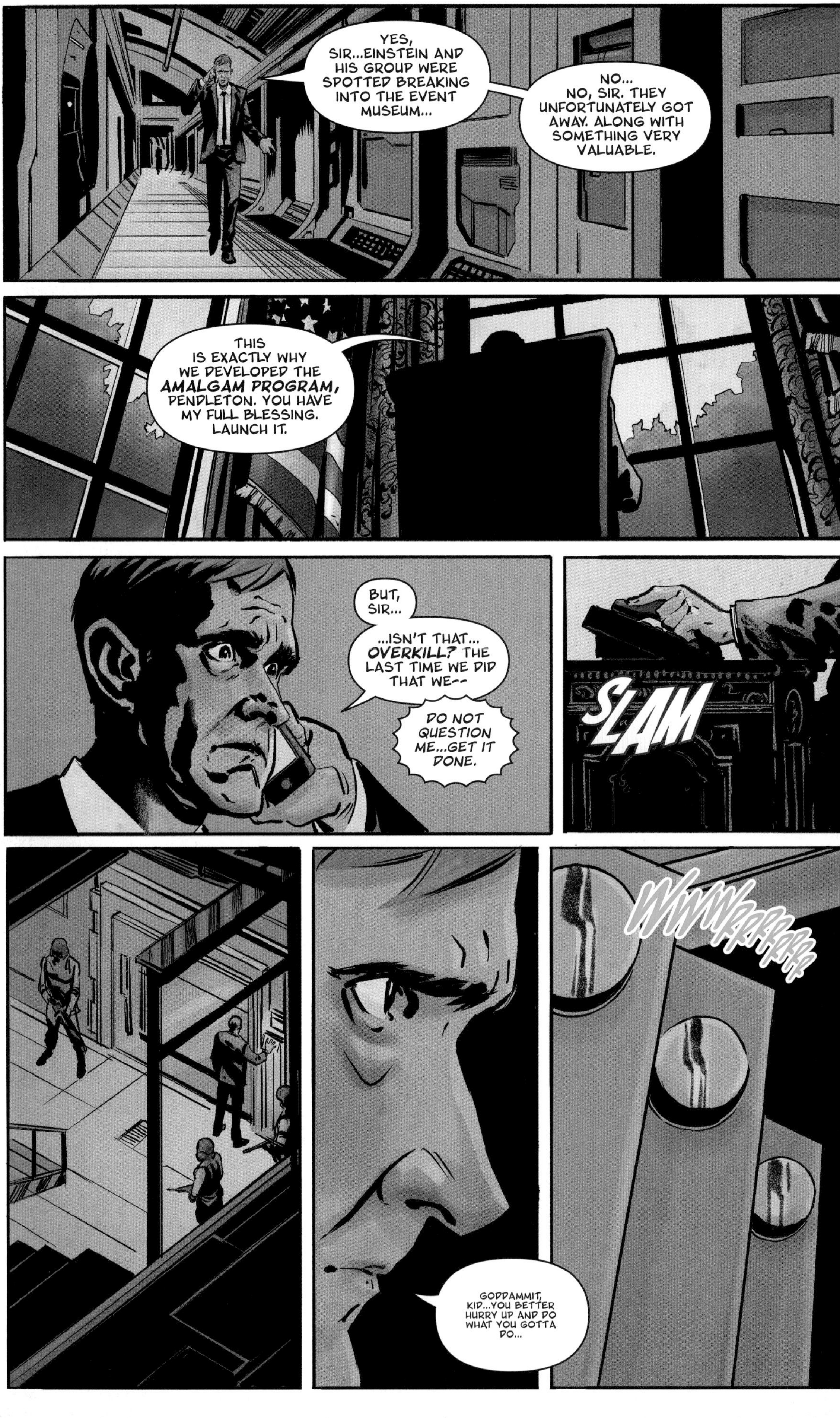
YES, SIR...EINSTEIN AND HIS GROUP WERE SPOTTED BREAKING INTO THE EVENT MUSEUM...
NO... NO, SIR. THEY UNFORTUNATELY GOT AWAY. ALONG WITH SOMETHING VERY VALUABLE.
THIS IS EXACTLY WHY WE DEVELOPED THE AMALGAM PROGRAM, PENDLETON. YOU HAVE MY FULL BLESSING. LAUNCH IT.
BUT, SIR...
...ISN'T THAT... OVERKILL? THE LAST TIME WE DID THAT WE--
DO NOT QUESTION ME...GET IT DONE.
SLAM
WWWRRRRRR
GODDAMMIT, KID...YOU BETTER HURRY UP AND DO WHAT YOU GOTTA DO...

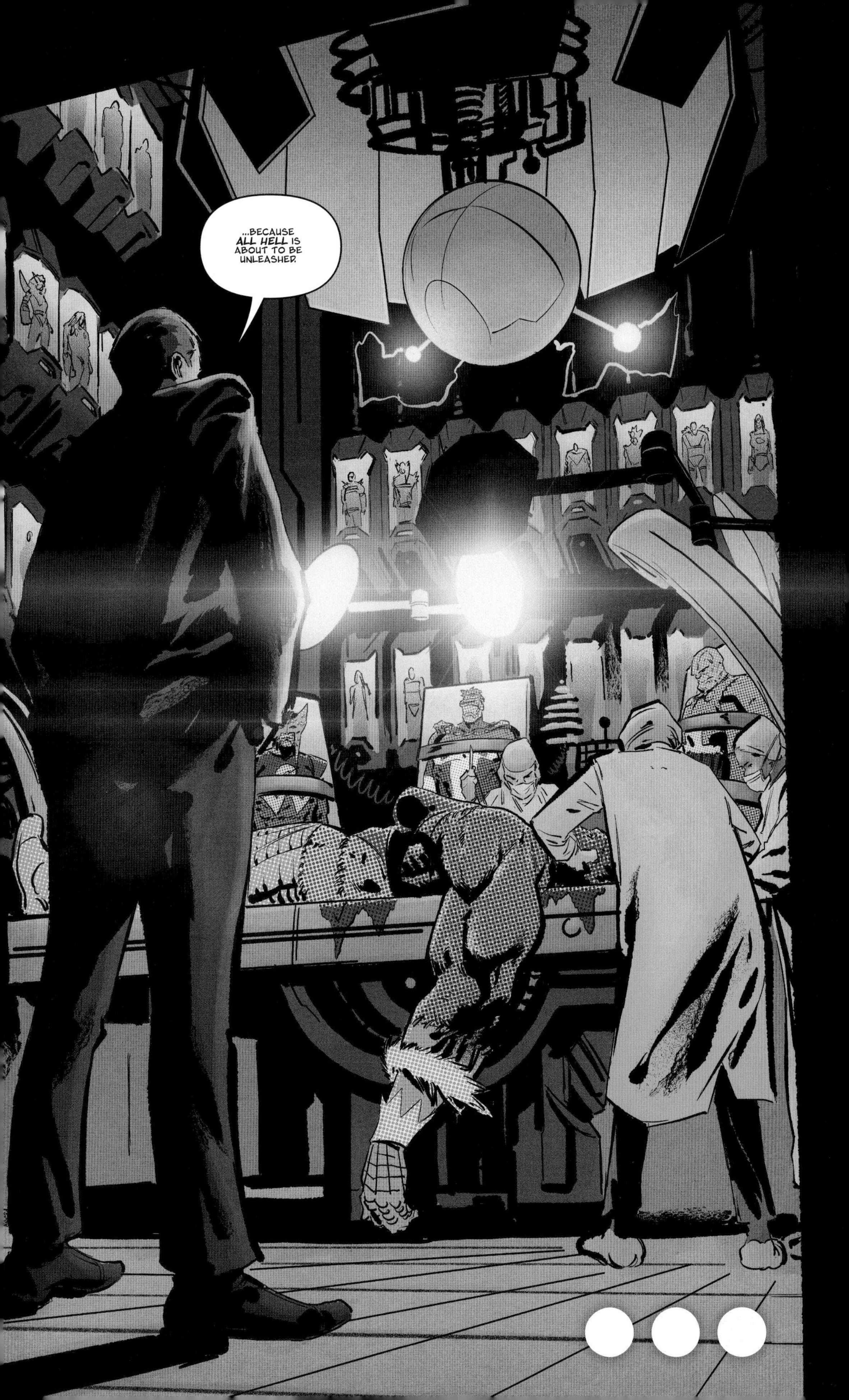
...BECAUSE ALL HELL IS ABOUT TO BE UNLEASHED.

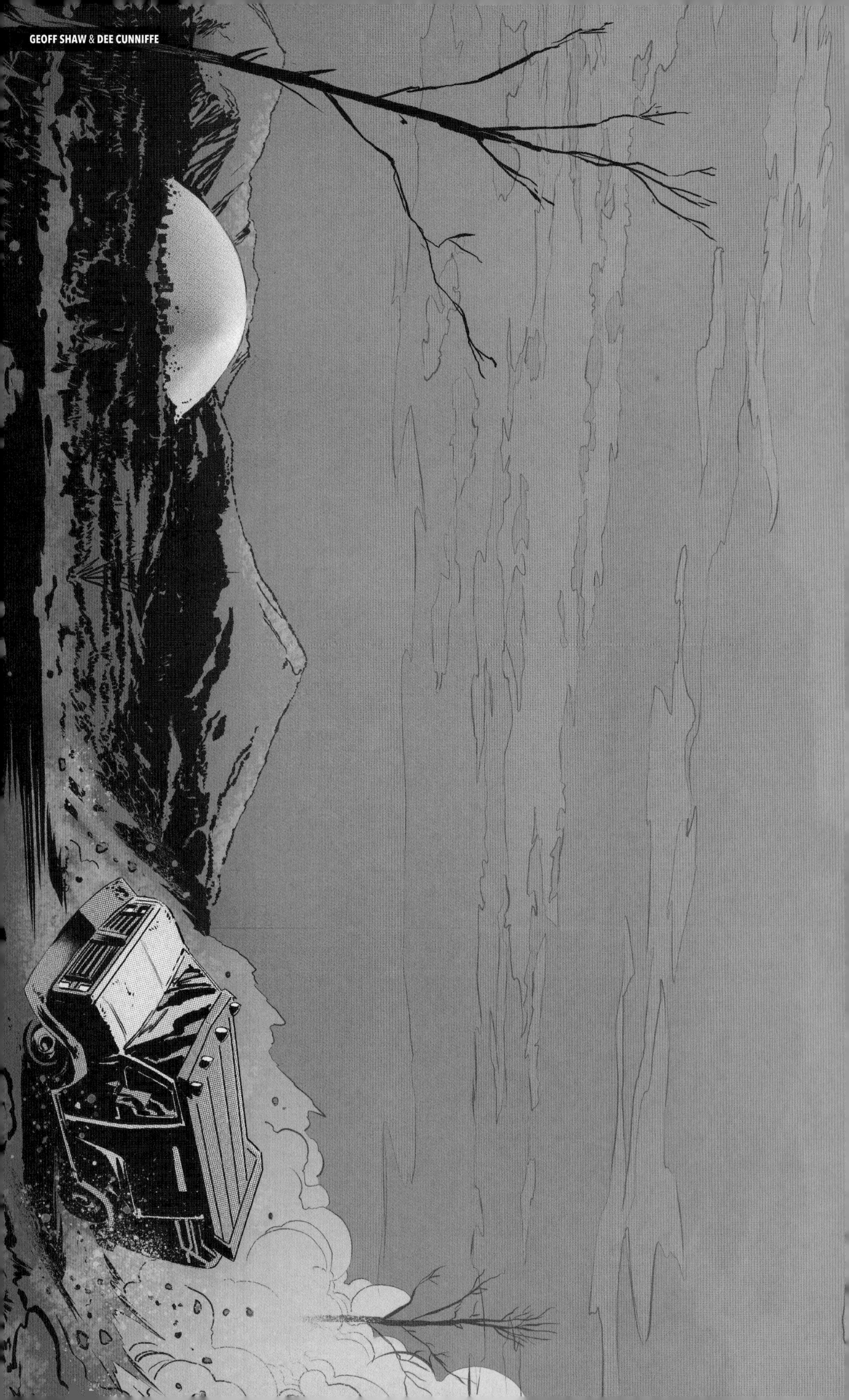

KIDS LOVE CHAINS

CHAPTER FIVE

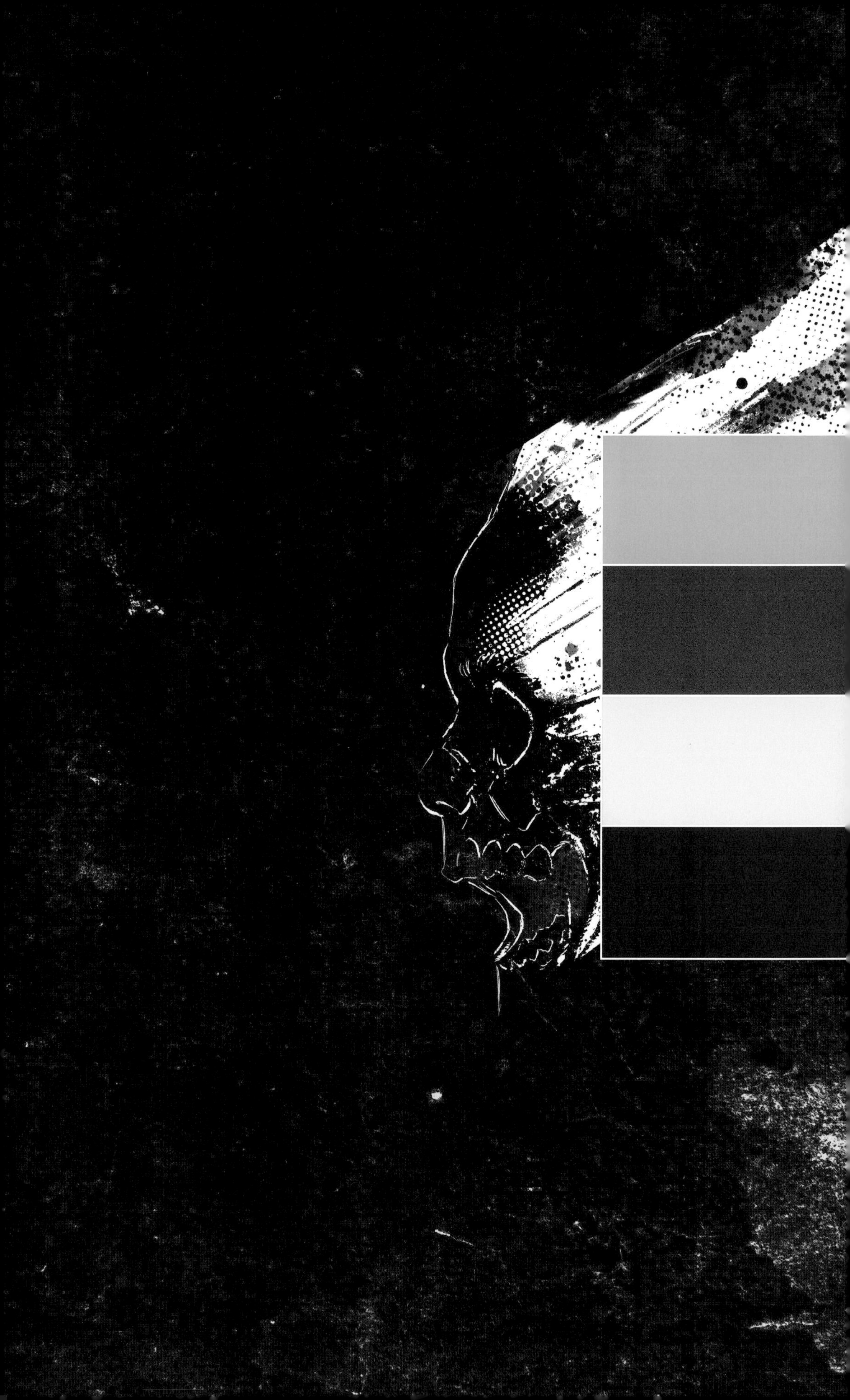

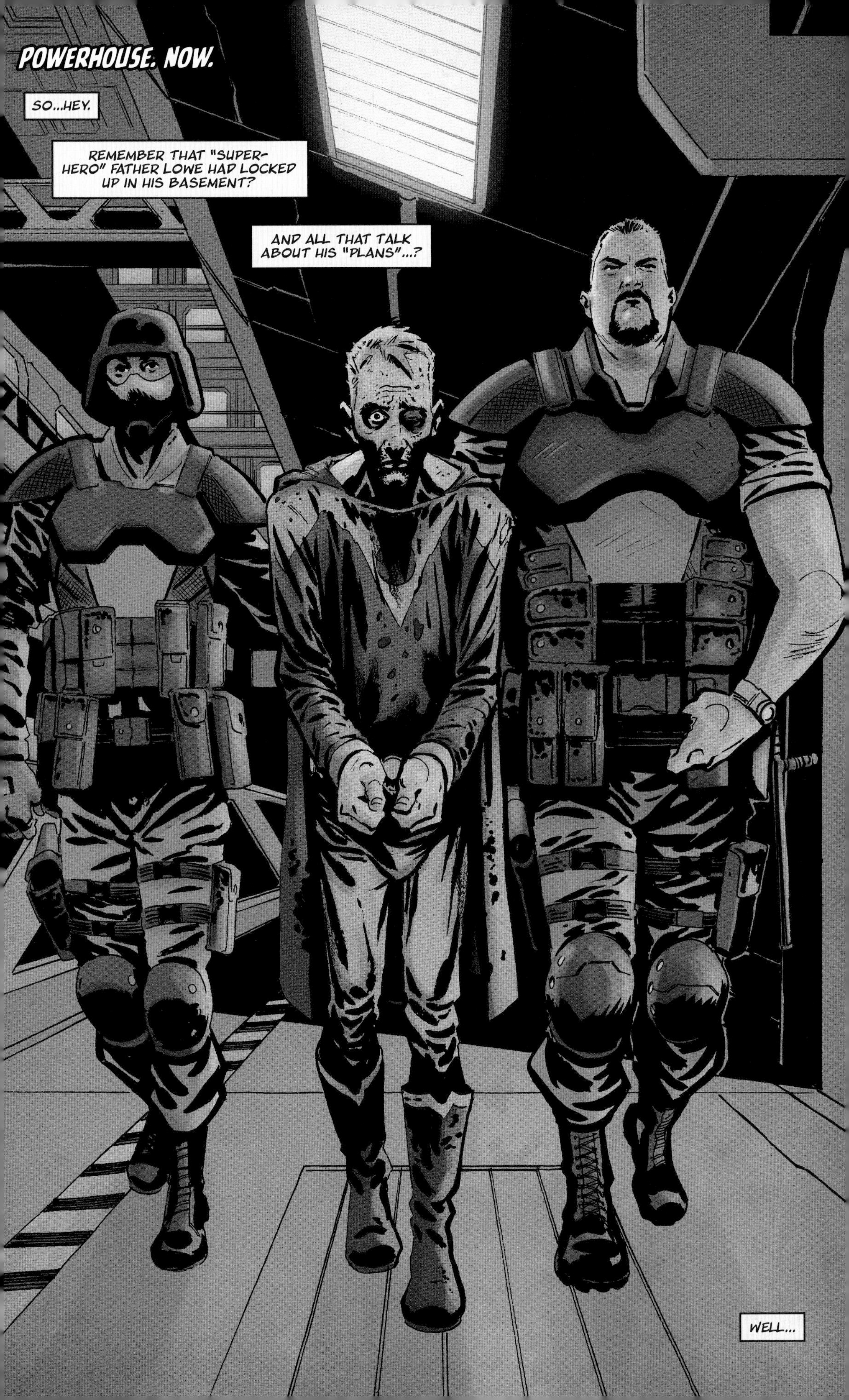
POWERHOUSE. NOW.
SO...HEY.
REMEMBER THAT "SUPER-HERO" FATHER LOWE HAD LOCKED UP IN HIS BASEMENT?
AND ALL THAT TALK ABOUT HIS "PLANS"...?
WELL...

SORRY. BUT, UH...

...THIS IS ABOUT TO GET *REALLY BAD.*

NEW ONE, HUH?

YUP. CITIZEN CALLED HIM IN. SAID THEY FOUND HIM ACTING *CRAZY.* WANDERING AROUND IN THE STREETS OR SOME SHIT.

WHAT'S HE SAYING? HE GOT A NAME?

WELL, HE AIN'T SAYING *SHIT* NOW. POOR BASTARD'S TONGUE'S BEEN CUT OUT.

SEEMS OUR "CONCERNED CITIZEN" SHOWED A LITTLE *TOO MUCH...* CONCERN.

OR THE *RIGHT AMOUNT.*

JESUS *CHRIST,* GUYS...

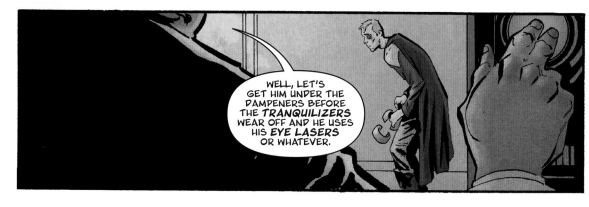

WELL, LET'S GET HIM UNDER THE *DAMPENERS* BEFORE THE *TRANQUILIZERS* WEAR OFF AND HE USES HIS *EYE LASERS* OR WHATEVER.

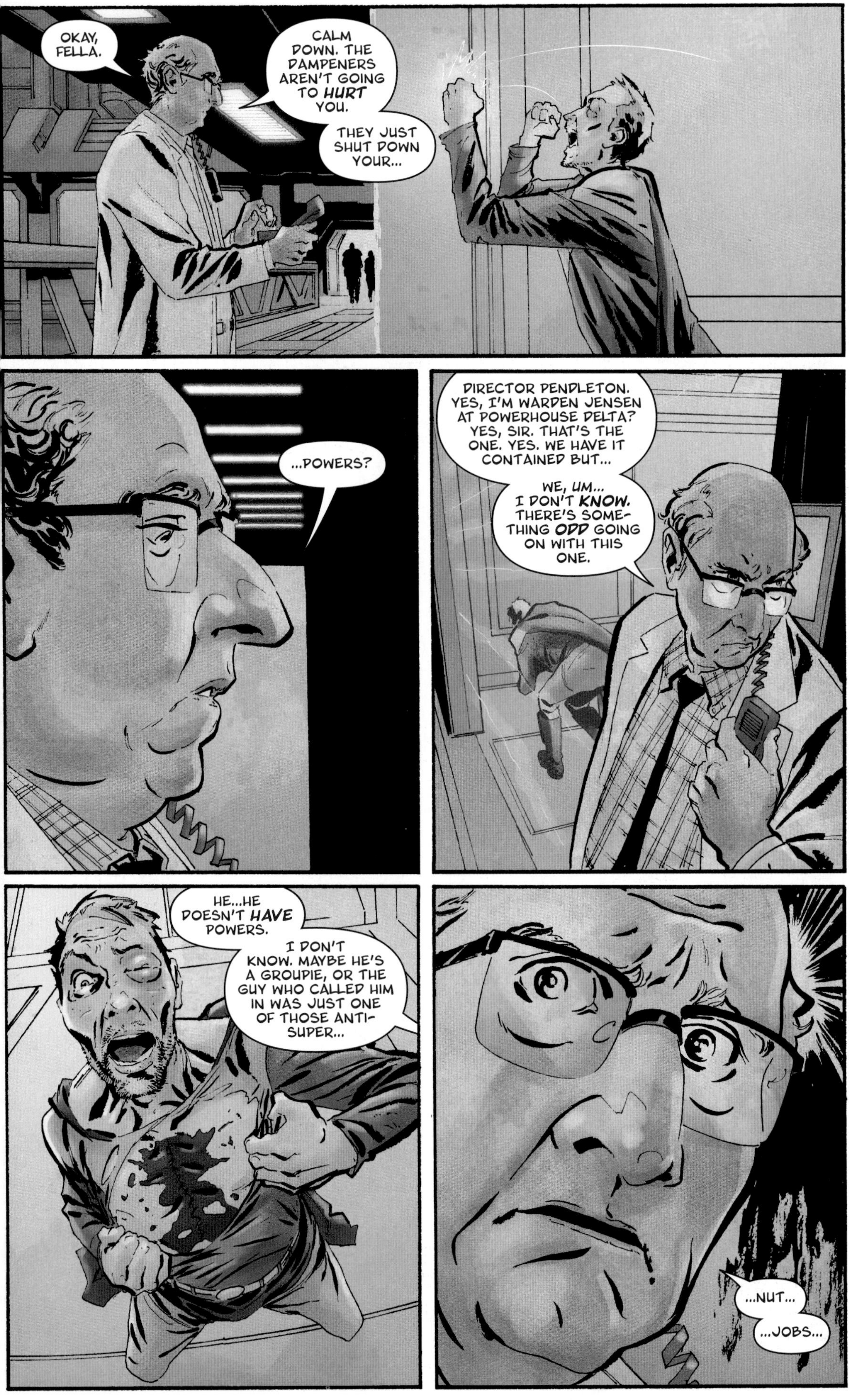
OKAY, FELLA.
CALM DOWN. THE DAMPENERS AREN'T GOING TO *HURT* YOU.
THEY JUST SHUT DOWN YOUR...
...POWERS?
DIRECTOR PENDLETON. YES, I'M WARDEN JENSEN AT POWERHOUSE DELTA? YES, SIR. THAT'S THE ONE. YES. WE HAVE IT CONTAINED BUT...
WE, UM... I DON'T *KNOW.* THERE'S SOMETHING *ODD* GOING ON WITH THIS ONE.
HE...HE DOESN'T *HAVE* POWERS.
I DON'T KNOW. MAYBE HE'S A GROUPIE, OR THE GUY WHO CALLED HIM IN WAS JUST ONE OF THOSE ANTI-SUPER...
...NUT...
...JOBS...

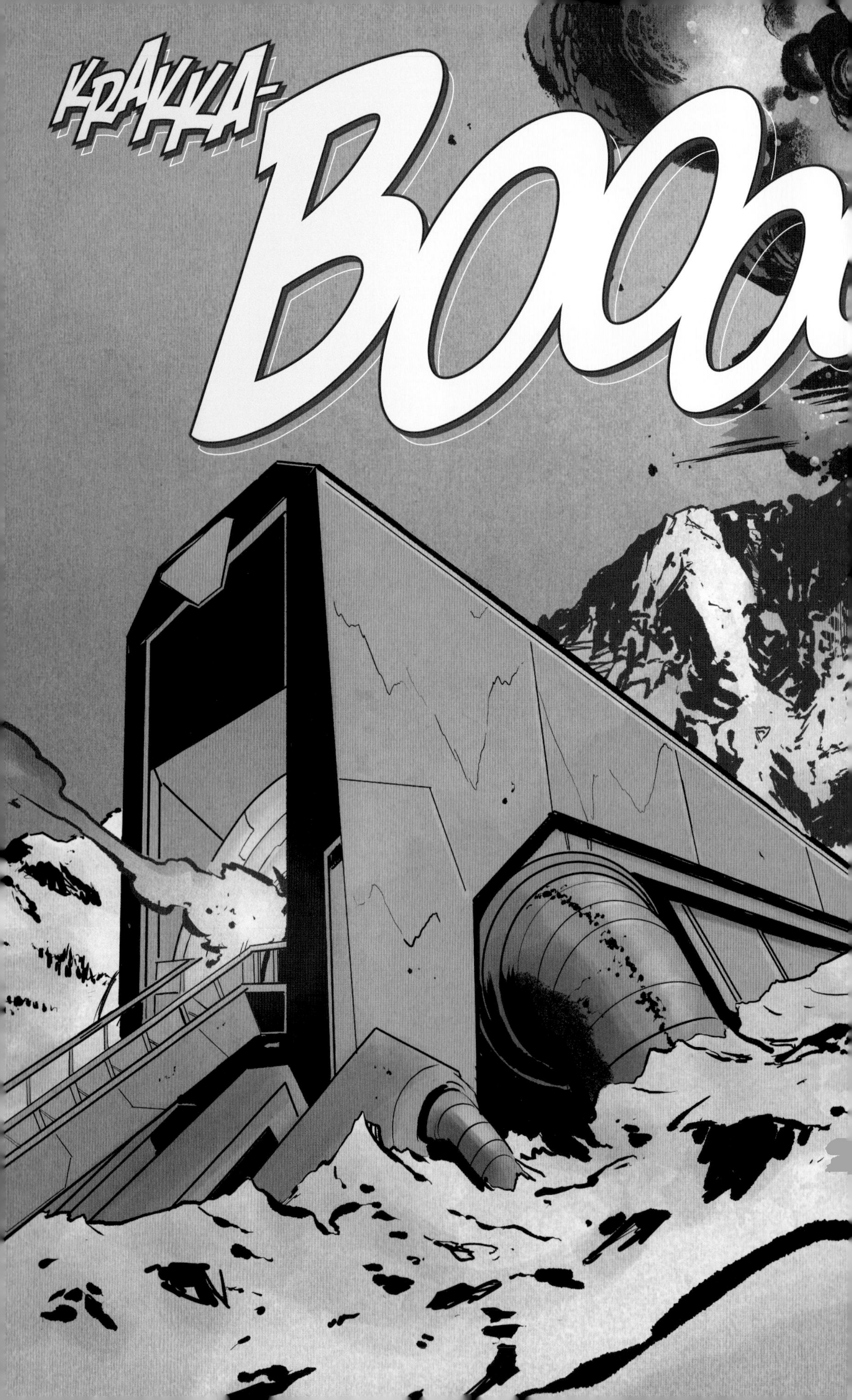
KRAKKA-
BOO

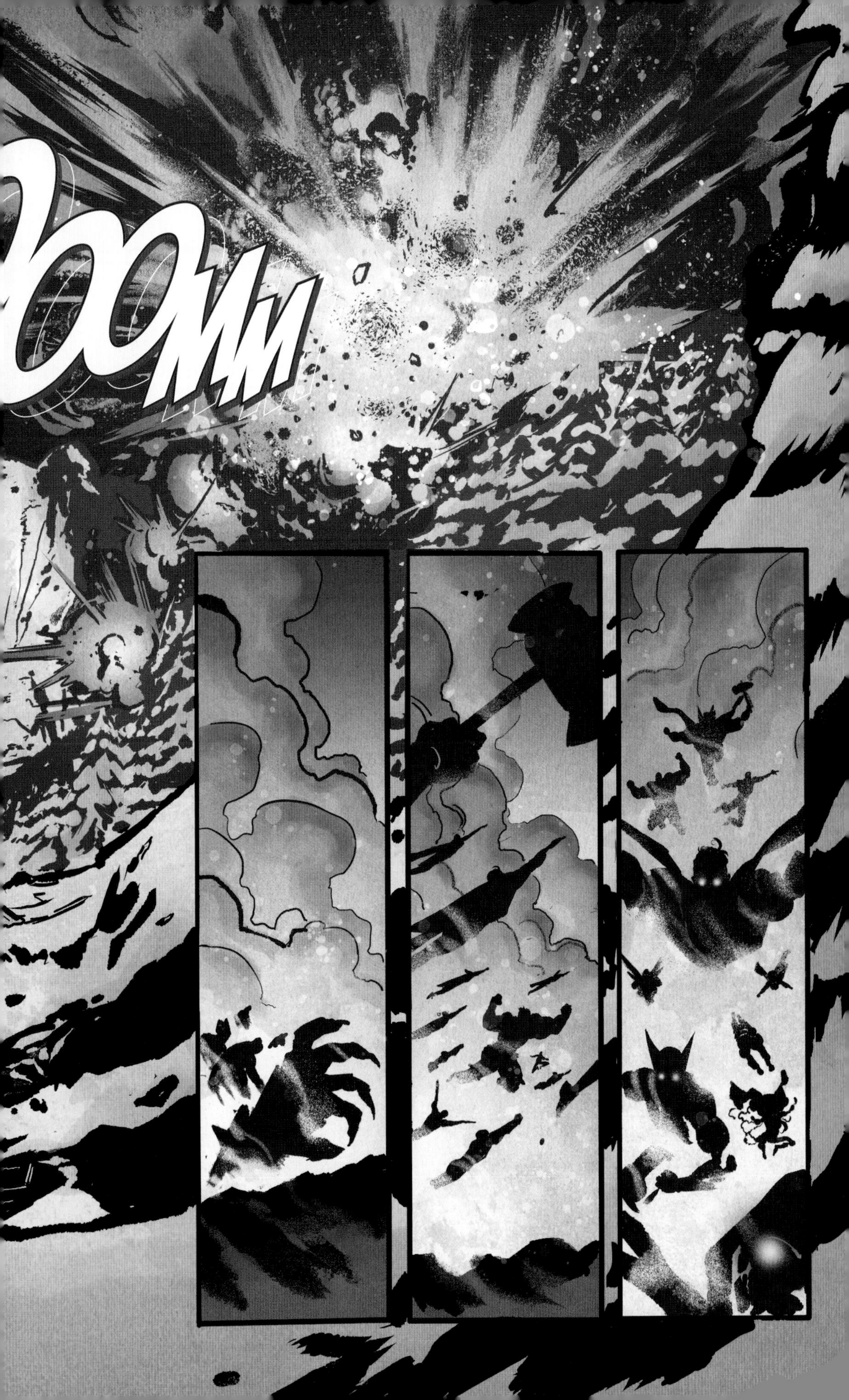

OOMMM

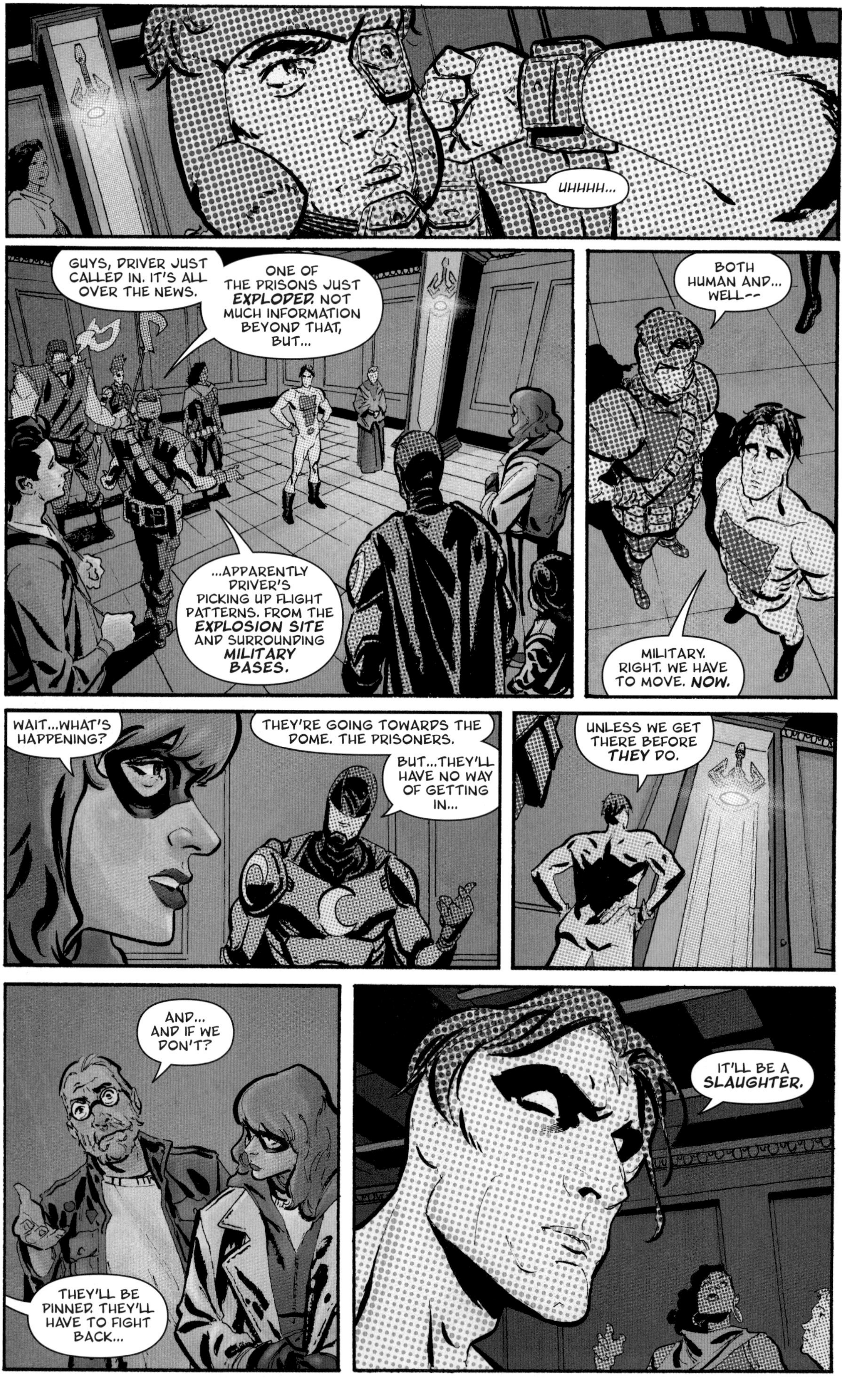
UHHHH...
GUYS, DRIVER JUST CALLED IN. IT'S ALL OVER THE NEWS.
ONE OF THE PRISONS JUST EXPLODED. NOT MUCH INFORMATION BEYOND THAT, BUT...
...APPARENTLY DRIVER'S PICKING UP FLIGHT PATTERNS. FROM THE EXPLOSION SITE AND SURROUNDING MILITARY BASES.
BOTH HUMAN AND... WELL--
MILITARY. RIGHT. WE HAVE TO MOVE. NOW.
WAIT...WHAT'S HAPPENING?
THEY'RE GOING TOWARDS THE DOME. THE PRISONERS.
BUT...THEY'LL HAVE NO WAY OF GETTING IN...
UNLESS WE GET THERE BEFORE THEY DO.
AND... AND IF WE DON'T?
THEY'LL BE PINNED. THEY'LL HAVE TO FIGHT BACK...
IT'LL BE A SLAUGHTER.

WH–WHAT'S *HAPPENING?* WHY IS EVERY-THING ALL RED, ARE WE––?

WE'RE IN LOCKDOWN. THEY KNOW WE'RE HERE.

EVERY SECOND *COUNTS.*

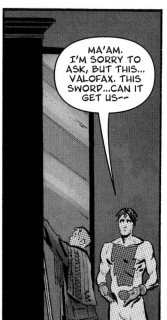

MA'AM. I'M SORRY TO ASK, BUT THIS... VALOFAX. THIS SWORD...CAN IT GET US––

YES. YES, I CAN.

I WILL PROVIDE YOU PASSAGE TO SAFETY. BUT AS YOU SAID, WE MUST BE SWIFT ABOUT IT.

HOLY SHIT, IT *TALKS?* WHY DON'T *WE* HAVE A TALKING––

DEE, ARE––ARE YOU *SURE?* I READ YOUR–– I MEAN...

I KNOW HOW MUCH THIS SWORD MEANS TO YOU AND YOUR FAMILY...

IF YOU KNOW THE *STORY,* THEN YOU KNOW IT WAS NEVER ABOUT THE SWORD.

MY GRANDFATHER WILL ALWAYS BE HERE.

HE'S JUST A *STORY* NOW.

AND *STORIES* NEVER LEAVE YOU.

NOW, GO. GO AND FIND YOUR FAMILY, HONEY.

THERE'S NOTHING ON EARTH MORE IMPORTANT.

SO, SORRY, THEN. I'VE NOT READ THE BOOK...HOW *EXACTLY* IS THIS SWORD MEANT TO WORK?

IT'S NOT JUST A SWORD. IT'S *ALL* SWORDS.

IT'S THE *GOD OF BLADES...*

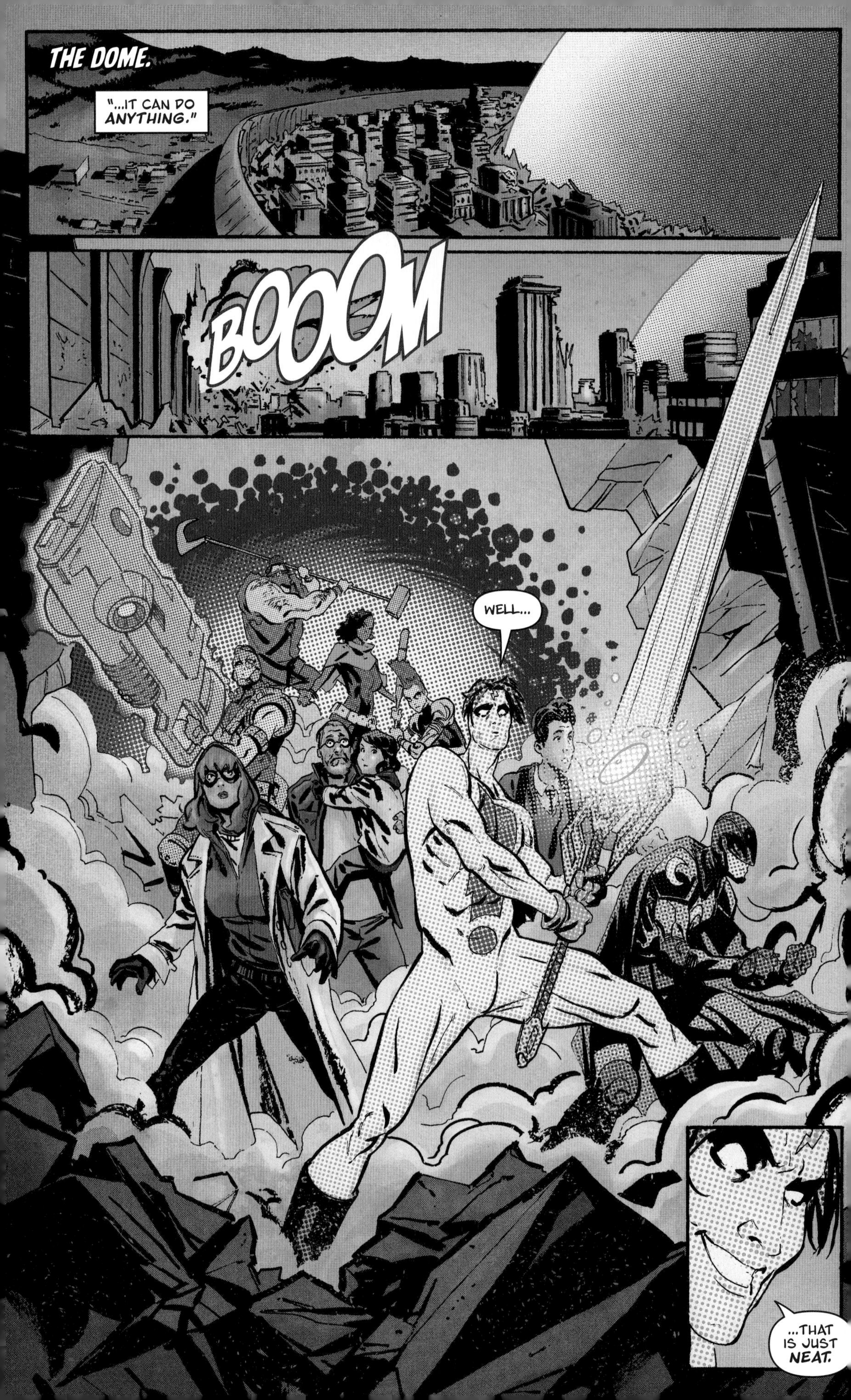
THE DOME.
"...IT CAN DO ANYTHING."
BOOOM
WELL...
...THAT IS JUST NEAT.

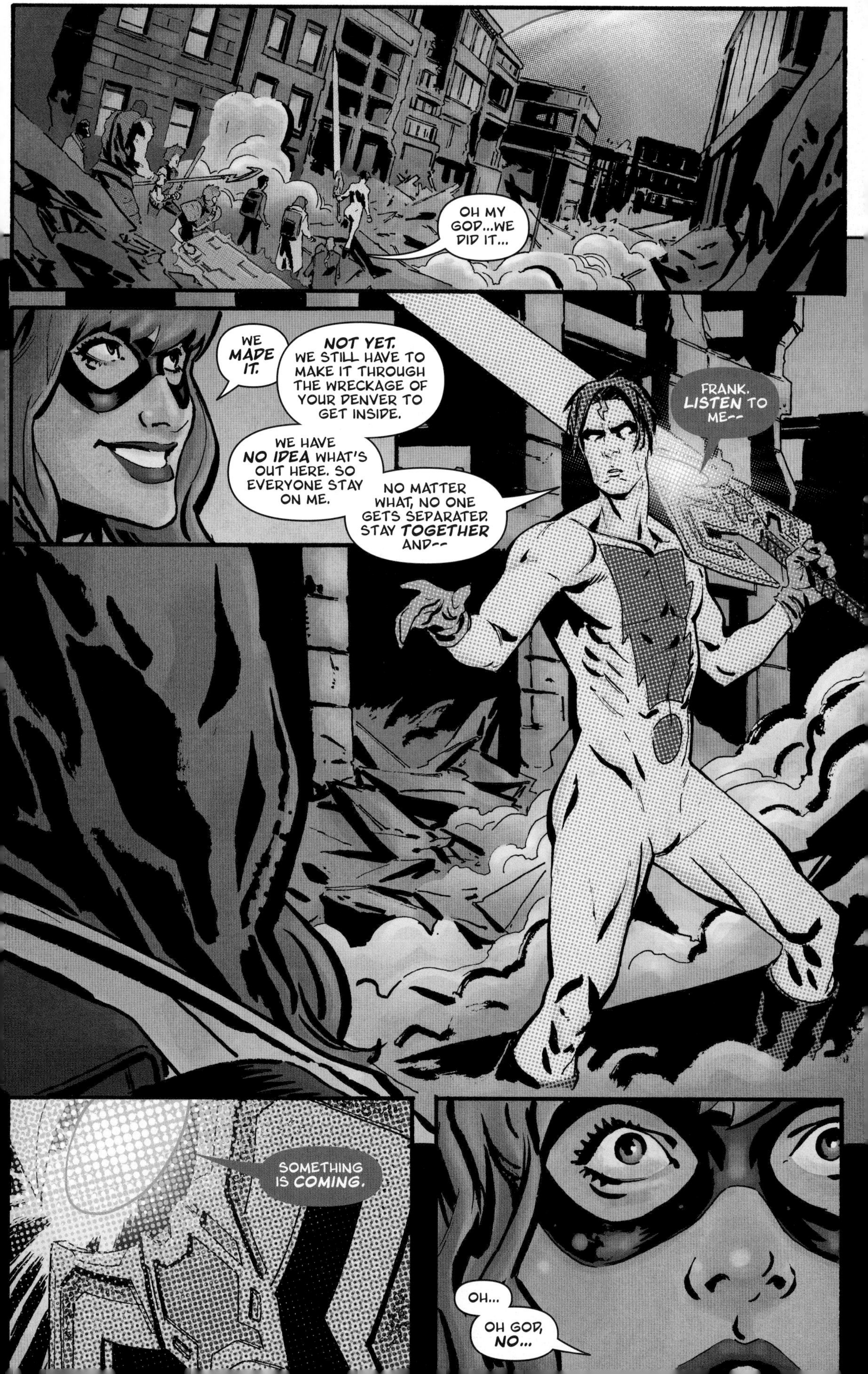
OH MY GOD...WE DID IT...
WE MADE IT.
NOT YET. WE STILL HAVE TO MAKE IT THROUGH THE WRECKAGE OF YOUR DENVER TO GET INSIDE.
WE HAVE NO IDEA WHAT'S OUT HERE. SO EVERYONE STAY ON ME.
NO MATTER WHAT, NO ONE GETS SEPARATED. STAY TOGETHER AND--
FRANK. LISTEN TO ME--
SOMETHING IS COMING.
OH...
OH GOD, NO...

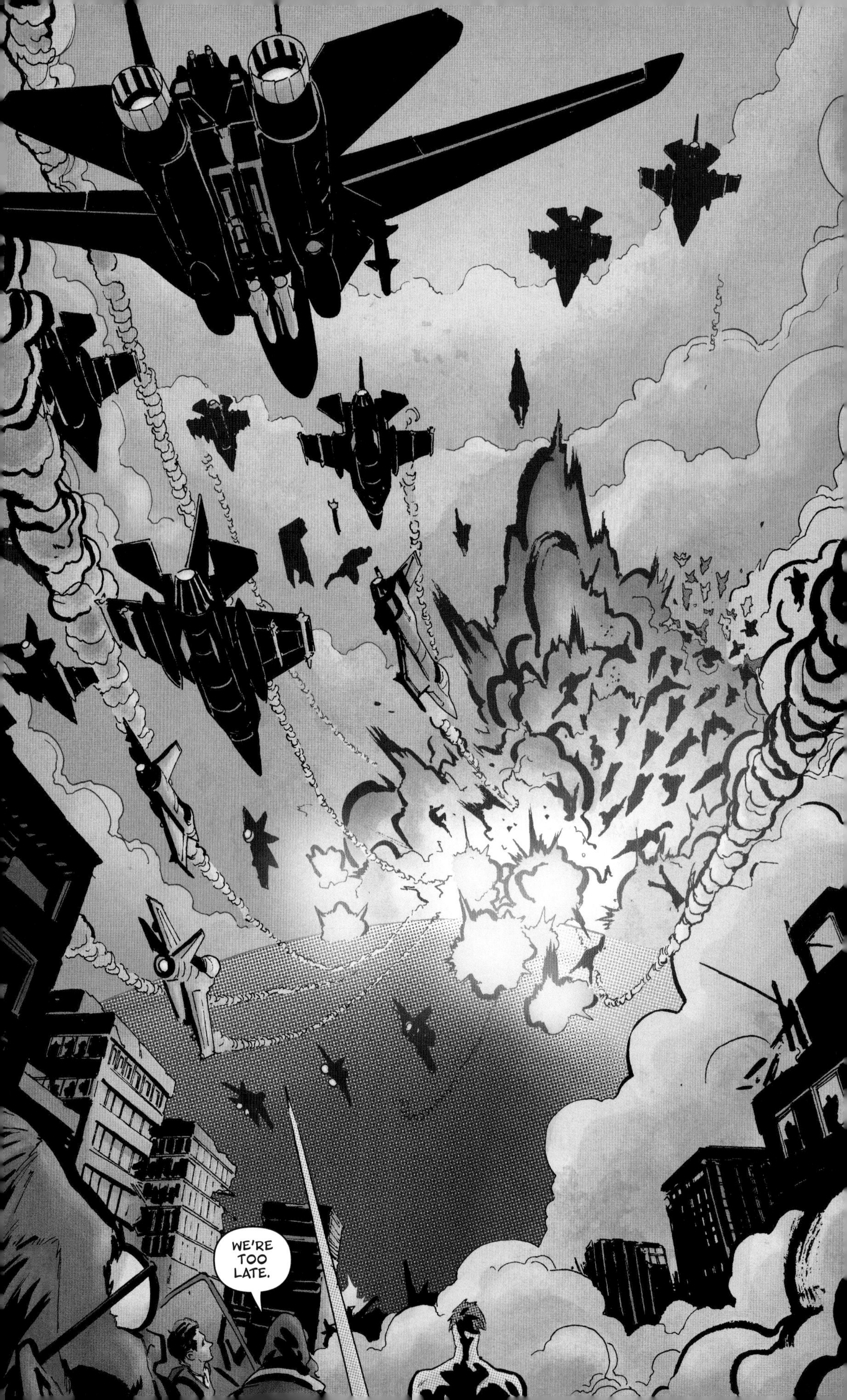
WE'RE TOO LATE.

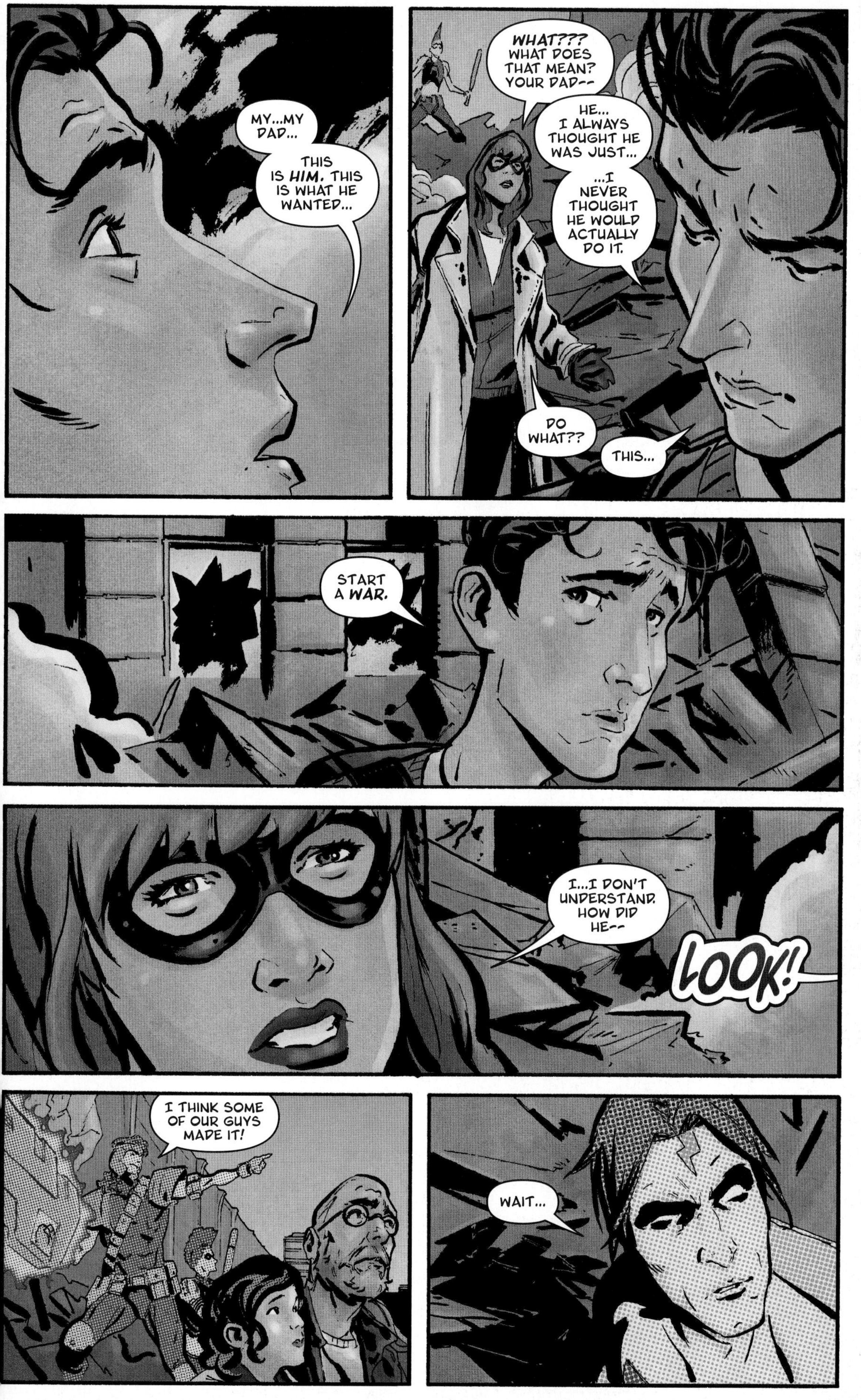
MY...MY DAD...
THIS IS HIM. THIS IS WHAT HE WANTED...
WHAT??? WHAT DOES THAT MEAN? YOUR DAD--
HE... I ALWAYS THOUGHT HE WAS JUST...
...I NEVER THOUGHT HE WOULD ACTUALLY DO IT.
DO WHAT??
THIS...
START A WAR.
I...I DON'T UNDERSTAND. HOW DID HE--
LOOK!
I THINK SOME OF OUR GUYS MADE IT!
WAIT...

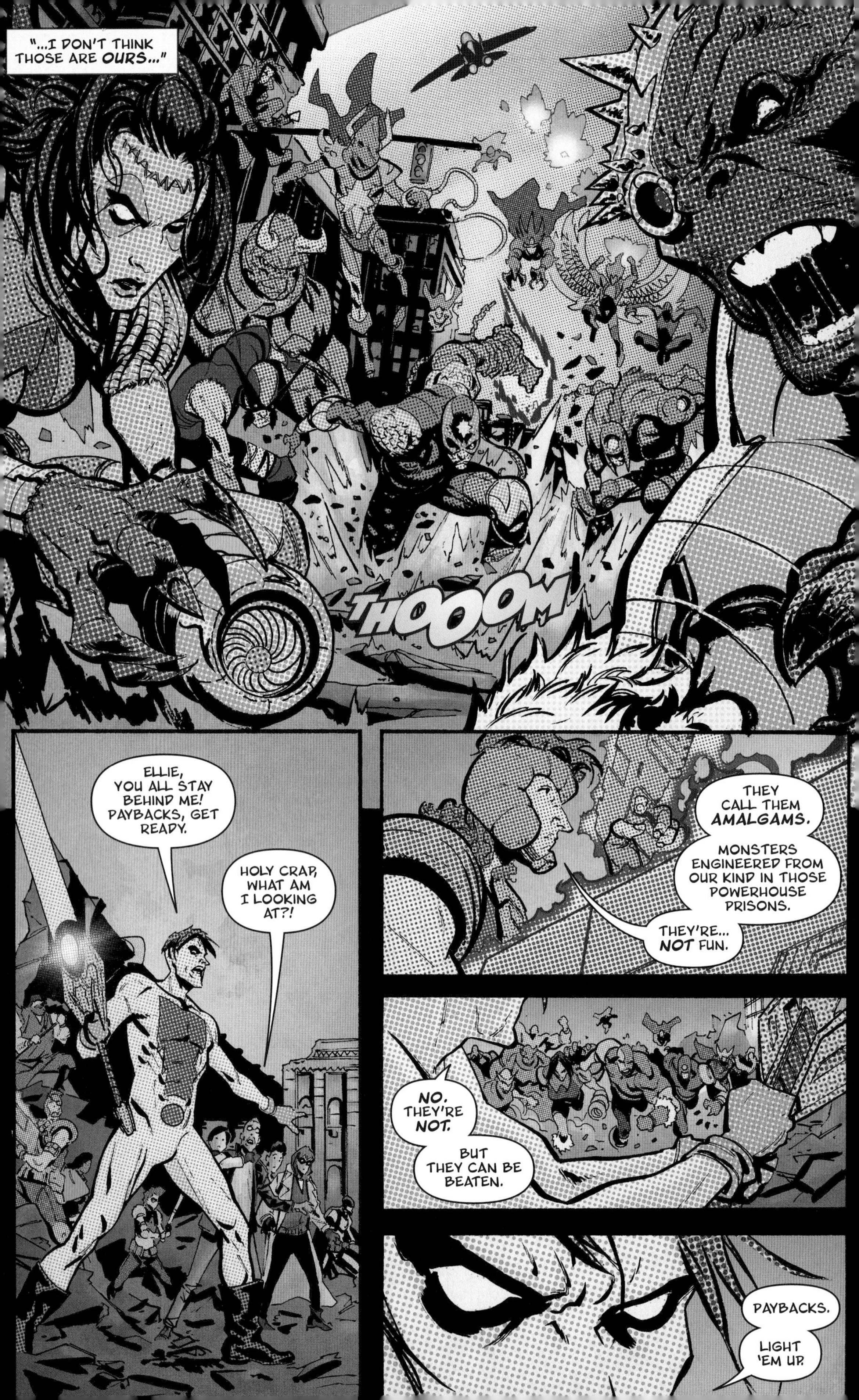
"...I DON'T THINK THOSE ARE OURS..."
THOOOM
ELLIE, YOU ALL STAY BEHIND ME! PAYBACKS, GET READY.
HOLY CRAP, WHAT AM I LOOKING AT?!
THEY CALL THEM AMALGAMS.
MONSTERS ENGINEERED FROM OUR KIND IN THOSE POWERHOUSE PRISONS.
THEY'RE... NOT FUN.
NO. THEY'RE NOT.
BUT THEY CAN BE BEATEN.
PAYBACKS.
LIGHT 'EM UP.

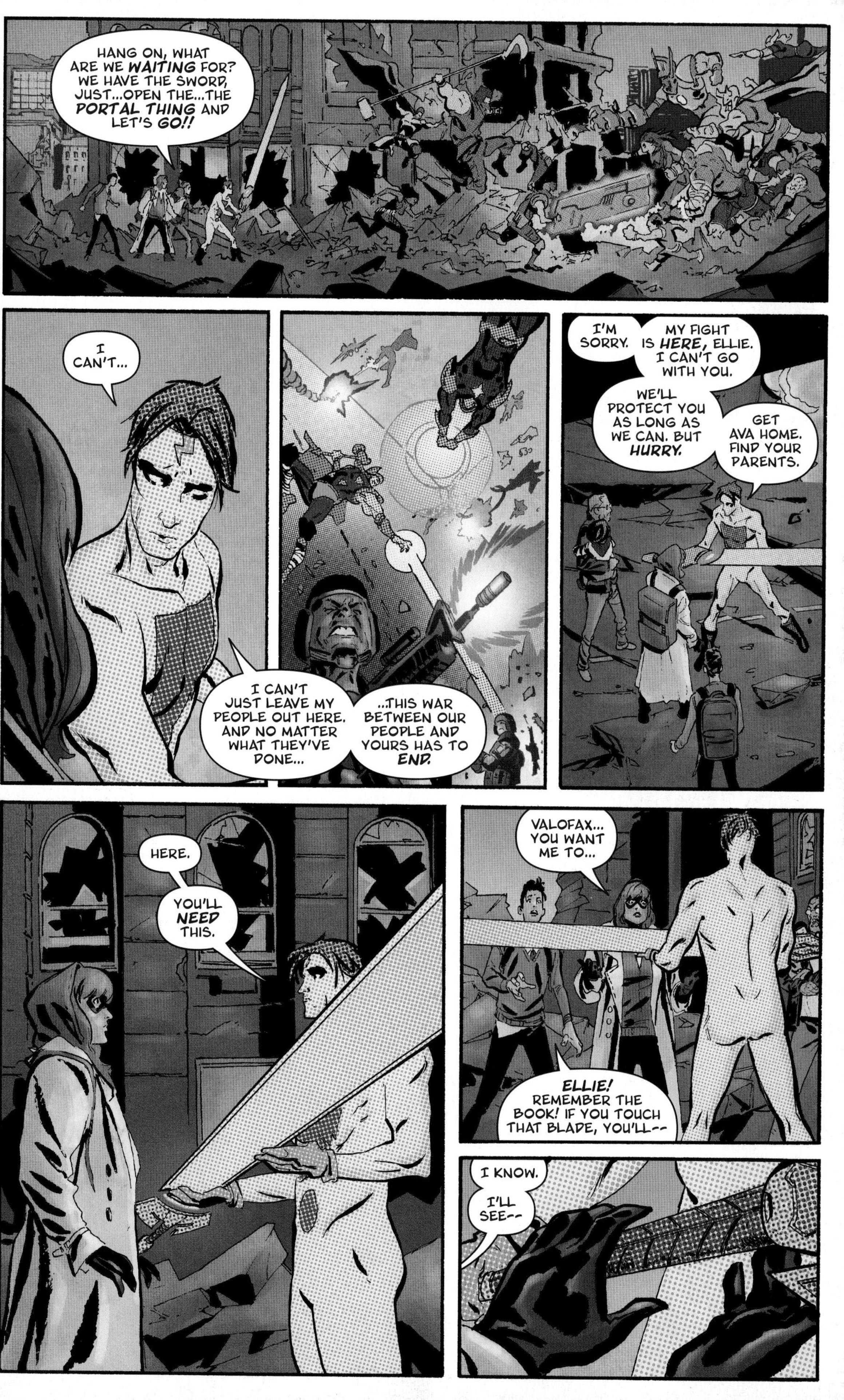
HANG ON, WHAT ARE WE WAITING FOR? WE HAVE THE SWORD, JUST...OPEN THE...THE PORTAL THING AND LET'S GO!!
I CAN'T...
I CAN'T JUST LEAVE MY PEOPLE OUT HERE. AND NO MATTER WHAT THEY'VE DONE...
...THIS WAR BETWEEN OUR PEOPLE AND YOURS HAS TO END.
I'M SORRY.
MY FIGHT IS HERE, ELLIE. I CAN'T GO WITH YOU.
WE'LL PROTECT YOU AS LONG AS WE CAN. BUT HURRY.
GET AVA HOME. FIND YOUR PARENTS.
HERE.
YOU'LL NEED THIS.
VALOFAX... YOU WANT ME TO...
ELLIE! REMEMBER THE BOOK! IF YOU TOUCH THAT BLADE, YOU'LL--
I KNOW.
I'LL SEE--

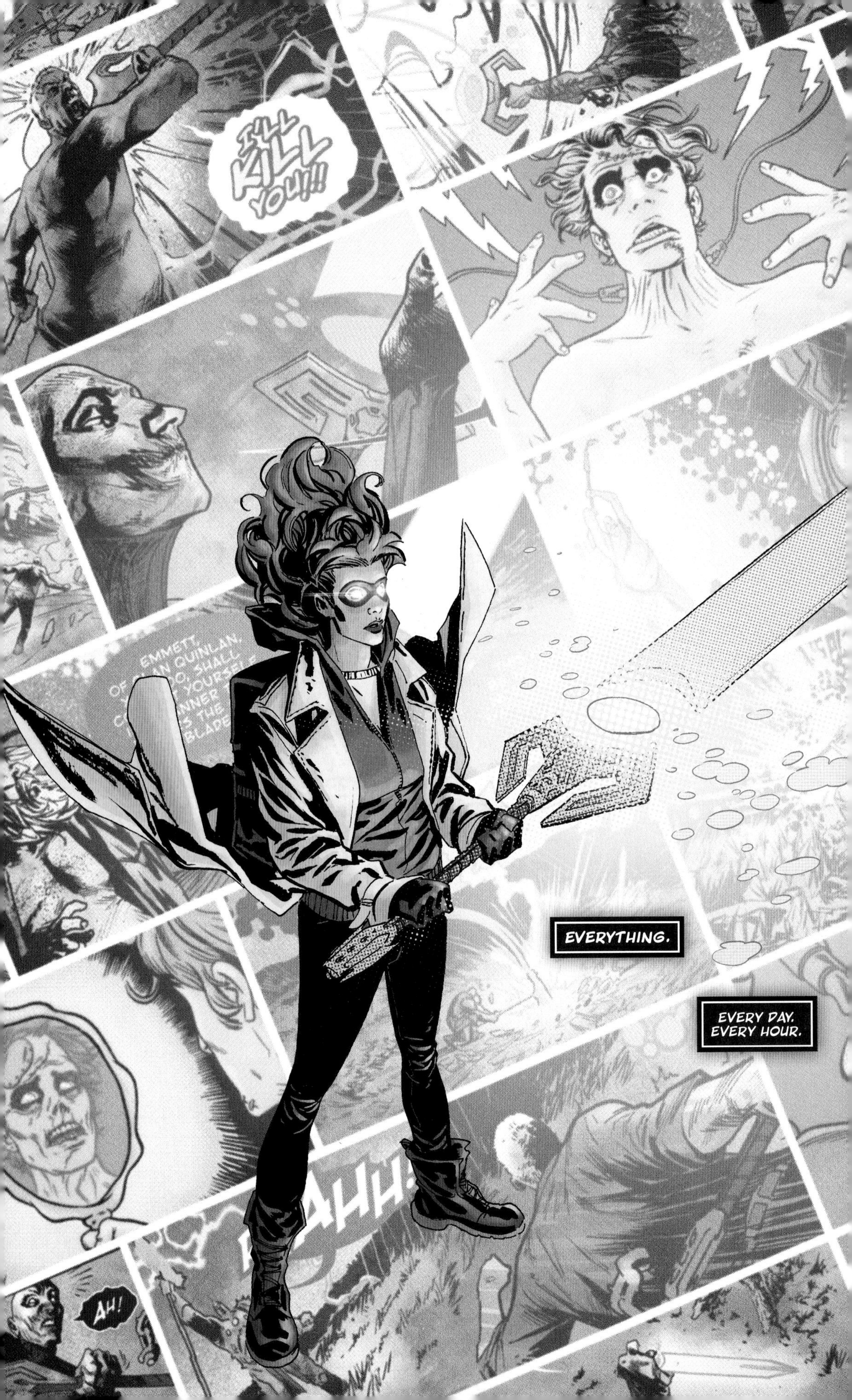
I'LL KILL YOU!!!
EVERYTHING.
EVERY DAY. EVERY HOUR.
AH!

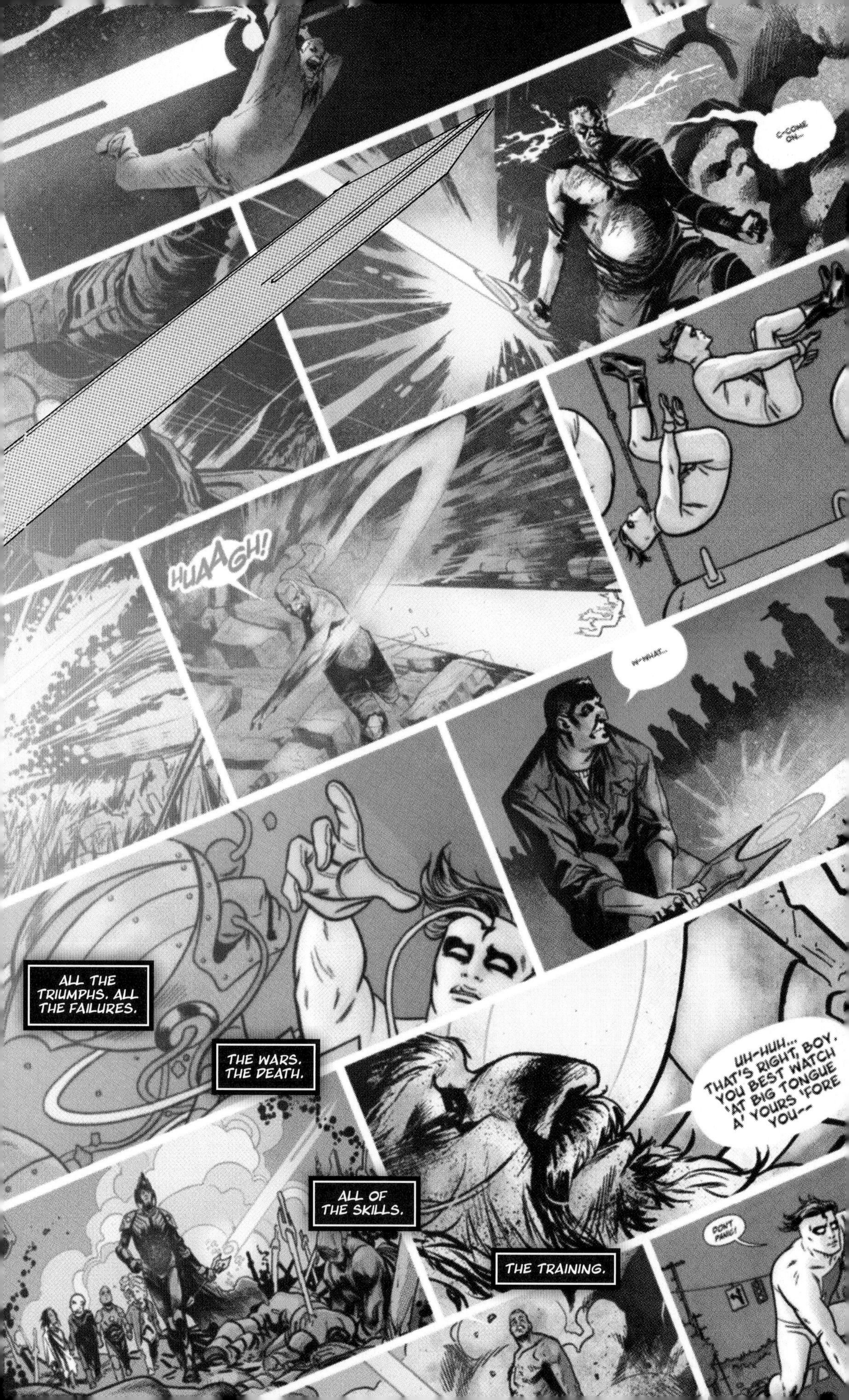
C-COME ON...
HUAAGH!
W-WHAT...
ALL THE TRIUMPHS. ALL THE FAILURES.
THE WARS. THE DEATH.
UH-HUH... THAT'S RIGHT, BOY. YOU BEST WATCH 'AT BIG TONGUE A' YOURS 'FORE YOU--
ALL OF THE SKILLS.
THE TRAINING.
DON'T PANIC!

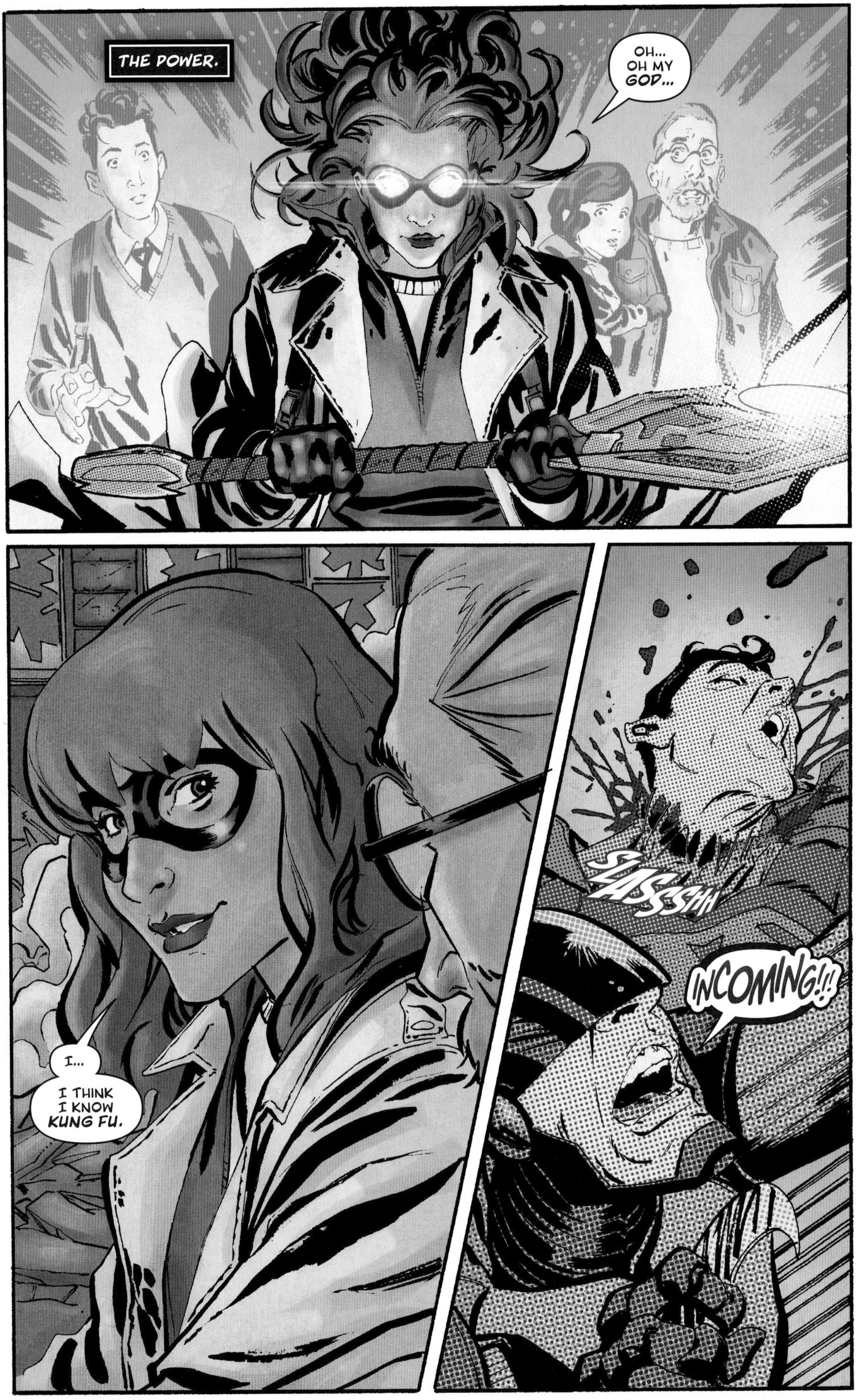
THE POWER.
OH... OH MY GOD...
I... I THINK I KNOW KUNG FU.
SLASSSHH
INCOMING!!!

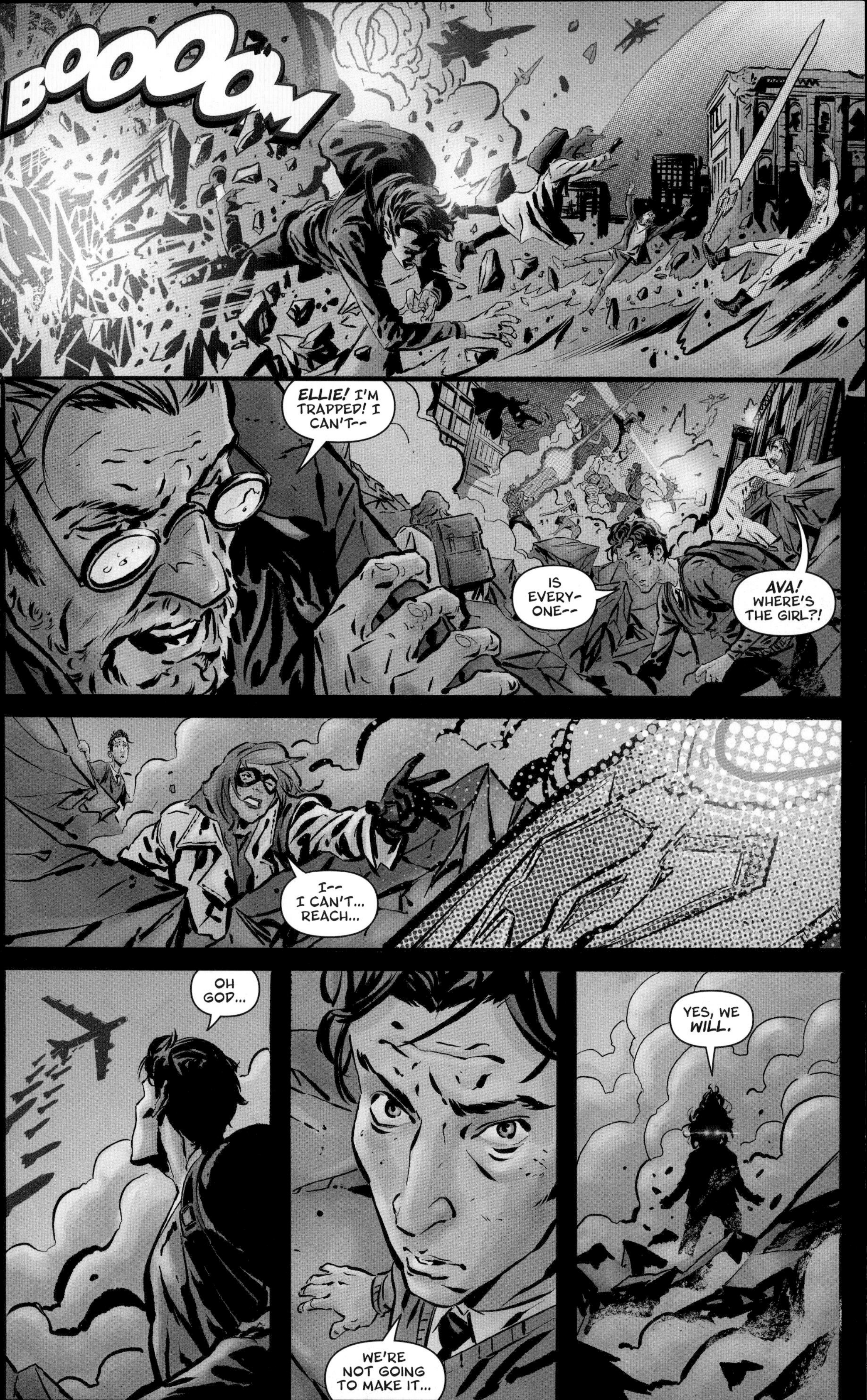
BOOOOOM
ELLIE! I'M TRAPPED! I CAN'T--
IS EVERY-ONE--
AVA! WHERE'S THE GIRL?!
I-- I CAN'T... REACH...
OH GOD...
WE'RE NOT GOING TO MAKE IT...
YES, WE WILL.

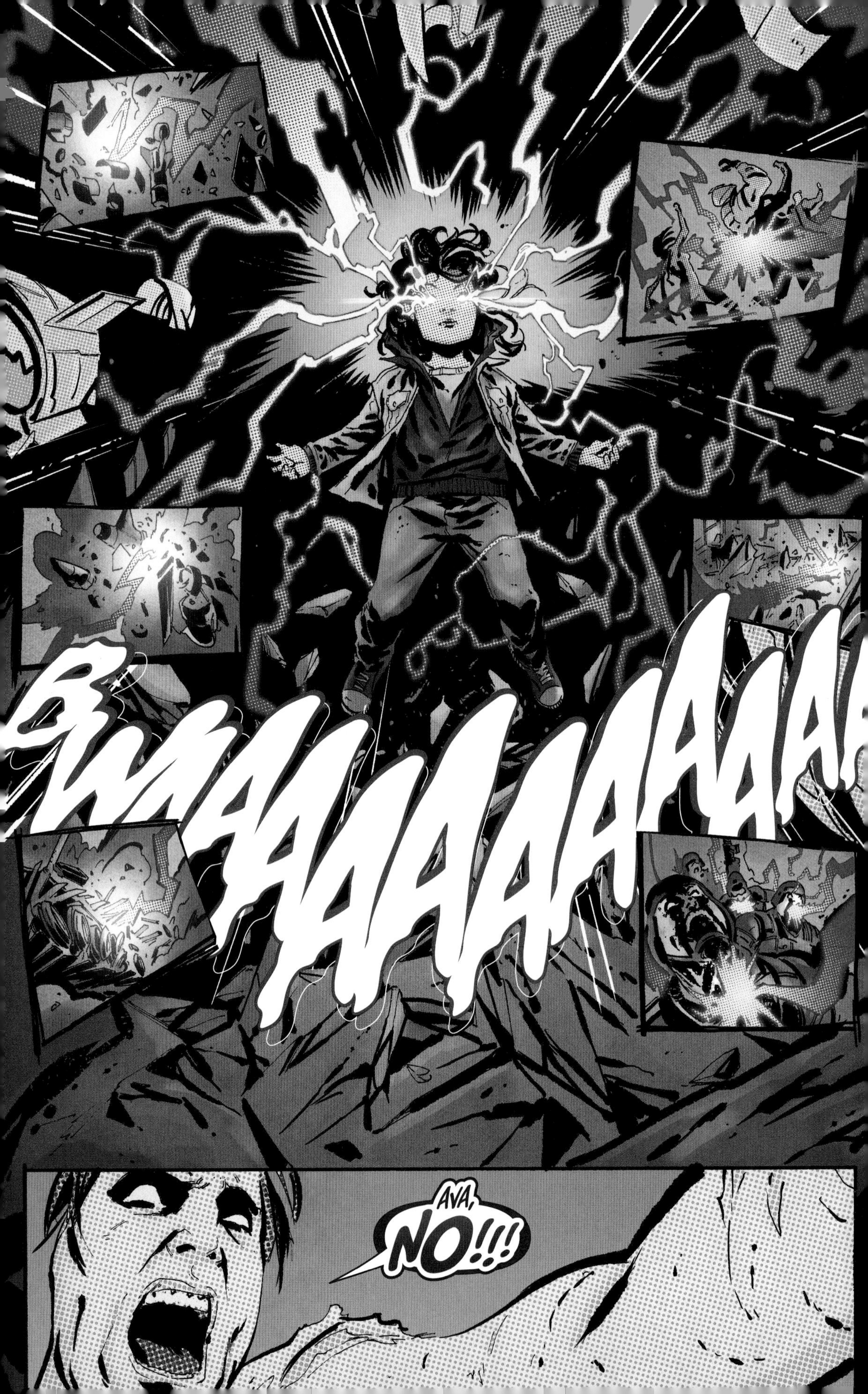
BWAAAAAAAAAAAA
AVA, NO!!!

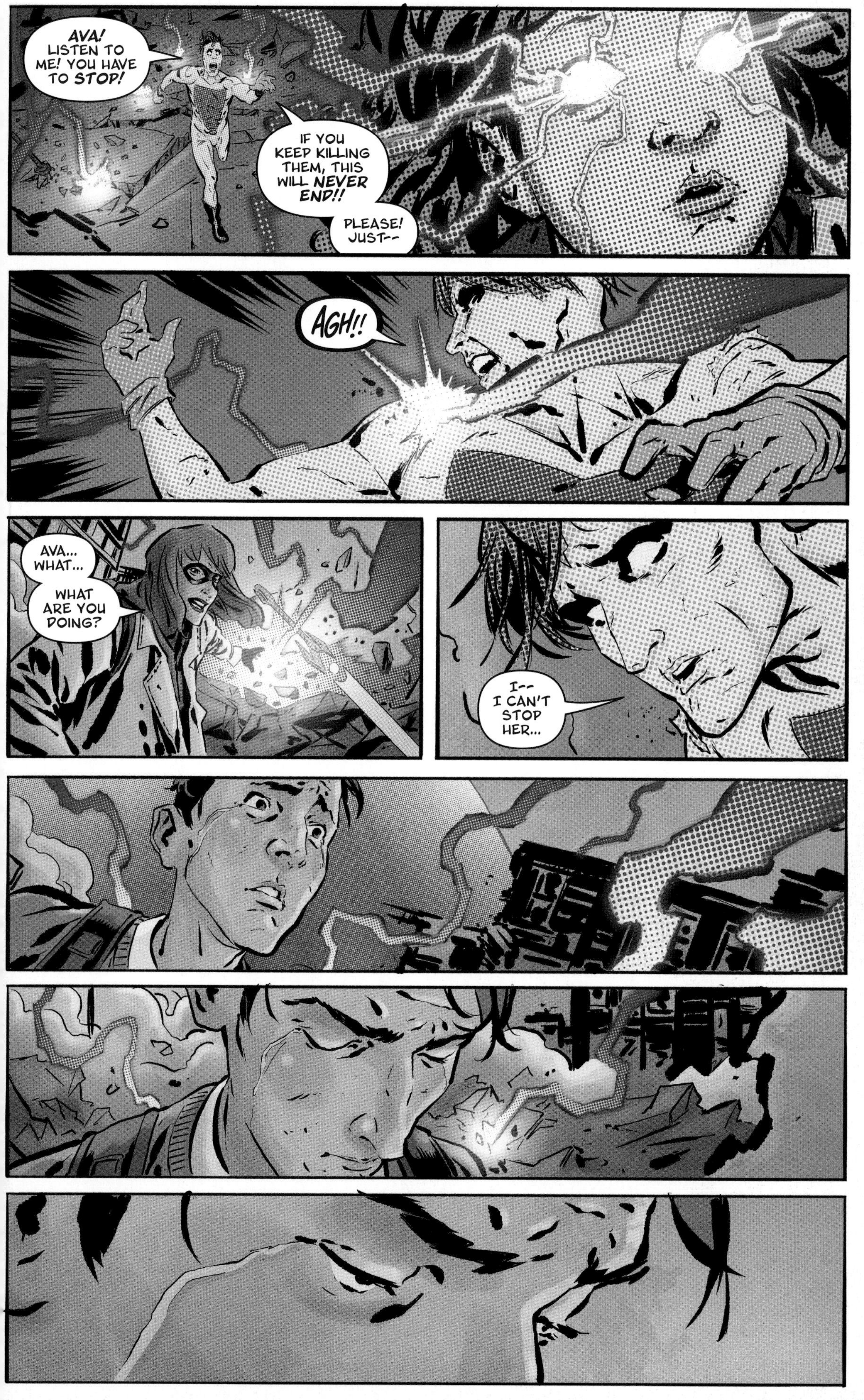
AVA! LISTEN TO ME! YOU HAVE TO STOP!
IF YOU KEEP KILLING THEM, THIS WILL NEVER END!!
PLEASE! JUST--
AGH!!
AVA... WHAT...
WHAT ARE YOU DOING?
I-- I CAN'T STOP HER...

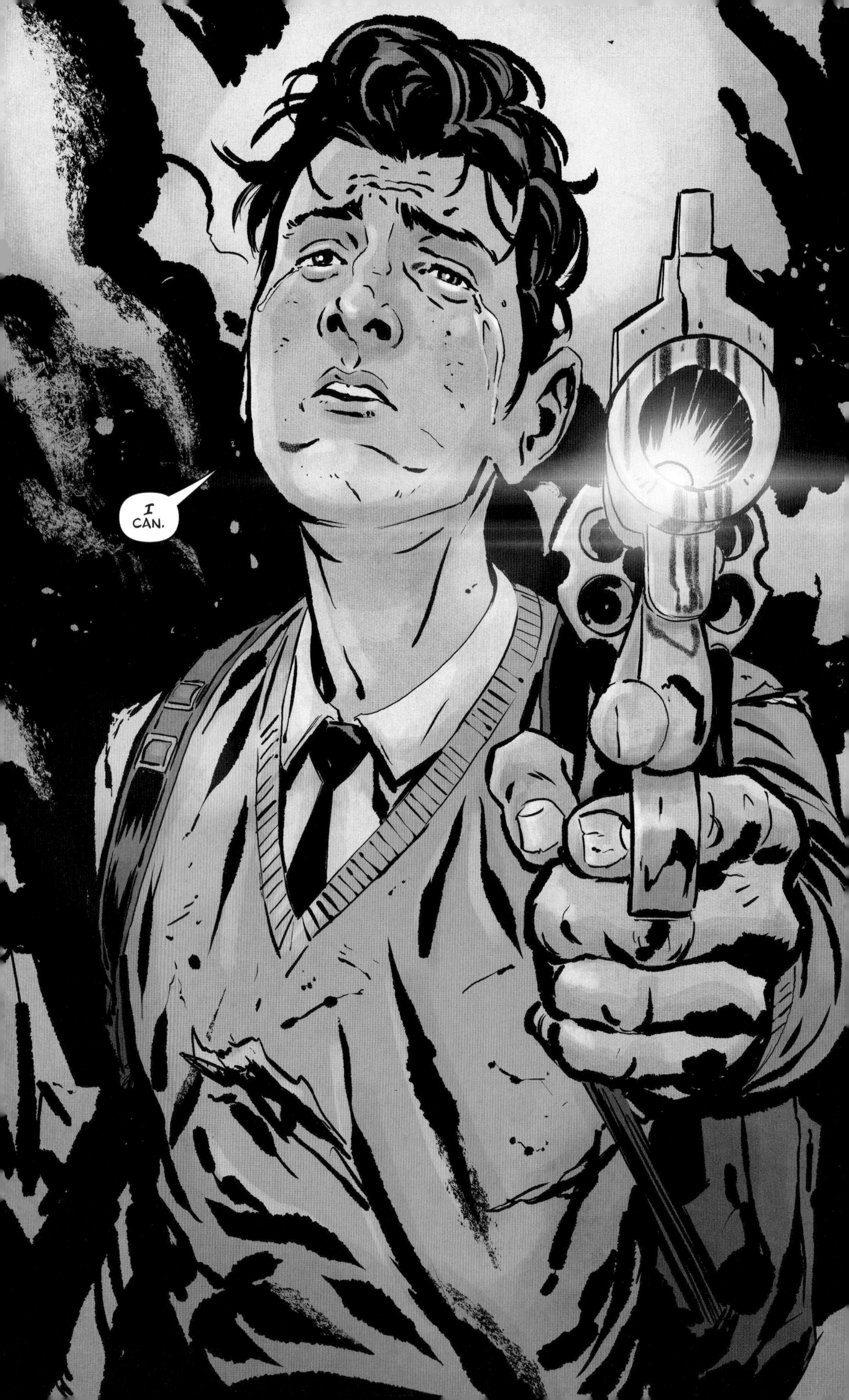
I CAN.

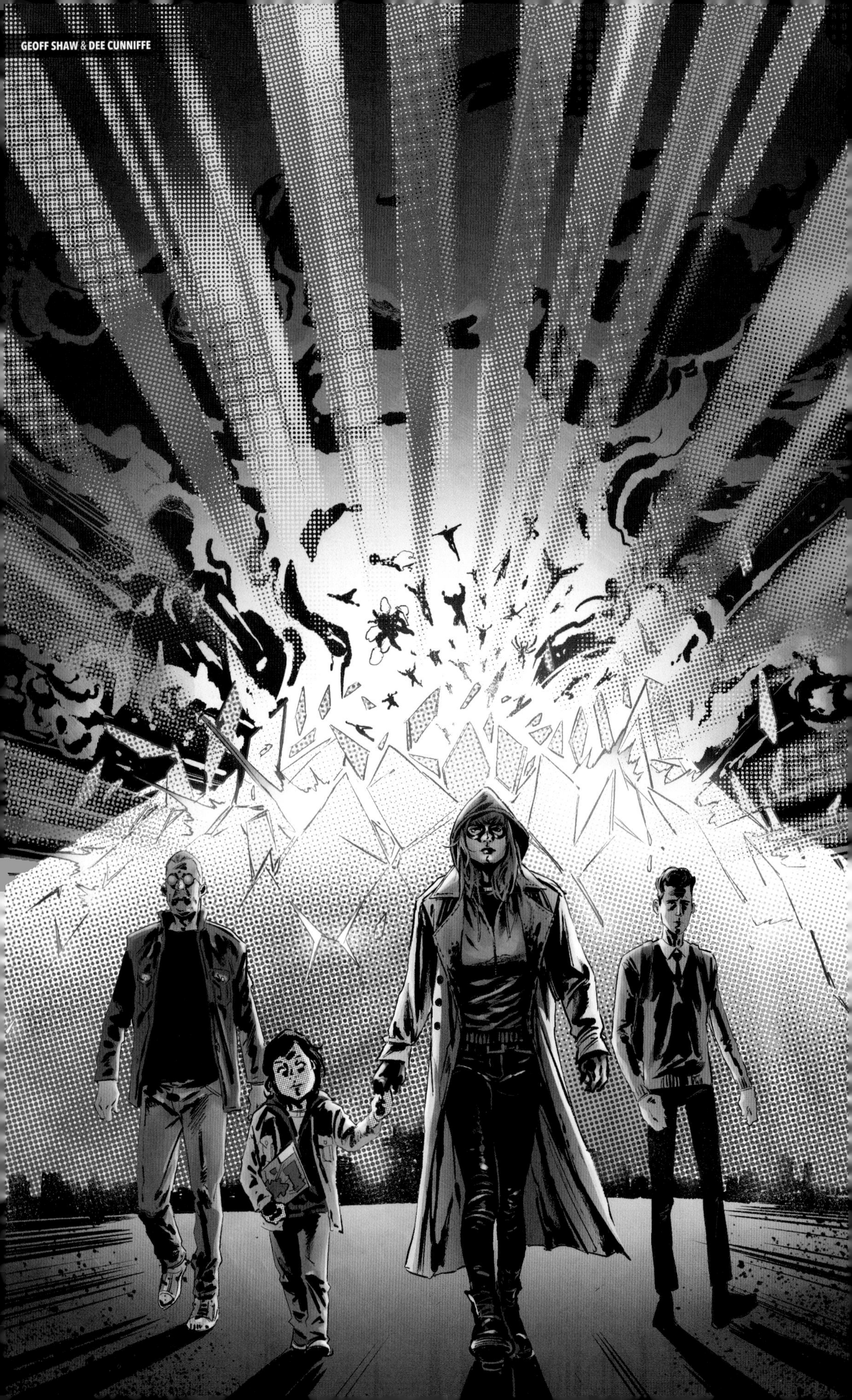
GEOFF SHAW & DEE CUNNIFFE

KIDS LOVE CHAINS

CHAPTER SIX

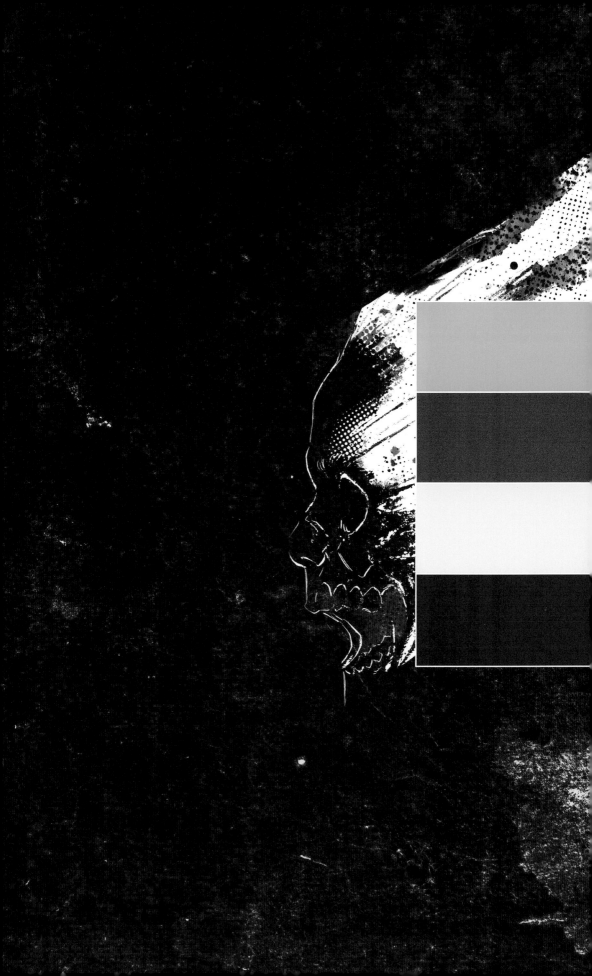

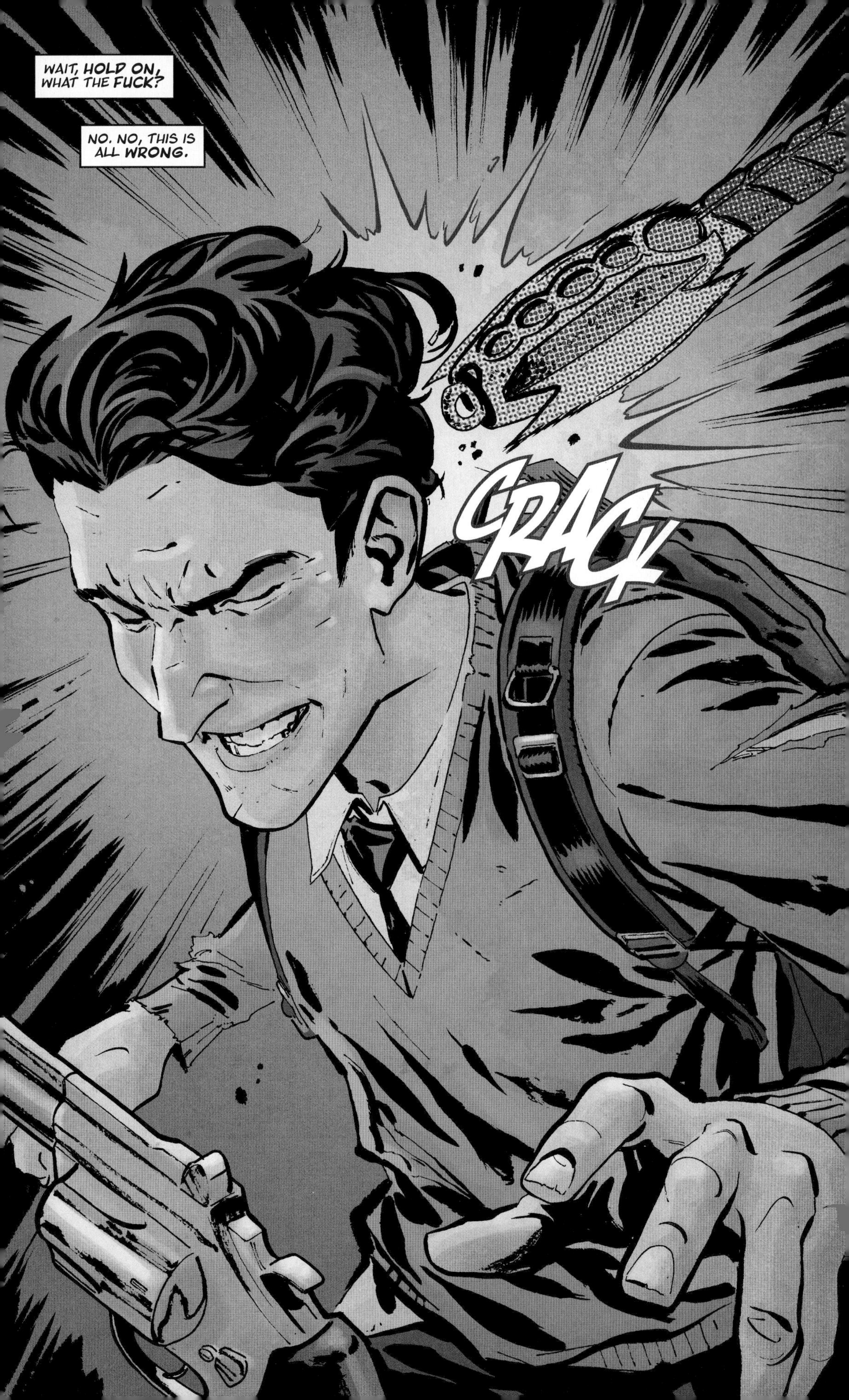
WAIT, HOLD ON, WHAT THE FUCK?
NO. NO, THIS IS ALL WRONG.
CRACK

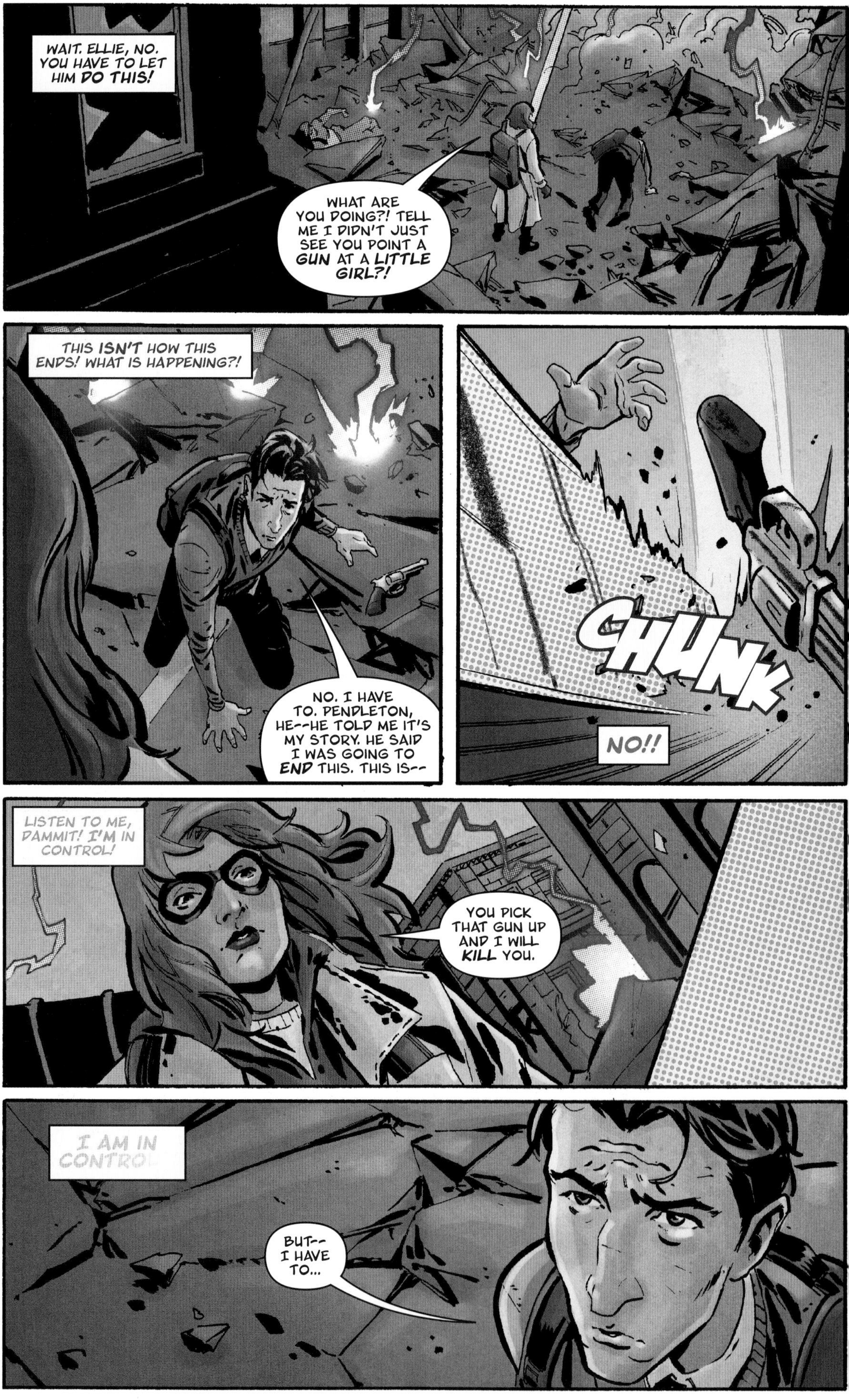
WAIT. ELLIE, NO. YOU HAVE TO LET HIM DO THIS!
WHAT ARE YOU DOING?! TELL ME I DIDN'T JUST SEE YOU POINT A GUN AT A LITTLE GIRL?!
THIS ISN'T HOW THIS ENDS! WHAT IS HAPPENING?!
NO. I HAVE TO. PENDLETON, HE--HE TOLD ME IT'S MY STORY. HE SAID I WAS GOING TO END THIS. THIS IS--
CHUNK
NO!!
LISTEN TO ME, DAMMIT! I'M IN CONTROL!
YOU PICK THAT GUN UP AND I WILL KILL YOU.
I AM IN CONTROL
BUT-- I HAVE TO...

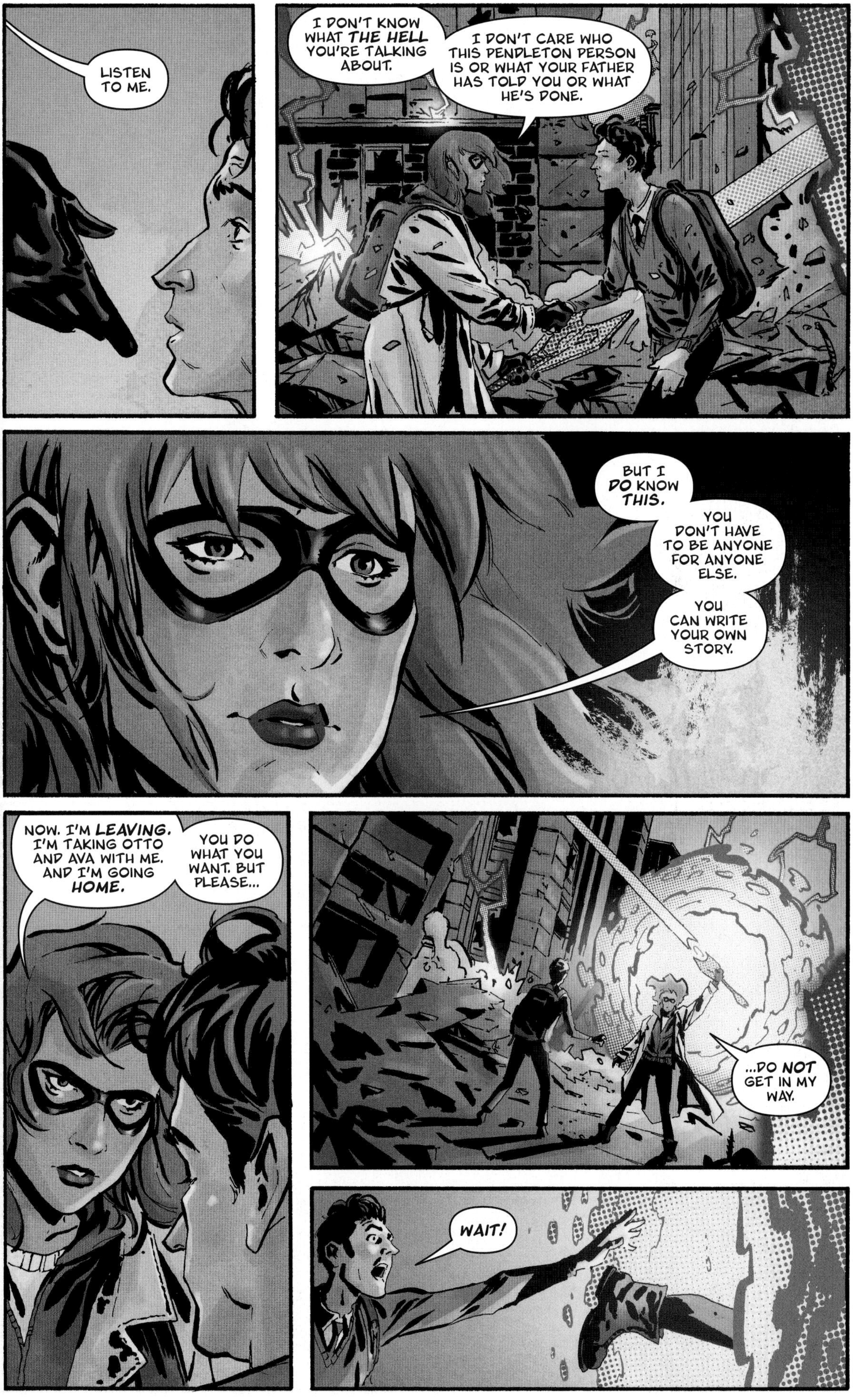
LISTEN TO ME.
I DON'T KNOW WHAT THE HELL YOU'RE TALKING ABOUT.
I DON'T CARE WHO THIS PENDLETON PERSON IS OR WHAT YOUR FATHER HAS TOLD YOU OR WHAT HE'S DONE.
BUT I DO KNOW THIS.
YOU DON'T HAVE TO BE ANYONE FOR ANYONE ELSE.
YOU CAN WRITE YOUR OWN STORY.
NOW. I'M LEAVING. I'M TAKING OTTO AND AVA WITH ME. AND I'M GOING HOME.
YOU DO WHAT YOU WANT. BUT PLEASE...
...DO NOT GET IN MY WAY.
WAIT!

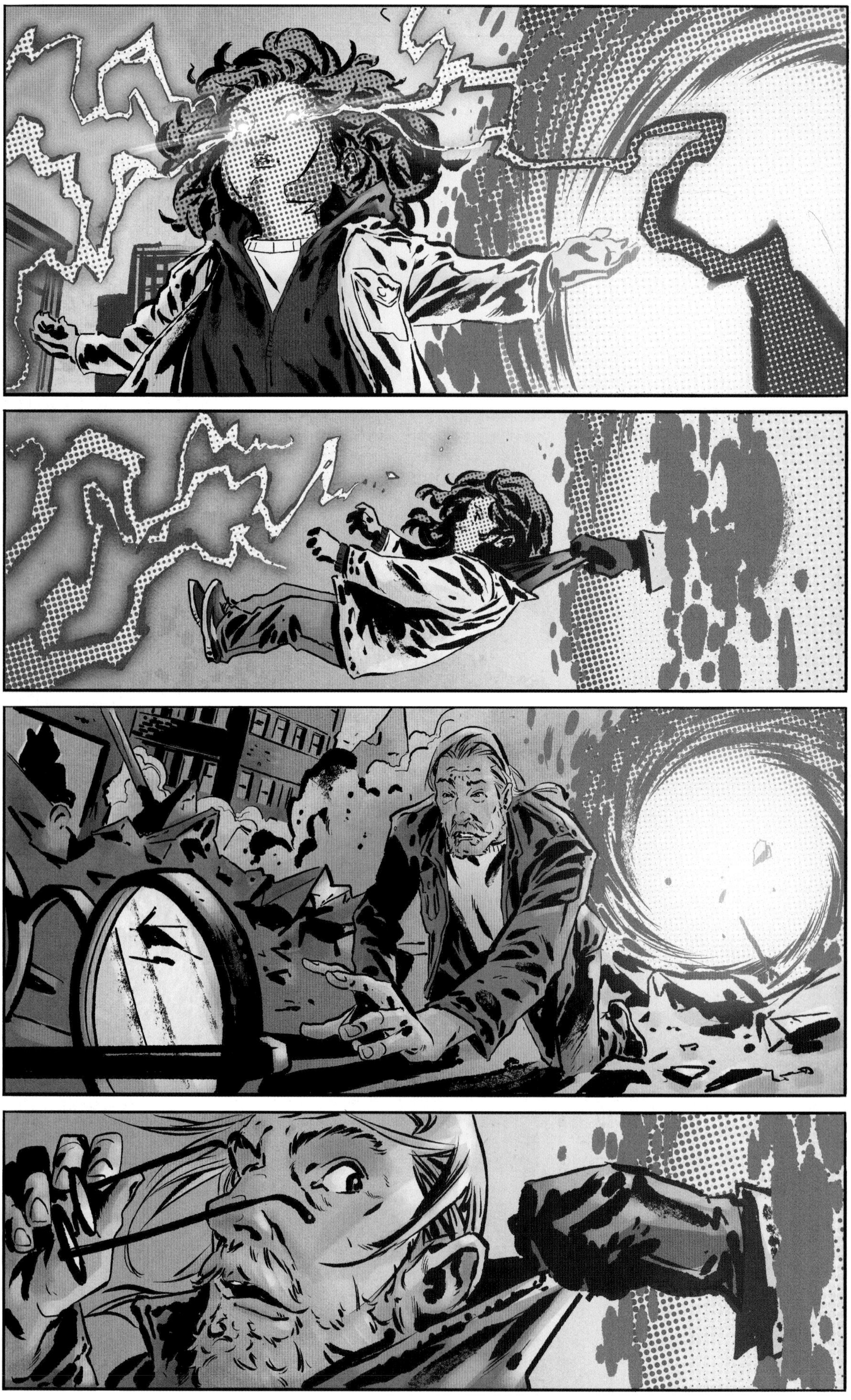

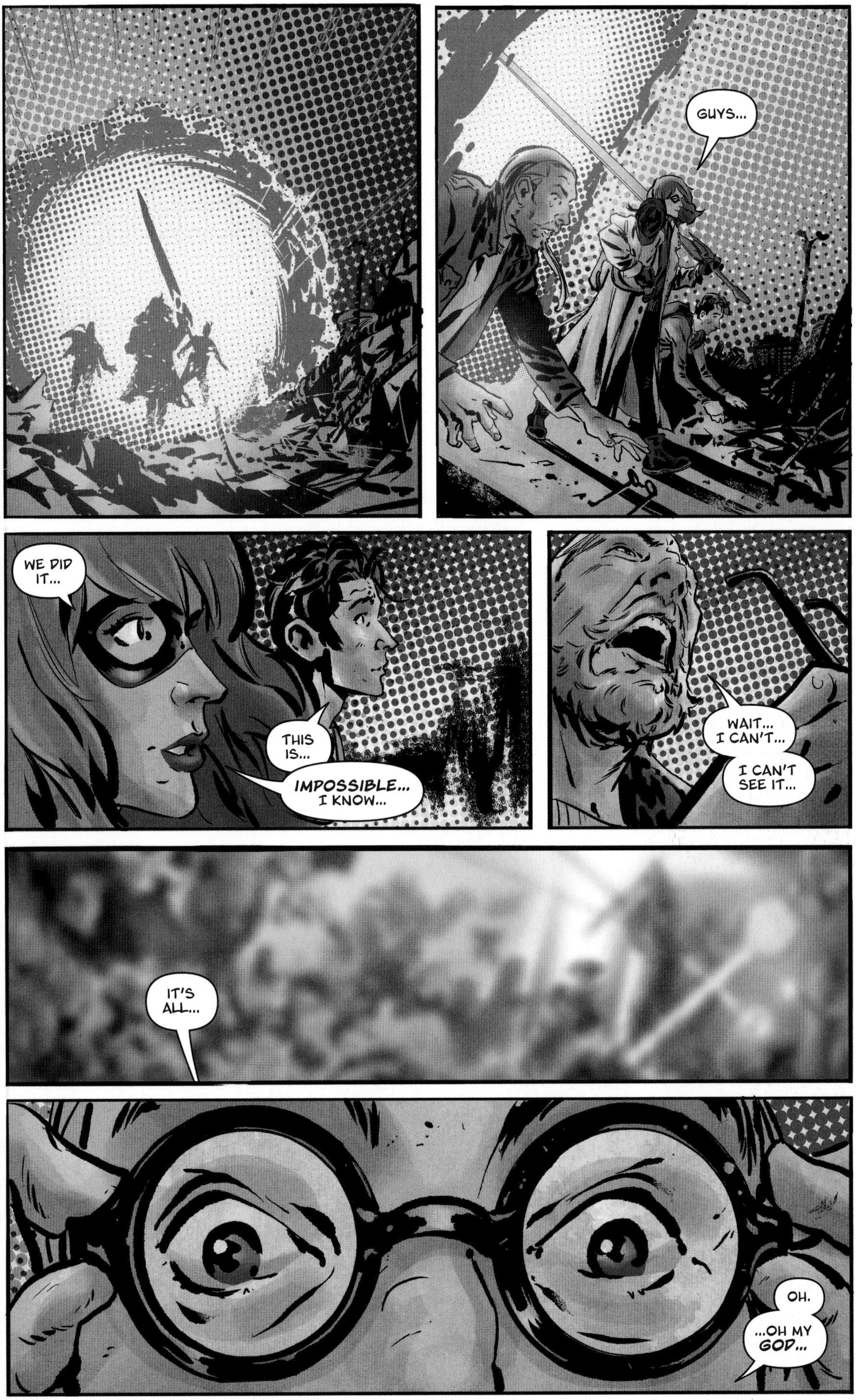
GUYS...
WE DID IT...
THIS IS...
IMPOSSIBLE... I KNOW...
WAIT... I CAN'T...
I CAN'T SEE IT...
IT'S ALL...
OH.
...OH MY GOD...

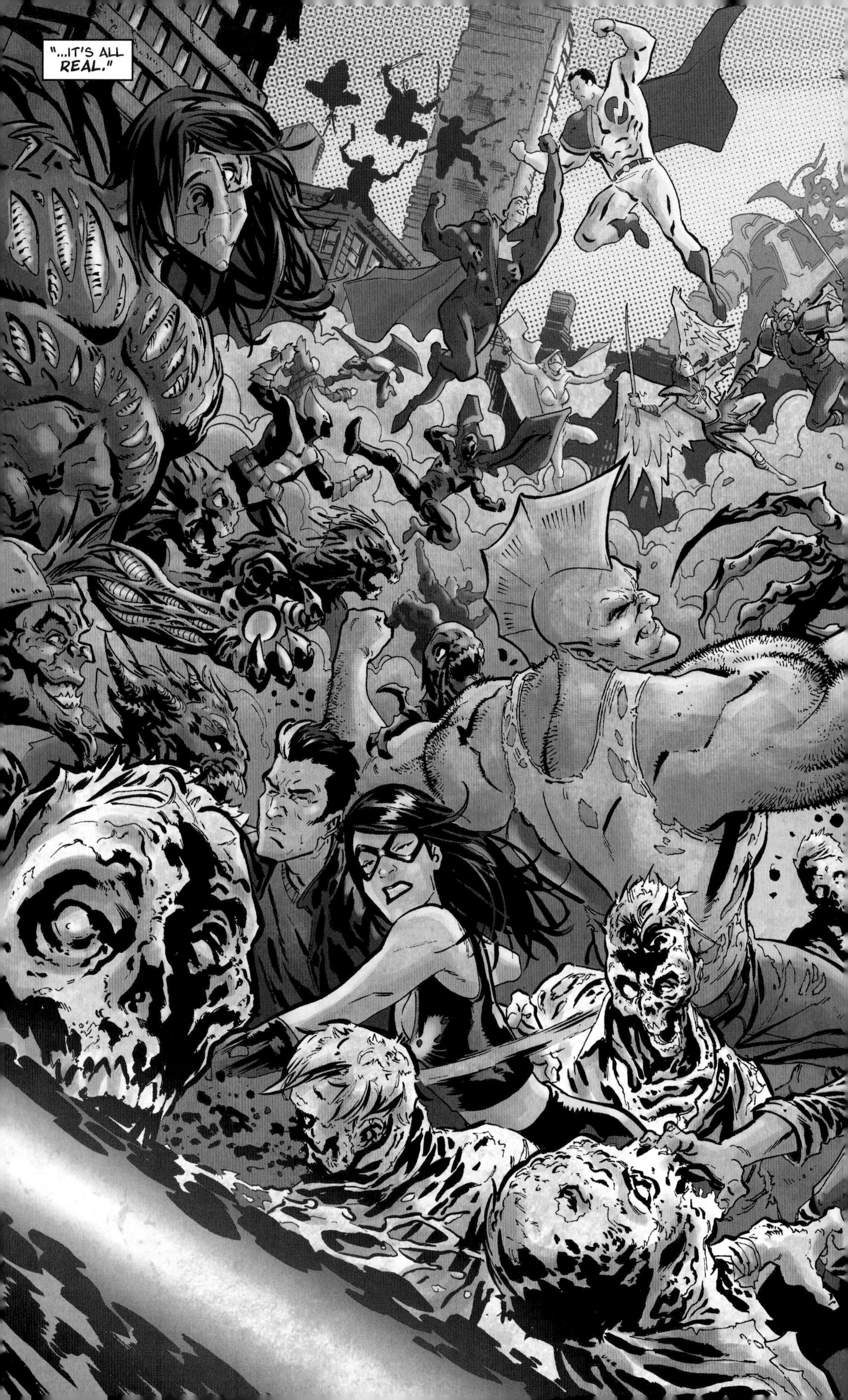
"...IT'S ALL REAL."

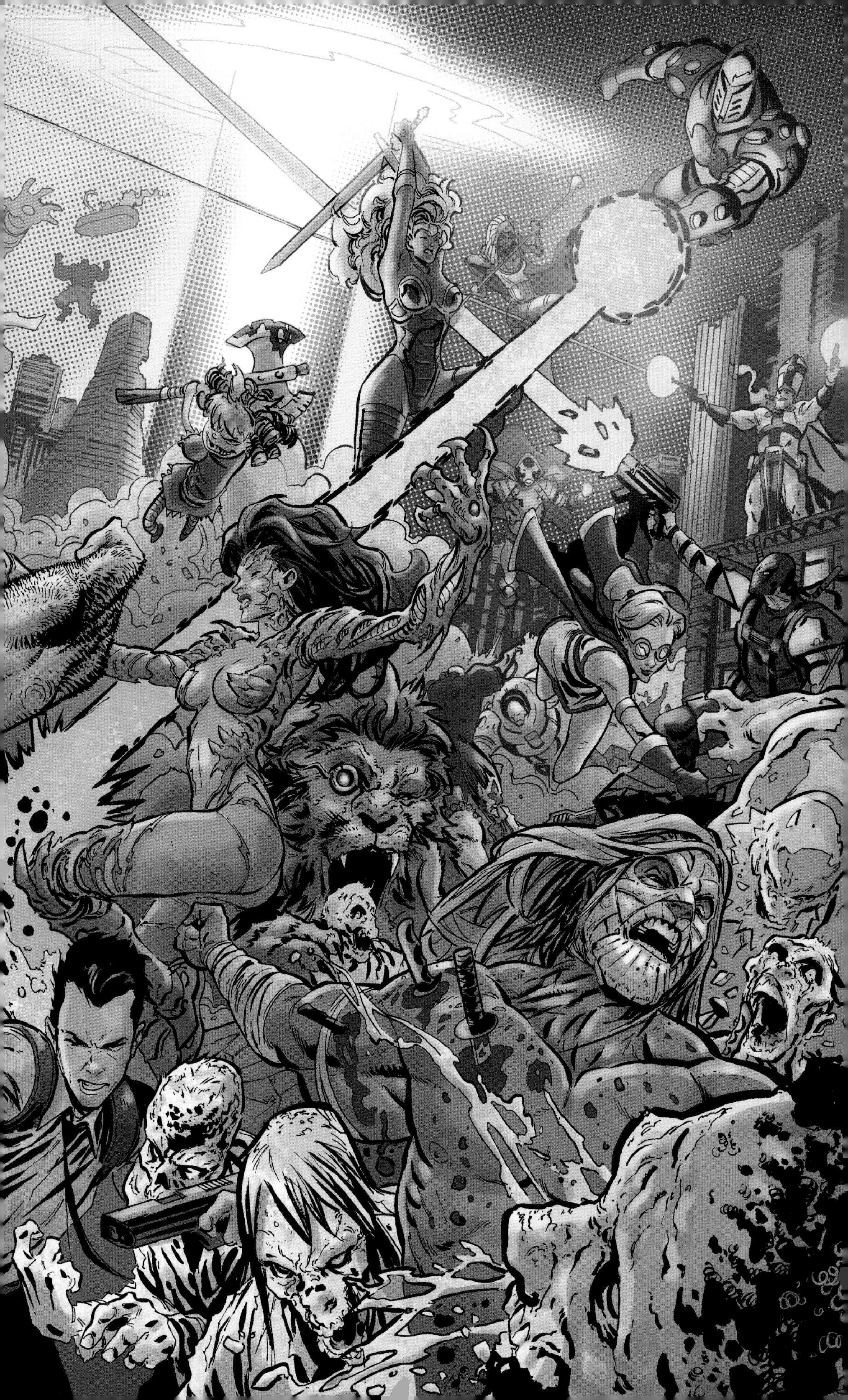

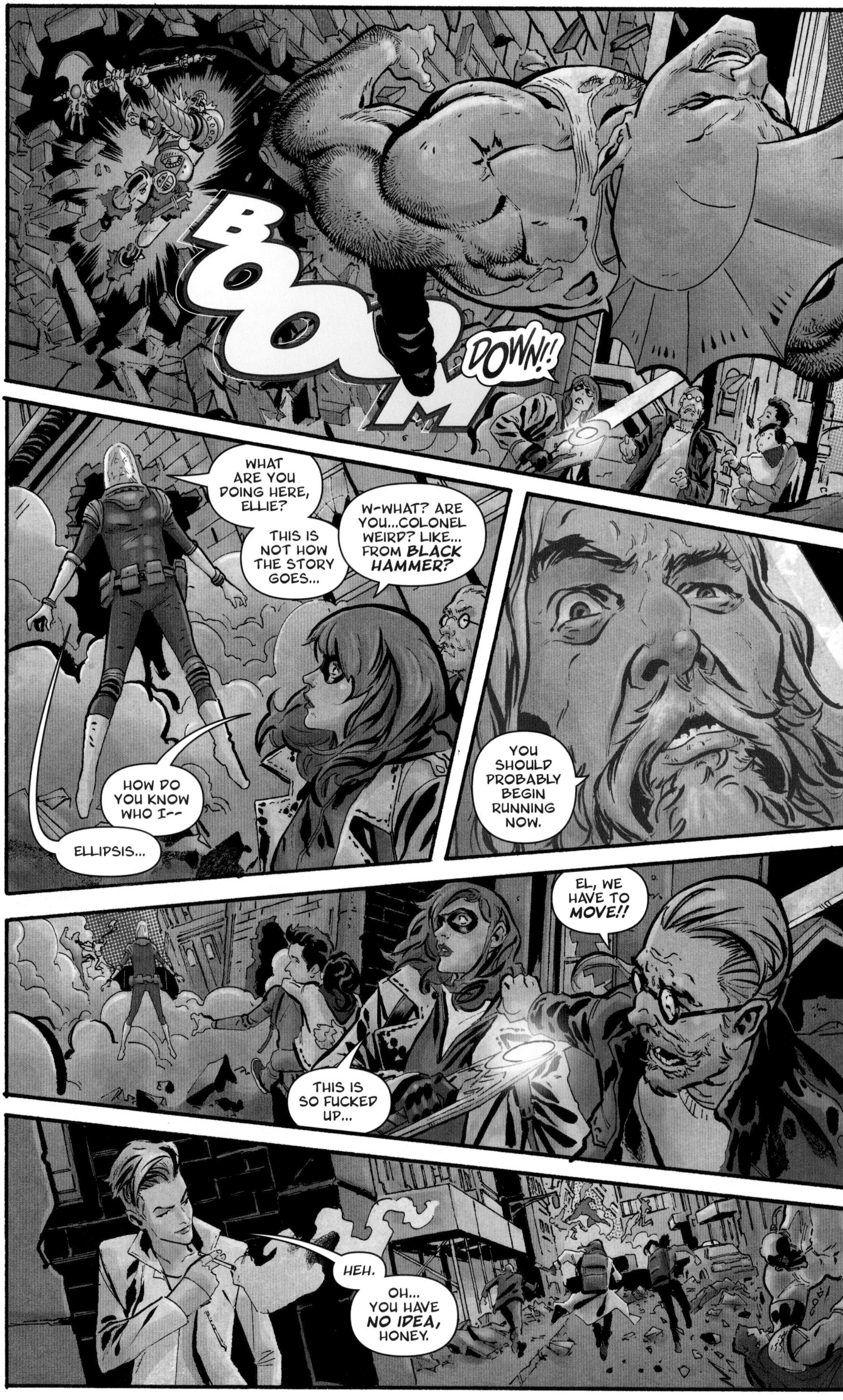
BOOM
DOWN!!
WHAT ARE YOU DOING HERE, ELLIE?
THIS IS NOT HOW THE STORY GOES...
W-WHAT? ARE YOU...COLONEL WEIRD? LIKE... FROM BLACK HAMMER?
HOW DO YOU KNOW WHO I--
ELLIPSIS...
YOU SHOULD PROBABLY BEGIN RUNNING NOW.
EL, WE HAVE TO MOVE!!
THIS IS SO FUCKED UP...
HEH.
OH... YOU HAVE NO IDEA, HONEY.

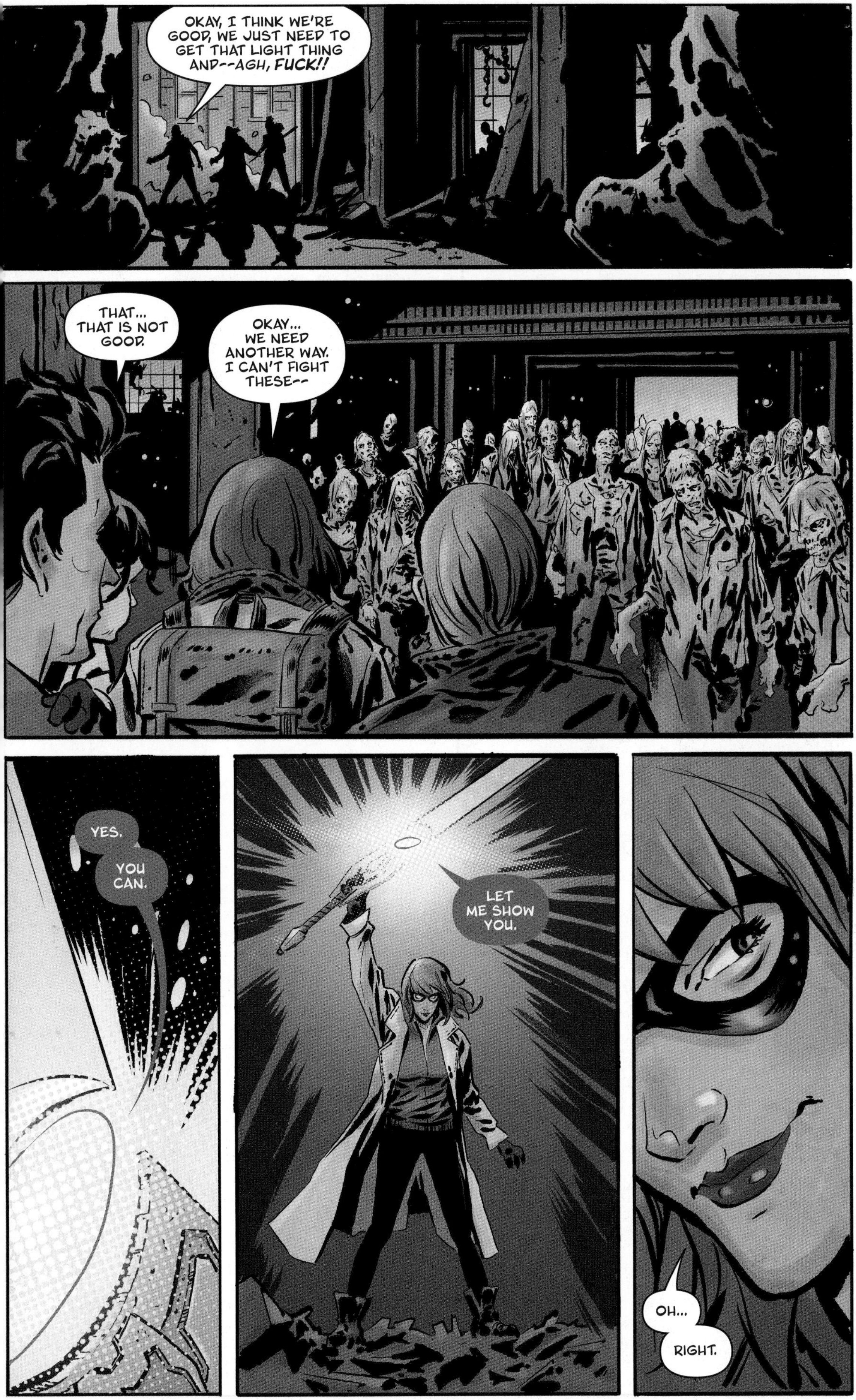
OKAY, I THINK WE'RE GOOD, WE JUST NEED TO GET THAT LIGHT THING AND--AGH, FUCK!!
THAT... THAT IS NOT GOOD.
OKAY... WE NEED ANOTHER WAY. I CAN'T FIGHT THESE--
YES.
YOU CAN.
LET ME SHOW YOU.
OH...
RIGHT.

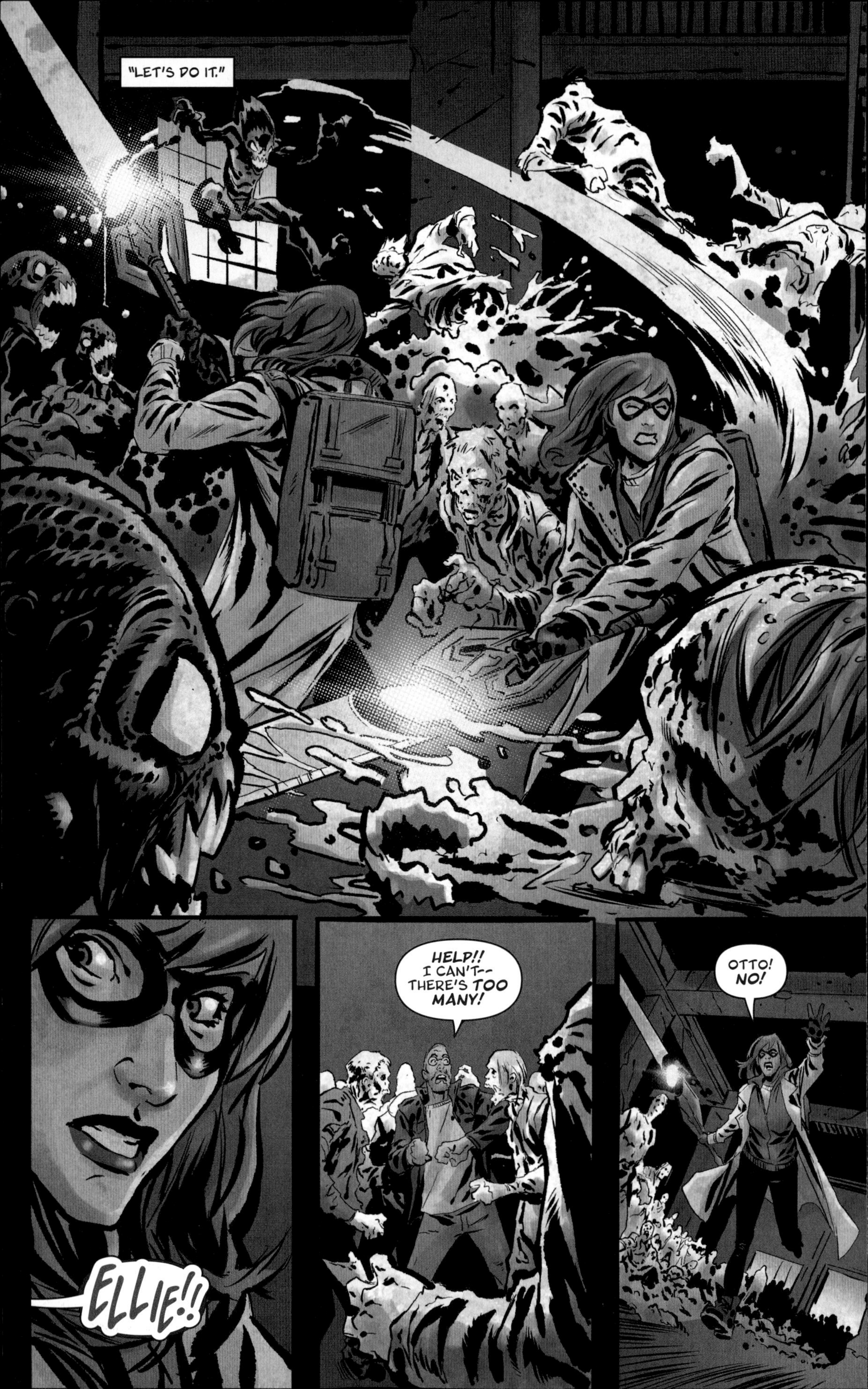
"LET'S DO IT."
ELLIE!!
HELP!! I CAN'T-- THERE'S TOO MANY!
OTTO! NO!

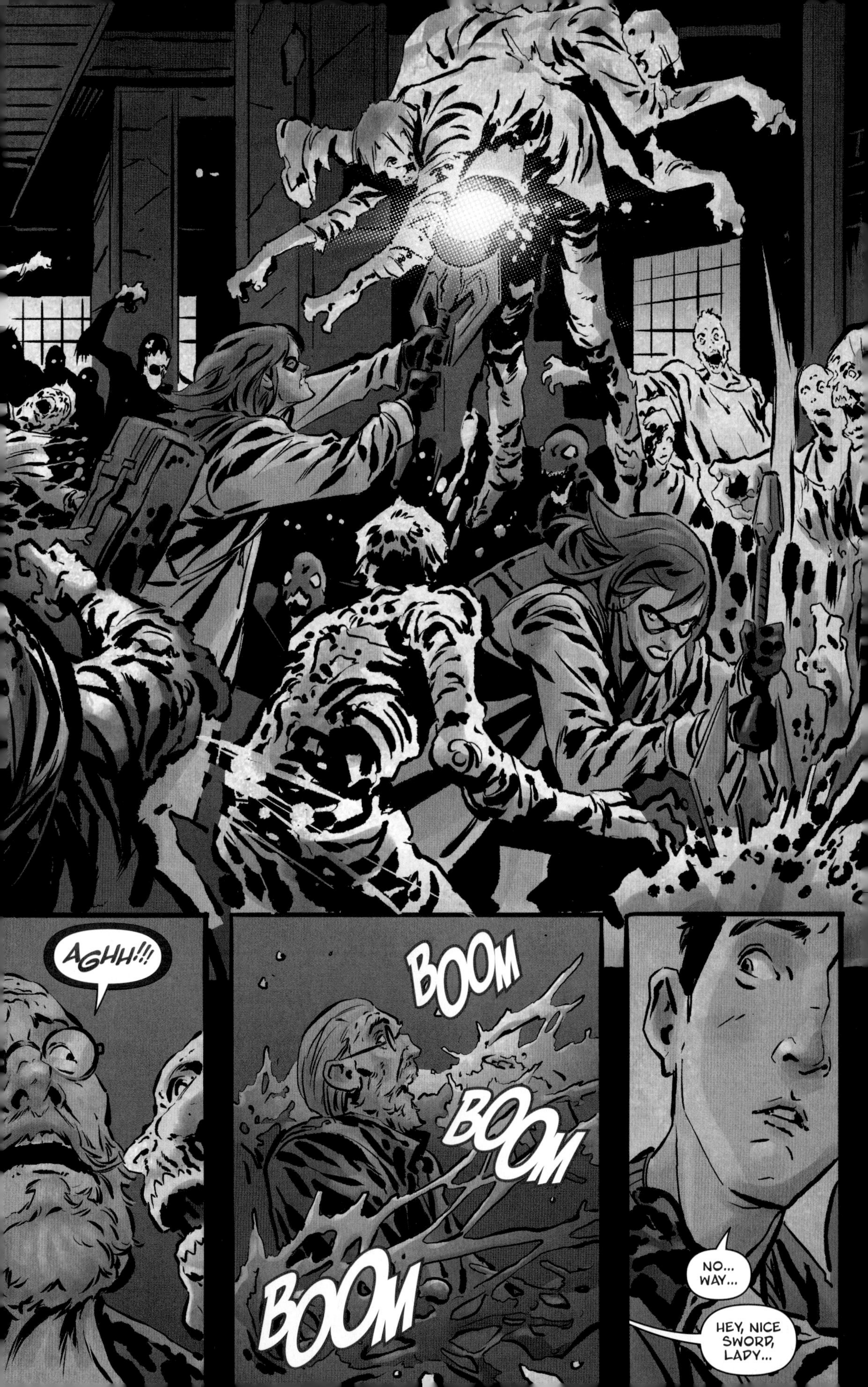
AGHH!!!
BOOM
BOOM
BOOM
NO... WAY...
HEY, NICE SWORD, LADY...

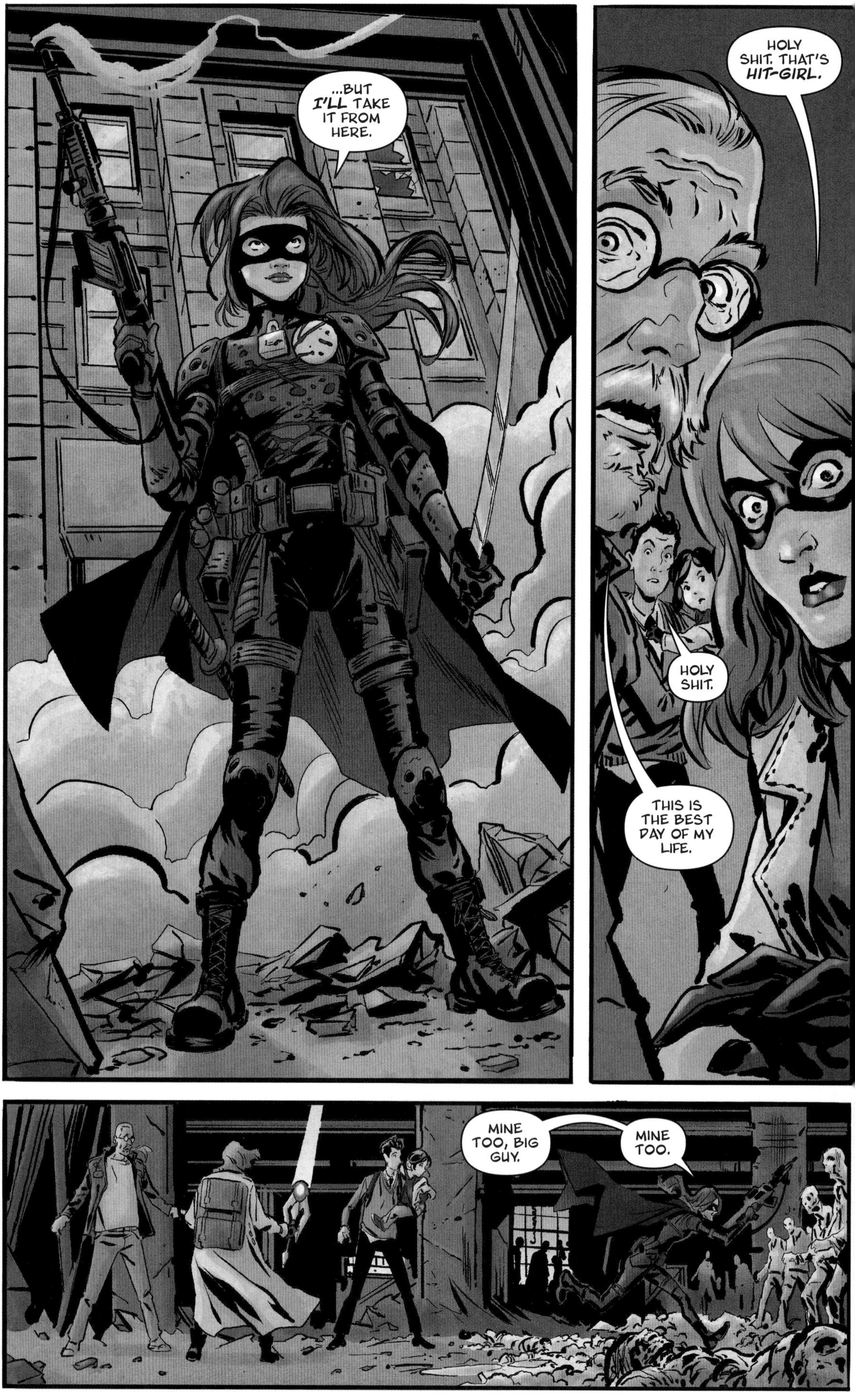
...BUT I'LL TAKE IT FROM HERE.
HOLY SHIT. THAT'S HIT-GIRL.
HOLY SHIT.
THIS IS THE BEST DAY OF MY LIFE.
MINE TOO, BIG GUY.
MINE TOO.

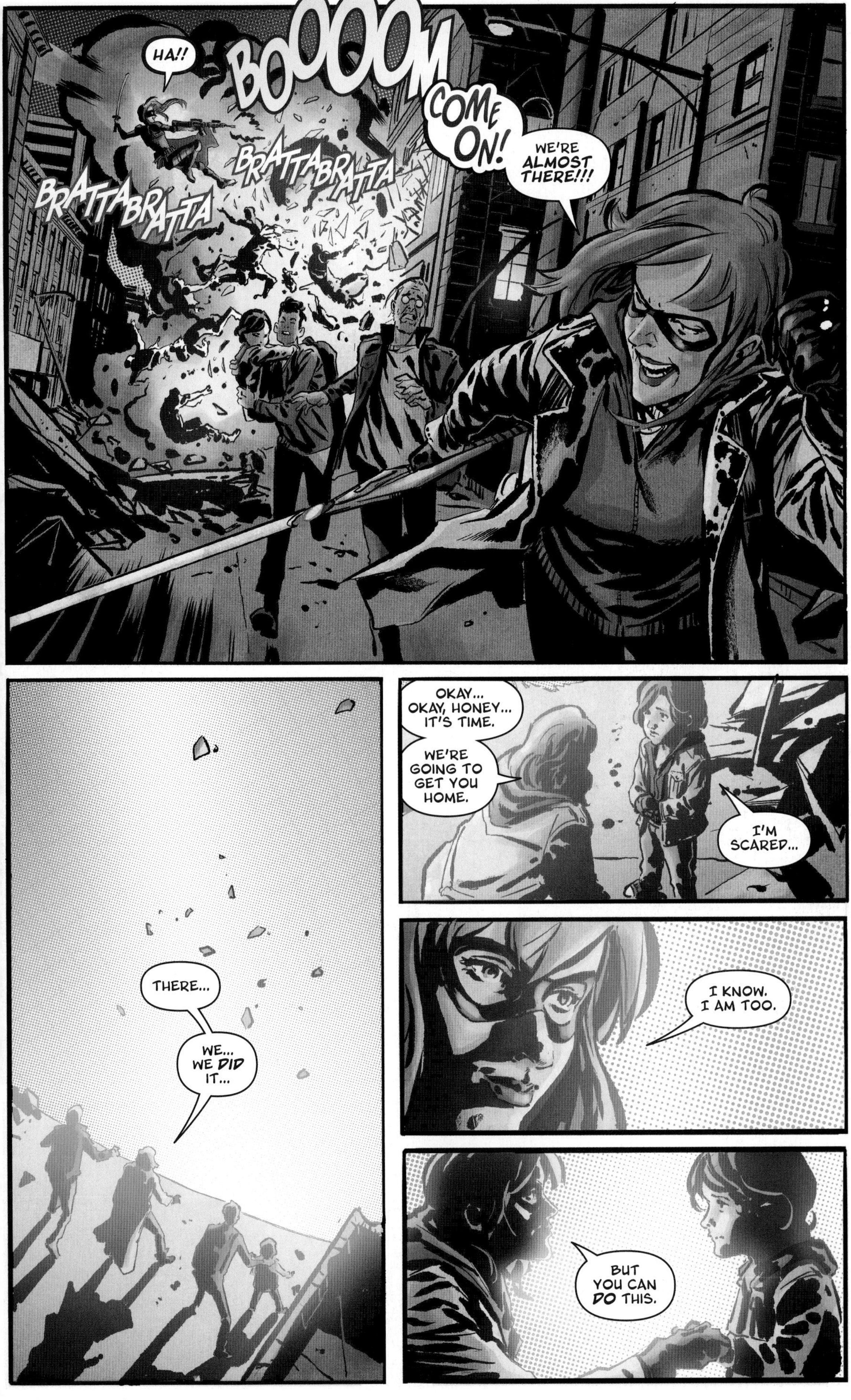
HA!!
BOOOOM
BRATTABRATTA
BRATTABRATTA
COME ON!
WE'RE ALMOST THERE!!!
THERE...
WE... WE DID IT...
OKAY... OKAY, HONEY... IT'S TIME.
WE'RE GOING TO GET YOU HOME.
I'M SCARED...
I KNOW. I AM TOO.
BUT YOU CAN DO THIS.

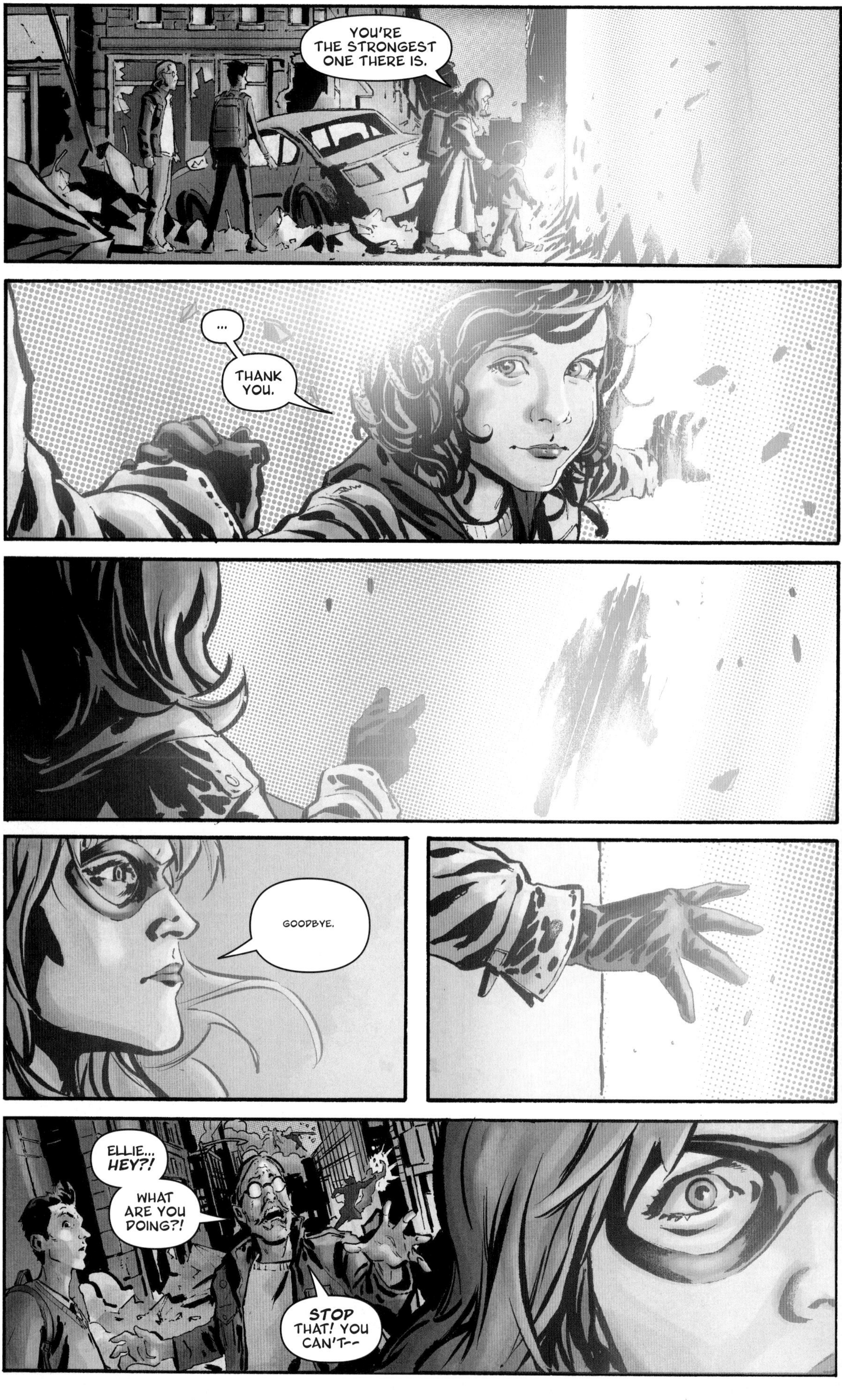
YOU'RE THE STRONGEST ONE THERE IS.
...
THANK YOU.
GOODBYE.
ELLIE... HEY?!
WHAT ARE YOU DOING?!
STOP THAT! YOU CAN'T--

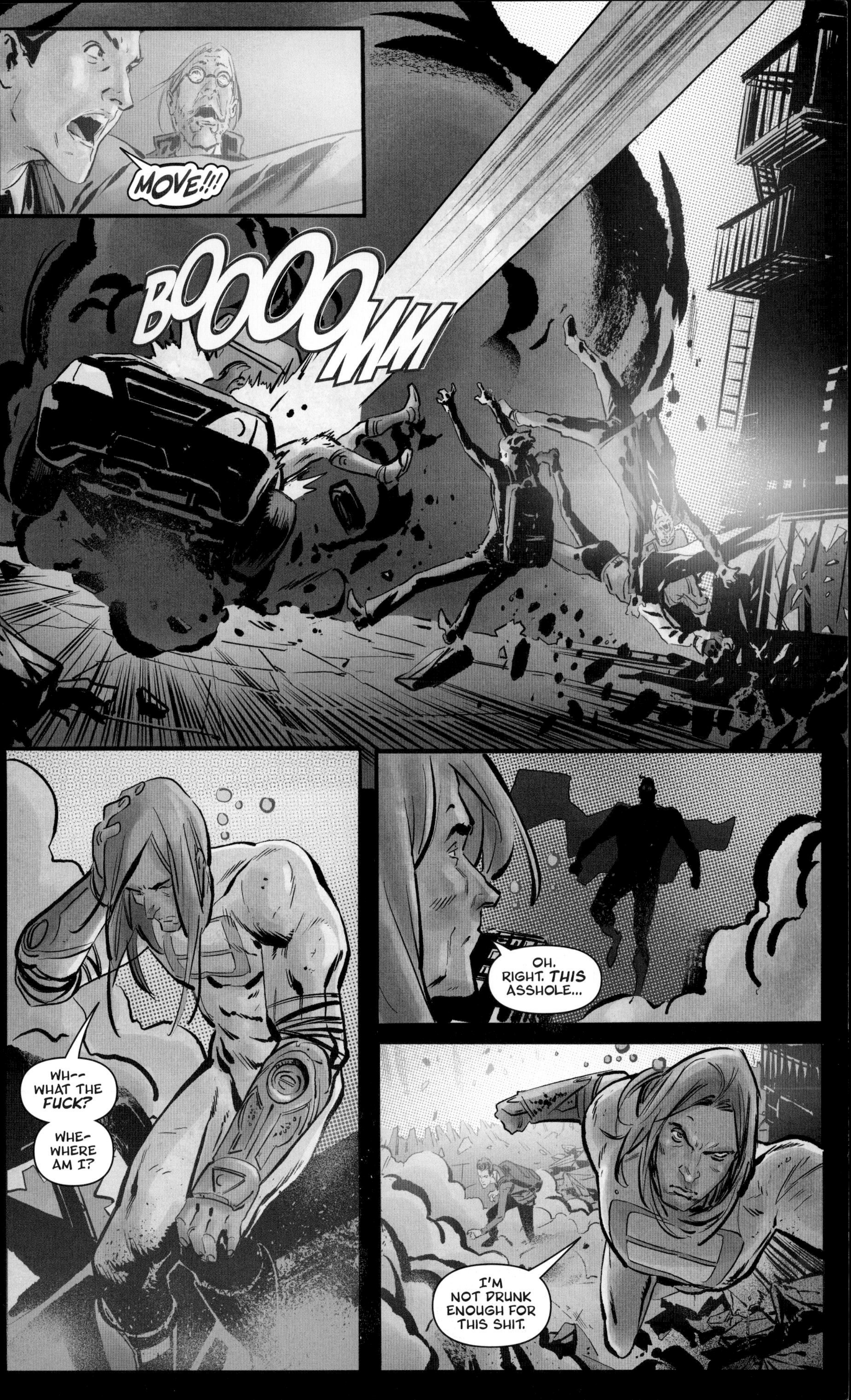
MOVE!!!
BOOOOMM
WH-- WHAT THE FUCK?
WHE- WHERE AM I?
OH. RIGHT. THIS ASSHOLE...
I'M NOT DRUNK ENOUGH FOR THIS SHIT.

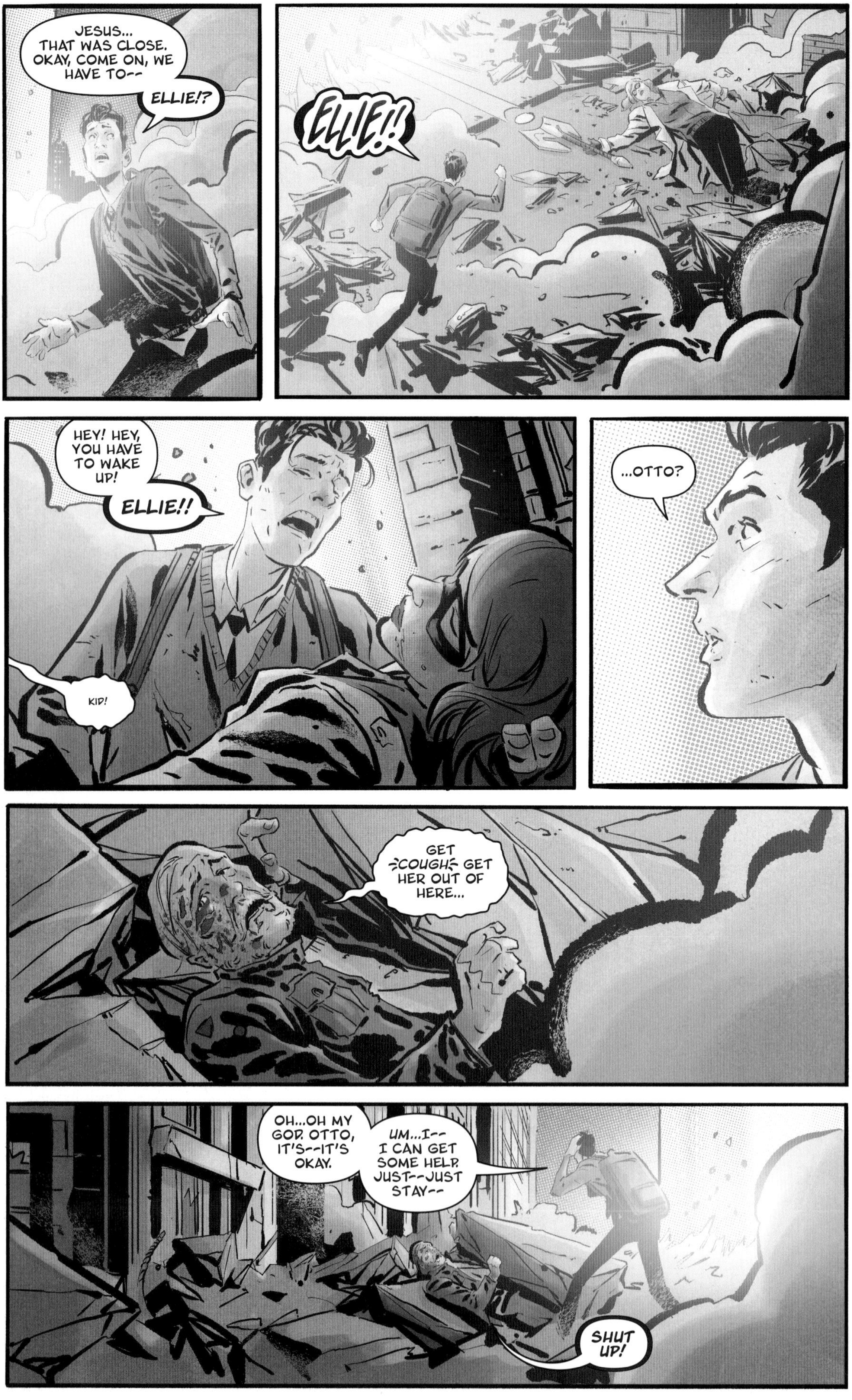
JESUS... THAT WAS CLOSE. OKAY, COME ON, WE HAVE TO--
ELLIE!?
ELLIE!!
HEY! HEY, YOU HAVE TO WAKE UP!
ELLIE!!
KID!
...OTTO?
GET *COUGH* GET HER OUT OF HERE...
OH...OH MY GOD. OTTO, IT'S--IT'S OKAY.
UM...I-- I CAN GET SOME HELP. JUST--JUST STAY--
SHUT UP!

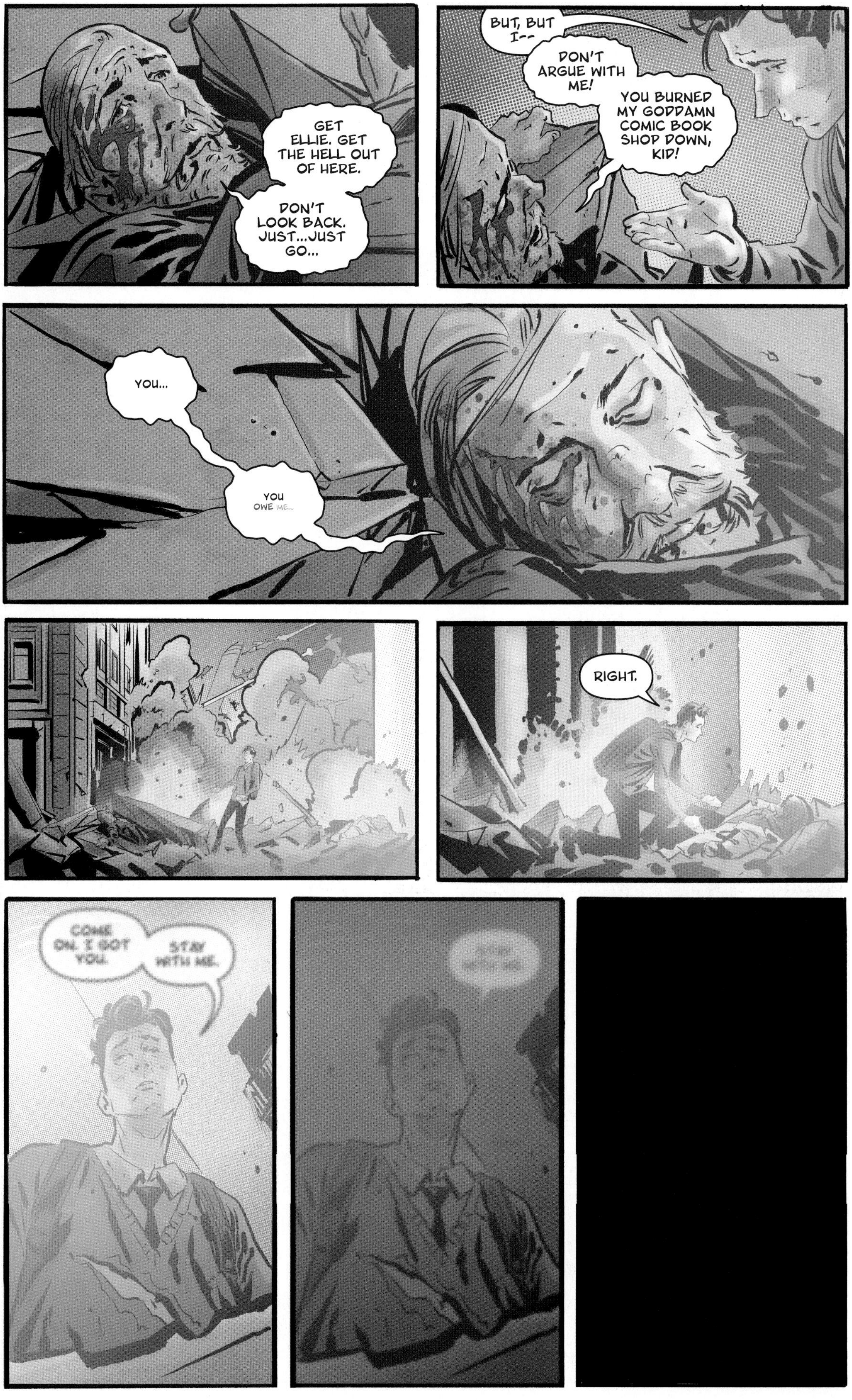
GET ELLIE. GET THE HELL OUT OF HERE.
DON'T LOOK BACK. JUST...JUST GO...
BUT, BUT I--
DON'T ARGUE WITH ME!
YOU BURNED MY GODDAMN COMIC BOOK SHOP DOWN, KID!
YOU...
YOU OWE ME...
RIGHT.
COME ON. I GOT YOU.
STAY WITH ME.

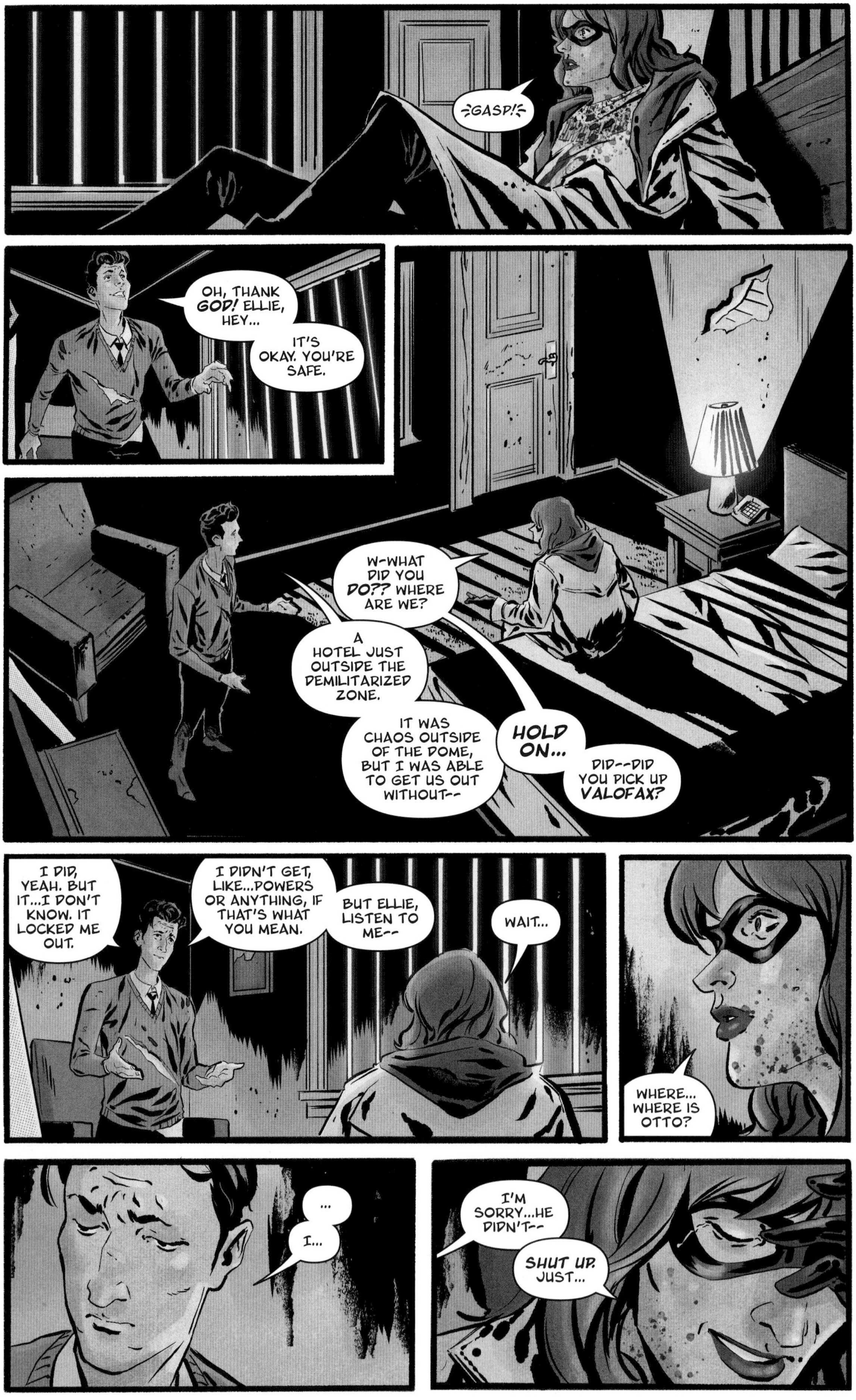

GASP!
OH, THANK GOD! ELLIE, HEY...
IT'S OKAY. YOU'RE SAFE.
W-WHAT DID YOU DO?? WHERE ARE WE?
A HOTEL JUST OUTSIDE THE DEMILITARIZED ZONE.
IT WAS CHAOS OUTSIDE OF THE DOME, BUT I WAS ABLE TO GET US OUT WITHOUT--
HOLD ON...
DID--DID YOU PICK UP VALOFAX?
I DID, YEAH. BUT IT...I DON'T KNOW. IT LOCKED ME OUT.
I DIDN'T GET, LIKE...POWERS OR ANYTHING, IF THAT'S WHAT YOU MEAN.
BUT ELLIE, LISTEN TO ME--
WAIT...
WHERE... WHERE IS OTTO?
...
I...
I'M SORRY...HE DIDN'T--
SHUT UP. JUST...

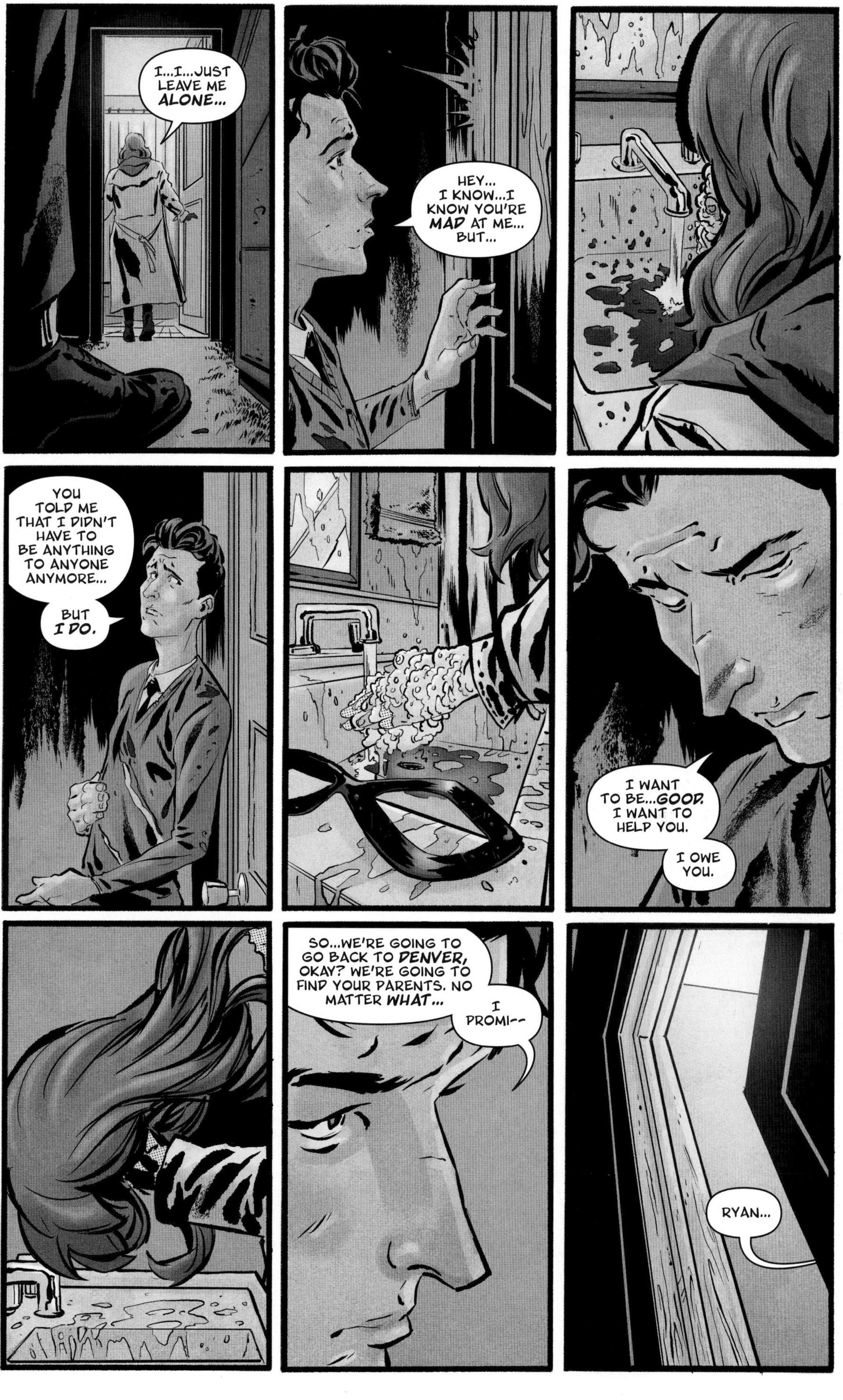
I...I...JUST LEAVE ME ALONE...
HEY... I KNOW...I KNOW YOU'RE MAD AT ME... BUT...
YOU TOLD ME THAT I DIDN'T HAVE TO BE ANYTHING TO ANYONE ANYMORE...
BUT I DO.
I WANT TO BE...GOOD. I WANT TO HELP YOU.
I OWE YOU.
SO...WE'RE GOING TO GO BACK TO DENVER, OKAY? WE'RE GOING TO FIND YOUR PARENTS. NO MATTER WHAT...
I PROMI--
RYAN...

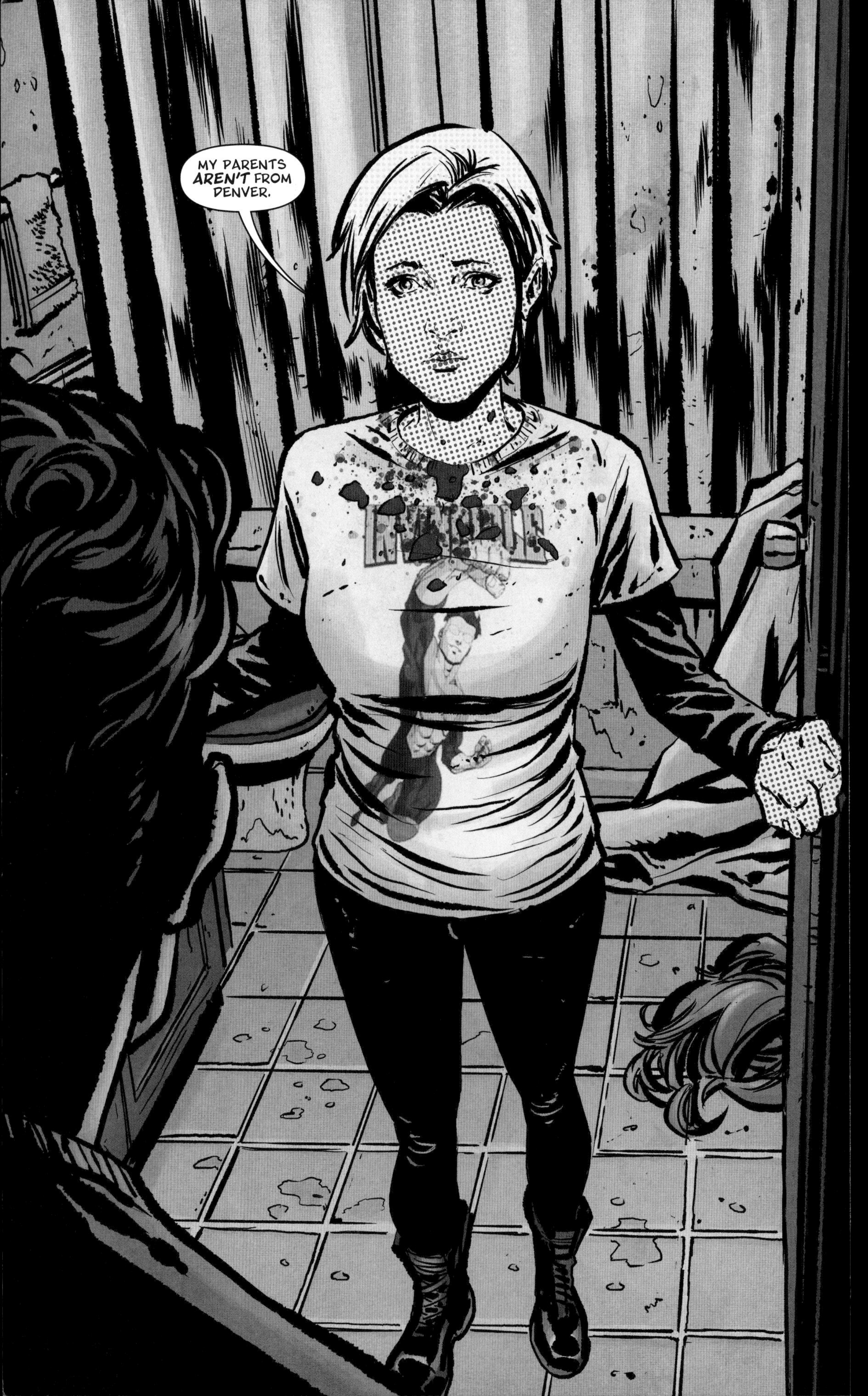
MY PARENTS **AREN'T** FROM DENVER.

THANK YOU FOR LETTING
US PLAY WITH YOUR TOYS...

MICHAEL ALLRED
MADMAN

IAN BEDERMAN
ATOMAHAWK

BRIAN MICHAEL BENDIS &
MICHAEL AVON OEMING
POWERS

KURT BUSIEK
ASTRO CITY

KIERON GILLEN &
JAMIE McKELVIE
THE WICKED + THE DIVINE

JUSTIN JORDAN &
TRADD MOORE
LUTHER STRODE

ROBERT KIRKMAN &
TONY MOORE
BATTLE POPE

ERIK LARSEN
SAVAGE DRAGON

JOHN LAYMAN
CHEW

JEFF LEMIRE &
DEAN ORMSTON
BLACK HAMMER

ROB LIEFELD
AVENGELYNE
BERSERKERS
BLOODSTRIKE
BLOODWULF
BRIGADE
GLORY
PROPHET

MARK MILLAR &
JOHN ROMITA JR.
HIT GIRL

ELIOT RAHAL
THE PAYBACKS

MARK REZNICEK
BUZZKILL

MIKE RICHARDSON
GHOST / X

MARC SILVESTRI
THE DARKNESS
WITCHBLADE

JIM VALENTINO
SHADOWHAWK

MARK WAID
INCORRUPTIBLE

SKOTTIE YOUNG
I HATE FAIRYLAND

ONE / VARIANT COVER
GEOFF SHAW

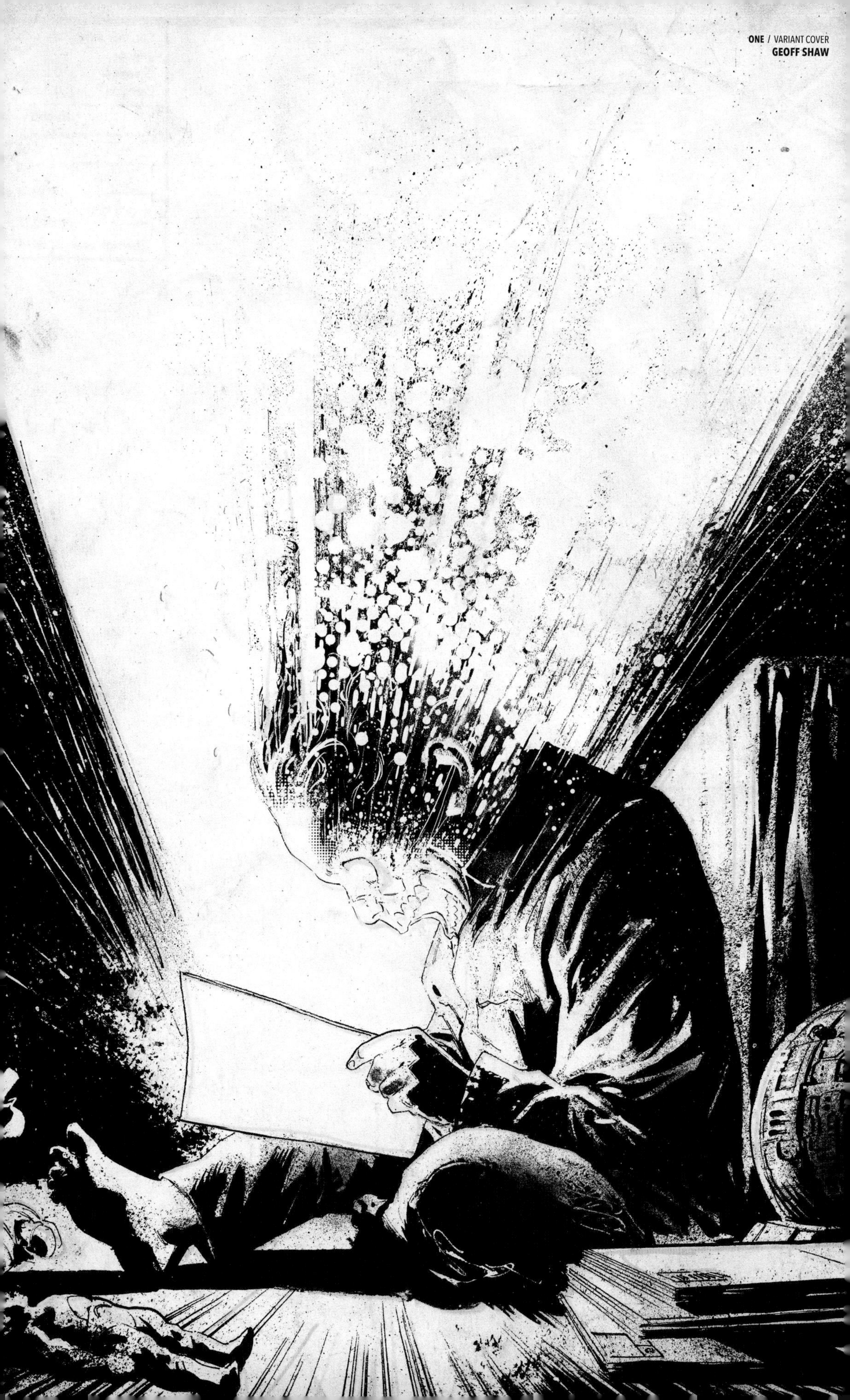

ONE / VARIANT COVER
RYAN STEGMAN & DEE CUNNIFFE

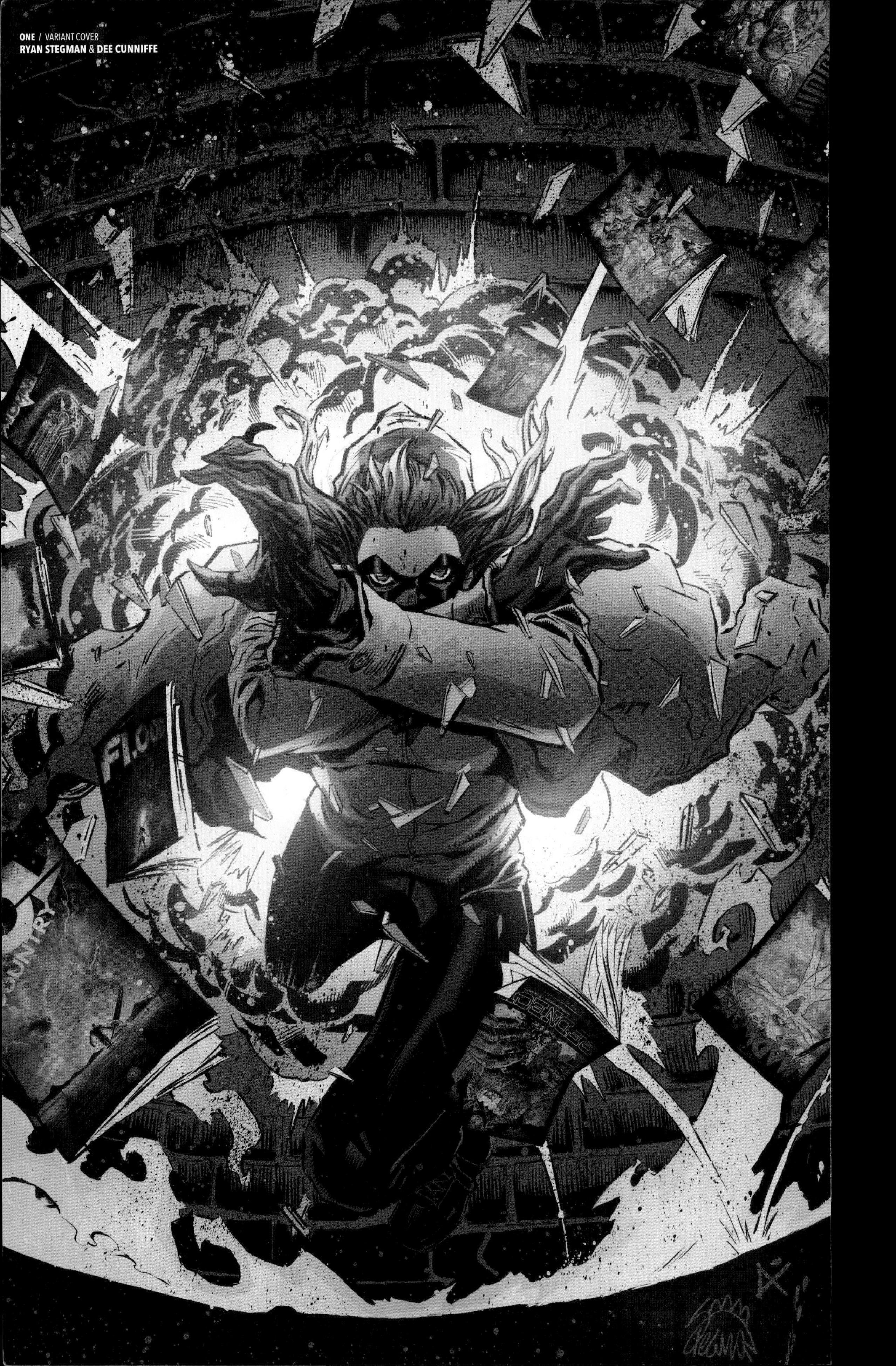
COUNTRY

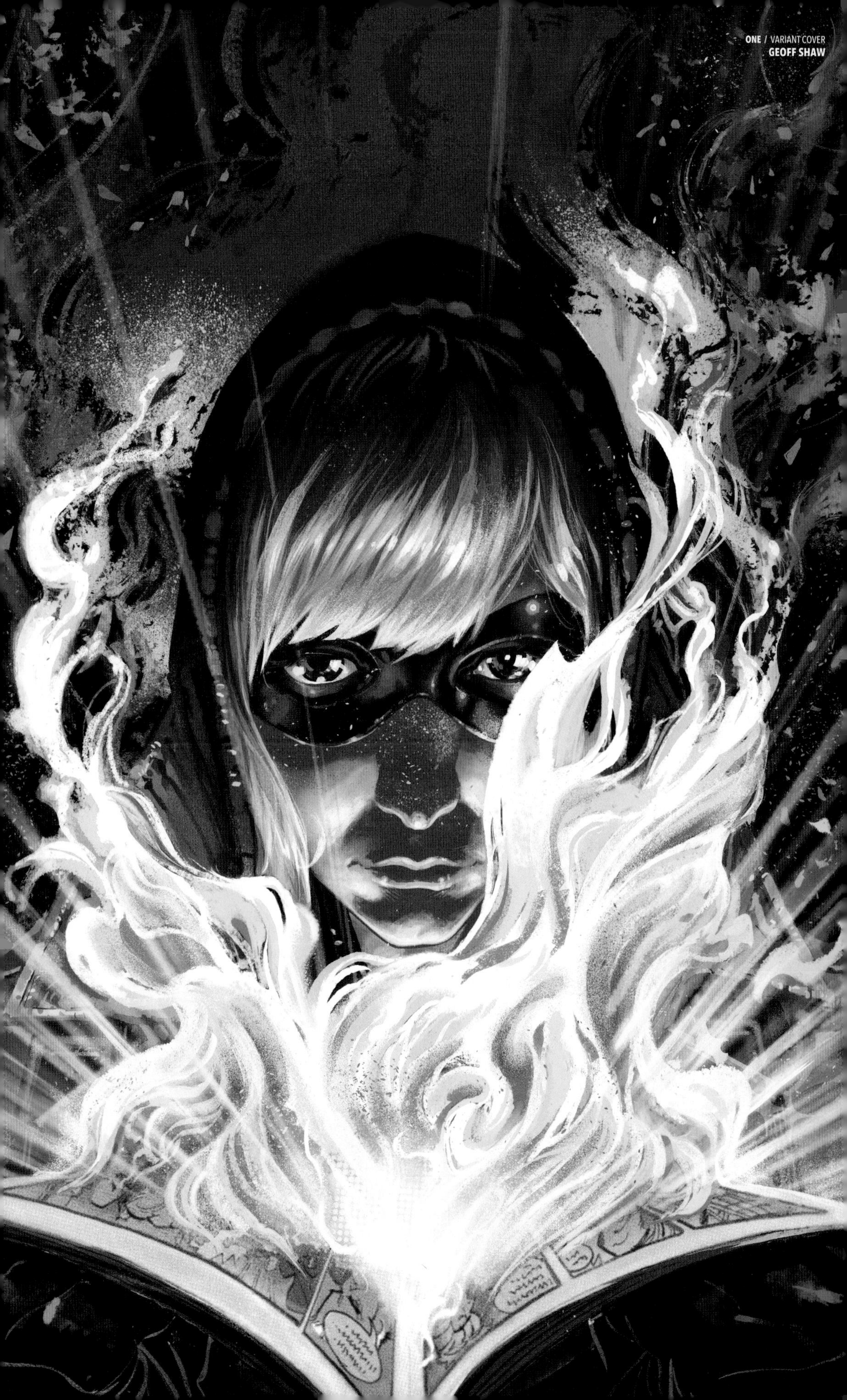

ONE / VARIANT COVER
GEOFF SHAW

ONE / VARIANT COVER
DANIEL WARREN JOHNSON & **MIKE SPICER**

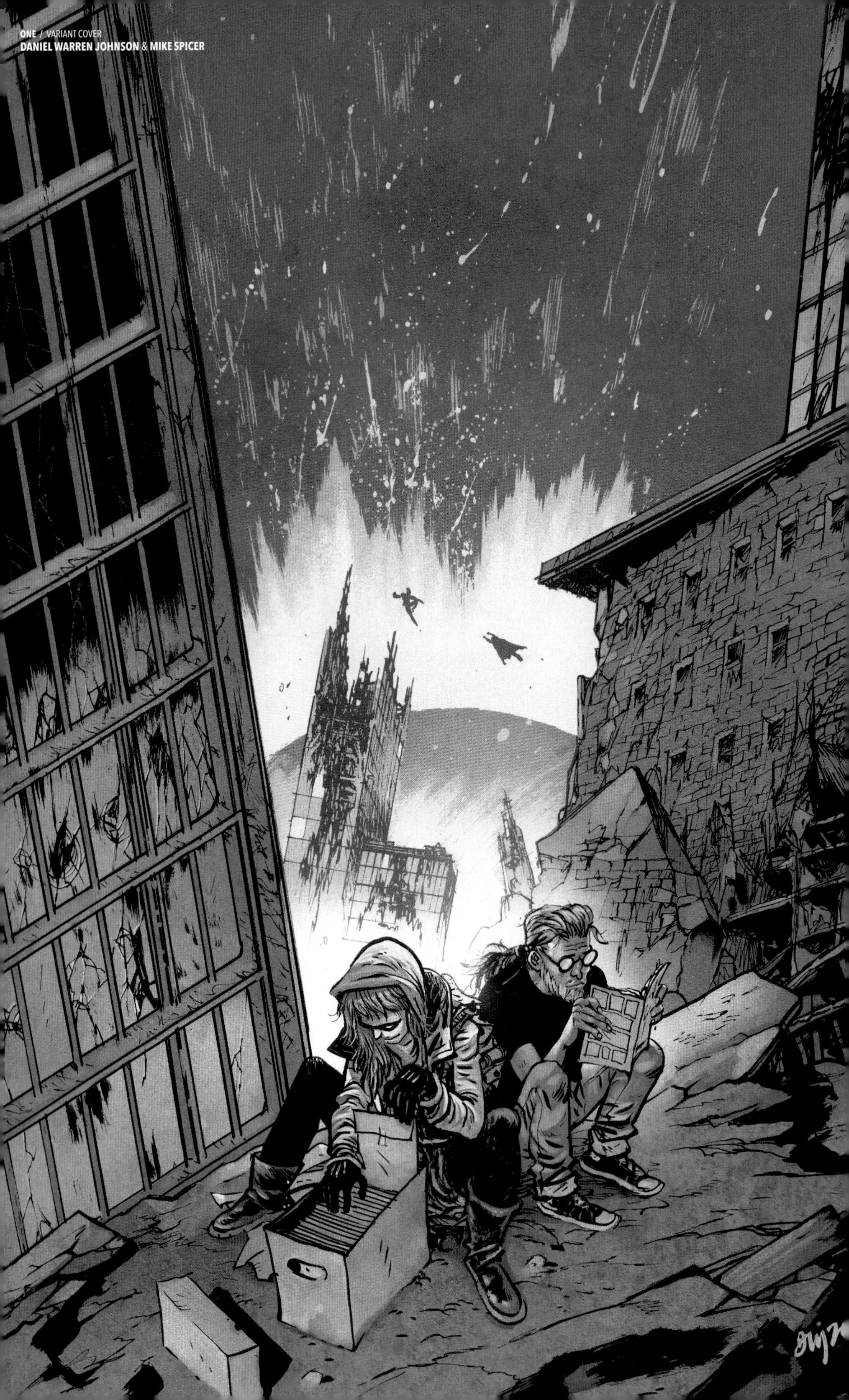

ONE / VARIANT COVER
TRADD MOORE

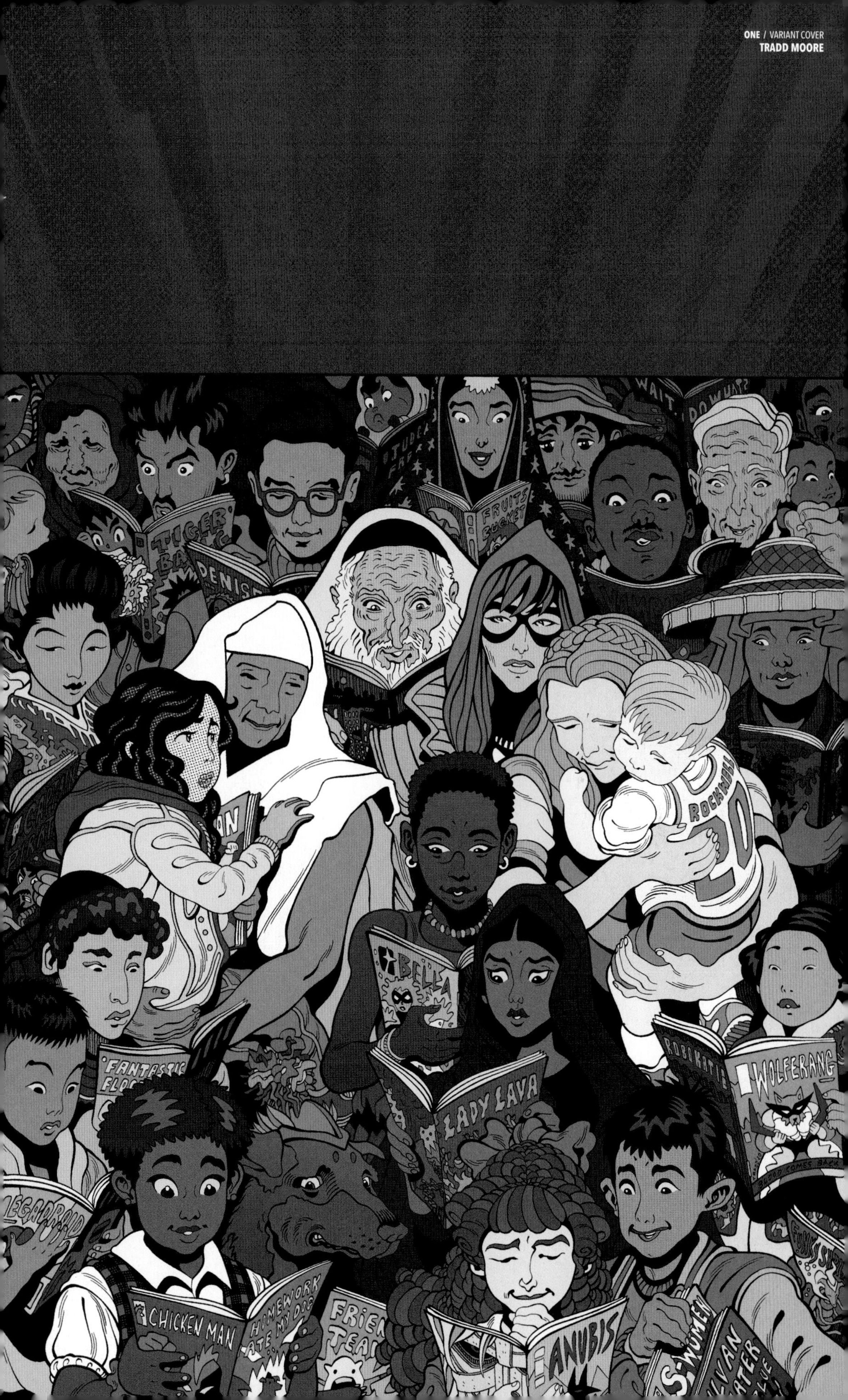

WAIT. DO WHAT?
FRUITS BUCKET
DENISE
BELLA
LADY LAVA
WOLFERANG
CHICKEN MAN
HOMEWORK ATE MY DOG
ANUBIS
S-WOMEN

ONE / VARIANT COVER
RYAN OTTLEY & DEE CUNNIFFE

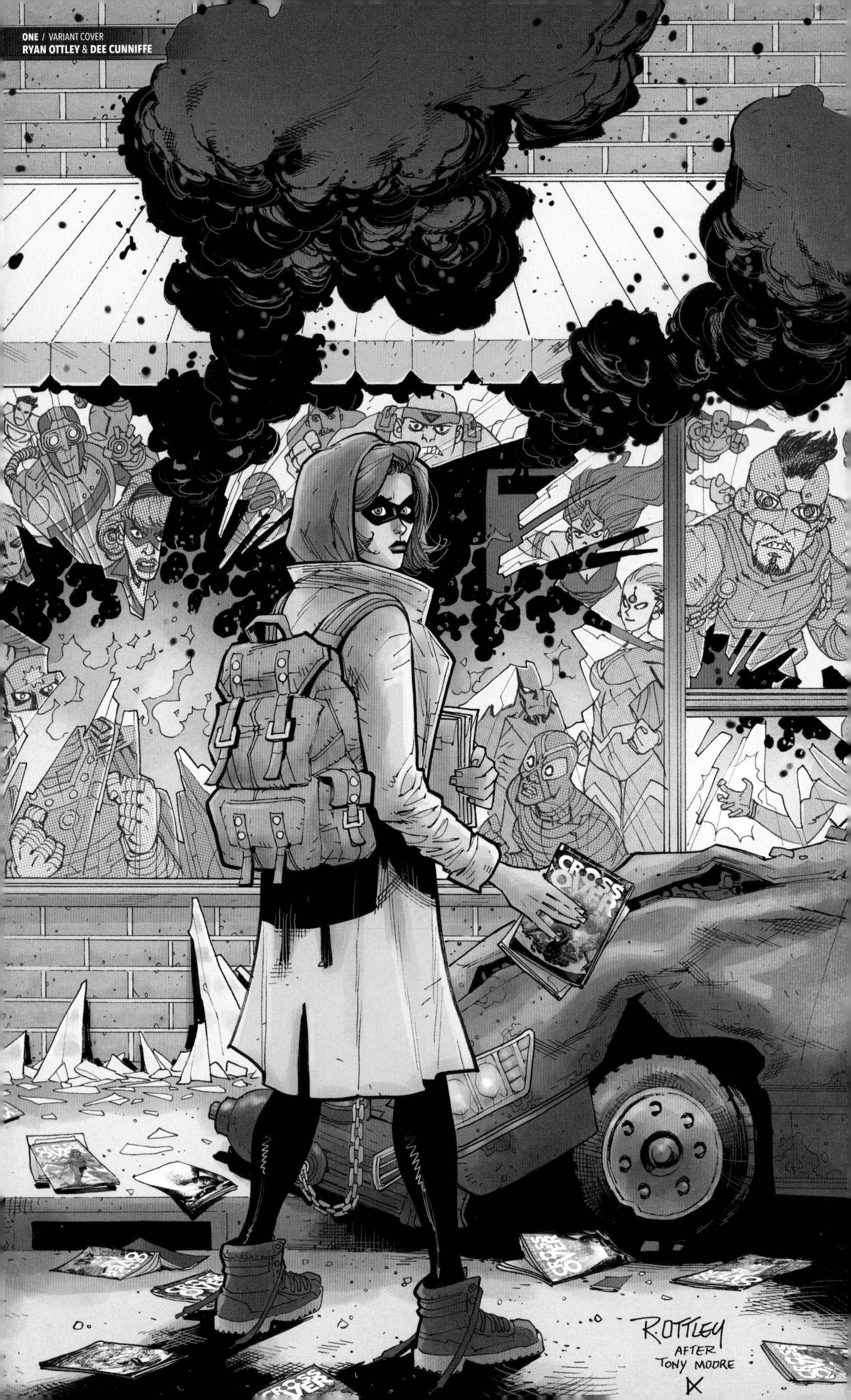
CROSS OVER
R. OTTLEY
AFTER
TONY MOORE

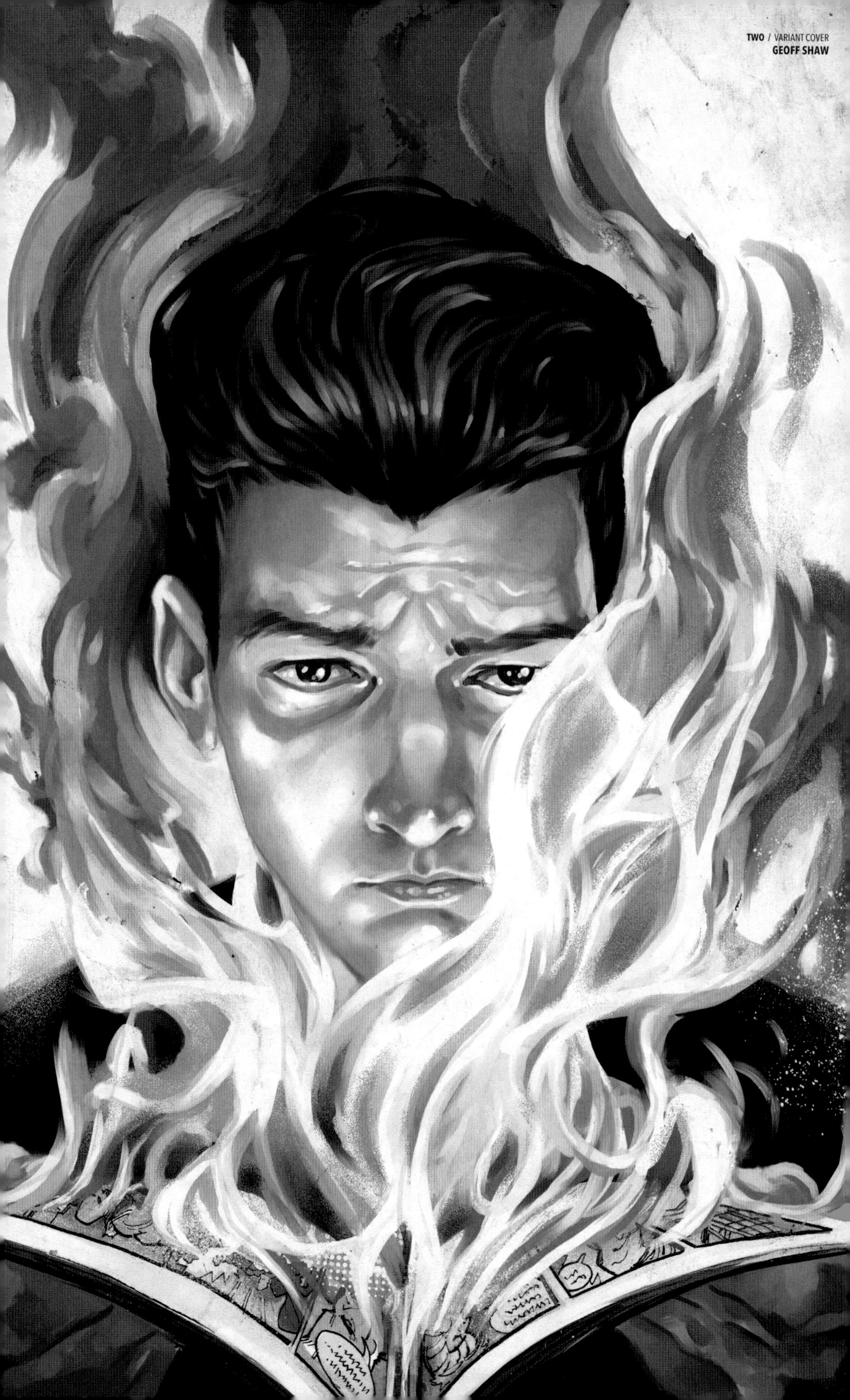

TWO / VARIANT COVER
GEOFF SHAW

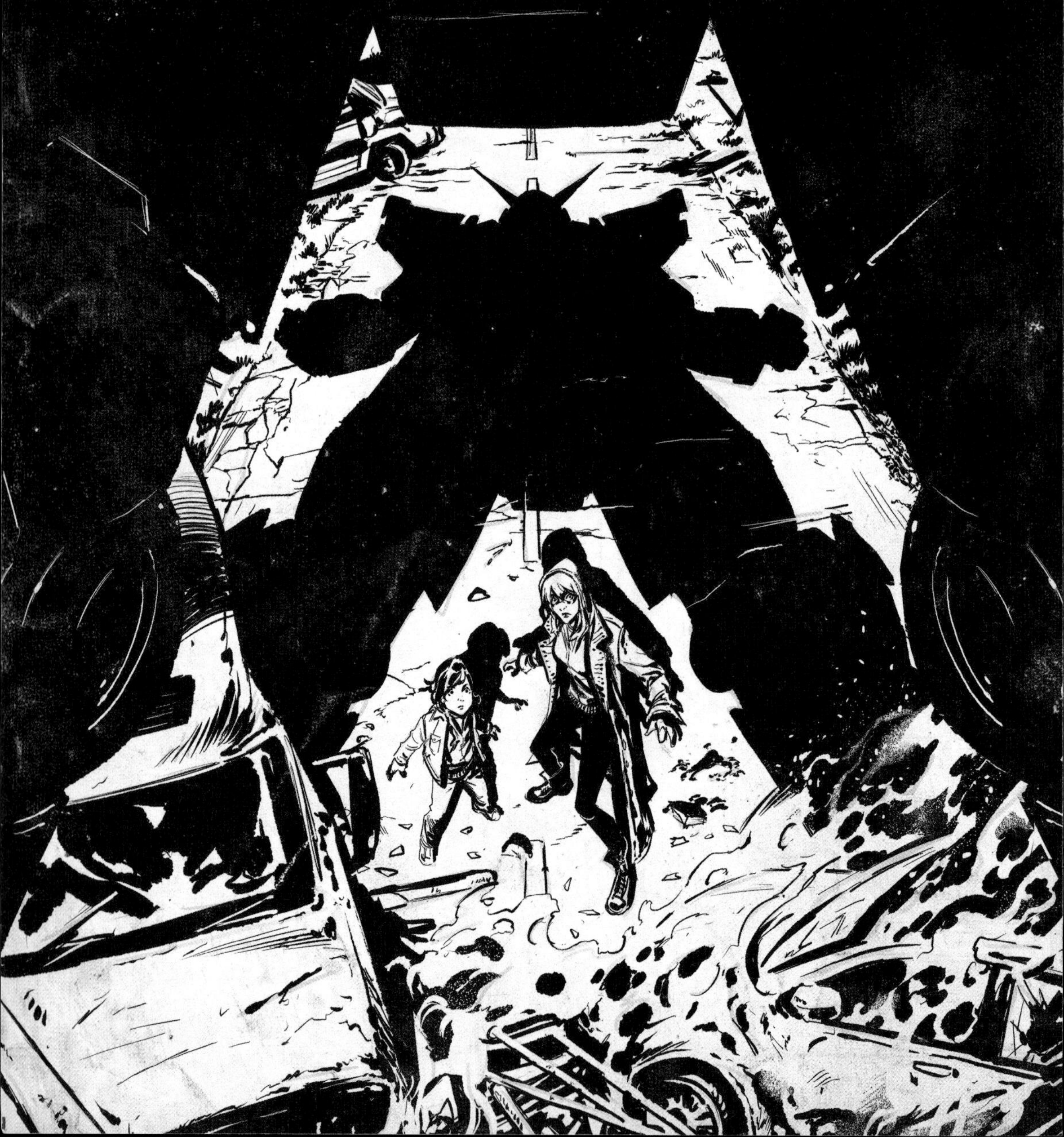

THREE / VARIANT COVER
TODD McFARLANE & **DEE CUNNIFFE**

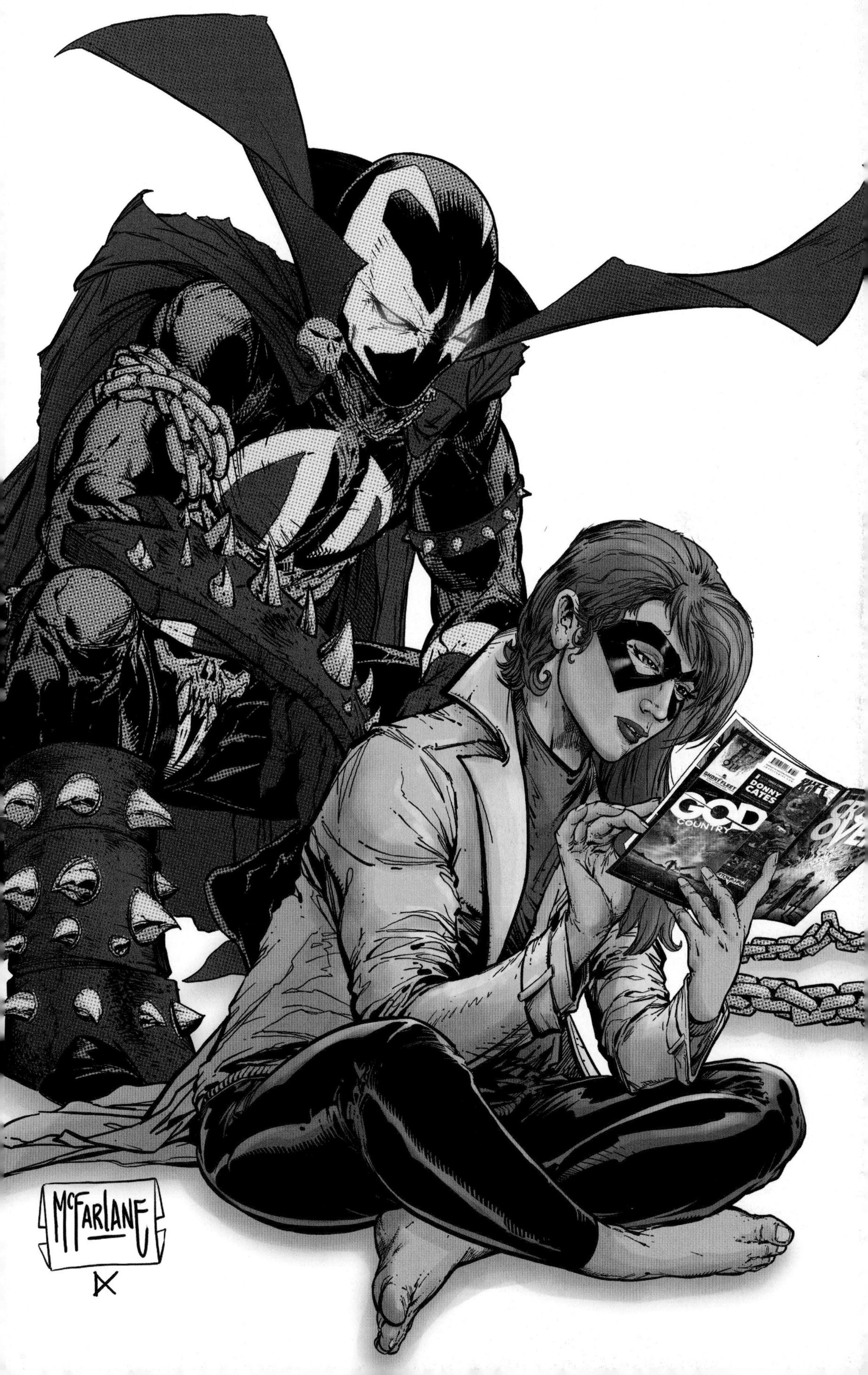

FOUR / VARIANT COVER
GEOFF SHAW

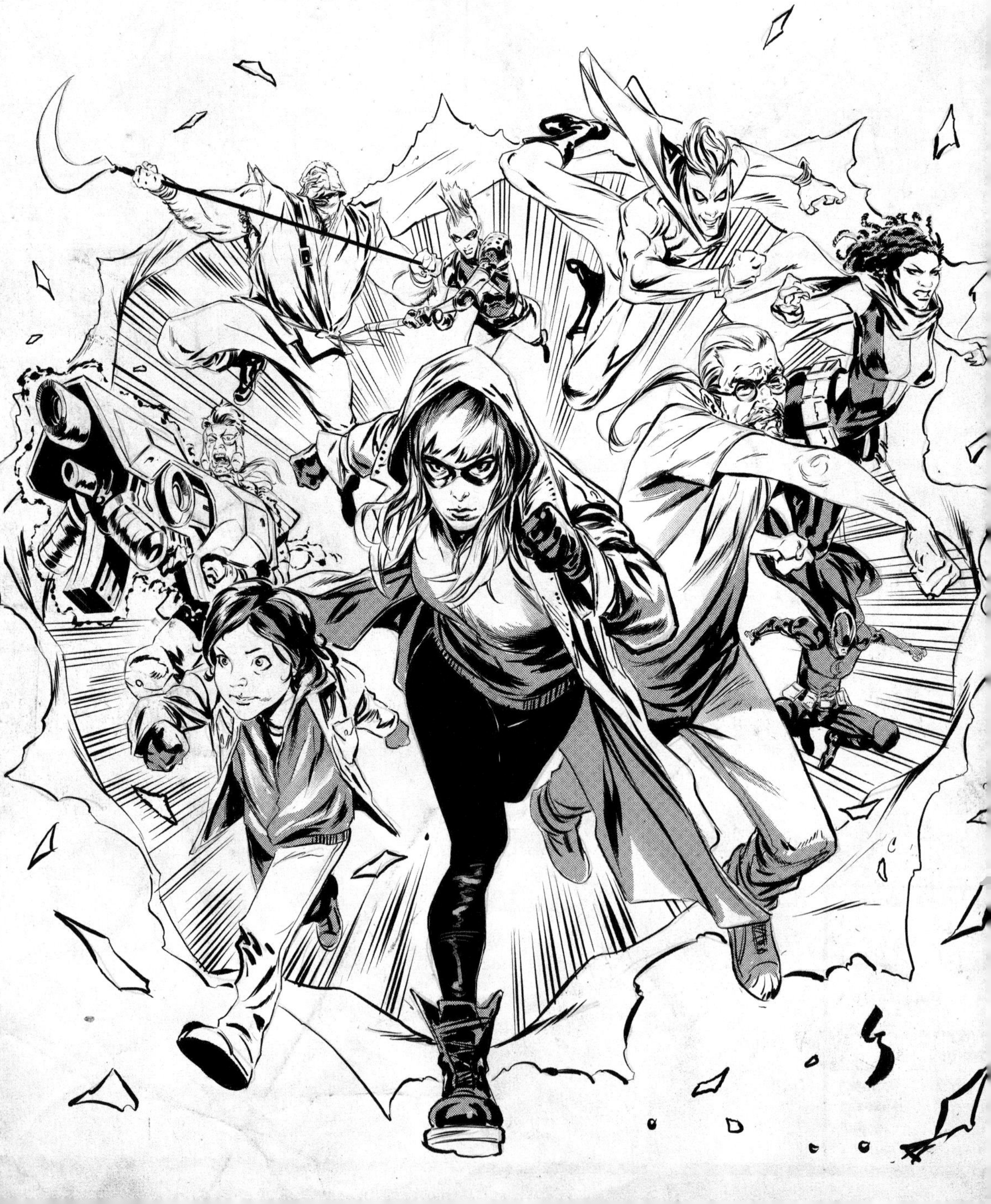

FOUR / VARIANT COVER
MICHAEL ALLRED & **LAURA ALLRED**

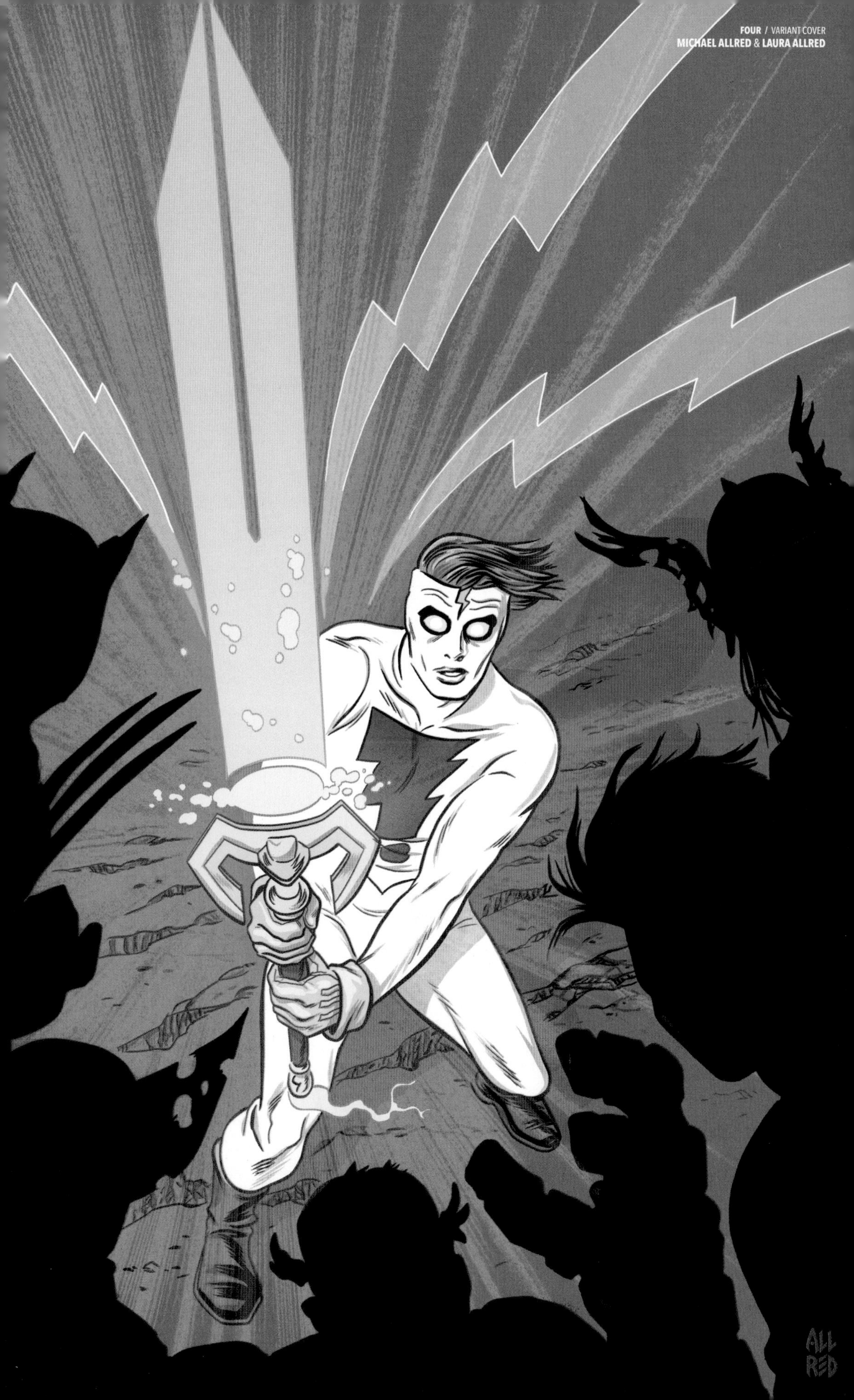
ALL RED

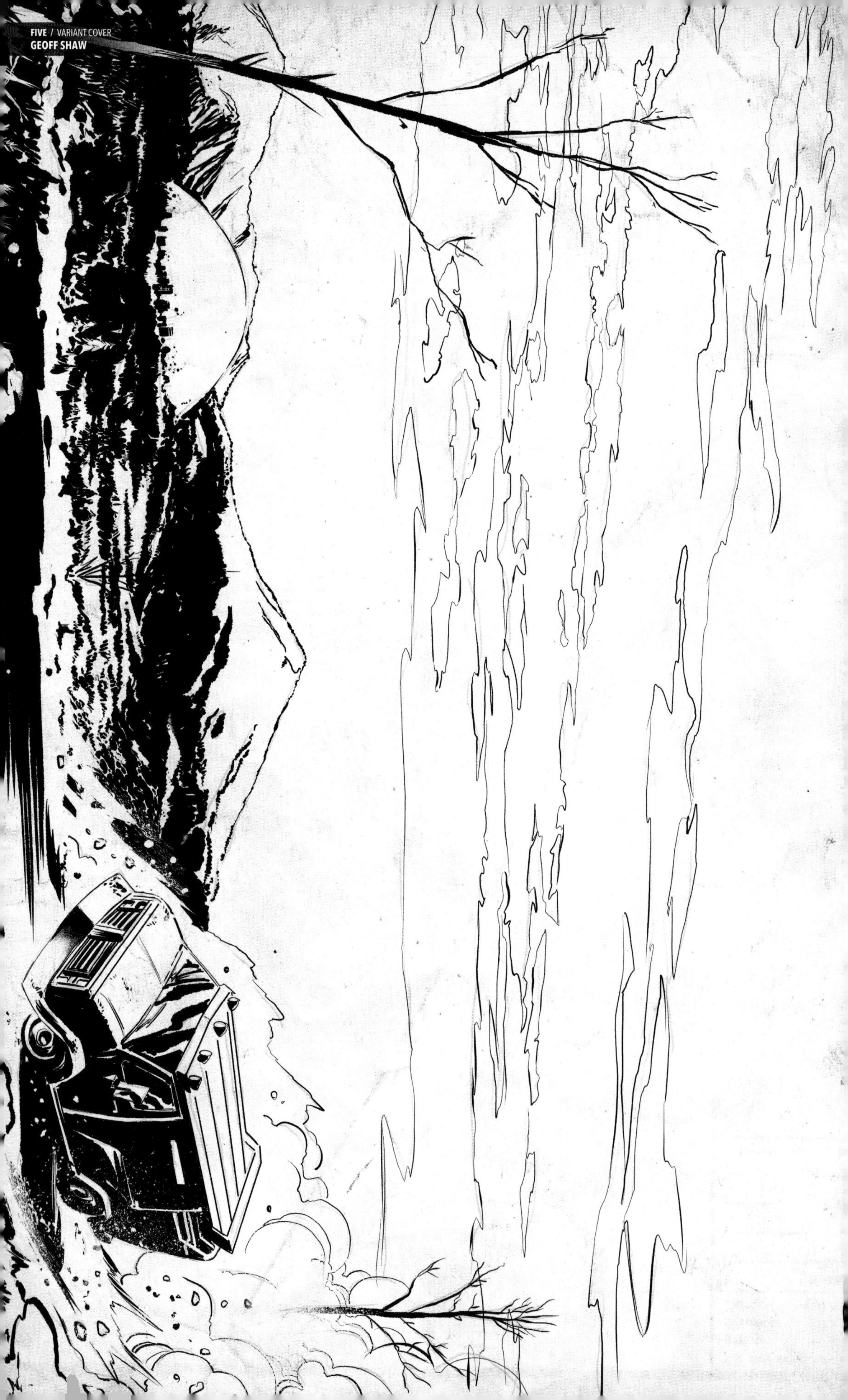

FIVE / VARIANT COVER
GEOFF SHAW

SIX / VARIANT COVER
GEOFF SHAW

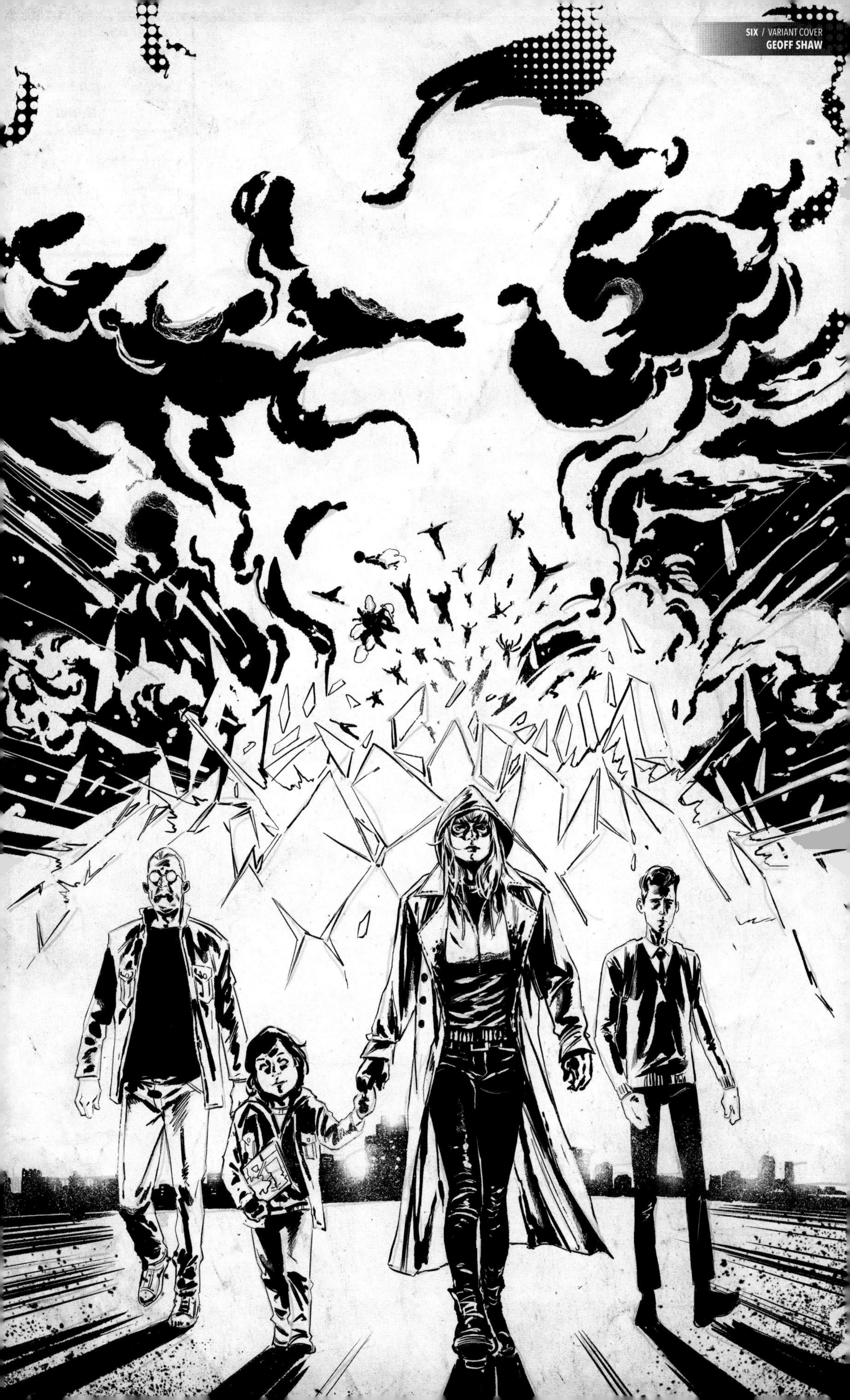

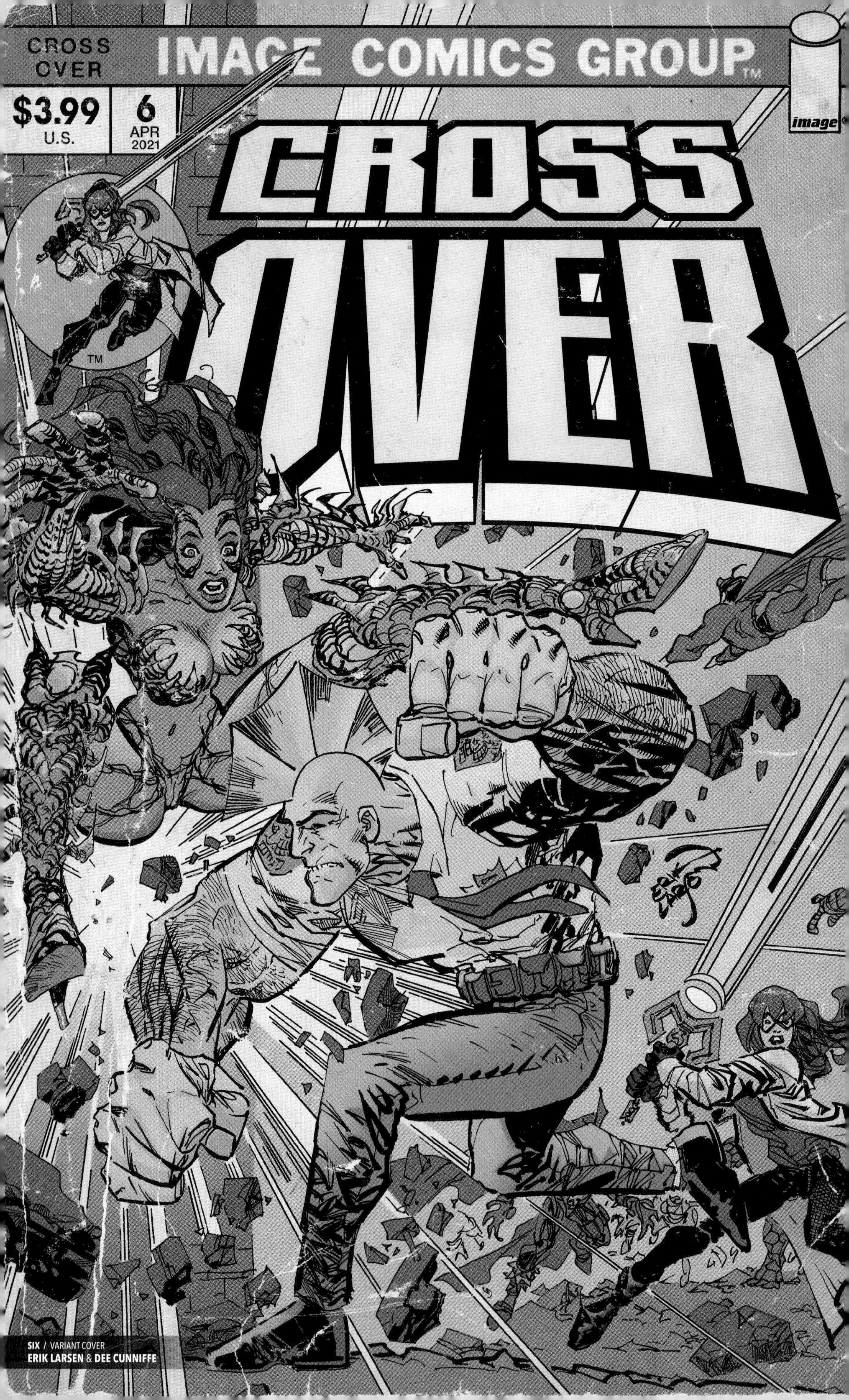
CROSS
OVER
IMAGE COMICS GROUP
TM
$3.99
U.S.
6
APR
2021
image
CROSS
OVER
TM

SIX / VARIANT COVER
ERIK LARSEN & DEE CUNNIFFE

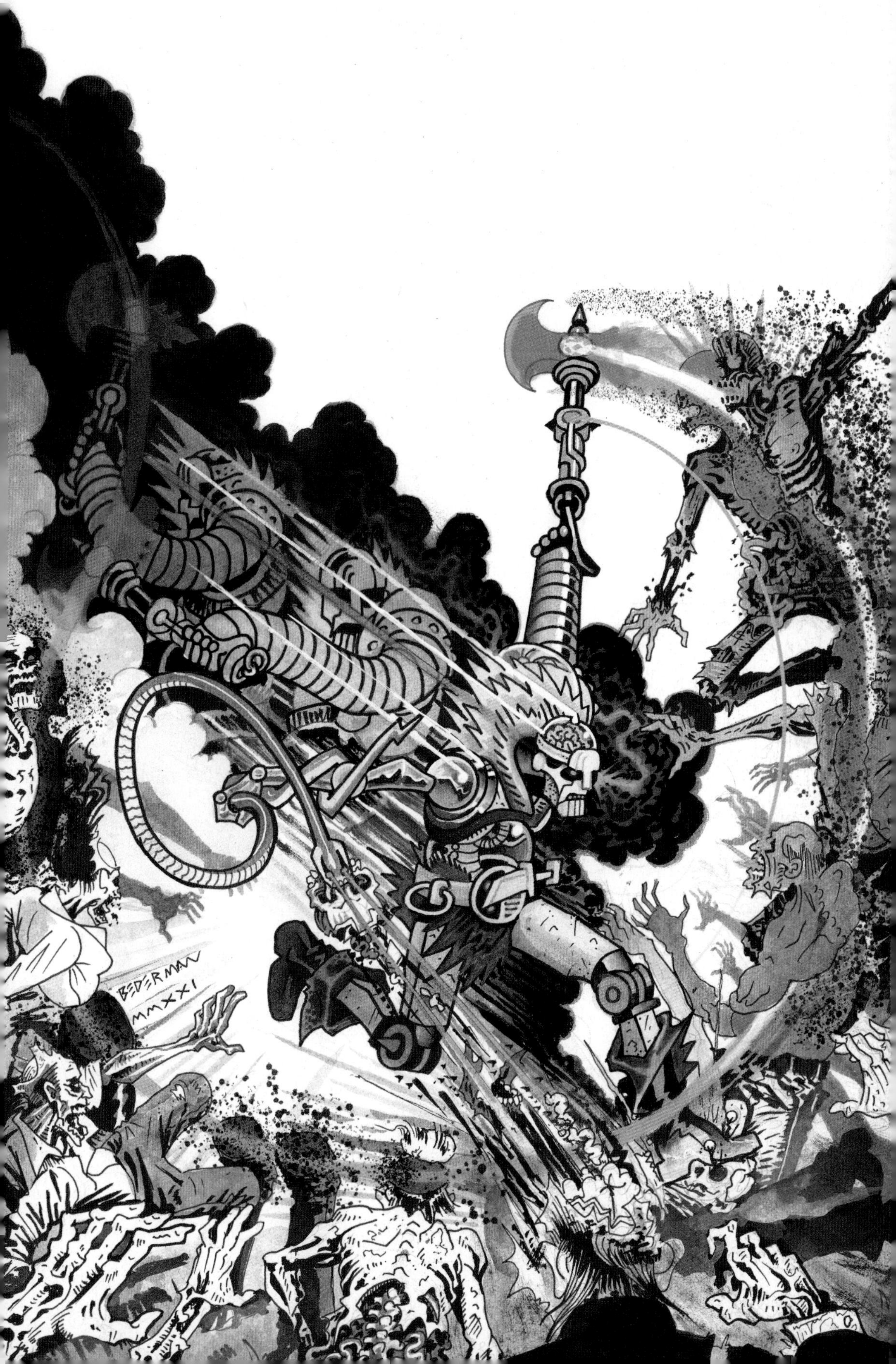
BEDERMAN
MMXXI

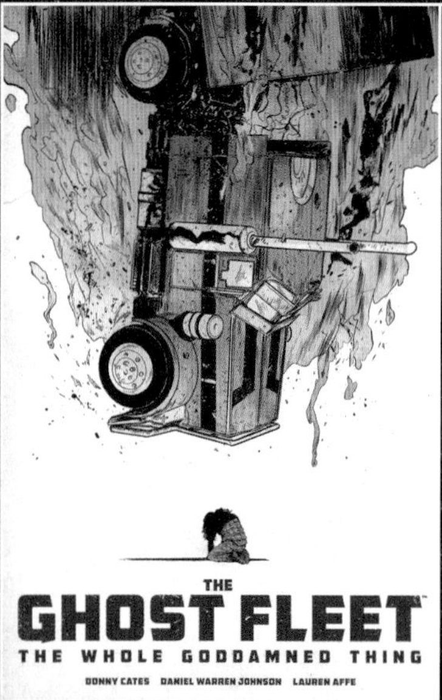
THE
GHOST FLEET
THE WHOLE GODDAMNED THING
DONNY CATES DANIEL WARREN JOHNSON LAUREN AFFE

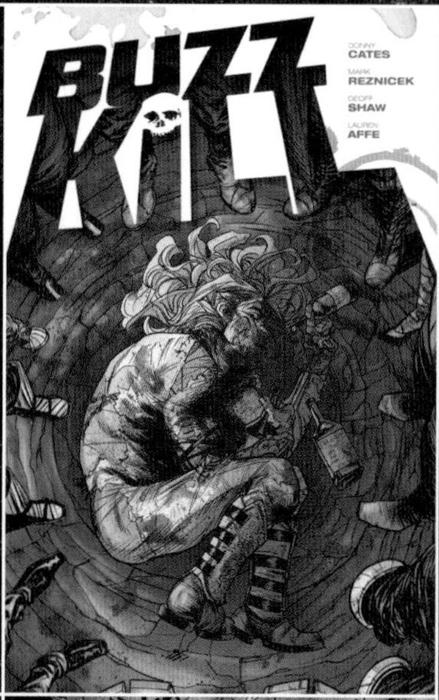
BUZZ KILL
DONNY CATES
MARK REZNICEK
GEOFF SHAW
LAUREN AFFE

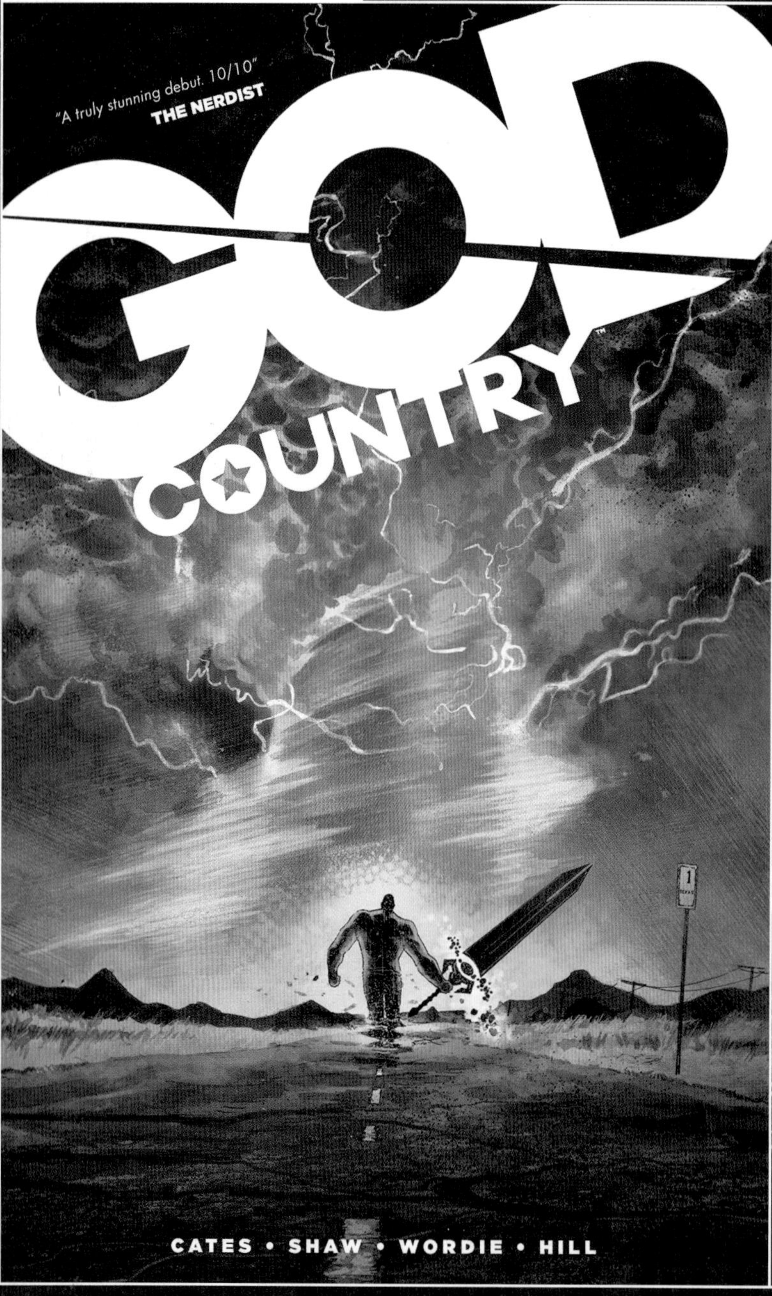
"A truly stunning debut. 10/10"
THE NERDIST
GOD COUNTRY
CATES • SHAW • WORDIE • HILL

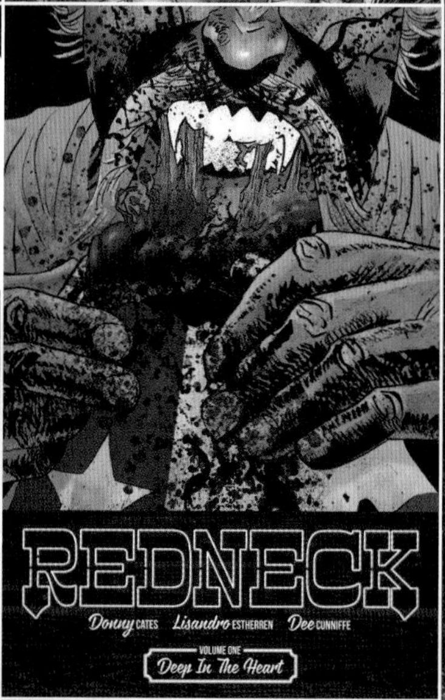
REDNECK
Donny CATES Lisandro ESTHERREN Dee CUNNIFFE
VOLUME ONE
Deep In The Heart

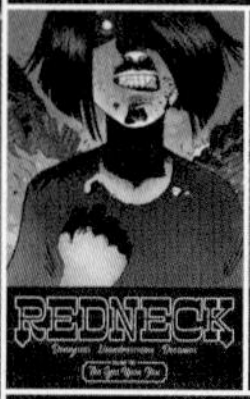
REDNECK

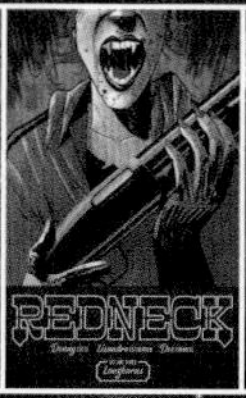
REDNECK

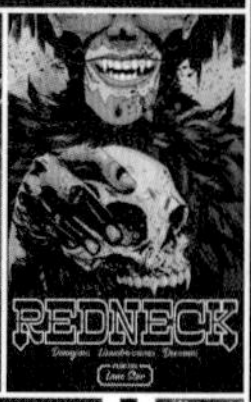
REDNECK

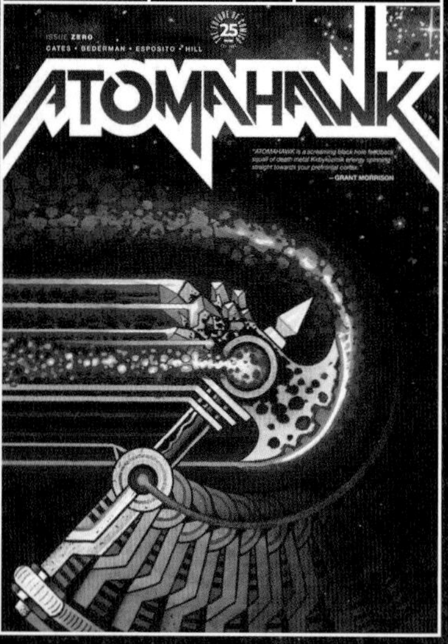
ISSUE ZERO
CATES • BEDERMAN • ESPOSITO • HILL
ATOMAHAWK
—GRANT MORRISON